SERIAL KILLER CONFE

He only hurts th̶ ̶̶̶ ̶ ̶̶̶̶

MARTYN MARTELLO

JESSICA —
Thanks for your
friendship and support.
Thanks for the very
strange experience meeting
you the first time...

SERIAL KILLER CONFESSIONS: Just Friends
Copyright @ 2016

Published by: Twirly Hug Productions

Martyn Martello
www.MartynMartello.com
ISBN: 978-1530373895
Library of Congress:

Editor: Tyler Tichelaar

Cover Design: Shelafoe Designs
Cover Photography: Emily Martello
Cover Models: Craig Grabarczyk, Eliisa Gladwell,
Melissa Neal, Sarah Paquette,
Whitney Wirkula

Printed in the United States of America
First Edition

Dedication

To my lovely bride.   Thanks for your support through this process.   Couldn't have done this without you cheering me on. I just wish you weren't afraid to read it.

Acknowledgments

Abby, for being my first eyes/reader. Your input really shaped the final product.

Monica, for saving my butt when my computer crashed. Glad you had my manuscript saved. And my back all these years.

Chelsea, for being my "first victim".

Sierra, for being my "second victim".

Alicia, for your eyes and perspective and notes.

Kerry and Marci, for helping me make my conversations sound real.

Tyler, for being a great and sensitive editor.

Carmen, for believing in me for 40+ years, even when I couldn't.

Gery, for going above and beyond every step of the way.

PROLOGUE

She was starting to accept her death. Her struggling lessened and then ceased. Her attempts to breathe became less insistent. Her body went limp. But her eyes remained fixed on mine. She stared helplessly, hopelessly, directly into my eyes. Her look was one of abject fear coupled with bewilderment. Her trust has been shattered. Her universe ripped apart. I could tell that she wondered why I was doing this. How could I? I was such a nice man, such a close friend. Why were my hands wrapped around her throat? What had she done? Why was her friend trying to snuff out her existence? Why? Why?

I was enjoying this immensely. The trust giving way to fear. The familiarity fading to terror. The pleading. The questioning. The bargaining. The struggle. The feel of her throat in my hands. The incomparable rush as I felt her very life ebbing. I was careful not to let her slip away too quickly. This girl was special. She had played along at first, thinking that I was going to surprise her in a good way. She'd been a little leery when I led her to my special place, but she'd known me for a long time and didn't think she had any real reason to worry. Her first look of actual fear had come when I slid the bolt on the door into place, clicked the padlock shut, and spun the combination dial. She had started to question me but stopped when I had put my finger up to my lips to shush her. When I had motioned to her, she had quietly hopped onto the small platform in the center of the room, wary but still trusting. It wasn't until I had started to tie her feet together that she had begun to struggle. Scream. I had told her to calm down, that it would all be OK if she just listened and followed my instructions. I was her friend. I wouldn't, couldn't hurt her.

I lied.

I loosened my grip on her throat. I felt hot blood rush beneath my fingers. Her arteries pulsed with life. She gasped in a breath. A little more time before Jess would meet her maker. I controlled every last moment of her life, and I was going to savor this. Like a cat toying with a mouse before making its final kill, I let air and blood sustain her for a little while longer. Still her gaze never left mine. She looked angry now. Angry that she was going to die? Angry that I was going to prolong it? I didn't know and really didn't care. I was enjoying the last few moments that Jess had, the last few moments that I let her have. I squeezed my fingers together one last time. Slowly, I felt her pulse weaken and stop. She went totally limp. I watched the life fade from her eyes. Jess had been the best so far. I climaxed just as she was dying. It was perfect. I loved my new hobby….

IT BEGINS

On June 3, 2009, I took off my wedding ring. It had been three years since the accident that had killed Gwen. Taking off the ring was an important step for me. Taking it off was, I think, symbolic of my actually accepting that she was really gone. Up to that point, I had empirically understood that my lovely bride was gone, but I don't think I really had crossed the line emotionally. I kept telling myself I was OK, that I could move on, but until I took off that ring, I was just treading water.

Gwen and I met here at Michigan North College in New Worcester on the shores of Lake Superior. I came to MNC because it had a great History Department and offered me a fast track to tenure. She was a professor in the Fine Arts Department. She was stunning, intelligent, talented, and interested in me. It was love at first sight. She became more than my "better half." She was my soul. It wasn't long before we were engaged, married, and had a couple kids. I never bought her an engagement ring. Instead I presented her with a choker style necklace. I like the way they look.

THEATER AND THE NEW HOME

As the kids had grown, I had started to dabble in theater a bit. I had never forgotten how much I enjoyed the audience at graduation and just kind of marked time until there was time for me to try acting. All through my teaching career, I continued to take a class or two each semester. I found that spending time in the classroom observing other professors really helped me hone my craft. In the early years I just took classes almost randomly. I took Introductory Russian, a few business courses, some incomprehensible math theory courses, a few P.E. classes…there was no real pattern. Then I took Intro to Theater. I was hooked. From that point on, I only took theater classes until I had exhausted the entire selection. I was awarded a BA in theater because I had fulfilled all the requirements. More initials after my name. As my children's time demands lessened, I got involved in theater more and more. I found that I enjoyed the theater folk more than just about anyone else. I became part of another family and enjoyed the feeling. The five or six weeks of intense preparation was a bonding experience for all. Gwen liked coming to my shows and enjoyed my performances on stage. While I never thought of myself as a great actor, I took great pride in every role I was cast in. After a while, the staff at The Pearl, an old vaudeville and movie house in nearby Northton, asked if I was interested in directing a show there. The Northton Players were a well-respected community theater group and owned and restored The Pearl to its former splendor. I had directed a few one acts and short shows as part of my theater program at NMC, but I had never directed a long show for the main stage. It was a challenge, but I found that I loved it.

Gwen and I spent more and more time at the

theater. She used her artistic talents to help with scenic design and set decoration. I alternated between acting and directing. I tried my hand at the technical side of the game, but I found that I had no real flair for design or construction. The kids came to the theater with us for rehearsals and on build days. They both did a few youth shows, but neither pursued it any further than that. Before too long, Gwen was the President of the Northton Players Board and was also their Artistic Director for a time. She was well-loved by all in the Players and was the heart and soul of the organization. I was proud of her. She was also painting and sculpting and was developing quite a following in the art world. One time when the funding well was running dry at The Pearl, Gwen donated several of her canvases and other works to The Pearl so they could be sold at auction. Gwen and I never discussed how much she was making from her art. She handled all the finances and I simply signed where I was told to each year at tax time. So I was caught a little off-guard when her donations to The Pearl had netted the organization almost $20,000.

"Gwen, I know that you are quite successful as an artist, but I never knew that your art was in this much demand. How have I not noticed this all these years?" I kissed my lovely wife and went on. "Not to pry, but you hardly need my meager salary to survive on if you can sell your works for this kind of money. Why do you keep me around? Why are we still teaching?"

"Because we both love the classroom. You'd die if you couldn't teach, James; you know that. Me too. I love to work with fresh young artists and watch them grow. I hope that I am some kind of influence on them. And I haven't sold that much over the years." She kissed me and looked into my eyes. "James, don't you ever look at the bank statements? Ever?"

"No, I just deposit my check, keep a little spending cash, and let you take care of it from there. Our bills are always paid and you never complain that things are getting tight, so I just don't think about it. I did enough of that when we were young and things were tight. I was so glad when you asked if you could handle the money. Just like my mom, you are so much better with it than I am, or my dad was for that matter."

"Well, James, I'm not going to live forever. You should take a peek once in awhile. I should take some time and show you where all the bodies are buried, so to speak."

"Young lady, you are going to live forever, or at least outlive me. If genetics has anything to do with it, I'll be dead before I can retire. Every male in the Martin family for the past five or six generations has been dead before he turned sixty-six. Dad was in the ground at sixty-four. Your family lives a long time. You will have to bury me, not the other way around." I laughed and kissed her again. I hoped that I could beat the odds and live a long life, but I had my doubts….

We both had to throttle back our involvement at The Pearl when we bought our new place. "The Martin Compound," as we called it, was a great place, but it did need some TLC. The older couple who had owned it for the past twenty years had not been able to keep up with the yard work and maintenance on the house the way they should have. The fence was falling down, the roof needed attending to immediately, all the walls needed paint, the floors needed to be refinished. Most of all, the house needed to be aired out. The house smelled of dogs and cigarettes and old people. We were sure the owners had never opened the windows in the last twenty years. All of them were swollen shut. It took careful persuasion with a hammer and putty knives and even chisels to get them all to function again. It was a labor of love, though. We were enthralled with the setting, and the lovely old trees that graced our lot were magnificent. The maple at the end of the driveway had to be ten feet around at the base and its crown, was home to a whole army of squirrels and birds. There were white pines and birches, hemlocks and cedars. The university property behind us was completely undeveloped. Part of it was cedar swamp and home to many deer and other animals. We saw foxes, raccoons, and woodchucks on an almost daily basis. We had to move a skunk colony that was living under the foundation of the tumble-down garage. I got fairly adept at trapping and moving them to the woods along Bay Road, only getting slightly sprayed once. Our two cats quickly adapted to life in the great outdoors. We hardly ever saw our old tomcat, Bart, except when he came in to eat. He left us various "presents" from time to time. He was so proud of the dead chipmunks and baby rabbits he deposited at our door. I could have done without his devoted tithing.

I wanted to add on to the house so Gwen could have a proper studio with more natural light, but she said she was satisfied using one of the smaller bedrooms. We put a large bay window in it so she did get increased light, but it was never like the sunny "Florida room" of our first cottage. Gwen spent more time painting out in the backyard than she ever did inside, anyway. Her output was amazing during those years. I never figured out how she found the time between working full-time, rehabbing the house, and doing a little theater. But she cranked out canvas after canvas. I told her we were going to have to buy a gallery for her because her works were going to crowd us out. She laughed and told me she was planning to do just that. A great old storefront on Main Street that she had always loved was coming up for sale soon, and the owners were going to offer it to her before they put it on the general market. Gwen said she could afford the building and it would be a good investment. I smiled and nodded. There wouldn't need to be any discussion; Gwen would have already made sure that the financials made sense before she even casually mentioned the idea.

After a couple of years, the house was essentially done. We still had plenty to tackle in the yard, but the house was now as we had envisioned it and comfy as could be. We spent more time at the theater again. We had our theater friends over quite a bit. Young and old, they all loved "The Martin Compound" as much as we did. Some of the students who did theater with us treated our place like their home away from home. We were "local parents" to countless kids. It was fun having that extended family around us. Our life was idyllic.

GIMME SHELTER

Gwen and I had the inside of the house under control and most of the yard as well, so we decided we finally had time to put in a vegetable garden. As much as I hated to do it, I felled several trees to give us enough sunshine to make a garden viable. I cut the main branches and trunks into fireplace lengths, split them, and stacked them to dry for our fireplace. I started hauling the brush into the woods to make shelter for little critters like rabbits and chipmunks. I know that making rabbit shelter was counter-productive as we were putting in a vegetable garden, but I liked hauling the brush to the perimeter of our property and making a natural barrier between our land and the university's tract. No fence, just rows of brush forming a natural fence. It did provide good cover for all sorts of woodland creatures and helped me "mark my turf" in an environmentally-appropriate way. One day, as I was hauling brush into our woods, I tripped over an iron ring protruding from the ground. Gwen and I had been all over our property, but we had never noticed this ring sticking out of the ground. I got up, brushed myself off, and took a better look. The ring seemed to be secured to the ground. Odd. I kicked some of the dirt and debris away from it. A flat metal surface lay beneath the forest floor. I went back to the shed and got a shovel and a hoe and started to clear around the ring. I spent the better part of the afternoon toiling. Gwen finally came out into the woods looking for me.

"James, you have been out here forever! Do you have a girlfriend out in these woods?" She looked sternly at me, well, as sternly as she could pretend to look.

"No, love, you are my one and only. You know that. But look at this." I pointed to the metal hatch that I was slowly unearthing. "I wonder what the heck this thing is?"

Gwen helped me with my archeological exploits. By the end of the day, the entire hatch was exposed. I got some WD-40 and some penetrating oil from the garage and liberally applied it to the hinges and the hasp. A large pair of bolt cutters dispatched the rusty old lock. The door had rusted itself to the frame. We had to use a sledge and a pry bar to break it free. When we finally did, we grabbed a couple of flashlights from the house and ventured down the steep concrete stairs we had revealed.

"I feel like Nancy Drew," said Gwen. "Nancy Drew and the Mystery of the Hidden Hatch. What do you think is down here?" She could barely contain herself. I was giddy myself. At the bottom of the stairs, we encountered another metal door. It wasn't quite as rusty as the hatch—it had been sheltered from the elements. I figured we must have come down at least fourteen feet before we reached the landing and the other door. I had a theory about what this was, but I didn't volunteer anything. I cut the lock off of the second door and pried it open. We both swung our flashlights into the room. What we found was a concrete bunker, a '50s era bomb shelter. There was a musty smell, but the place seemed dry enough. From the entry, we could see a table and chairs, some shelves, and a couple of doors.

"A bomb shelter! How cool!" we both exclaimed at once. We laughed because we sounded more and more alike as we lived together. We were each adopting the other's speech patterns and mannerisms. It was like we had become one being in the twenty-some years of our marriage. We entered the shelter and took a quick look around. It was obvious that no one had been in here for a long time. We wondered why the Makis hadn't told us about the shelter. We figured that the original owners were embarrassed to admit that they had built such a thing and hadn't told the Makis when they had bought the place, or that the Makis had simply forgotten it in their advancing years. Either way, it was a neat surprise and discovery.

"Gwen, I am going to get our work lights and string together enough extension cords so we can actually see this place. I'm excited. It's like we just found a hidden treasure in our backyard."

"It is a hidden treasure. I hope it is in as good a condition as it appears to be at first glance. I'll come back to the house with you. I want to get into jeans and a long sleeve shirt. God knows what we'll find." Gwen took my hand and we trotted back to the house together. I gathered about 200 feet of heavy-duty extension cords. I could never find one when I needed it, so I tended to buy one before each project. After we had built the tool shed and organized it, I found that I had hundreds of feet of extension cords. And multiple hammers, saws, and other tools that I had "lost" over the years. Now I could almost open my own hardware store with all the surplus I had accumulated. I plugged a cord into the outlet in the shed and started to unreel it. Two hundred feet came close to reaching the shelter, but I had to get another twenty-five-foot cord to make it down the stairs and into the shelter. Then I hooked up our two 500-watt halogen work lights. The place came to life.

The walls were covered with flaking old paint, lead-based I was sure. There were light fixtures on the ceiling and switches on the wall. I flipped one for fun and was surprised when one of the old fluorescent bulbs tried to flicker to life. The old ballast made a loud buzzing sound, and the light never came fully on, but we were both surprised that there was power at all.

"Mystery solved, Gwen," I said. "The 'mystery fuse' in the box must be to this place." For years, we had wondered what the last fuse in our old style fuse panel did. We had turned everything in the house on and pulled the fuses one by one to try to figure out what went where. We never could figure out what the "mystery fuse" was for. It never disconnected anything. We labeled it with a question mark. I later added a small subpanel so we could make coffee and use the microwave at the same time. The mystery fuse was a "round to it" project—I would someday figure out which wire leaving the fuse box was the mystery wire and follow it wherever it went. Now I no longer had to. I unplugged our work light from the extension cord and plugged it into one of the outlets on the wall. It worked. Gwen and I were pleased.

Gwen and I spent the balance of the day looking around. We found that the shelter was hooked up to city water and had its own cistern. The cover to the cistern was hidden under brush, just as the entrance had been. The water in the cistern was not potable, not at least by our tastes, but it was interesting to note the care that had been taken in the building of this shelter. A diverter valve switched between the city water and the cistern. There was a fresh air system, and exhaust fan (not operational), plenty of rusty old cans of long-expired food, some books and first aid supplies, long dead 12-volt batteries and an old generator. No expense had been spared when this place was built. Gwen and I decided that we would restore the bomb shelter and, after we were done, share it with our friends. We thought of all sorts of theme parties we could have down here. We were both amazed at the level of paranoia in the '50s. That anyone would go to this much trouble to try to survive a nuclear exchange was rather remarkable. I had always said that if the nukes started to fly, I would simply go on the roof and look toward the airbase so I could enjoy the last show. I wondered whether there were still any weapons targeted on the site, no longer a SAC base, but our local airport since the mid-1990s. I figured that New Worcester had no more strategic significance with the base gone, unless pasty pies had somehow gained strategic value.

We found the shelter in early April of 2004. We finished preparing the garden and other outdoor projects before we started in on the shelter. It was a fun project, but not very high priority. The garden took more time to create than either of us had anticipated. Getting all the roots and stumps pulled from the garden site was tiring, backbreaking work. Screening all the soil to get the last of the foreign matter was also a time-consuming activity. We had planned a fairly large garden, 24' x 36'. Neither of us had started a vegetable garden from scratch, so we had no idea just how much work was really involved. Cutting sod, pulling weeds, screening…it never seemed to end. Then there was the matter of a deer and rabbit fence. We had critters in abundance in our area, so a stout fence was a must. I hauled loads of treated 4x4s, 1x4s, fence fabric and the like from our local Menards. I rented a power auger, laid out the fence posts, and started drilling the post holes. Gwen and I set them together, setting every other one in concrete. We built the fence a full seven feet high with thirty-two inches of rabbit fence at the bottom. We put concrete pavers vertically below grade to keep burrowing marauders out of the garden. Our garden fence was, like our shelter, over-built and over-engineered. We figured that if any critters did get in, they deserved whatever they could eat. Because we underestimated the time it would take to develop the garden, we got a very late start planting. Nothing was in the ground before July 1st. Needless to say, our first year's garden was not a huge success, but we both loved working it.

We started working more seriously on the shelter in the late fall. Of course, school was back in session, so the work went slowly. We first started by hauling everything out of the shelter. We covered it all with a tarp and then started stripping the walls of paint. We got proper respirators, gowns, and gloves, and dug in. It was slow going. The paint that had started to flake was easy. The stuff that hadn't was truly tenacious. I was all for renting a sand blaster, but Gwen wisely talked me out of that. We soldiered on using scrapers and wire brushes until we had the walls and floor ready for fresh paint. We tried to paint it in the original colors—a palette of white, cream, and institutional green. It looked clean and tidy when we were done. The work stretched out over the winter and into the next spring. We took periodic breaks from working on the shelter. It was meant to be a fun project, not a slave labor camp. When I had time between work and shows I reworked the wiring, installed a new propane furnace, and checked and repaired plumbing. We had decided that this little hideaway would be a fun place to get away from it all without ever going anywhere. In a pinch, the shelter could serve as a guest house. We would have to develop a proper walkway to it, but that could wait. We decided to keep the shelter's very existence a secret until we were ready to unveil it at our first gathering in it. It was fun to have a secret project and place to conspire about.

TROUBLES

Our life together was not entirely conflict-free. I doubt any marriage ever is. When we first met, I was acerbic and essentially friendless. As time went on, Gwen had drawn me out of my shell and helped me normalize my relations with other people. I'll never figure out why she had taken an interest in me in the first place, but it certainly changed my life. I had been starved for human contact, but didn't know it. I had convinced myself that I didn't need others and that they were beneath me. I was brighter than the vast majority of those around me and allowed that to be my only yardstick of worth. Throughout my youth, I withdrew further and further. I became the oddball the other kids teased me about being. After Gwen and I got together, however, I started to realize how important socialization really was. Gwen had a large circle of friends, and she went out of her way to make sure I was integrated into it. I became more and more social and more and more accepting of others. I no longer disdained people and dismissed them as unworthy because they weren't on a par with me intellectually. I became a social animal, and that proved to be a source of friction between Gwen and me in years to come.

After meeting Gwen, I started to notice women for the first time in my life. Before Gwen, men and women were kind of lumped together as simply "other people." Until Gwen woke me up, I never really looked at women "in that way." As time went on, though, I did. As I learned more about social graces and became more personable, I discovered that I had a certain amount of charm. I'm not much special to look at, pretty much just an average guy, but I am articulate and know what to say to make people feel at ease. I am persuasive and sincere. I found that

very curvaceous woman—in fact can appreciate nearly all women on some level—my tastes run more toward the svelte and sylphlike. A woman with a spare, athletic build and a unique face is more likely to turn my head than a Playboy bunny. Jess definitely did not have the bunny build. She was petite, about 5'5" and maybe 110 pounds, soaking wet. She was practically flat-chested with just a hint of cleavage when she wore a low-cut dress or blouse. Her nose was slightly too large, if one were to judge using conventional standards, and her mouth was as well. Yet, somehow, the whole physical package worked, and I found her quite striking. She was very bright, wise beyond her years, and very talented. She was also one of the most driven and focused young people I have ever met. She reminded me of me. When we first spoke, I found her to be a good conversationalist and exceptionally well-read for her youth. When I saw her on stage, I was even more impressed. This kid had the chops to be a professional. I liked her very much and enjoyed her company. I told myself that I was not attracted to her sexually and, besides, I had no desire to risk my marriage to Gwen. But there was a connection there that went beyond the casual. I couldn't explain it and I couldn't get enough.

As time went on, Jess and I became very good friends. I know it sounds strange that a forty-something man and a seventeen year old could have such a close relationship, but there it was. She was comfortable enough to tell me everything. I knew the inner workings of her very dysfunctional family, knew about her boy troubles, her experimentation with bisexuality, her hatred of drug use, and her love of Star Wars. I suppose I was her surrogate mother and father, her actual parents being very distant and not very supportive. We worked on every show together that we could. Gwen found her delightful as well—at first, anyway—and invited her to our home for dinner or just to chat. We hosted her eighteenth birthday party at our place, filling the house with college kids till 3:00 a.m. It was a gas, and I was glad we were able to do it for Jess. When Jess had herded the last out the door, she found me in the hallway and pulled me aside.

"James, you and Gwen are the best thing that has ever happened to me. I love you so much." She hugged me and put her arms around my neck and kissed my cheek. She let go and started down the hall to make her exit. Gwen was standing in the kitchen, at the end of the hall, arms crossed. She did not look happy. Not in the slightest. I wondered what she had seen and, more importantly, what she *thought* she had seen.

"James, can I see you? In our room? Now, please…." Her request was an order, one not to be refused. I followed her into our room. She shut the door behind me as soon as I had cleared it.

"James, an eighteen-year-old child? Is that what you really want? What are you thinking?" She glared at me. She had been a little touchy about some of the theater kids before, but I'd never seen anything like this.

"Love, I have no interest in anyone other than…." I couldn't finish the sentence.

"Liar! I saw that. I heard that!" She took two steps closer and stabbed my chest with her finger. "You can't deny that she just said 'I love you so much' and kissed you. I am not stupid. I have eyes and ears. Why?" She started to cry.

"Gwen, if you had seen and heard everything, you would know that she was saying 'thank you' to both of us. She had just told me that we, you and I, were the best things that had ever happened to her. That she loved us so much. And besides, if there was something going on, would she just kiss me on the cheek? Honey, you took this out of context. There is nothing going on between us. I...."

She turned on her heel and bolted into the bathroom. She locked the door and I could hear her sobbing behind it. I realized there was nothing I could say that would make any difference. She had made up her mind that I was silly enough to risk our marriage on a child. Hadn't all the years together shown her anything? Yes, I was a little bit of a flirt, but I had never, not ever, crossed the line. Not once had I ever done anything inappropriate with any of the female companions I'd had over the years. I decided that, since I was indeed innocent, I would say nothing. I went to bed and waited for Gwen. She never came. I have to assume that she waited until I was asleep and went to the guest room to sleep.

It was very icy the next morning. I tried to talk to Gwen, but she was having none of it. I left for the gym, kissing her on the forehead as I left. She glared at me and visibly wiped the kiss from her forehead. I went to the gym and furiously worked out. I kicked and punched the heavy bag like it was my worst enemy. I pounded the weights faster than ever, barely resting between sets. I was so angry. I could understand her jealousy if I had done something wrong, but she was wrong. Jess had done nothing inappropriate and neither had I. I was less and less concerned about Gwen's hurt feelings and more and more upset at how stupid she was being about all this. If she chose not to believe the truth, so be it. I couldn't change reality, and I wouldn't lie to make her feel better. I had done nothing wrong, and I would not bend. She would have to figure this out, not me. I was right; she was wrong. End of story. I finished my workout and took a sauna. The steam and heat did a lot to soothe me. I felt almost normal when I showered and headed home. I did have a rehearsal later that evening, and I was not looking forward to the confrontation I was sure would come before I left for it. Gwen was not involved in this show. She hated *Oklahoma* even more than I did, so I was sitting this one out. I was doing the show only because the director had asked me to. He needed as many strong male voices as he could find, and he was having trouble fleshing out the chorus. Even a bad show was better than no show and, in truth, *Oklahoma* wasn't all that bad. Hell, it was light years better than *Kismet*, the prior show. And besides, Jess was playing one of the secondary leads.

"James, what is up? You look pissed and tired." Jess met me in the lobby as I arrived. "Gwen looked upset last night. Did we all stay too long?"

"No, we were glad to have you guys. It was a fun party. Don't worry. I'm just old. I can't party that late without paying the price the next day. Don't ever get old, Jess." I did my best to smile at her, but I don't think it was very convincing.

"James, your nose is growing. What's really up?" Jess and I couldn't lie to each other. We knew each other too well. She was calling my bluff.

"OK. You're right. Things aren't good. Gwen isn't talking to me. She's mad about our affair…."

"Our what! What affair? What the hell? Where'd she get that idea? James. What the fuck? Oh, God, did she see me thanking you for the party and think…? Oh, God. James, do you want me to talk to her?"

"No, Jess, that's the last thing I want. She'd only think I had coached you. I'm just going to have to ride this thing out. Sorry to drag you into it. I mean, well, don't trouble yourself over it. I am innocent. You are innocent. It's not like we're Lancelot and Guinevere. We are friends, just friends. OK, maybe I am your adopted father. But certainly not lovers. Ever. But, for a while anyway, we need to cool it on all levels and let Gwen figure shit out on her own." I kind of scowled at the stupidity of the whole thing. Jesus Christ, what was that woman thinking? I would never screw a student, certainly not a kid. I was getting angry all over again.

Rehearsal dragged. My heart wasn't really in it. I could tell that Jessica was disturbed, too. The director kept asking the cast where our energy had gone. He was frustrated with us. I guess the negativity flowing from us was having an effect on the whole cast. I'd had it happen to me when I was directing a show. A couple would have a quarrel and the whole cast would feel it. This was just the same, only Jess and I weren't a couple and hadn't argued. Gwen and I had argued about Jess and made her uncomfortable. I tried my best to snap out of my funk, but it just wasn't happening. I finally asked the director whether I could be excused. I told him I was feeling a little off and I could tell I was rubbing off on the rest of the cast. I alluded to some domestic issues without being specific. He let me go at our break time. I was glad to be out of there, but I didn't want to head home. Jess followed me out. I motioned her off, but she followed me anyway.

"James, I feel awful. You and Gwen shouldn't be fighting over us. I should call her. Maybe the three of us can get together and work this out. I don't want you to have any trouble because of me." She looked into my eyes with a helpful expression.

"Jessica, you've never been married. You're a great kid, but believe me, the last thing I need is 'the other woman' coming to my defense. I somehow think that that would only make things worse. Thanks, but I'll have to try to work this out with Gwen on my own." I got into the car and headed back to the war zone. I was not looking forward to the coming confrontation. I had no idea even how to start to deal with this. I could argue rationally and logically, but I was in the dark when it came to defending my innocence against baseless and senseless accusations. I just saw the whole thing as stupid. I knew Gwen would pick up on that and it would only get worse. I drove back to New Worcester very slowly.

"You're home early. Bored with your girlfriend already?" Gwen glowered at me.

"Gwen, I don't know what to say. You heard a snippet of conversation and jumped to a ridiculous conclusion. The only words I can use are the truth, but you've already rejected those. So what do you want me to do?"

"Drop the show. Stop seeing her. And never see her. Period." She crossed her arms and stood, waiting.

"Gwen, where is the woman I married? I've never seen you this irrational before." As soon as I said the word "irrational," I knew the shit was going to hit the fan.

"Irrational! I'm being irrational?" she screamed. "You're fucking some little eighteen-year-old twat and I'm being irrational? Maybe I was irrational when I let you have a party for your little tramp! But I'm not now. I am just claiming my rights as your wife. You do remember that I am your wife, don't you?" Her face was an ugly red. I was dumbfounded. I could understand this outcry had I done anything wrong, anything out of the ordinary, but I could see nothing different about the way I interacted with Jessica from how I interacted with any other female friend. I had no ammunition, no way to combat this. "The truth shall set you free…." What a crock. The truth apparently had no place here and now. I tried to gather my thoughts and speak to Gwen as calmly and rationally as I possibly could. In retrospect, maybe I would have been better served

27

by yelling back. Maybe my calm tone was an irritant—fuel on the flames.

"Gwen, I am not having an affair with Jessica or anyone else for that matter. You were the first woman I was ever with. You are the only woman I've ever been with. I love you and only you and have no desire to stray. I'm sorry you got the notion into your head that I'm having an affair with Jessica. Yes, she's an appealing little girl and I do like her company. But I am not sleeping with her. Not now. Not ever. Nor shall I ever." I stopped and waited for my rational wife to return and talk to me. I was calm and rational; I expected her to be the same.

"Are you going to drop the show? Are you going to stop seeing her?" Gwen had not calmed down one iota.

"No and no. If I had done anything wrong, I would throw myself at your mercy and do whatever you asked. But, since I've done nothing wrong, I've no need to change a thing. I will do the show, I will still be Jessica's friend, and I will continue to be the faithful husband I have always been. And, hopefully, you will come back to being Gwen, my lovely bride." Needless to say, my words had no positive effect on the situation. Maybe I should have genuflected and said, "You're absolutely right, dear; I'm sorry," but, in truth, I wasn't, and I had nothing to be sorry for. So we had a standoff for the next several days. I wasn't going to back down. She wasn't, either. Something was sticking in her craw about Jessica, and she was not going to let it go. I was so taken aback by her outburst that I just dug my heels in. We slept in separate rooms for a while. In time, things thawed and we talked a bit. Gwen finally told me that she felt threatened by Jessica, that I was too emotionally involved with her. She felt that my relationship with Jessica was like having an affair, even though Gwen did finally concede that there really was nothing physical going on. Things returned to a semblance of normal.

I tried to keep my distance from Jess, even though I still believed I was wholly in the right. I didn't want to rub Gwen's nose in it. So I kept at an arm's length from Jess. I dealt with her as minimally as I could during rehearsals, and I kept my distance at social gatherings of the theater clan. It was hard. Jessica had become my closest confidant. I felt lost without my daily conversations with her. In retrospect, I guess I understood why Gwen was feeling a little out of sorts, but Jessica and I were simply friends. Close, personal friends. I didn't want her as a replacement for Gwen. I kept telling myself I didn't want to have sex with her, appealing as that thought might have been. I was very happily married. Jessica simply had a different, fresh perspective that Gwen didn't. Gwen and I had been together for twenty-plus years. There was a certain predictability to our interactions that Jess and I didn't have. I liked Jess's spontaneity and life. It was nice to have someone who was a close friend, truly close enough to share everything with, who wasn't my spouse. She sadly happened to be an attractive, eighteen-year-old girl. My life would have been much simpler had Jessica been "Joseph."

As time went on, I was able to normalize my relationship with Jessica. She needed me as much as I did her. She was a bit of a loner and did not open up easily to others. She trusted me completely and viewed me as more of a father than she did her own. I did my best to be discreet; I did not want another Gwen explosion. Once again, I firmly believed I was not doing anything wrong, that it was Gwen who drove Jessica and me "underground." I felt bad keeping anything from Gwen. Other than surprises for her, I had never felt any need or desire to keep any secrets from my wife. But Jess was different. I needed what Jess had to offer me. It was a counterpoint to my other relationships, a complement or supplement. I thought of Jessica as a "social vitamin" for my soul. I was a better person, a better husband, a better partner when I had Jessica in my life. I did not look forward to the day that she would graduate and move on. That would be rough on me.

In May of 2006, Jessica called me on my cell. We had, since her eighteenth birthday, agreed that I could call her, but she should never call me unless it was an emergency. Gwen was still a little prickly when Jess was in a show with me or we saw her at a cast party. If she knew I had almost daily conversations with Jess, I'm sure she would have kicked me out in a heartbeat. Jessica had had another tiff with her boyfriend, Marcus. I had disapproved of Marcus from the very start. The kid struck me as a retarded ape with manners to match. I never knew what she saw in the brute. I thought she should be with someone who could actually carry on a conversation, someone whose knuckles didn't leave giant furrows behind him when he walked. This kid was coarse and common. I suppose he was attractive on a purely animal level, but I thought Jess deserved so much more. When I saw her number on my cell, I silenced the ringer. I didn't dare answer in front of Gwen. I waited until I had a private moment and returned Jess' call. The moment she answered, I could tell something was not right. Her voice, normally strong and clear, was very weak and timid sounding. When I asked what was wrong, she simply said that this wasn't a good time—that she would call later. She hung up. Now I knew something was seriously wrong. I anxiously waited for her call. I decided I would answer, regardless of whether I was in a private setting or not. I knew she was in trouble. I knew she was calling for help.

A couple of hours later, just after dinner, my cell rang. I looked. Jess. I answered it and wandered outside.

That was not out of the ordinary. I would either wander around while I was on the phone or, if I couldn't wander, doodle. Nothing should have raised Gwen's alert level.

"James…I am sorry to call…. I need to talk. Can you come see me? Can you come to my apartment? Please?" She sounded very distraught.

"Jess, coming over would be more than a little awkward for me. What's wrong?"

"James, I really can't talk about it on the phone. I need a friend. I need to talk. Can you please find a way?" I could tell she had been crying.

"Jessica, Gwen and I were just heading out to a movie. I don't know how I could even bring it up to her that I was going over to see you instead of going to the movies. Can I bring her along?"

"If you have to, but I really need to talk to someone, talk to you. It's…I'm…oh James, please…."

"Jess, I'll try." I hung up the phone. How the hell was I going to manage this? It sounded serious to me. I knew Jessica would not have called if she didn't think it was important enough to risk it. And while I had never lied to Gwen about Jess and me, I certainly had not been forthcoming about the close nature of our continuing friendship. I was guilty of lying in spirit and lying by omission, nothing more. But I couldn't bail on my movie date with Gwen without a good reason, and I didn't think she'd find Jess to be a valid reason. I decided simply to tell her the truth and hope she would remain rational.

"Gwen, I just had a disturbing call from a student. I think she is in trouble and needs to talk…." I waited for the Inquisition…

"Who is it? What's wrong?" Gwen looked concerned.

"Gwen, don't be upset, but it is Jessica." I could see

31

Gwen's mood visibly darken. "She sounded like she had been crying and she said she really needed a friend. She asked if I could come over. I told her I would have to talk to you. I really think I should go, but the ball is in your court."

"Why did she call you, of all people? Why not one of her girlfriends? James, I am not comfortable with this. Not at all. Are you still seeing her? Have you been lying to me all this time?" She was pissed. I lied to her for the first time in our marriage.

"No, Gwen, I only see her when we're in a show together or if we run into each other on campus. She did take a class from me last semester. But she still trusts me. And I don't think she has much of a circle of friends here at MNC. You were her friend once, too, before…well, just before."

"Am I supposed to believe that she, out of the blue, decided you are the only one she can talk to about whatever is bothering her? That she really has no one else and that you two aren't still seeing each other?"

"Gwen, you are going to believe whatever you choose to believe. You are your own woman. That's one of the things I respect most about you. If you want to, come with me. If you still don't trust me after all these years, just come along. I have nothing to hide from you." I waited for her response. I was surprised by it.

"Look, I don't like this. Not one bit. But, James, I do trust you. I don't trust her, but I do trust you. So go if you must. Call me if you need me, but I'll stay here." I kissed her and headed out to the car.

I had dropped Jessica off at her apartment before, but I had never been in. I rang the bell and she buzzed me in. I knew she lived on the third floor, but I didn't know which way to turn when I got up there. I didn't need to;

Jess was waiting at the top of the stairs for me. Her eyes were puffy from crying. Her cheeks were streaked with tears. Her lip looked suspiciously swollen, and the top of her T-shirt was freshly ripped. I couldn't help but notice that, for some reason, she was more beautiful than ever. Broken bird that she was, she looked fragile and beautiful and enticing. I quickly dismissed these thoughts from my head as inappropriate. They were disturbing, though. Why would the sight of this little girl, obviously in physical and emotional distress, excite me? I was moved on both an emotional and a physical level by the sight of her. Yet I should have been repulsed or saddened to see my friend like this. What was wrong with the way my brain was wired?

"James, thank you. I'm sorry to have called. I'm sorry; I'm sorry; I'm sorry. Please…I'm sorry, James; I'm so sorry…." With that, she buried her head into my shoulder and started to sob. I picked her up like I had my daughter when she was young and carried her through her open apartment door. She was like a feather; Jess was so slightly built that a good wind could blow her over. I gently placed her in a chair, closed the door, and knelt in front of her. Once again, I was struck by her beauty at the moment. Her tears and puffy eyes were having quite an effect on me. I had to shift to avoid her seeing my growing member beneath my shorts. I was embarrassed.

"Jessica, what is wrong? Why have you been crying? Tell me, kiddo, what's wrong?" She tried to talk, but only unintelligible syllables came out. She cried harder and buried her head once more in my shoulder. I squeezed into the chair next to her and rocked her gently, wiping the tear soaked hair from her beautiful face. I rubbed her shoulder and told her she'd be OK, that she had all night to talk, just to calm down. I liked holding her close, feeling her life in my arms. She was warm and soft and…damn it! I was losing sight of the fact she was hurt and I was there to help, not to be aroused. But there was something powerful going on, something I'd never felt before with her.

"Jess, can you try to tell me what's wrong? Slowly. Just let it out…."

"James, I'm sorry. I'm so sorry. I'm so stupid. I'm in trouble. I'm…I'm…I'm…oh, God, James, I'm pregnant. Two months. And Marcus is being such a jerk. He asked me if it was his! I've never slept with anyone else and he knows it. He called me a slut, asked who else I was fucking. Called me stupid for getting knocked up! Like it doesn't take two!" She practically screamed the last couple of sentences and then collapsed in my arms, sobbing. I tried to soothe and reassure her.

After a while, Jess was able to talk again. She told me about finding out that she was pregnant, the worries she had about telling Marcus, her fights with Marcus and, incredibly, how much she loved him. I really was baffled. This man was a boor, a jerk, and rude to a fault, but she still insisted that she loved him. What the hell? I hadn't asked, but I assumed that the puffy lip was a result of him hitting her. Where was the strong and independent young woman I knew? How could she still love this animal? I never will understand women. They are the strangest (and most fascinating) creatures. Jess told me she planned on having the baby, but was going to give it up for adoption. She didn't want to have an abortion; she didn't believe that she could live with herself after making that decision. She knew it wasn't the right time for her to have a child, that she wasn't ready to raise one, and that Marcus certainly was not.

"That's what our fight was about, James. The baby. Marcus wants me to have an abortion. He doesn't want me

to have the baby. He told me he'd beat it out o
didn't have an abortion."

"And then he hit you." I said it as a statement, not a
question.

"He didn't really, James. He wouldn't really hurt
me. He couldn't. He's so sweet most times. No, he grabbed
me. He was angry. When he grabbed my shirt, his hand
slipped and hit my lip. That's all. He didn't hit me." She
wasn't convincing me.

"Jessica, really? You expect me to believe that? We
know each other better than to let each other lie. I've gotta
call you on this one. You just told me he was angry and
yelling, and now you're telling me it was an accident? I'm
not buying it, Jess."

"James, Marcus loves me. I love him. He wouldn't
hurt me. Trust me. He wouldn't do anything like that on
purpose. I know you don't like him, James; we've talked
about that before. But he wouldn't hurt me."

"He'd better not. I know a couple of officers on the
New Worcester PD and several of the cops on campus. I
would not hesitate to call if he ever did hurt you. Jessica,
you know how important you are to me. I don't want to see
you hurt. I don't want to see you end up at a safe house,
worrying about where Marcus is. I don't trust him. I'll keep
my eyes wide open." And I would. I knew he was a bad
seed. I was sure he had hit her intentionally, and I was
concerned he would again. I never could understand how a
woman could find herself in this position and still defend
the abuser.

When I was sure she had calmed down and could be
alone, I left for home. I told her to call me if Marcus tried
anything else. I told her to call me for any reason, that I
would be there for her. I told her I loved her and wanted her
to be safe and healthy and well. I drove home slowly,

thinking about how screwed up her whole situation was. I knew she was pro-choice, so I was surprised by her choice. I thought she would have aborted, but maybe her love for Marcus clouded her judgment about the baby. Maybe the thought of terminating his child was beyond her ken. I just didn't know.

"James, you've been gone over three hours. What the hell?" Clearly Gwen was not amused.

"Gwen, it was ugly. She's confused and in trouble and needed a friend. Gwen, she's pregnant and—"

"Pregnant! So why did she need to call you? Is it yours?" Gwen's eyes were fiery and dark, all at the same time.

"My God, Gwen, how could you think that? Mine? I've never touched the girl. She's a kid. A nice kid. A good friend. But that's all. I have *never* had sex with her. I've never done anything inappropriate with her. If you're patient, you can have a DNA test done after it's born. She's not aborting; she is going to have it and put it up for adoption. Christ, if that's what it will take, I'll ask her to have a DNA test. I think they can do them in-utero. I just don't believe this bullshit, Gwen. This kid is in trouble, but all you can do is think that I'm the cause. Do we have to go here again?" I stormed out of the room, went out the back, and out to the shelter to be alone. We were making good progress on the shelter, and it struck me that it was the only place I could go and think in peace and quiet. I hadn't even had time to tell Gwen about Marcus and my suspicions about abuse. Gwen still had some deep-seated mistrust of me and of Jessica. I certainly didn't understand it.

I slept out in the shelter. It was actually a pretty cozy little nest. I'd never thought I'd have to use it as my "doghouse," but it served well that night. In retrospect, I'm certain it was the wrong choice on my part. When I came into the house, Gwen was nowhere to be found. I did find a note on the kitchen counter:

> James,
> I am going to go to Copper Harbor for a couple of days. I need to think.
>
> Gwen

"Jesus Christ! Gwen!" I yelled to no one. This was out of control. Stupid bullshit. The only thing I was guilty of was being a friend. Trying to help out someone in need. And for that, my wife left "to think." I hoped she would think and realize how silly she was. I wouldn't try to call. I knew there was nothing for me to say. She would have to parse this out on her own. I just hoped she would come to the right and truthful conclusion. I couldn't imagine life without Gwen. She was truly my better half, and I needed her. If she left me, especially over a silly misunderstanding, I would be ripped apart and left without a soul. I honestly didn't know how I'd go on without her; she'd become so much a part of who I was.

Gwen came back a few days later. She apologized for thinking the worst and jumping to conclusions. She told me that she trusted me, that I had never done anything to make her truly think I had strayed. She told me again, however, that something about my relationship with Jess still bothered her. She felt that, even though Jess and I shared no physical intimacy, we were having an "emotional affair," so she would be more comfortable if I promised to stop any communications with her. She felt that was not an unreasonable request. I thought it ignorant, but I held my tongue. Gwen was my life. Jessica was important, too, but not as important as my wife. I told her I would let Jessica know she couldn't call me or see me, that I would not do a show she was involved in, and that we were finished. I wasn't sure I could actually do that. Jess was also a part of me. Not a threat to my marriage, not a replacement for Gwen, just something different, something of my own that I didn't share with Gwen. I still don't know why that was so important to me, but it was. I needed to have just one friend, one connection, that wasn't shared. I didn't know if I could sever the ties.

JUNE 3, 2006

Things had gotten pretty much back to normal between Gwen and me. I had tried to toe the line and not talk to Jess, but I did "fall off the wagon" a few times. Jess was still having trouble convincing Marcus that she was really going to give up the child for adoption. He thought she was going to have it and try to use it to hold on to him or extort money from him or some such. I kept Jessica at arm's length; I didn't want to upset Gwen's applecart again. I worried about Jessica, but I worried more about my marriage. Gwen and I were working on our garden and on the shelter. School was out and that afforded us the free time to do as we pleased. I had elected not to teach any summer classes and was taking a little break from the theater as well.

Gwen had bought me a new motorcycle back in March, but we hadn't ridden much since she got it for me. Winter hung on late in 2006. There was still snow on the ground through all of April and even a few days into May. The ice on the harbor didn't break up until May 15th. We had a few nice days scattered in there, but no stretches of nice weather until the end of May. So my shiny new Suzuki just sat in the garage, waiting for proper motorcycle weather to arrive. I swore to Gwen that I could hear it crying out to me, begging to be ridden.

June 3, 2006 dawned bright and clear. A Saturday, although when school was out the days really didn't much matter. Gwen and I took the Suzuki out for our first long ride of the season. We put on our new helmets, turned on the communicators, and headed out. We were on the no-plan plan as I like to call it: we were headed wherever the road took us. Our only firm destination or deadline was being back at the house by 6:00 so Gwen could get ready for her dinner date with "the girls." One Saturday a month, Gwen and six or seven of her friends would get all dolled up and treat themselves to a girls' night out. They would have cocktails at 7:00, dinner at 8:00, and then head to a club to dance or catch a late movie. Some nights they would retire to one of their houses for dessert and a lively evening's conversation. Gwen loved her girls' night and wouldn't miss it for the world.

So we rode south toward Escanaba, continued past till we got to the family-owned zoo just north of Menominee, cuddled with the new baby tiger cub and petted their new goats in the children's zoo, and then rode back home. We pulled in at 5:58, right on time. Gwen hopped off the bike, pulled off her helmet and leathers, and went in to shower and get ready. I changed the Suzuki's oil and cleaned up the bike before putting it away for the night. We'd put a couple of hundred miles on the bike and I wanted to get the initial break in oil out and put in a good quality synthetic. I am fairly anal retentive when it comes to my motorcycles and their care and feeding. This Suzuki was the first I'd ever gotten new, so I wanted to make sure I treated it right, right from the start. I was just finishing up when Gwen came out to kiss me goodbye.

"Gwen, I still don't know why you bought me this bike. I'm sure I don't deserve it. I know I don't deserve you. I love you, honey." I kissed her and held her close.

"James, I bought it because I could and you were like a little boy when you first saw it. I thought you would pee yourself every time we went by the dealer. I just had to get it for you. It was a surprise, wasn't it? Just like this was." She pointed at the opal choker necklace I had surprised her with all those centuries ago when we were still kids. I kissed her again and held her close.

"I know you will go out tonight no matter what, but

I wish you were staying home. It is such a lovely night. I want to sit out under the stars and just hold you all night long."

"Silly boy, you know I'll be home soon. Before you know it. Maybe we'll sleep in your old tent tonight…." She kissed me goodbye and got into her car to leave.

"No parties while I'm gone!" she called out as she drove off.

"No boys, only men!" I called out to her as she left, echoing a joke we used to tell babysitters when we left for the night. I smiled and went inside to make myself some dinner.

I spent most of the evening curled up on the couch with a new Anne Rice book. I loved her lush writing style. Only she could make the act of killing a human seem seductive and sexy. Her descriptions of the vampires plunging their fangs into their chosen ones and sucking the life from them was almost orgasmic in nature. I wished that I had her writing skills. I wanted to be one of her vampires. Every touch, every sensation was described in exquisite detail. The pages practically dripped with sex and blood and romance. I dozed off, book on my face.

A loud scream and a violent knocking on my door woke me with a rude start. I caught sight of the clock. It was a little past 10:00. There was a loud moan again and a bang at the door. I rushed over to answer it. It was Jessica. She looked horrible. Her left eye was swollen almost shut and her lips disfigured. Her dress was torn and she was barefoot. Her car was in the driveway, butted up firmly against mine. I didn't try to assess any damage; Jess was more urgent. I grabbed her, helped her in, and placed her on the couch.

"My God, Jess, what happened?" I already knew. Marcus had tried to make good on his threat to beat the baby out of her. As soon as the word left my mouth, a dark red stain started to grow on her dress. She was hemorrhaging heavily. I grabbed my cell and dialed 911 and let the operator who answered know the situation. I raced to the linen closet and grabbed a towel and raced back to the couch to try to staunch the heavy flow. I put pillows under Jessica's little bottom to prop her up and try to get gravity on our side. I didn't know how long the EMTs would take to arrive, but I knew I had to stop her blood loss or it would be too late, no matter how quickly they got here. I pushed her legs up, one on each of my shoulders, pushed her dress out of the way, and put the towel between her legs. I applied pressure to try to slow the blood loss. It seemed to help, although the towel was quickly turning dark red. Jess moaned and writhed from the pain. I bent down so my face was close to hers and I could talk to her softly. I wanted to calm her as much as I could— to tell her the ambulance was on the way and she would be OK. She moaned, "Oh, God, James…. Oh, God…James…. It hurts…. Oh, God…James…James…James!" And that's when Gwen walked in. The final, loud "James!" From her vantage point, Gwen saw Jess' feet on my shoulders with me bending down, my face hidden by the back of the couch. She heard Jessica moaning my name and heard me saying hers. It must have looked for all the world like I was having the time of my life with the lass. Gwen had no way to tell I was trying to save a life.

"You filthy fucking PIG! You're fucking that little whore on my couch! In MY HOUSE! I hope you both rot in HELL!" Gwen screamed louder than I had ever heard any human scream. Her face erupted in a spiderweb of bulging veins. I popped up over the back of the couch just in time to see a heavy, bronze, antique doorstop come hurtling toward my head. It grazed my ear, but didn't do any serious damage.

"Gwen, it's not what it looks like. Oh, God, no, it's not at all what you think! She's—" A piece of pottery came whizzing past.

"Don't you ever speak to me again! YOU FUCKING ANIMAL!" With that, Gwen ran out the door, slamming it loudly behind her. I wanted to get up and follow her; I wanted to stop her, but I couldn't take my hands off Jessica. She would surely bleed out if I took my hands and the towel away. I had to try to save her. I could try to save our marriage later, later when Gwen would have to see the truth. If the police report and the ambulance log and the bloodstain on the couch didn't prove my case to her, nothing would. I heard Gwen's motor race and then heard a crash as she rammed her car into another. I would find out later that Gwen had rammed Jessica's car several times and mine once before leaving. I then heard gravel fly and tires squeal as Gwen peeled away and went screaming down the road. Moments later, I heard the wail of the ambulance and a police car's siren.

"Jess, you've got to hold on a few more minutes. Just a few more. The ambulance is almost here. It's almost here. Hold on…. Hold on…!" I pleaded with her. I couldn't bear to see her die like this. She was so bright and beautiful and special. It would be such a waste of a young life. The EMTs burst through the door and immediately started working on Jess. I stood there, dumbfounded, watching as they tried to save my young friend. They got a couple of IVs started and started pushing fluids as fast as they could. They hung a bag of saline and one of blood and prepared her for transport. I asked whether I could come with them to the hospital. They nodded, so I got into the ambulance next to Jess and held her hand the whole way to New Worcester Memorial. They got her into the ER and then into an OR so quickly that my head was spinning.

*

I waited for what seemed like a week in the waiting room. I paced and fretted, hoping she would be OK. Finally, a female doctor came in to talk to me.

"Dr. Martin, you probably saved her life. She had serious internal bleeding. Putting pressure on her like that was the only thing you could have done, and it was the right thing. She lost a lot of blood and lost her baby, but she will live. Her eye took a couple of stitches to patch up, and we had to use butterfly bandages on her lip, but she'll be OK. She'll be going to Recovery and then into the ICU for observation. You should go home and get some rest. There's nothing you can do here. We'll call you if anything happens...." I thanked the young doctor and told her I would probably wait until morning to make sure Jess was OK. I asked whether there was some place I could stretch out and take a nap. I also needed to wash up. My hands were covered with crusted blood. The doctor started to tell me where to go when her pager went off.

"I'm sorry; I've got to get to the ER, NOW. Someone will come and get you later." With that, the young doctor scurried off. I sat down to wait. I picked up the waiting room phone and dialed for an outside line. I called Gwen's cell. This number wouldn't appear on her caller ID, so maybe she would answer. I was sure she'd never pick up if she knew it was me. Her phone rang eight times and then turned me over to voicemail. I tried again. Same thing. I broke the hospital rules and got my own cell out and dialed. Same result. I put it away and sat down to wait. As it turned out, I didn't have to wait for long.

"Dr. Martin, I need to talk to you...." The young doctor had returned. "I...." She paused.

"Is it Jessica? Has something happened?" I was

concerned that she had taken a turn for the worse. "And please call me James. Dr. Martin sounds a little silly around here when I'm a PhD, not a physician." I smiled at the young lady in front of me.

"OK, James…umm…this isn't going to be easy…." She walked over and shut the door. "I think you should sit down. I think we both should." My stomach leapt into my throat. I sat.

"Dr. Martin, I need you to come into the ER. I need you to identify someone. I think it is your wife." The young doctor looked down at the floor.

"What! I don't understand. My wife? Here?" I stood up quickly. "What do you mean?"

"James, a red Subaru Outback was found crashed into the bridge on Bay Road, the bridge over the Hemlock River. The car had been there for a little while. Central Dispatch sent out a crew as soon as it was called in. They had to use the Jaws of Life to get the driver out; the car had been going at a very high rate of speed when it hit the bridge. The page I got when I was talking to you…I had to go and pronounce the driver dead on arrival. The ID in her purse said 'Gwen A. Martin'."

It took a moment for it all to sink in. I fell to the floor—out stone cold.

When I came around, I was on a gurney under the harsh lights of the ER.

JUNE 4, 2006

"James? Dr. Martin? Are you awake?" A young man's face peered into mine. He had on scrubs, so I assumed he was a nurse or intern. I moved my head slightly and felt a nasty pain shoot through me as I did. I let out a yelp.

"Dr. Martin, you're in the ER. You took a nasty tumble when you passed out, hit your head on the coffee table in the waiting room. We've put in a couple of stitches. The doctor will be here shortly to talk to you. Is there anything I can get you?" The young man looked at me helpfully.

"Uh, my wife. Call her. Let her know I'm here. I need to talk to Gwen...." I tried to sit up, but a wave of pain and nausea forced me back down onto the gurney. I reached my hand up to touch my forehead, the center of my pain. I found a bandage and tape there. "Sorry, I didn't get your name," I said to the young man. "You have the advantage; you know who I am."

"Dr. Martin, I'm Rick. I'm one of the nurses here in the ER. Please don't try to sit up again for a little while. I promise it won't be pleasant if you do. You're pumped full of pain meds and have had a pretty good head trauma, so I'd just relax as best you can. Dr. Barton will be in in a minute."

"Thanks, Rick. You're right; this isn't pleasant just lying here, but I don't think I'll try to get up again for a bit. Could you please call my wife for me?" Rick stood mute, a puzzled look on his face. Then I remembered what the young ER doc had told me before I passed out. Gwen was dead. There would be no calling her. She was here, too, on a gurney just like I was. Only difference was that I would walk out of here under my own power and she would never wake again. I started to cry, softly at first, but it soon escalated into a full-fledged wail. My feet had been knocked out from under me, and my world had come crashing down. My wife, my sweet lovely wife, was dead, and I was alone. How could I possibly go on without her? She was my soul mate, my spirit, certainly my better half. I sobbed uncontrollably.

Dr. Barton entered the room. She came and sat by the bed and took my hand in hers.

"I am so sorry for your loss, Dr. Martin. I didn't know your wife, but I went to her gallery several times. I loved her artwork. I read about the good things she did for the theater in Northton. She was a lovely woman. I'm so very sorry." I stopped sobbing long enough to croak out a feeble "Thank you" and tried to roll on my side. My body was having none of that. I got dizzy from that simple act and vomited on the floor next to the bed.

"I'm sorry; I'm so sorry; I…" and I vomited some more. The pain medications clearly were not agreeing with me, nor was the grief. Every time I wretched, pain would shoot through my body. I knew that my injury couldn't be that severe; it took just a couple of stitches to close. How could it hurt this much? The pressure inside my head was unbearable. My head ached and throbbed. I blacked out again. When I came to, Dr. Barton was looking worriedly at me.

"I don't like this, not one bit. Dr. Martin, I'm going to take you down for a head CT. You shouldn't be in this much pain. You hit the table pretty hard, but this seems excessive to me. They'll be wheeling you down for your CT in a couple of moments." She scurried off as a couple of orderlies came to whisk me off to get my scan. I just wanted to see Gwen, wanted to hold her one last time. That's all I could think of.

The scan revealed a slight fracture in my skull. A bone spur from the fracture was pressing against a nerve and causing my pain. They had to reopen my wound and do a quick repair, basically grinding away the burr that was pressing into the nerve. I had several more stitches than before, but much less pain now that the nerve was not being agitated by the bone splinter. I was in the recovery room at about 7:00 in the morning when my friend and colleague, Vince Spatafore, came in to see me.

"James, the things you won't do for attention! Man, what a stunt. Did you miss me that much?" Vince was always a joker. He got serious quickly, though. "Tough break about Gwen. Joe Higgins found her. When he couldn't get you on the phone, he called me to ask if I knew where you were. After he found you here, he called me back to tell me about Gwen and told me to hightail it over here. I am so sorry, James. You know, if there's anything I...." With that, Vince broke down and started to cry. I ended up calming him instead of the other way around. When we could talk again, he asked me why I was in the hospital in the first place. I told him about Jess and about Gwen storming out of the house.

"Oh, shit, James. Shit. She thought you and Jess were...uh...oh, shit. James, that is awful. That she would fly off the handle and drive away crazy like that. On Bay Road, no less. Oh, God, James, I just don't know what to say. I just don't know." He sat silently for a moment. "Is Jess OK? Did she make it? Did she...?"

"I think she's OK. She was the last time I heard, before they told me that Gwen was here. Before I passed out. Before my world disintegrated. But I just don't know for sure. No one has said anything since I got into Recovery. I hope so. Young kid. Bright. Shame to lose her, too." And it would be. Waste of a young life if she hadn't made it. Still, I didn't know how I would handle seeing her the next time I did. In a way, Jess was responsible for Gwen's death. I didn't know if I could deal with seeing her any time soon, no matter how close we were. Rational or not, I would always see her as being responsible for Gwen's death. I loved Jess' friendship, but because of how I had valued her, I had lost the love of my life. How to deal with all the guilt? I had no idea.

Dr. Barton came back in to check on me. Vince excused himself and left for the cafeteria. Dr. Barton looked at my charts, checked my vitals, and asked how I was feeling. I told her that physically I felt much better; the pain in my head had diminished dramatically. I told her that emotionally I was a wreck; that I felt lost and alone. She nodded and looked sympathetically back at me. She asked whether I wanted her to refer me to "someone to talk to." I told her I had just lost the only person on the planet I could really talk to, the only one who mattered at all. I started to cry again. I'd cried more in the last twenty-four hours than I had in the previous twenty-four years. I asked whether I could see Gwen, whether I could say "goodbye" to her. Dr. Barton told me that it would not be a good idea, that the crash had been so severe that seeing Gwen would only disturb me. I cried harder.

"James, you really should let me send someone in for you to talk to. A grief counselor at the least, or one of the hospital social workers. I'd rather you let me refer you to one of our psych—"

"No!" I shouted. "I don't want to see any of them. I just want my wife. I don't want to talk to some shrink. They don't know me and they didn't know her! Just let me *be*!" I crossed my arms over my chest and closed my eyes. "If you could please leave now, Dr. Barton, I'm going to try to rest. Isn't rest something that you would prescribe?"

Dr. Barton said nothing. She patted my hands and quietly left the room. I just lay there, numb. I had no idea what would happen next. I really didn't care. Everything seemed so pointless with Gwen gone. We were both still young. Full of life. We'd really never talked about death and life without the other. We had made wills and trusts and all that legal stuff, but we never really thought much about dying. I had to get my shit together. I had a lot to do. I needed to make a list. I needed to call the kids. I needed to make arrangements. I needed to get out of here. I pressed the call button and waited for a nurse. A pretty young thing came into the room in just a few moments.

"Dr. Martin, how can I help you? You buzzed." I had a hard time believing this little girl was an RN, but her nametag said "Rebecca Allen, RN."

"Can I have a pad of paper and a pen or pencil? I need to write down some notes, got to start arranging things. Need to write it down before these drugs make me forget what I was thinking about."

"Sure, no problem. Anything else? Your breakfast will be here in a few moments. Not much, you're going to be on liquids for a couple of meals at least. Hope you like JELL-O!"

"When you see Dr. Barton, could you ask her to stop back in? I've got a few questions for her."

"No problem, Dr. Martin. I'll be right back with your writing supplies and one of the aides will bring your breakfast."

"Thanks, Ms. Allen. I really appreciate it." She scurried off and, as promised, an aide came in with a tray for me. JELL-O, coffee, milk, and some chicken broth. Not a very appealing breakfast, but I wasn't really very hungry. I sipped the broth and coffee. The milk held no attraction for me, nor did the JELL-O. The broth was OK. The coffee weak. In a couple of minutes, Nurse Allen returned with a legal pad and a pen.

"Dr. Barton will be in in a moment. Anything else?" She smiled pleasantly at me.

"If you don't mind me asking, just how old are you, Ms. Allen? You don't look a day over sixteen. Your tag says you're an RN, but I'm finding it a little hard to believe." I did my best to coax a smile from my face, but I think I only managed a grimace.

"Dr. Martin, I don't expect you to remember me, but I was in your 200-level American History class in 1997. I was pretty quiet and sat in the back, so I don't imagine you remember, but I am almost twenty-eight now. I've been an RN here for several years."

"I apologize for asking and for not recognizing you, but that class is always a blur to me. One hundred kids in a lecture room every semester. I hardly remember anyone from those classes. Sorry."

"No worries. I get carded anytime we go to a new bar or restaurant. I don't mind. My mom still looks very young. I got it from her. When I had my son, some people on the ward looked at me like I was a twelve year old with a kid. It was rather amusing, actually." She smiled again. Dr. Barton came back into the room and Ms. Allen left.

"Dr. Barton, I want to apologize for earlier. I was a little rude to you. I know you are doing the right thing by offering to refer me to a psychologist. I'm still trying to take all this in. I didn't mean to be rude. Will you forgive me?"

"James, with all you've been through in the last twenty-four hours, you have held up remarkably well. No need to apologize for anything."

"How long will I need to be here? I mean, I've got a lot to do, arrangements to make. I've got to call my kids. I don't know how I'm going to tell them that their mother is dead. I've got to make funeral arrangements…. Oh, God, there's so much to do and so much of it that she would normally take care of." I started to cry again. I choked back the tears and waited for Dr. Barton's answer.

"Your surgery was really rather simple. I just had to drill a very small hole in your skull and remove a bone spur. You seem to be doing great now that the nerve pain is relieved. I want to observe you for twenty-four hours. You should be able to go home tomorrow morning, if everything goes well and you are eating solid food, passing urine and stool, and your vitals continue to be strong. I would like for you to have someone with you for the next twenty-four hours after that, but I'll bet that won't be a problem; you'll have more company for the next few days than you'll know what to do with…."

"Thanks. And thanks for taking care of Gwen. And Jess. Is she OK? I kind of lost track of what actually brought me here…."

"Jess is fine. She lost a lot of blood and the baby, but you saved her life. She's been asking to see you…."

"I'm glad she's OK. I don't know if I'm ready for company. I am glad Vince is here; I'm going to make him regret it by using him as my 'eyes and ears,' but I don't think I'm ready to see Jess. The whole thing is a little raw right now. Gwen crashed her car because she thought Jess and I were having an affair. She saw me bent over this girl with my face next to hers and thought I was…ummm…well, you get the picture. I'm not sure I can handle seeing Jess right now. Tell her I'm glad she's OK, but I'm really not seeing anyone right now. Could you do that for me?"

"Sure, I can do that. I didn't know about, well, the nature of your wife's accident. I'm really sorry. If only

52

she'd known the truth...." Dr. Barton's beeper went off. She looked down at it and frowned.

"I have to answer this page. My shift was supposed to end soon, but it looks like I'll be here for a while. A couple of kids being brought in from Lake Superior. Swimming at Treasure Point. It's going to be a long summer...." She hurried off.

After a time, Vince came back in to see me. He asked what he could do for me, told me to treat him as if I owned him. Told me he'd get even with me some day. We both laughed a little. I asked him to run to the house and pick up some clothes and my toothbrush and the like. I also asked him to call Mark Lundberg at the funeral home for me. I told him to contact our family attorney and to call Grace, Gwen's gallery manager and best friend. He wrote down what I asked and headed out. I thanked him for being a good friend. After he left, I made a "To-Do" list. I dreaded calling the kids, so I busied myself with the list for a few moments while I steeled myself for the worst phone calls I would ever make in my life.

"Brian, good morning. Sorry to wake you...."

"Dad, what the hell? It's like 9:30. On a Sunday. Can't I sleep in? What the hell? This better be important...." He was not amused. He would be less so in a moment.

"Brian, I don't know how to say this. Brian, there's been an accident. Two, really. I am in the hospital with a slight concussion and a fractured skull, but that's not what I called about." I could hear him sputtering in the background. "Brian, your mom has been in a serious auto accident. She wrecked her car on the Bay Road, at the bridge. Brian, she didn't make it. She died from her injuries, son. I'm sorry."

"Dad! What! She WHAT? She died? Oh, shit. Oh,

shit. OH, SHIT! FUCK! I...." Brian dropped the phone and I could hear him crash into a chair or table, sobbing. He picked his phone back up. "Dad, I'm coming home. Today. I'll grab some stuff and I'll be home later tonight. Are you OK? Does Gretchen know? Oh, God...." His voice trailed off and he started to wail.

"Brian, please take your time; don't rush home. See if you can get a friend to come along and drive. Please. I want you home in one piece. Be careful." I said goodbye and dialed Gretchen's number.

"Dad? You never call this early on a Sunday? What's wrong?"

"Gretchen, I need you to come home for a few days. I can't sugarcoat this. Your mom has had an accident. It was serious. She didn't make it, hon. I'm sorry." I waited for Gretchen's reaction. She stayed surprisingly calm, considering.

"Dad, are you OK? Were you in the car with her? What happened?"

"Well, dear, I'm in the hospital, but I wasn't in the car with your mom. I brought a friend here last night, and they brought your mom in while I was in the waiting room. When they told me about her, I fell and cracked my head against a table. I'm OK, just hurt and look a little stupid, but I'm OK."

"Where was mom when she...ummm...where did she crash? What happened?"

"She crashed into the bridge on Bay Road. No one really knows how or why yet, but she was going very fast when she hit the bridge. I'm sure that she didn't suffer, hon; I'm sure that it was all over quickly. I'm so sorry; I hated dialing the phone to call, hated to tell you this over the phone, but I really need you here right now. Are you OK, Gretchen?"

"I'm in shock, Dad. I'll be home tomorrow, early as I can. When will you get out of the hospital?"

"If everything goes OK, I'll be leaving tomorrow morning. As long as I can eat and have no fever or anything like that. Call me if you need anything. Do you have enough money to get home?"

"Yeah, Dad, I'm OK. I'm not rich, but I'm doing OK. I'll be OK. I'll see you tomorrow. Love you." With that, she hung up and I was done with the calls I dreaded most.

I spent the rest of the day on the phone, calling family and friends. Mark Lundberg came to see me and we made the arrangements for Gwen's funeral. It was all a little surreal. Vince came and went several times. He was indispensable; it was just like I had grown an extra set of hands and eyes. He was the best friend I could have asked for. Everything fell into place as the day went on. We would wait a few days before having Gwen's memorial. I wanted to make sure I would be out of the hospital and give her family and friends time to get here. Mark was really great, too. He really understood his profession. He was sympathetic without being maudlin, helpful without being cloying. We put together a service that Gwen would have approved of. There would be no viewing, Gwen was too battered for that and, besides, we both hated the ritual. We would have the parlor at the funeral home decorated with pictures of Gwen and the kids, pictures of her life. We planned to make this a celebration of her life, not a dreary mourning of her death. I would have the kids select their favorite paintings that Gwen had done to put up as well. It would be as upbeat as Gwen had been.

The doctors and nurses were very respectful of my needs that day. They took my vitals, checked me over as they needed to, but quickly left me to go about my business. The whole staff was really great. I made a note to send them a thank you note and flowers after Gwen's memorial service. My years with Gwen had given me a sense of proper social graces. I can't imagine what I would have turned out like if she hadn't taken an interest in me all those years ago. When the day came to a close, I was exhausted. Most people complain that they can't sleep in a hospital. I slept like exactly what I was, a tired, distraught man bereft of his mate and drained by all of the day's details. I closed my eyes at around 9:00 and, other than when the nurses would take my vitals, slept soundly until 9:00 the next morning. I slept right through breakfast. Dr. Barton came in to check me over and told me that I would be going home at noon. Vince would come pick me up. Mark's people had already picked up Gwen. We were both leaving the hospital, but only one of us got to go home.

THE BLUR

The couple of weeks following Gwen's death I simply call "The Blur." I really can't recall everything that happened. I know the kids came home, I got out of the hospital, and we had Gwen's funeral, but it was all a jumble of disconnected actions to me. I lost track of how many plates of deviled eggs friends brought over, or how many bad store-bought lasagnas ended up half-eaten and in the trash. How many times I said, "Thank you so much for your kindness," or "Yes, she was wonderful; I will miss her…." I came to the conclusion that funerals are a stupid waste of time. They are for the benefit of the living, not for remembering the dead. I spent more time calming and soothing other people than they did me. Friends of ours, students of hers, family members, I seemed to be their solace rather than they mine. I held more sobbing women and told them that they would be OK than I can count. My world had been ripped apart, my very soul stripped from me, and yet the mourners seemed to need my counsel and succor. By the time it was all over, I was ready for them all just to vanish, just to leave me the hell alone. I wanted to sit alone, quietly, silently in my own house with no hustle and noise. I was glad the kids were going to stay for a while; I welcomed their company. I was just glad to be free of the other foolishness.

I had to start dealing with all the various paperwork associated with a person's passing. I called our attorney for help with this. Fred Johnston had set up the various trusts and the like for me and the kids, and I wanted him to handle things as much as possible. I would need guidance about how to close down Gwen's gallery and all the legal BS that would follow. He came over to the house to meet with me the Monday after her funeral.

"James, I just want you to know how much this all pains me. I mean, it's nothing like what you're going through, but over the years, I've come to think of you and Gwen as family. I just can't believe that she's gone. And so young. I am so sorry for you and the kids." I thanked Fred for the condolences. He was practically family. Gwen and I would have been the guardians of his children, had anything happened to Fred and Julia. They would have been Brian and Gretchen's guardians had we both expired. We had dinner with them at least twice a month. We went to their camp during the summer. Fred was truly broken up by Gwen's death, and I didn't resent him the way I did some of the others I had dealt with in the past week. His feelings were genuine, justified, and heartfelt. He actually cared about both of us, so I felt OK sharing my grief with him.

"Thanks, Fred. I really don't know what I'm going to do without Gwen. You know that she truly is my, was my better half. You didn't know me 'pre-Gwen,' but I was a prickly bastard. Self-absorbed. I didn't really have any social skills. Gwen made me a human being. I still don't know what attracted her to me in the first place, but I'm sure I'd be a hermit in an apartment full of arcane textbooks and crumpled papers if she hadn't come into my life. I'm not joking. She made me who I am today. I am fucking lost, Fred, lost. I just don't know what I'm going to do. I don't know why the hell I should even want to live any more. I've got nothing left. Nothing." With that, I started to sob. Fred held me and patted my back. I cried for at least a half hour. Fred patiently waited and did his best to soothe me. I was cracking. I'd stayed strong all week during the blur. Now it was my turn. The tears flowed and my body shook as sobs wracked my body. When I was finally able to get a grip, Fred and I just talked for a while before we got back to the business of Gwen's affairs.

"Now, James, I know that Gwen was the financial brains of the outfit. She told me when we were drawing all this up years ago that you never even looked at the bank statements. So I suppose that some of what we're going to discuss will be kind of a shock to you."

"What do you mean? Did Gwen have a secret gambling habit or something? Are we broke?" I was joking and hoped that Fred saw it that way. He laughed.

"No, James, quite the opposite. Your wife had a good head on her shoulders. That and quite a bit of talent. Her gallery did very well and her artwork continues to rise in value all the time. In round numbers, the value of your share of her estate is around $2,400,000, not including the value of the artwork still in the gallery. When we sell the gallery and whatever artwork you choose not to keep, I expect that your total will climb north of $2,750,000 or so. Add to that her life insurance and you have well over $3,000,000. The kids have trusts worth about $250,000 each. Gwen was very careful with her investments, and as I said, her artwork has risen steadily over the years. I know that none of this makes losing her any easier, but she has left you quite a gift." Fred paused to let it all sink in. "You really had no idea what Gwen was worth? No idea how much her art was bringing in?"

"Honestly, Fred, I never gave it much thought. I simply signed my paycheck, kept a little mad money, and let her handle the rest. We found out early on that she was better with money than me. I knew we were comfortable, but I had no idea. Gwen would always tell me 'I sold such-and-such this week,' but I never asked how much she got for it. I felt it rude to ask. So I would just congratulate her on the sale and we'd talk about our days. When she told me we didn't have to worry about a mortgage on this place, I just assumed that we had made enough on the old house to pay cash for this one. When she bought the gallery property, on her own and without getting the bank involved, I assumed that she'd 'broken the bank' to do it, but I wasn't worried. I figured we both had good incomes and her art was selling, so it would be OK. Little did I know that she could buy the place with 'petty cash.' I guess I should have quizzed her a little about the finances, but it just didn't matter all that much…."

"Well, James, I'm glad I could be the bearer of some good news. Obviously, I've always known how well she was doing, but she told me to keep it mum. She said that she was going to surprise you someday, but she never told me just how. Now we'll never know. Pity." Fred took another sip from his gin and tonic and sat back.

"Fred, I really don't know what I should do with her art. Should I sell it off so others can enjoy it? Should I keep it so I can have a little more of her around? I don't want to keep the gallery; that much I do know. But how do I decide what to keep and what to sell? How do I go through her things? What about her clothes? Her shoes? What about all her files? God, I just don't know where to start. I don't even know if I can. How do people do this?"

I slumped in my chair. The thought of someday having to pack her things and erase her very being was appalling to me. There wasn't a "Surviving Spouse 101" class that I could take at MNC to help me with this stuff. I'd lost my rudder in that car crash. Gwen was my practical side, my human side; she was my everything. And now I had to face the task of trying to put together a life without her and try to move forward without her. Everything ended in "without her." Everything looked bleak. I didn't care how much freaking money she'd made or left with me, she'd left me and I was alone. I was angry that she was gone, angry that she had driven off so stupidly that night, angry that she died thinking the worst and not knowing the truth. I was angry with myself for not seeing how Jess affected her and being a little more sensitive to it. I was angry with Jess for causing me to lose my wife. I was mad at myself for blaming Jess. Why did women have to be so confusing? Why couldn't they see things with their eyes instead of their hearts? Why was the truth not enough? Why couldn't Gwen see that I was just trying to save a young life, not screw a young girl? Why? Why? Why? I fell forward, my head "thunking" the desk rather loudly. Fred was caught off-guard and let out a short yelp when I did.

"James, are you OK? What the hell was that?"

"I am not all right. I will never be all right. Not ever again. My wife is dead. I have nothing!" I banged my head loudly against the desk. I jerked my head up and shouted at Fred, "I am *not* all right! I won't ever be again! Why did she have to die! Why? Fred...I.... Shit...I just want to crawl in a hole and hide. I don't want to deal with any of this. Fred, I'm sorry, but could you leave now? I just want to...."

"I don't think you need to be alone right now, old friend. Maybe I'm not the right one to have around, but—"

"Fred, just go. Let me wallow a bit. I've spent the last fucking week putting on a show for everyone! I just want to be alone. I want to be left alone...."

"James, please, I'll go, but you shouldn't be alone right now. Where are the kids? They should be here with you. Someone. Is there anyone I should call?"

"Fred, I'm sorry. It's not you. It's me. I just don't know how to deal with this shit. I'm falling apart. You're one of my best friends, Fred. If I wanted anyone around, it would be you. I really just need to stew in my own juices for a while. The kids just went out for a bite with some friends. They'll be back later this evening. Till then, I just want to sit in a dark room and sulk. I'm not fit company for man nor beast. I'll be OK. I won't be all right, but I will be OK, Fred. Thanks for coming over. You know I'm going to have to lean on you a lot in the next little while.... Thanks." Fred patted my shoulder and left the room. After a few moments, I heard his car pull out of the driveway.

I pulled the shades, turned off the lights, and put my head down on the desk. I just stayed that way for a while. The silence was welcome. Not having to interact with anyone else, a blessing. After a while, I went to the kitchen to mix myself another drink. I'm not a heavy drinker, but I do enjoy a good drink now and then. I'd only been drunk once or twice in my life and paid the price heavily the next day, so I avoided drinking to excess. Tonight, however, I wanted to be numb. I wanted to stop thinking. Wanted to stop remembering. I was still taking some pain meds after my fall and surgery—nothing too strong—so I didn't think that throwing a few more drinks into the mix would be a problem.

Gin and tonic is a nice summer drink. Refreshing. Goes down smoothly. Kind of a "stealth drink"—the tonic and lime tend to overshadow the taste of the alcohol. I drank several, downing them like a cold soft drink on a hot day. They seemed to be having no effect. I wanted another, but the gin was gone. Whiskey time. I cracked open a bottle of Jameson's. Delightful stuff. I'm glad that the Emerald Isle is populated by a bunch of creative drunks. I poured myself a double and started to sip. It went down faster than I planned, so I poured another. And another. Very soon I was shit-faced. The world started to be unstable, and I was getting unsteady on my feet. I had a hard time going from the couch to the kitchen. I spilled while trying to pour my fourth. I thought I should eat something to offset the alcohol. I definitely had that thought too late. I grabbed a couple of leftover deviled eggs from the fridge and wolfed them down. Had a little lunchmeat from a tray that I had contemplated tossing out earlier that day. No sooner had I eaten it than my stomach began to churn. I gagged a few times and tried to race toward the bathroom. I tripped and puked on the way to the floor. Vomit was all over the hallway and all over me. The smell of it made me wretch and vomit some more. I didn't even try to get up and move to the bathroom. The damage was done, the hall was a mess. Another load wasn't going to make a difference. When I had emptied the contents of my gut all over the hall, I tried to get up to go to the bathroom to get some towels to clean myself up a bit. I got a couple of steps when another wave of nausea hit. I dry-heaved and fell to my knees. This was not going to be pleasant. I wondered how my students consumed as much alcohol as they did and still functioned. Training, I guessed. I laughed at my own inner joke and tried once more to find my feet. I was successful this time. I staggered into the john and sat down on the toilet. I leaned over and rested my head on the sink. I turned on the water and waited for it to warm up. I passed out waiting.

"Dad! Dad? What the hell? Dad!" I opened my eyes and saw Brian looking down at me. I had fallen to the floor at some point. The room was spinning, he was spinning, and I was spinning. All on different planes and in disparate directions, it seemed. I closed my eyes. The room didn't stop, but at least I didn't see Brian spinning counter to the room any more.

"God, I feel like shit. Brian, I'm sorry. Can you help me up?"

"Dad, what the fuck! You're drunk. The hallway

looks like a vomit hurricane hit. Jesus, I've never seen you this way. Let me get you to bed." Brian bent down and helped me up. I leaned on him, keeping my eyes closed, and we made our way down the hall to the bedroom. Brian helped me sit on the bed and then lie down.

"Let me get you a towel and a bucket, Dad. You're worse than my roommate Glen was after homecoming my freshman year!" He scurried out of the room and got a towel and a wastebasket for me. I kept my eyes firmly shut against the spinning universe around me. It didn't help much. I was rather embarrassed. I slipped away again. Each time I lost consciousness, I saw Gwen in her casket or Gwen in her car. I'd see Gwen screaming at me and tossing things at me. I saw Jessica on the couch, blood everywhere. I'd wake with a start and pass back out, and the nightmares would start all over again. I saw Jess on the gurney being whisked into the ambulance. I saw Gwen's Subaru, crushed and torn by the crash. I saw Gwen entombed in the wreck, Jess sitting calmly, unhurt in the pristine passenger seat, her lap full of blood. I woke with a scream that brought both kids running. They both stared at me as if they'd seen a hideous monster. I passed back out. The night went on like this until I finally fell into something resembling a normal sleep state at dawn. I slept until the early evening.

*

"Morning, Dad, or evening actually. You were quite a handful last night." Gretchen smiled slyly at me. "Didn't think we'd ever get you cleaned up. And the hall—UGH! You never get to tease us about our college partying days again, that's for sure!" I tried to sit up. My head was splitting and the world was still spinning.

"I'm sorry you kids had to deal with that. I really didn't plan on getting quite so smashed. The drinks went down way too fast…."

"Hey, Dad," said Brian as he popped in the door, "how are you feeling?"

"Awful. Look, kids, I'm sorry. You never should have had to see that. No one should have to pick up their drunk father and put him to bed.... I'm so sorry. I'm—"

"Dad, shut up. You did worse for us when we were little. You told me that I once finger-painted all over my bedroom with the contents of my dirty diaper. And how many times were Gretchen and I sick and puking while we were growing up? I think we can let you slide on this one. Have you ever been drunk before? I don't remember Mom ever talking about you partying in college or anything...." Brian paused and looked over at Gretchen.

"Only once or twice. I hate the way I feel right now. That's kept me pretty much on the straight and narrow over the years. Last night, however…ugh! I've never been that shitfaced before. I just had enough of the bullshit act, dealing with all the chaos over the last week. I just wanted to escape. I don't think I'll do it that way again...." I slowly got out of bed and unsteadily made my way to the kitchen to get a drink of water. My lips were dry; I was sure I was dehydrated. My stomach was growling, but food held no appeal for me. I had a couple of glasses of water and made my way back to my bed.

"I don't care what your mom used to say about you, you kids are all right. I'm going back to bed. See you in the morning."

I slept like the dead until the next morning.

DETAILS, DETAILS

As the weeks dragged on, I dealt with all the detritus of my shattered life. I sorted through all of Gwen's clothing and personal items. I was fairly ruthless; I only saved a few items that had some shared significance. I kept the opal I had surprised her with all those years ago, a shirt of mine that she used as a smock while painting, a cup of her paintbrushes, and a couple of unfinished canvases. I encouraged the kids to keep whatever they needed or wanted, and I donated all the rest to our local St. Vincent's, Goodwill, and Salvation Army. I wasn't trying to erase Gwen from the house, but I didn't want to wallow in her personal items like so many widows and widowers do. I had all of our photos and lots of her art on the walls to keep her alive in the house. I had a head full of memories. I didn't need to see her clothes or smell her scent on them. I didn't need a shrine to Gwen. I needed Gwen.

After a couple of weeks, the kids went back to their homes and lives. They called every few days to check on me. Gretchen was dealing with her mom's loss better than Brian was. She was more like me, practical and able to compartmentalize her feelings and deal with them as she wished. Brian was definitely his mother's child. Sensitive. Caring. Emotional. He was taking this hard. He was moody and sullen. He was listless. He was angry. I worried about him. I hoped he would seek the counseling that he so obviously needed. Since he was his mother's child, I was sure he would.

Fred was indispensable during this time. He handled the closing of Gwen's gallery and her corporation (!). I didn't even know that she was a corporation, but she had formed one when it was obvious that her artwork was going to do well. The gallery and the artwork were held by Gwen

Martin, Inc. Her mom was the other officer in the corporation. Fred handled the legal mumbo jumbo, and he and Gwen's mom had an auction of the remaining artwork and then sold the gallery itself. Fred's estimate of my net worth proved to be a little low. After the final auction and the gallery sale, Gwen's estate was worth more than three million dollars, *before* the insurance. Fred kept whining about the tax bite, but I was floored by how astute and talented my lovely bride had been. I viewed it all as "found money." I had been unaware of just how successful and respected Gwen really was. I was rather humbled by it all.

The hardest thing I had to do was go to the university to clean out Gwen's office and studio there. Everything there was Gwen. Every note, every book, every lesson plan, all of it was Gwen. If Vince hadn't been there to help me, I never would have finished. Somehow cleaning up her "professional life" was harder than dealing with her personal one. Somehow this made it all more real. Cleaning out her office and studio cemented in my brain that this was the new reality. I was on my own. I was alone. Gwen was gone and I was alone at NMC. Things had come full circle. I was back to being the smartest kid in the room, with no friends and no social graces. I knew that wasn't really true; I did have a circle of friends, something I lacked when Gwen and I had met. I had an even larger theater "family" at the Pearl. I was only as alone and isolated as I allowed myself to be. But Gwen had been my ticket into the real world. She'd been my passport into social life and graces. Could I really maintain my relationships without her to guide me? I didn't know. Already I was turning inward. I politely declined most social invitations. I spent more and more time at home, writing or reading, or just sitting in my shelter, thinking. I spent the next couple of months living like a hermit, only talking to my kids, Fred, or Vince. I dreaded the start of the next semester. Would I even be able to go into the classroom and pretend to be a professor? The summer was quickly leaving, so I would have to face the classroom and people in a couple of more weeks. I could certainly afford to take a leave of absence for a semester or two. Our contract allowed us to take up to a year off, without pay, but with a guarantee of our job, without having any more cause than "I want to take the year off." I certainly had more cause than caprice. I could easily argue that I needed time to heal. But if I didn't return to the classroom, what would I do? Wallow around the house? Rattle around aimlessly and get even more depressed? Once I had finished with all the details after Gwen's death, what would I do to occupy my time? That was an even darker hole to look down than the prospect of having to deal with all the people at the university. So I decided to buck up and return to work.

THE BLACK HOLE

Months passed. I tried everything to be "normal" again. I taught. I went to the Pearl and worked on a show. I went to dinner with friends. Outwardly, I seemed to have adjusted to my new reality, life without Gwen. It was a good act. Inwardly, I was dead. Numb. Nothing reached me. Nothing touched me. I didn't care about anything. Nothing excited me. Nothing interested me. I was simply a shell of a man going through the motions of daily existence. I got some satisfaction from riding my Suzuki when the weather permitted. Gwen had given me the bike, and I really enjoyed it. My other two bikes languished in the shed. When I rode, it was only the Suzuki. I still didn't really feel while I was riding, but it came close. I got no pleasure from working at the Pearl. I felt nothing when I was on stage. I got better reviews of my acting than I ever had before, which I found amusing since I felt like a robot on stage and off. I bought a new camera and started to take pictures again. I had dabbled a bit when Gwen and I were first married. My old Canon and I were good friends; I took it everywhere. After the kids were born, I was the official family photographer. My new Nikon digital SLR was a neat piece of technology. I took the camera with me when I rode, took it with me when I drove, and kept it by my side at the Pearl when I was directing a show. But it was a hollow experience. I would scroll through the images and see just snapshots, no real feeling behind them, no "photographs." I spent more time at the gym. I toned up a bit. I tried to work out my frustrations by working the heavy bag. Still, nothing. I was an empty shell. The only things I really paid any attention to were the lovely young ladies in my classroom or at the Pearl. I didn't long for them in a physical way, but they were interesting. I enjoyed looking at their various shapes and colors and textures. Spending time in the company of young women in the prime of their lives was about the closest I ever felt to actually being a living being.

I had a hard time sleeping. I couldn't get used to the empty bed. I missed Gwen's lovely warm form cuddled up next to me. I bought a large, almost human-sized, pillow to sleep next to. It was no substitute. I tossed. I turned. I would read. I would watch TV. I listened to music. I tried to force my eyes closed. I would drink warm milk before bed. I tried Sleepy Time Tea. I tried over the counter sleep aids. I'd stay up later and later, hoping that the long hours would force me to sleep. Every few days, I would sleep a fitful night's sleep, not really getting any serious rest. And I would dream when I did doze off. I saw Jess on the couch, bleeding out. I saw Gwen in her wrecked Subaru, face bleeding from all the glass, arms broken and twisted in unnatural ways. I saw the Pearl burning. Gwen's canvases ripped. Shit smeared onto them. All manner of horrors filled my few sleeping hours. The bags under my eyes had bags of their own. I started using some of my stage makeup to disguise the hollows under my eyes. I did my best to keep up the masquerade, to keep the "OK" mask on, to prevent the world from finding out just how fucked up I really was. I stuffed it all in, stuffed my soul full of the bile and dread and horror that I experienced every day. I tried to distance myself from the horrific thoughts and memories in my head at the expense of having any feelings at all. I thought I could balance it all, walk a line that would keep things under control and me on an even keel, not let my inner nightmares bleed through to the outside world. But, in exercising that control, I lost the ability to feel the basics: Love. Pleasure. Want. Need. Desire. Lust. Happiness. All gone. Just going through the motions of being a living human being every day. Just going through the motions.

My work suffered. I was less tolerant of students in general, less sympathetic to their needs and situations. I was stricter about deadlines and more critical of their presentations. I relied more and more on PowerPoint. I wasn't a bad professor; I simply slid to average based on my apathy. In retrospect, I feel guilty for the students who had the bad fortune to have taken my classes while I was deepest into the black hole. For a couple of semesters, I probably wasn't worth their time. I tried to keep myself motivated, kept telling myself that I should care more, but, in truth, I just couldn't be bothered. I couldn't even make myself feel guilty about it at the time. Short of physically hurting myself, I don't think I could make myself feel anything at all, let alone make myself care about a bunch of students filling desk space in my classroom.

I went back into counseling. I went through the motions there, too. My shrink was a dolt, a dullard who had less insight into me than he did into a block of granite. All I really succeeded in doing was using up many dollars of taxpayer-provided health benefits without deriving any benefits of my own. The fool would sit there, listen to me disinterestedly, nod once in awhile to make me think he was processing it, look at his watch, and proclaim the session to be done. Then he would tell me to remember my dreams and tell him about them next time. Certainly, he didn't offer any plan to help me heal. After a while, I just started making up dreams to see whether he was paying any real attention to what I said. Most times, he was as impassive as ever. I would make up the most outlandish tripe and he would nod and murmur, "OK, Dr. Martin, how do you feel about what you just told me?" He never offered up any thoughts of his own, never questioned me any further than "How do you feel about what you just said?"

Then he would nod and grunt without commentary or further questions. I suspected that he was burnt out and simply going through the motions himself. I was certain that he wasn't astute enough to see that I was lying, that I was not participating either. He disgusted me. At least I felt that much.

Lin Jun, a colleague in the department, started to take an interest in me. I suppose that a "proper" amount of time had passed since Gwen's death; it had been almost a year and a half. Lin was forty-something, divorced a few years ago, and not unattractive. I suppose she had been quite attractive thirty pounds ago, before kids, middle age, and benign neglect took their toll. Her kids were off at Michigan State, a sophomore and a senior. She was an adequate professor, thorough and well-versed in her material, if a little dull in her presentation skills. At this point, she was probably better than I was, but I knew I was just off my game. If I ever shook my funk and got back some lust for life, I would be superlative in the classroom once again. She never would be. Lin would pop into my office now and again to check up on me. Sometimes, she brought me coffee. She'd stay for a while and we'd chat. One day, she asked me whether I would like to go to lunch with her. I smiled and said, "Sure, when?" It would be nice to have some company instead of eating at my desk like I did most days. We agreed to meet at the Flatiron Grille, a favorite of mine. Great smoked meats and barbeque. Nice atmosphere and reasonably priced.

"Nice to see you someplace other than work, James. Have you been waiting long?" Lin asked as she sat down. She'd obviously gone to some fuss over how she looked— she didn't look like she was just teaching that day. Her hair was loose and flowing, and her makeup looked newly applied. I caught a little whiff of fresh perfume. I had been waiting longer than I thought reasonable, 1:00 means 1:00, not 1:20.... Still, I did appreciate that she had gone the extra mile and tried to look nice for our lunch.

"No, I just got here a couple of minutes ago myself. I was worried that you'd think I stood you up," I lied. "Have you been here before?"

"No, but to hear you and Vince talk about this place, one would think that they served the best Kobe beef and the sauces were nectar."

"C'mon; we're not that over the top about it. But I think you will enjoy it. Terry has a way with that smoker of his. Even the corned beef gets smoked. I know it isn't traditional, but their Reuben sandwich is my favorite of all time. I just like the flavors—a lot."

"Well, I'm going to have to trust your instincts and let you order for me. You know what's best here, so I'll just go with the flow."

"Lin, that's a lot of pressure. Other than department functions, usually buffets, we've never shared a meal. I have no idea what you like—what you eat or don't eat."

"Good. Someone should throw you a curve now and then, James. Glad it could be me."

When the waitress came to take our order, I asked for a pulled pork sandwich for myself and a barbeque sample platter for Lin. I had no idea whether she even ate meat, but if she was silly enough to leave it up to me, well she'd just have to deal. I ordered a nice glass of wine for each of us. Middle of the day, but we were grownups after all. I didn't have any more classes for the day. I wasn't sure of Lin's schedule. She didn't object. We chatted while we waited for our food. The conversation was pleasant and uncomplicated. We talked a little about looming budget cuts at the university and how they might affect the department. We talked about my theater involvement. Lin came to quite a few of our productions at the Pearl and was a season ticket holder at MNC. We talked a little about Gwen's accident. Lin's kids. My kids. Just normal, getting to know you better kinds of topics.

"James, this is delicious. I can't believe I've never been here before."

"Glad you like it. With so many restaurants in New Worcester, it is easy to overlook a few. I hope you won't overlook this one anymore. This place deserves to succeed."

"I couldn't agree more. How can anyone be brave enough to take the leap of faith required to open a place of their own? I really like the security of knowing that I have a job and a paycheck and benefits. To just risk it all and open a store or restaurant, well, I just don't think I could do it." Lin paused and took another bite of barbequed chicken.

"James, I don't want to seem too forward, but would you like to go out with me this Saturday? If you're not busy…I'd really like to get to know you better. Can I take you to dinner?" I sat silently for a moment, not sure of what to say. I must have had a strange look on my face because Lin reacted as if she'd been scolded. She quickly said, "James, I'm sorry, I didn't mean to offend. I just—"

"Oh, goodness no, you didn't offend me in any way. I'm flattered. I'm a little out of the loop on how this whole dating thing works. I didn't expect to be asked out on a date. Thank you. I would enjoy that very much. Now I am a little embarrassed. I hope I wasn't being assumptive by calling it a 'date'."

"I'm happy you see it that way; I do. James, you know I have a lot of respect for you professionally, and I find you fascinating personally. And, I guess I can say it now that I've asked you out, I do find you rather attractive…." I smiled pleasantly and thanked her. I wasn't sure whether I was attracted to Lin or really interested in dating, but I thought it might be nice to at least try. Maybe I would feel something again, something positive and bright rather than the dark and depressing thoughts that dogged me every day.

Saturday came. Lin pulled into my drive and parked her Escape under the canopy of huge maples. She got out and came up to the door. I opened it before she had a chance to knock. She looked a little startled when the door opened.

"Welcome. Didn't mean to scare you. I saw you pull in and thought I'd just meet you at the threshold to my abode."

"You're lucky I didn't knock on your chest instead of your door," Lin laughed.

"Do you want to come in for a drink before we head out?"

"Rain check? Our reservations are for 7:00."

"Oh, OK, let me grab my jacket. Lin, you look nice this evening." After I said that, I thought that I should have left off the "this evening." To me, it sounded as if I had said "You look nice this evening, unlike your usual frumpy self…." I hoped she didn't take it that way.

"Thank you, James. You look wonderful yourself. Shall we?" I followed Lin to her car and we got in.

"Is it a mystery, or may I ask where we're going?"

"I like to be mysterious, so I am just going to kidnap you. You can put on the black hood in the center console." I liked that Lin had a sense of humor.

"Are you going to bind my hands or duct tape my mouth as well? This is an abduction, after all." We both laughed.

"No James, nothing like that. I won't put the hood on either. I like to talk to you, so I guess we'll let that all slide this time." We continued talking for a few minutes, and then Lin pulled up to The Waterstone, a new "gourmet" restaurant that had just opened downtown. I'd not been there, but I had heard nothing but raves about the menu and the atmosphere. I had my doubts about its viability in a small town like New Worcester. It was very pricey and I feared there wasn't going to be enough of a regular clientele to support it.

"Lin, how did you know that I wanted to try this place? I am very interested to see whether it can live up to its billing. If it does, it will certainly be an interesting addition to the local scene."

"I've wanted to try it myself, but I needed a special occasion to do so. And you're now officially a special occasion." We both laughed, got out of the car, and made our way to the door.

The Waterstone did not disappoint. The menu was varied and interesting, the presentation exceptional, and the flavors a delight. We were both impressed with the entire package. The wine list was extensive. We ordered a bottle of a rare 1964 Chateau Margaux that was like drinking liquid velvet. Our waiter was a former student of mine, one I had enjoyed having in the classroom. While Lin was in the restroom, I pulled him aside and instructed him to hold the bill at the desk; I would take care of it privately and discretely. I knew Lin had asked me on the date, but the bottle of wine alone was over $400. As we were colleagues, I knew approximately what her income was and did not want her to shoulder the financial burden of this date. I certainly had the wherewithal to pay and wanted to.

"Lin, that was beyond my wildest dreams. Thank you. I hope this restaurant can survive; I look forward to coming back." We chatted a little longer, and then I excused myself to use the restroom. I went to the desk and settled up and returned to the table.

"James, can I use that rain check now? After the waiter brings me the bill, I'd love to go back and see your home. I really don't want the evening to end…." I nodded and told her we should go.

"But James, we still haven't gotten the check. We can't leave quite yet."

"We could skip out. That sounds like fun." I grinned at Lin. She looked mortified.

"James, I couldn't. I didn't know there was a devil inside you."

"There isn't, and I couldn't. The check is taken care of; we can leave any time."

"James," she protested, "I was taking you out. You were not even supposed to see the bill."

"Don't be mad, but I took care of it already. You didn't look at the wine list, so I'm not sure that you were prepared for exactly what I ordered for us. Besides, unless you have a revenue stream that I am unaware of, I am better able to pay this one than you are. If you're not too mad at me and didn't have too awful a time, I'll let you pay for our next date, if you want another…."

"I am a little miffed, but I'll let it go if we can have a nightcap and you will let me take you out next time." She was smiling as she said this, so I knew she wasn't really upset. "And I am certain that I would like another date. Soon." We got up and drove back to my place.

"James, this house is beautiful. What a little gem. I can't see the yard, but when I pulled up, the trees were amazing. Who knew there was a setting like this right in the city? You really lucked out when you got this place."

"I know, we were so pleased when we found it. Large wooded lot, plus woods around it. I don't think the city or the university will ever do anything with the property around ours any time soon. We had to thoroughly restore it; the old folks who lived here were in no shape to keep it up, but it was a labor of love for us." Lin's smile had slowly faded. I realized that I had been speaking about "us" and "our," as if Gwen were still alive. I had hoped to keep Gwen's ghost at bay, but the house had so much of her in its very core that it was difficult. I quickly changed the subject.

"What would you like for a nightcap? I have a fairly well-stocked liquor cabinet; what's your pleasure?"

"Do you have any B&B? Maybe my favorite after-dinner drink."

"Lin, you are more interesting every minute. I have been a B&B drinker most of my adult life. My folks used to drink it in front of the fire. When I started to develop some actual taste, I tried it. I've had a bottle in some state of fullness in my home ever since. Do you take it up or on the rocks?"

"Up, of course. I'd never pollute it with ice or water." I nodded my approval and got two snifters, poured and offered Lin one, along with a comfy seat by the fireplace. I took a moment to light the fire that I had laid in the grate earlier that day. I usually kept the fireplace ready to go, tinder and kindling just waiting for a match. I liked to sit in front of the fire and just watch the flames. Sometimes, watching the fire dance would allow me to empty my mind of all the sorrow and dread and boredom and just be again. I sat on the leather club next to Lin's and sipped my drink.

"This has been lovely, James. Thanks. And thanks for lighting the fire. I always love a fire; it really doesn't matter what time of year it is. I wish my place had a fireplace." Lin snuggled deeper into her chair. If she'd been a cat, she'd be purring. We chatted about everything and nothing. It felt good to talk. In no time at all, it was almost one in the morning. When she noticed the time, Lin got out of her chair with a start.

"Oh my, James, I had no idea it was so late. I've got to get up early for church tomorrow. I don't want to run, but I must."

"May I walk you to your car?"

"I wish you would." She looked up at me with "that look." I took her arm and we walked outside. When we got to her Escape, she stopped and waited expectantly. I supposed that she wanted a kiss. While I'd had a nice evening, I wasn't sure I wanted to. I didn't feel any kind of attraction for her beyond friendship. She was reasonable looking and obviously interested in more. We were going to go out again, that had already been established, but I didn't know where it was heading. Worse, I didn't know if I wanted it to head anywhere other than friends. I decided that a simple kiss would be a sort of litmus test. I took her into my arms and moved to kiss her. She responded willingly. I wanted to kiss her more chastely than she expected, so it was a little awkward. After a couple of moments of strangeness, we settled into a mutually acceptable kissing posture. When we parted, I could tell she had liked it. I felt as if I had kissed my mom inappropriately or maybe Frenched the cat. It was not interesting or exciting on any level.

"James, you are a wonderful kisser..." she said dreamily. "Your kisses make me want so much more." She leaned in and kissed me again. I cooperated. I quickly decided that I could simply treat it the same way I would any role at the Pearl. I had enjoyed the evening's company and conversation. I figured I could fake the rest, a small price to pay if I wanted to get out of my hermit rut.

"James, I really do have to run. Can't have the biddies at church gossiping because I look like I was on an all-nighter. I need to sleep and then make myself up again. I'd rather stay here and skip early Mass, but that would be worse…." Indeed, it would. I didn't know whether I was that good of an actor without rehearsal. I had to encourage her to go home.

"Lin, we've had a lovely evening, but I do have a tutoring appointment fairly early myself. Don't know why I let this kid talk me into a Sunday session." That was the best lie I could come up with on short notice. "Good night. See you back at the slave ship on Monday." I gave her a final, chaste peck on the cheek and opened her car door for her. She got in and gave me a final longing look and drove off. I retreated to the house to process the evening's events.

I hadn't had a bad time with Lin. The conversation was easy and flowed well. She was bright enough and well read. She was, unless she was a better actor than I was, attracted to me and wanted more. For her age, she looked good; not as trim and fit as Gwen had been, but not unattractive by any normal standards. I simply felt nothing after spending the evening with her, nothing more than I would have had I spent the evening talking to Vince. I wanted to feel more. I needed to feel something again. I wanted the physical comforts of a female companion. I didn't want to be adrift in a black hole forever. I needed something to wake up my emotional self. I decided I would continue to see Lin, see where things led, and hope that the ice block that had replaced my soul would start to melt.

THE DATING GAME

Lin and I went on a second date the next weekend. It was much like the first, dinner and pleasant conversation. Drinks at her place afterwards. A few awkward kisses that she seemed to enjoy. Parting, leaving her obviously wanting more. Me wanting nothing more. I didn't find her company repulsive. She was well read and fairly interesting. But something wasn't there. No sizzle. No attraction. Nothing to make me want to pursue anything "deeper." Still, it was marginally better than staying home alone every night. When I was leaving after our date, Lin asked me out again. I mechanically told her that would be fine and made a date. She told me that she was in charge, that I should leave everything to her. I smiled, agreed, and left. Monday there was a small envelope in my in basket. Perfume scented. I opened it and found a card that simply said "Four more days…." Huh? Four more days? Till what? Tuesday there was another card with a three-day countdown. Wednesday the card said "Two more…" Thursday's card said, predictably, "One more day…" Friday's card simply said "Tonight…" This woman was going to a lot of trouble.

I went home to change and get ready for our evening out. Lin was going to pick me up at 7:00, so I didn't have to hurry. I showered, shaved, got dressed, and settled into my favorite chair with the day's evening paper. There wasn't much interesting in it. One of New Worcester's appeals was that the paper and TV news were generally pretty boring. A hiker lost in the woods, a snowmobile rider falling through the ice in the harbor, a very rare drug bust, a few traffic accidents, and once every decade or so, a murder. The deer harvest or the weather were more likely to be the lead story than a rape or murder.

A couple of years ago, a man shot his estranged wife a few blocks from the high school and then committed "suicide by cop" by holing up in his house and taking a few potshots out the window. He finally came out with his gun leveled at the cops surrounding the house and an over-eager young officer shot him. I'd often thought that New Worcester would be the perfect place for a serial killer to ply his trade since the police had no experience whatsoever in dealing with anything of the sort. Then I thought to myself, *I could be a perfect killer—no one would ever think that James Martin could hurt anyone.* After all, I was a "pillar of the community," a well-respected professor, well-liked with a large circle of friends in the community. I was active in the theater. I was too well-known ever to be a suspect. In an odd way, the thought appealed to me. And what did I have to lose? I really didn't care about much at this point, didn't feel anything, just going through the motions of daily life. I had nothing to live for with Gwen gone. The kids were on their own; they didn't really need me anymore. I had nothing to prove professionally. I'd been offered the chair of my department numerous times and turned it down. I'd been spoken of as a Dean or Provost, but I had quickly quelled any such nonsense. I was flattered that I was that well-respected, but I had no desire to get out of the classroom. Administrative tedium held no appeal for me. Sadly, nothing did as of late.

My doorbell rang promptly at 7:00. I strode to the door and opened it. Lin was there, and she had obviously spent quite a bit of time on her hair, makeup, and attire. I should have been impressed, should have been enticed by the clingy low-cut gown and the too-high heels. Instead, all I saw was a slightly too plump dowager vainly trying to primp her way into an unwilling partner's heart and pants. It all seemed fake and contrived and too planned. Her ample breasts were stuffed into a Wonderbra that made them appear like water-filled bags of flesh forced together. They jiggled like JELL-O when she moved. The form-fitting dress was not, in my eye, flattering in the least. The cut line of her underwear and the slight roll of tummy over the top of her panties was all too evident. I did my best to smile and look appreciative.

"Good evening, Lin. You look lovely."

"So do you, James. Better than you know…." She smiled dreamily at me. I choked back a little vomit, figuratively speaking. I really should have told her, "Thanks, but no thanks" and just stopped the charade, but I decided I would tough it out. Maybe make a game out of it. I had no reason to hurt Lin, but I couldn't really think of any reason not to….

She kissed me, took my arm, and led me to her Escape. She drove off toward downtown. We pulled up in front of the Landreu, the finest hotel in New Worcester. The valet parked the car and Lin led me to the dining room. A table was waiting for us, a chilled bottle of champagne and a shrimp cocktail already set. The waiter seated us, poured our champagne and excused himself.

"James, I want to propose a toast to us. I know we've only been seeing each other a short while, but I feel closer to you than I have to any man in a long time. I really like your company and hope you enjoy mine as much as I do yours. I want tonight to be very special. So…to us." She held her glass up for me to clink. I obliged, smiled, and sipped the champagne.

"This is very nice champagne, Lin. Thank you. I haven't dined here often; I'm glad you chose it. I look forward to what the evening has in store." I had decided that I would play along, treat it like a game or a role in a show and see how far she wanted it all to go and how far I could stand to take it. How good an actor was I?

I must say that we had an excellent dinner. The Landreu had recently hired a fairly well-known chef from Chicago, and he was doing wonderful things with their restaurant. Lin offered me samples of most of what was on her plate. I dutifully tried every proffered morsel and did not have to feign my enjoyment of them—the chef was worth whatever the Landreu had paid to lure him out of Chicago. I was less sure of how to handle the obvious "display" that Lin was offering. Every time she leaned forward to talk or provide me with a taste of her food, she quite deliberately was showing me more and more of her ample cleavage. I didn't know whether I should avert my eyes and show her that I was being a gentleman or stare at her unabashedly. Her breasts certainly held less than no appeal for me. The more the sheer enormity of Lin's bosom was presented to me, the more I thought of Gwen's high, firm, perky breasts. Kids and the years had had no ill effects on Gwen's bosom. To her last day, her body was lean and taut, inviting and youthful. I'm sure that if I were to superimpose an image of her twenty-year-old body over her forty-something body, there would be some difference, but not much. She'd always prided herself on being able to fit, not squeeze, but *fit* into her wedding dress. Lin, however, was a different matter. She was looking more middle aged every time I paid any attention to her, and that was not a good thing.

We had a couple of drinks after dinner, and then Lin excused herself for a moment. When she returned from the powder room, she paid the bill and we got up.

"James, I have a little surprise for you…." She took my hand and pulled me close to her. She pressed something into my hand. It was a room key. "James, I booked us a suite. Would you like to come up with me now?" She looked doe-eyed and hopeful. While I really didn't want to, I hadn't had sex since Gwen had died. Hell, I hadn't even pleasured myself since then. It would be wrong to lead her on, but even bad sex had to be better than none, so I whispered, "Yes" into her ear. She smiled and led me to the elevator. We rode to the very top floor. She had booked the penthouse suite, the nicest room in the city. I'd never actually been in any hotel room in New Worcester other than the room at the Ramada that Gwen's parents had booked for us for our wedding night. My folks had usually stayed at the Ramada as well, but we'd never gone to their room. They always met us in the lobby or at whatever restaurant we were eating in that night. And if my brother or sister had come to visit, they'd always stayed at our house. The room lived up to its billing. It was spectacular. Lavishly decorated, fine artwork on the walls, elegant décor, and all very tastefully done. I was impressed.

"James, would you like to join me in the tub? The suite has a hot tub in the other room."

"Uh, sure, but I don't have my suit...." I grinned. Might as well make the best of it.

"I'm sure that won't be a problem. There's no one here but us. Would you be a gem and unzip this for me?" She turned and waited. I walked over, screwed up my courage, and started to pull the zipper down. I was fairly certain I did not want to unwrap this package, but the prospect of sex after all this time did have a certain appeal. Surely, I could go through with it, derive some pleasure, and not let her know I really wasn't into it. Maybe Lin would surprise me and have some "hidden talents." I could only hope because as I pulled the zipper down, I was less and less enthused by what I saw. The slight roll of fat over the bra. The faded stretch marks. The lack of tone. It was all adding up to a terrible picture. She stepped out of the dress and waited for me to undo her bra. I hesitated and then soldiered on. I undid the clasp and she let it fall to the floor. She took my hands, placed them on her bare breasts, and backed up close to me, sighing and panting. Her breasts felt even worse than I had imagined. Formless pillows of fat with pencil eraser nipples on the ends. She moaned something about how much she wanted this. I thought how badly I wanted to run. She purred and turned toward me. The water balloons fell from my hands as she turned and reached over to undo my tie and shirt buttons. She finished and slid my shirt off of my shoulders. She slithered out of her panties and stood naked in front of me.

"Well...?" She waited expectantly. I decided that I needed to choose my words carefully. Tell the truth, but only as much of it as I needed to.

"Lin, you look remarkable. It's been a long time...." Remarkable isn't always a positive comment, and I certainly did not mean it to be such. She brushed up close to me and kissed my chest.

"Follow me, I'm going to go draw our tub." She spun on her heel and tried to slink into the other room. Her bottom was as sallow and disappointing as her breasts. Ripples of cellulite adorned her bottom and thighs. Again I thought of Gwen and how delightfully unaffected her lithe form had been by the passing of time. I really needed to get out of here, now. If I were any sort of gentleman, I would tell Lin that I was not interested, that she should put her clothes back on, and that she should take me home. Or would that be worse for her than faking it all? Would I hurt her feelings more by rejecting her right after she'd bared her body to me? She didn't deserve for me to hurt her or humiliate her. I couldn't be that much of a cad. Letting her think I was interested and having sex with her was bad enough, but to look at her naked form and simply say,

"Thanks, but no thanks" was rude beyond belief. I would have to play along through the night.

Thankfully, the tub was full and already hot. It only made sense; a hot tub takes hours to warm up. A simple jetted bathroom tub is another matter; you fill that like a regular bathtub. This was a full-fledged hot tub. I figured it would seat five or six comfortably. It was a relief. I wanted to spend as little time as possible looking at Lin naked. The jets and bubbles would conceal most of her body. She hopped into the tub and turned to me. I shucked off my pants and underwear and slipped in. As soon as I was seated, Lin was on my lap and kissing me deeply. Her hands traced my chest and shoulders and worked their way to my nether regions. I held her and tried to make it seem as though I was enjoying this. I ran my hands up and down her ample form and pulled her close. I initiated a kiss or two and tried my best to seem enthusiastic. Her hand found my member and she started to stroke me. Involuntary actions took over as my penis responded to a type of touch it had not felt in a long while. *At least it's a good actor*, I thought. She seemed pleased with what her hands had done.

After a few minutes in the tub, Lin suggested that I sit up on the side of the tub. I obliged. When I did, Lin took me into her mouth. I'd never felt any woman's mouth on my cock except Gwen's, so I had no idea what to expect. Gwen was my only frame of reference for any of this. I didn't know whether Lin was "good" or "bad"; I just knew she was different. Lin attacked my member like a starving woman might go after a meal. She vigorously gobbled and swallowed my cock. I was very aware and afraid of her teeth. I'd never felt threatened by Gwen's, but I worried that Lin might bite me in her ravishing of my member. There was never a time when her teeth weren't in contact with my skin. It was not pleasurable. It was, in fact, almost painful. I didn't want to be rude—this woman was simply trying to please me in a way only my wife ever had—but I was not comfortable. I was sure that Miss Manners didn't offer advice on how to tell the woman you are with that you are not enjoying the BJ she is giving you.

After a bit, Lin slowed down and eased up on me a little. I closed my eyes and tried to relax. She was not going to let me relax, though. As soon as I tried to, she resumed her assault on my cock. I opened my eyes and spied the perfect escape. On the wall hung one of Gwen's paintings. It was a picture of our yard and garden, the trees in fiery autumn glory, leaves lightly scattered on the grass. It was a pleasant scene, but I knew I could use it for more than just its beauty. It would be a prop in my escape from what was quickly turning into dating hell. I reached down and gently put my hands on Lin's shoulders and motioned her to stop. I summoned up a shuddering sob and put one hand on my face.

"Lin, please…I…." I stopped, pausing for effect. "Lin, I just saw it on the wall. I was having such a good time, but now I really can't…. I'm sorry…it's just too soon…."

"What is it, James? What's wrong?"

"There…." I pointed at the picture. "I don't mean to be maudlin, but that is my backyard, one of Gwen's paintings. It's like she's in the room with us and I'm cheating on her. I'm sorry, Lin; I am so sorry. I can't stay tonight. Can you please take me home?" She just nodded, looked at the picture and then back at me.

"James, I…." Her voice trailed off. "I understand. It must be a little jarring. Let me dry off and we can get you home." I nodded my thanks and made my way to the other room to get dressed. I really had no desire to see Lin get out of the tub. I'd already seen enough.

I quickly got dressed and waited for Lin. I thought about this whole dating game. I was lonely, that was too true. I wanted female company. I wanted to feel like a human again, wanted to feel like a man. I wanted Gwen back. I didn't want to have to go shopping for a mate. Gwen and I had just fallen together like it was meant to be. I'm not a spiritual man; I don't believe in a god or ghosts or fairies or the great monkey overlord, but I did feel that Gwen and I were meant to be together. Something in the universe deemed it should be so. And it was good until she couldn't see the truth and stupidly killed herself in the car.

"James, I'm ready to go. I'm sorry to see you like this. I am a little confused, though. You live in the house that you always have; you have pictures and her artwork there. We've kissed there. What is so different here and now?" She took my arm and opened the door to the suite. "What is so jarring about that picture? Or is it me? Don't you like me?"

"Lin, home is home. It is empty, but it is where I am most comfortable. Yes, we've kissed in Gwen's nest, but we never went any further. Truth be told, I felt a little uncomfortable kissing you there, but I thought it would pass, thought I was ready to move on. But here, just seeing one of her paintings unexpectedly, and one of our own backyard, while I am naked with another woman and doing something that I'd only done with her before…well…I now know that I am not ready to move on. I am…I don't know how to say it, but I haven't given up on Gwen yet. I know that sounds weird, but I just can't let go. Not yet. I'm sorry." What a crock of dung I was feeding her; I just hoped that she would buy it.

"James, I'm sorry too. I really like you. A lot. It wasn't like me to be as forward as I was, but I wanted, no, want you so badly. I thought we had a connection, and I wanted to share myself completely with you. Bad timing, I guess…" We made awkward small talk on the way back to my place. It was uncomfortable and tense.

A PLAN OF ACTION

I withdrew from the dating world. That one experience was quite enough to convince me that I wasn't ready, nor really interested. I was getting back on track as a teacher. Finding my way at the Pearl as well. I still was numb. A husk of a man, devoid of any actual feeling. I needed something to break through if I were ever going to survive as an actual person again. I tried a couple of different therapists, yoga, a spiritual retreat in Sonoma…nothing. Nothing reached me. Nothing stirred me. Nothing got into my inner being and made me feel alive. The closest I came to feeling anything was when I'd look at a winsome young lass and feel an old familiar stirring down below. But that really was just physiology and chemistry, not any kind of emotion. Still, it was better than being numb. Jess was my one true savior through it all. It had taken a while after Gwen's death for our relationship to normalize, but I couldn't stay away from her for long. We fell into the same old pattern, talked about life, talked about her boyfriends, talked about nothing.

A conversation with a student in a class on Victorian England made me think. When the subject of Jack the Ripper came up, and this student and I got into a long discussion of what it was that had motivated him and other killers. What had they gotten out of the killing? Was it just the challenge? Were they angry? Repressed? Sociopaths? Was it different when they killed people they knew versus strangers? Why did some capture and torture their victims and others commit random mass killings? How did they function in society between killings? The whole subject was fascinating.

After class ended, something about the subject still seemed to reach out to me. I'd never hurt anything beyond a marauding crow or a raccoon that was getting a little too comfortable around the place. I began to question whether I could. Would I? Would I get some satisfaction from it? Could I get away with it? I was bright enough, I thought, that I could evade capture. And If I couldn't, I could certainly plan for an escape if the "heat" was getting to me. It was all just an internal intellectual "discussion" in my head…but I began to wonder. Could I…? And what would I derive the most interest from? Random strangers? Too easy. Too common. *No real challenge*, I thought. Anyone could just pick out some stranger somewhere, kill her, dispose of the body and get away with it. If the person was truly random, if you had no connection and had any knowledge at all about police methods, that would be a breeze to do. There had to be more. What about someone you knew? What about breaking the trust of a long friendship? There was a lot to be had with that approach. The challenge of not getting caught when someone close to you was discovered dead or missing. Fitting into society, dealing with the police, your other friends, their families. Crushing their dreams and beliefs, seeing their look of incredulity when they realized that you meant to do them harm.

And how to do it? A gun was the simplest and surest, but guns are noisy. And sighting up someone and pulling a trigger was detached, almost like a video game. Anyone could do that. A knife was a better choice. You had to be close in; you would feel the person's blood spill. Strangling. Strangling was the best. You would have to feel her die. You would have to do it with your own hands. You would have to be committed to the act. Own it. Take ultimate responsibility for it. And get the most pleasure. Of course, it was all just an intellectual exercise. I'd never really do it….

Since Gwen's death, I had spent a fair amount of time in the shelter. It was private. No one could bother me there. No phone. No one even knew it was there. No cell service that far under dirt and concrete and steel. Solitude. Silence. Bliss in many ways. The first time I entered the shelter after my discussion with my student about serial killers, I looked at the place a little differently. If I were to consider playing the game I'd thought about in my head, this was the perfect place. And the cistern would be a great place to put the bodies. The police knew nothing of the shelter. The city and county didn't either. Gwen and I had done some research—looked for any permits that had been pulled or plans that had been filed. We found nothing. No paper trail of any sort. We both had found that amusing. No one, other than ourselves and the person who had built the shelter, most likely long-dead by now, knew it was there. There was no trail from the house back to it. Gwen and I had never put in the path we'd discussed before her death. I'd never bothered after. I just kind of wandered around the yard and would end up in the shelter from time to time. I seldom took a straight line from the house to the shelter. I liked looking at the different woodpiles and brush piles that I'd made over the years. Liked seeing what kind of "critter condos" they had become.

I looked around the shelter one evening and figured out a good placement for a video camera. Hidden, but with a good view of the room. I thought that multiple cameras might be needed, but I could start with one. Not that I was going to do this. Just thinking. Planning. Kind of a fun exercise. The camera could go there, the recorder over here…. And then I could relive the experience when I wanted to. Watch the video. See the scene play out. Any time I wanted. I thought that my playmates, I didn't want to think of them as "victims," would most likely be young ladies. Students? Not close to many of them. Actresses from the Pearl? That was far more likely. I was as close to them as family. They relied on me. Trusted me with their secrets. Looked for my counsel. It was not uncommon for several of the theater kids to hang out at my place after a rehearsal, so it would not seem out of place to ask one over some evening…if I were thinking of actually playing this game. I tried to shake it out of my head, dismiss the idea that I would ever do anything like that, but I found the idea more and more appealing. They certainly didn't deserve to die, but neither had Gwen. The thoughts of my hands on one of their lovely young necks, holding them down, squeezing their throat until the life started to ebb…. I found myself growing hard thinking about it. I wouldn't have sex with them, that wasn't the point, but steal from them their sanity and their lives. But for some reason that was making me hard. My erection grew uncomfortable in my pants. Involuntarily, I pulled my rigid member out of my jeans and began to stroke myself. It felt good. I imagined one of my theater friends in my hands and stroked harder and faster. I'd not pleasured myself since Gwen's passing. I was excited beyond belief and I came in torrents. My knees buckled from the release. I felt alive….

I bought a high grade camera and DVR. I installed them in the shelter. It was a fun fantasy to think that I might actually use them someday. Record a sweet young thing's face as it went from trust to disbelief to terror to death. I'd never really do it. I mean, how could I? How could I? I thought long and hard about that. I delighted in laying out the plan, in picking my playmates. Deciding who would be the first. Planning on how to get them here, alone, without arousing suspicion. How to handle getting them from the familiar surroundings of my house to this temple of solitude. How much lime would it take in the cistern to prevent the smell of death from pervading my property? How would I deal with class the next day? What if the police did talk to me? Could I "poker face it"? Was I a good enough actor? Could I eliminate the DNA evidence from the house? Did I need to? It was common enough knowledge that anyone I might choose for a playmate would probably have been to my house at some point in time. I agonized over all the details as if I were really going to go through with it. I started to research creating a new identity someplace else in case I needed quick escape. I found myself masturbating quite a bit during the time that I planned it all. I was starting to feel. Starting to feel like I had a purpose again. Starting to feel alive again.

BETH

I could feel my pulse quicken as I pulled up to the theater. Tonight was the night, the first time I'd act on what I'd been planning for all these months. I had thought about nothing but this night for days. I'd gone over every aspect of my plan, thought about all the possible ways I could get caught, hoped I had figured out all the angles. I knew it was risky. My actions would be right out in the open. No stalking in a quiet back alley. No cloak and dagger. No skulking in the shadows. That stuff was for the average man. I was better than that. I was smarter than that. I felt like I was superior. I could do this and get away with it. Who'd imagine that James Martin could do anything to hurt anyone?

I parked my bike and took off my helmet. I stowed my helmet and got my script and notebook out of the top case. I headed into the theater. My stage manager, Sarah, met me and gave me the night's conflict sheet. Only a couple of people would be missing rehearsal tonight. One had called to say that he'd be a couple minutes late. Not bad. Almost a full cast. Rare this early in the rehearsal process at the Pearl. I wasn't really interested in the rehearsal, though. I was interested in Beth. Beth would be the first. I'd thought long and hard about who would be first. I really wanted it to be someone close, really close to me. I wanted to push it all to the very limits. I didn't even know whether I could go through with it, and I wasn't certain that I really could get away with it, so I wanted to make sure I got the most out of it. If Beth ended up being my first, my last, my only, I would be oddly satisfied. So much more so than a stranger. How much pleasure could you get from the terror of a stranger? Certainly violating the trust of someone close to you, crashing her world around her, showing her that everything she knew to be true was wrong, revealing the monster inside the person she thought she knew would be so much more rewarding than killing a stranger….

I managed to get through the rehearsal. I was distracted, but Sarah kept things moving for me. *Guys and Dolls* was one of my favorite shows, and I was looking forward to opening night, but I was looking forward to this night even more. Time dragged. I could hear the blood pounding in my ears. My heart beat faster and faster. I was a little sweaty. I tried to keep it together, tried to act like I was OK, that everything was normal. I hoped I pulled it off. Finally, it was 9:00.

"That's it, folks. Time to call it a night. We'll pick up right where we left off on Monday." I dismissed the cast. "Hey, Beth," said I as Beth walked up the aisle toward the exit. "Beautiful night for a ride. I remembered my spare helmet. Want a lift home?"

"Cool. Let me tell Lainey that I'm not riding home with her. How'd you know that I really wanted a ride tonight?" asked Beth.

"Might be that you've been bugging me to bring an extra helmet all week…." I grinned.

Beth rushed off to tell Lainey that she was riding home with me. I couldn't help but notice how nicely she filled out her Levi's. I thought about how nothing looked quite like a young girl in the prime of her youth. The fresh taut skin. No ill effects of gravity. No wrinkles. The glow. The inviting curves. The sparkle in her eyes. I loved every aspect of a young girl's beauty. Beth was an especially fine example. Lean, nicely proportioned. Honey blonde hair and dark brown eyes. A mouth that always seemed to smile. Slender waist and long legs. High firm breasts. Sweet kid, too. I'd really grown quite fond of her in the past of couple years. We had a bond beyond friendship. She trusted me with everything. Boy troubles. Roommate problems. Parent issues. She felt totally at ease with me and I with her. She could tell me anything and knew that I would understand and that her secrets were safe. I was her closest "grown up" friend, after her mom.

"Hop on. Got your helmet on right?" I double-checked the strap on her helmet. Beth had ridden with me several times before, but she still had trouble getting the straps cinched just right. When I was satisfied that she was ready, I stood up on the bike and waited for her to saddle up. She dropped onto the passenger pillion and put her arms around me. I smiled to myself and fired up the Suzuki. Everything perfectly normal. No different than many other summer nights. Me taking one of my young friends home on my beloved motorcycle. Lots of my college-aged friends rode with me. I missed having Gwen to ride with me. I also truly wanted as many of my young friends as possible to have a good first ride on a motorcycle. I figured that college-aged boys were too jazzed up on testosterone and adrenaline to take young ladies out for their first ride. I was a safe rider. I wanted to live to ride again. I had nothing to prove and had long since accepted that I was not invincible. Twenty-year-old men had no such realization. They still thought that they could conquer the world and that nothing could ever harm them. They still believed they had a bright future. They still wanted to impress the girls. They were stupid.

I twisted the throttle and we headed out of Northton and onto the county road to New Worcester. "Let's take the back way. Too nice a night to ride home on the highway," I called back to Beth.

"Great. I love it at this time of the year. Besides, I'm in no hurry to get back to my apartment. Kendra left this morning. Field studies trip. Won't be back for a week." Beth practically had to yell to be heard over the engine and the rushing wind. I already knew Kendra would be gone for a week. That was part of why I planned for tonight to be the night.

I nodded and enjoyed the ride, enjoyed the anticipation of what was yet to come.

"Do you want to stop over for a drink?" I asked as I pulled up to Beth's apartment. "I could use the company. It's a rare Friday night. I don't work tomorrow...."

"I really could use one, but I have a paper I need to get finished for my Theater History class. It's not due until next Friday, but I've really been dragging my feet." Beth looked at me like she really wanted to be talked out of homework. I knew the look. Most of my college-aged theater friends had it from time to time. I had been counting on this. I knew it would not take much persuading to get Beth to come over.

"I've got the rum you like, Coke and limes. All with your name on them." I grinned. "Besides, you could consider an evening at my place as research for your Theater History class. Hell, I'm old enough to have been around for all the shit you're studying!" I paused.

"Well, if you're going to twist my arm...OK. And you're not old, damn it! Forty-eight is not old. OK, so you're older than my dad, but you're way cooler. Let me just drop my stuff off and change. I came to rehearsal straight from work, so I'm tired of smelling like sub sandwiches."

"No problem. I'll just wait here." I started to pull the bike over to a parking place.

"James, I need to take a shower too. Why don't you just head home and I'll be over in a little bit. I'll walk. It's only a few blocks and that way neither one of us will have to drive after we've had a few. I sure don't need a DUI after the MIP I got when I was sixteen!"

"You sure you don't want me to wait? I don't want a fair young thing wandering the 'mean streets' of New Worcester late at night." I joked. The streets of New Worcester couldn't be safer. It was like everyone who lived here knew the town was something special and no one wanted to break the spell. No one but me.

"James, sitting out here in this parking lot for a half hour sounds both boring and rude. Waiting for me in my messy apartment would be even worse. Kendra is a real slob sometimes. So just head home and I'll be right over." Beth got her backpack out of the top case and put the helmet in.

"Anyone else you want me to invite?" I asked. "Or are you OK having drinks alone with a dirty old man like me?" I hoped that she didn't feel like a bunch of company. That would queer the whole deal. I asked so everything would seem normal, so she wouldn't have a hint of anything untoward.

"You're always a gentleman and you are not old! No, I'd really just like to have a quiet evening with a friend. OK with you?" I was relieved and suddenly nervous at the same time. This was really going to happen. No more planning. No more fantasy. No more waiting. I was really going to do this thing. Tonight. I could still back off if I wanted to. In all the scenarios in my head, I was able to carry it out, but could I really? Tonight would be the acid test.

"Right. I'll head home, grab some munchies, and tidy up a bit. My place isn't the neatest right now, either. See you in a bit." I started the bike back up and pulled out of the parking lot. Everything was going according to plan. I was sure the apartment complex had surveillance cameras; just about everyone did nowadays. I wanted the tapes to show Beth arriving safe and sound and me leaving without her.

I rode carefully home. It was less than a mile, but I didn't want to get a traffic ticket tonight. I was hyped up enough without having an encounter with a cop. I thought that if I even saw a police car, I'd get so distracted that I'd lay the bike down or something stupid. Who was I kidding? Did I really think I was going to pull this off? That I could keep my shit together when the cops inevitably questioned me about Beth's disappearance? That I could maintain my cool at work? That I could keep my "game face" on when I was with the rest of the kids in my cast, the rest of the kids I hung out with? That I could converse about Beth getting abducted with my adult friends and coworkers? This was really an impossible task. I would crack under the pressure. I would get caught. I was an idiot even to think I had any chance. And yet none of that mattered. I needed this. I was so numb and bored with life that only something this huge, something this horrible, something this powerful, only an act this hideous might touch me. I had convinced myself that this was it, the only way I'd ever feel again.

I really did tidy up a bit when I got home. I was neat and organized by nature, but cleaning helped me focus. Doing something familiar helped me concentrate on the evening's grand events. I put out some fresh veggies and a dill dip I was fond of. Mustard pretzels for Beth. She always loved them. Glasses. Rum. Ice bucket. Coke—Diet for me and regular for her. Small plates and napkins. It was going to be a party of sorts. Her last. My first.

The forty minutes or so that I was home waiting for Beth seemed like an eternity. Hot blood pounded in my ears. My palms got sweaty. I had to change my shirt a couple of times because I was breaking out in a body sweat.

If I didn't get a grip on myself, Beth would turn tail and run when she first saw me. I imagined that I resembled Jekyll and Hyde, alternating between calm and neatly groomed, and looking like a sweaty, filthy beast. I just hoped I could keep my cool until I had Beth in the shelter. After that, it wouldn't matter anymore. She'd never leave that room alive. I wanted her to see the beast. I wanted to feel her terror.

I almost jumped out of my skin when Beth knocked. I barked my shin on the coffee table when I got out of my chair. "Shit!" I exclaimed as I made my way to the door. Not a very auspicious start. I completed the journey to the door without any further complications. Time was oddly stretched out. It took seconds to get from the chair to the door in real time, but to me, it seemed as if hours passed. So many thoughts running through my head. What was she wearing? What did her skin smell like? What would strangling her feel like? Would she sense something was wrong when she first saw me? Could I really end her life? Would I enjoy it the way I thought I would? Would I chicken out? Would I feel guilt? Remorse? Anything?

I opened the door. Beth was wearing a denim skirt, sandals, and a gauzy peasant-style top that reminded me of the stuff girls were wearing when I was in high school in the '70s. Funny how styles kept going round and round. Whatever was old was new again. Beth was kind of a latter-day hippie, and her clothes usually reflected that. Casual. Earthy. Sometimes tie-dyed, some peasant stuff like she wore tonight, and some more modern styles. Once in awhile, she wore what I considered "Dungeons and Dragons" clothes, frilly Middle-Ages styled dresses with a cinched waist and laced bodice, emphasizing her modest cleavage. I always found her style to be fascinating and free. How could I even think of hurting this beautiful young thing? What kind of monster was I trying to be?

"Oh, God! You're bleeding!" Beth screamed. I looked down at my leg. Sure enough, when I'd hit my shin on the table, I had whacked it hard enough to draw blood, and now it was spreading on my light khaki slacks.

"I hit my leg when I got up. I guess I dozed off and the door startled me. Didn't think I had hit it that hard. Damn. Come in. Sorry. Not a great way to start an evening." I couldn't believe my luck. No way could I pull this off if I couldn't even get my prey into my house without hurting myself. Might as well just tell Beth, "Hey, look at me! I'm a serial killer wannabe! But I'm too clumsy and stupid! Run for your life!"

"Where's your first aid kit?" Beth asked. "I've dealt with a lot worse than this the summers I've life-guarded."

"I'll be OK. I'll just go into the bathroom and clean up. Make yourself at home. Be right out...."

"James, you are bleeding a lot. Christ, you're making a puddle! Let me help."

I looked down and saw that she was right. I was standing in a small pool of my own blood. The entry rug was ruined.

"Beth, could you grab a towel out of the linen closet? They're all old, so don't worry about which one you grab. Just get something so I won't bleed all over the house as I get into the bathroom. Thanks...." I felt like a dolt. Did Ted Bundy ever have this stuff happen to him? Did Richard Speck have to ask his victims to nursemaid him so he could kill them? What the fuck! Beth sprinted to the closet and came back with a towel. She wrapped it around my leg and helped me to the bathroom. We managed to get there without leaving a bloody trail. I laughed to myself about the irony of that.

"James, I think you need to take off your pants so I

103

can clean you up."

"Great. I have a beautiful twenty-something telling me to take my pants off and it's for this? What the hell did I do in my last life to deserve this?" I laughed. "Let me roll up the pant leg. That will be just fine."

"James!" Beth protested. "You are wearing underwear, aren't you? What's the big deal? Are you really that shy? Christ, how many times have you had to make a fast costume change over the years? We've all seen your legs. Stop arguing with me!"

I complied. When I did, I noticed that the gash on my leg was much worse than I'd imagined. How the hell had I ripped it that much with my pants on? The corner of that table must have been like a freaking razor. Beth was very gentle as she cleaned up my leg. The wound was "Y" shaped and looked deep. Beth kept telling me I should go to the ER and get stitches. I insisted that butterfly bandages and gauze would be fine. I promised Beth I would go to the walk-in clinic in the morning if my leg didn't seem like it was going to heal OK. She finally agreed and expertly bandaged my shin.

"I'm impressed," I said when she was finished. "You stayed so calm and you did a great job. I bow to you, Beth." I was impressed. She was as cool as a cucumber during the whole thing, and the bandage job looked like it had been done at the hospital, not in my bathroom.

"I had first aid training when I was a Girl Scout," she teased, "and more when I was a lifeguard. I was a lifeguard every summer from the time I was sixteen until last summer. Last summer was the first that I spent here rather than back home. And the park district wasn't hiring. That's how I ended up at the sub shop."

"Thanks. Do you want a drink now? God knows I really want one!" I hobbled back out to the living room and started to make a couple of rum and Cokes with a little lime. Beth took hers and drank eagerly. The evening had, so far, been a total disaster.

"Let me go get some pants on. God knows none of you kids will ever come to see me again if word gets out that I'm flashing!" I went to the bedroom and put on another pair of summer weight khakis. When I came back out, Beth had refreshed her drink and mine. She looked a little shaky now. Somehow, that made her more appealing.

We sat and talked for a while. I made sure that her glass was always full while I was careful to nurse my drink. I wanted her a little tipsy, not sloppy drunk. I needed to keep my wits about me. I had to control the situation. When I felt she was appropriately "lubricated," I began to set my trap.

"Beth, would you like to see something really cool? Something I've never shown anyone else here in this house?"

"Uh, sure…I think…. What is it?" Beth looked puzzled.

"OK, I misspoke a little. It isn't exactly in the house. But it is here on the property. We need to go out back. Put your sandals on and follow me." I started to get up. My leg hurt far more than I expected, so I started to fall back into my chair. Beth broke my fall and helped me to stand up. I gingerly put my full weight on my leg. It stung, but I was prepared for it this time.

"Are you OK? Are you sure you want to go outside?" Beth looked concerned.

"Yeah, I'm fine. Just took me a little by surprise when I got up. Smarts. But it is a little better now. I think moving it will help my leg loosen up. Let's go. Follow me." I grabbed a small flashlight as I led Beth out the back door. I flipped it on when we got to the edge of the woods at the back of the yard.

"Are we hiking in the woods? At midnight? With you on a bum leg? Are you nuts?" Beth asked. "Can't this wait until daytime? Another day?"

"Are you afraid of the dark? Think the boogeyman is out here in my woods?" I teased. "I'm OK. My leg feels much better. And we don't have to go far."

I led the way back to the hidden door. I pulled it up and flipped on the light. Beth peered into the opening and saw that there were neat concrete stairs leading down to a steel door.

"What is this? A storm cellar like in *The Wizard of Oz*? 'Toto, I don't think we're in Kansas anymore…'"

"Follow me. I just found this a couple of years ago, and I've lived here for years. This leads to a '50s bomb shelter. A Cold War relic. The house was built in the mid-1940s. The airbase opened in the early '50s. No one ever confirmed it, but it was a SAC base and probably had nukes, so people around here figured that they were living at ground zero. Right here on the shores of Lake Superior, far away from "civilization," and we were at ground freaking zero. Building bomb shelters was a small industry in the '50s and early '60s. A lot of them have been turned into wine cellars or just filled in. This one was just kind of ignored after the original owners of the house sold it. Don't know if they ever even told the folks we bought the place from that it was here. Hell, I lived here for years before I stumbled on the door; it was that overgrown. I found it almost by accident. Gwen and I had cleared a space for a vegetable garden, and I was hauling brush to the far end of our woods to make brush piles for rabbits and the like to live in. I saw the corner of the hatch under some weeds and decided to check it out. I was blown away when I found it. Took a while to get the hatch open. Weeds and brush and rust. But I did and I went down to check it out. No one had been in here for years. It was dry, but it smelled a little musty. There were still some canned goods and other supplies and…Hell, let me just show you. This is so friggin' cool."

I made my way down the steps. Beth followed, keeping very close to me. I liked feeling her near. I was looking forward to getting much closer…. I opened the heavy steel door and flipped on another light switch. The fluorescent tubes flickered to life and lit the room quite well. Beth could see neat shelves and a bunk on the far wall. I motioned her in.

"I spent about a year cleaning the place up and painting it. It had power when it was built, but I rewired it and refinished the old cabinets. It has an air filtration system, running water from a cistern outside, a real toilet…all the comforts of home. Great place to hole up in if the Soviets started lobbing nukes at the base. Safe. Quiet. Self-contained. There were old 12-volt batteries and lights and stuff, too, for when the power went out. The original owners spared no expense. This place was pretty much state of the art for 1955. You could stay down here for weeks, and no one would ever know you were here…."

Beth entered and looked around. "It is rather cozy. You have lots of books and stuff down here to keep you entertained. Food. Water. Do you ever stay down here?"

"Beth, I am not nuts. I kind of keep it around as a museum. Just a reminder of what the world was like. You're too young to remember disaster drills at school, but when I was a kid, they'd have us get under our desks with our hands clasped over our necks and keep turned away from the windows. We'd have to stay in that position for what seemed like forever to an eight year old. And that was supposed to help us ride out a nuclear attack. So I kind of kept this place like it would have been back then. Ready for something that was never going to happen."

"Crazy. I'd heard that people had these things, but I never thought I'd see one."

"Here, let me give you the full experience." I closed the heavy steel door and slid the bolt home. "This door was meant to keep the neighbors out. Bomb shelters weren't arks. They were, for the most part, rather selfish things. The owner got to choose who was going to live or die, who would get to wait out Armageddon in safety, and who would die a horrible death from radiation sickness. The owners were God." I clasped the lock into the bolt and spun the combination dial. "I'd rather use this door to keep people in...." I looked at Beth.

"OK, I—I get it. Now open the door. I feel a little claustrophobic. This place isn't that small. It's really rather nice, but knowing I can't get out makes me a little uneasy. What if you couldn't get the lock open? What if you used the wrong one or forgot the combination? Then what?" Beth looked more than a little concerned. I liked it.

"If I couldn't get the lock open...well...we'd both be screwed. There's no other way out. A cellphone won't work down here. Too much steel, concrete, and dirt over the top. Nobody outside can hear what's going on in here. And sooner or later, we'd run out of food and water. Sooner, actually. It would be the Donner party in a couple of weeks. Sure hope you taste good because it would come to that if we were trapped here. No one even knows this place is here, so no one would even look for us. I hope it is the right lock. Hope I know the combination. I certainly plan on leaving here...." I stared at Beth. Her eyes were starting to dart around the room, scanning to see whether there was any other way out.

"I...Please. Let's go back inside. I'm really

uncomfortable now. This is weird. Can we just go inside now? I think I'm going to be sick. I'm getting dizzy. Never felt this claustrophobic before. Open the door. Please?" Beth was almost pleading. The more she squirmed, the better I liked it. I'd never felt this way before. It was intoxicating. I could stop the game now, unlock the door and smile, and go back to being plain old James, and nobody would be the wiser. Beth would be fine. I would have had some fun. No harm, no foul. I hadn't gone too far yet. Just a tiny scare, not much worse than in a Halloween funhouse. But it wasn't enough. Now that I had started, I knew that I wanted more. Beth's fear would be my elixir, my tonic. Her collapse would rebuild me. Through her death, I would be reborn and would feel again. I was ready to move forward.

"Beth, I have to tell you a sad truth. I really don't plan to unlock the door and take you back inside. I like things just the way they are. You. Me. This little room. A self-contained little universe. I get to be God. You get to be my toy. And when I'm done playing, I will simply cast my toy aside." I sat quietly down at the table and just stared at Beth. I waited. Beth stared back in disbelief. She shook her head. Her hands trembled a little.

"OK. Enough. This game isn't fun anymore. Funny for a moment, now it is just wrong. I don't know why you thought it would be…."

"Quiet! I didn't tell you you could talk." I got up from the chair and crossed to Beth. I grabbed her wrist and put my hand roughly over her mouth. "I don't think you understand me. This isn't a game, at least not for you. This is very real, kid. The only thing you get to decide is how easy or hard your last few hours are going to be." I delivered these words with a quiet power. I didn't yell. Just the tone of my voice was enough to let Beth know that I

109

was serious. I didn't know where that voice had come from. My voice was normally higher-pitched and pleasant. Soothing. About as non-threatening as a purring kitten.

Beth bolted away from me. The suddenness of her action caught me off-guard. She screamed and ran into the storage room, slamming the door behind her. I strode over to it and calmly said, "Beth, there's no lock on that door. I will simply push it and you aside, and I will have you again. I know this sounds funny, but I don't want to hurt you. I mean, umm, I don't want to have to hit you. I have no anger or rage; I certainly like you. I just need a few moments of your time. I need you to listen and be very good. Maybe you don't have to feel any pain. Maybe I will let you go. Just calm down and come on out…."

"Are you fucking nuts? What kind of sick game is this? I…what have I ever done to deserve this? What the hell is wrong with you? I thought I knew you. I thought we were friends," Beth sobbed.

"Beth, you are one of my best friends. That's why I need you. You are the first. Maybe the only. I need to share this with someone close, someone special. With you. This can be easy. Pleasant even. Or it can be awful. Your choice. You can come out here and we can talk. Or I can force my way in and things will get ugly. You decide. I can wait." I went back to the table and sat down calmly. I listened to Beth's sobs through the door. I knew it was wrong, that her sobs shouldn't make me happy. I shouldn't get pleasure from this. But I did. It was more potent than any drug. I wondered how it would feel when I had my hands around her throat. I could wait….

*

After a few minutes, Beth's crying diminished. It stopped. I went to the door and gently rapped on it. "Ready to come out? Want to talk about the next few hours?" I

110

paused. The door started to open. Slowly. Beth's eyes were red and swollen from crying. Tears stained her gauzy top. She was beautiful. I gasped at how beautiful she was at this moment. Somehow, terror and bewilderment had made her even more appealing than ever before. I smiled. A big toothy grin. Beth looked repulsed by my demeanor. She stepped back farther into the storeroom. She started to close the door.

"Beth, don't do that. Don't make this any harder on yourself than it has to be. Come out so I can see you. You have no idea just how radiant you are at this moment. Your skin is glowing. You look amazing. So much better than I'd imagined. Come out; sit down. Let's talk about this. Could you use a drink? I could." Too late, I noticed the arc of her hand as it came toward me bearing a can of beans. She missed my face and the blow landed on my chest. I staggered back a step as she pushed past me and grabbed a chair. She brandished the chair like a circus lion tamer and backed up to the door.

"Dear child, there is no place for you to go. I wish you hadn't tried to bean me with those beans, but I should have expected that. I'll plan better next time. No canned goods down here next time."

"Next time? What?" Beth screamed. "What next time? What the fuck are you talking about?"

"Another truth. I plan on this becoming a hobby of sorts. I haven't even touched you yet, but this is more thrilling than anything I've ever done. This is rich. I can't wait to get serious about this whole thing. So far this has just been, for lack of a better term, foreplay. The real fun comes later."

I closed the gap between Beth and me. I was mindful of the chair in her hands, but thought I'd best her. Beth swung the chair full force at me. She put every ounce of her strength into her roundhouse swing. The mass of the chair and the force of her swing caused her to spin to the ground. I pounced and pinned her. She screamed and struggled to break free. I grabbed her shoulder, lifted myself slightly, and turned her over so I could see her face. It was wet with tears, and she was sweating from the exertion. I put my knees on her shoulders and took her wrists into my hands. She kicked her feet and twisted her torso. She tried to buck me off. She tried to bring her knees up to impact my back. She did everything she could to try and escape, but I held fast. I was aroused by the struggle. This was more than I'd imagined. I was happy for the first time in a long time.

"Why, why, why, why?" Beth moaned. "Who are you? What the fuck? Why, why, why….why…?" She sobbed. She stopped saying any discernible words and just made a guttural keening. The sobs wracked her body.

"Don't fight, Beth. The final outcome is inevitable. You don't have to make it awful. Just relax. It will be OK and it will be over soon. Too soon." I spoke as soothingly as possible. "I'm going to move my knees off your shoulders so you won't be so uncomfortable. If you cooperate, I will do things to make you even more comfortable. If you fight, it will get worse. Your choice. You do have some control over your destiny. I just hold the final say…." I did as I had promised and took my weight off her shoulders and lifted to let her breathe more easily. She took some deep sobbing breaths and seemed to calm slightly. She stared at me. She looked directly into my eyes as if she were trying to pierce directly to my soul. She seemed to be searching for the James she knew somewhere deep inside me. She was not having any luck.

"What do I have to do? To live? What do you want?" Beth asked. "Is it sex? Do you want to have me? Is that what this is all about? Some fantasy? Just do it. Fuck me. Get it over with. Let me go. I promise I won't say anything; just do it and let me go. James, please. Just don't hurt me anymore. I feel your erection. Rip off my clothes. I'll be whatever or whoever you want. Just let me live. Just let me go..." Beth pleaded.

I didn't think of myself as a rapist. While I certainly found Beth attractive, I had never thought of her in that way. How quickly she had tried to bargain her body for her life. How fast to give up one's dignity in the hopes of keeping one's life. Killing her, strangling her with my bare hands, that had been the object. I wanted to experience death, her death. I wanted to feel again. I wanted this act to jumpstart my emotional being. I wanted to be powerful. I wanted to be more than an afterthought. I was tired of going through the motions of life. I was tired of being numb. The challenge of this act, the thrill of it all was what I was after, not forced sex with an unwilling partner. While I didn't have a "code" I was following, somehow it felt wrong to force myself on this young woman, felt more wrong than killing her.

"Beth, my dear, you just don't get it. I don't want to rape you. I haven't had sex for a long time, but that's not it. Sorry. I want something so much more intimate. I want to feel your life in my hands. I want to be with you when you die. I want to feel you die, see you take your last breath, watch you slip away. Don't ask me to explain it; I probably can't...."

I paused and watched her face contort in horror. I smiled. She screamed. She twisted and jerked more violently than before. Once again, she caught me off-guard. She bit my arm hard. I instinctively grabbed at my arm to defend it, letting her arms go. She shoved my chest and pushed me aside. She turned and kicked at my wounded

113

leg. Her foot found the bandage and she kicked again. Harder. Pain shot up my leg. It was my turn to scream. She kicked again and I felt the gash tear back open. I screamed again and grabbed blindly. My hands found purchase in her hair and I pulled with all my might. When she crashed into me, I let her hair go and put my hands on her throat. I squeezed. She sputtered and gasped and kicked and strained. I tightened my grip and felt her resistance lessen. Her eyes started to glaze and her struggles ceased. She passed into unconsciousness. I let go—I wasn't ready for the kill. I hadn't originally planned it, but I decided that she deserved to suffer a little longer. It all could have been so easy for her. All she had to do was cooperate. It could have been peaceful. She made it ugly.

I picked up her limp form and carried her to the table. I got the rope I had stashed and tied her to the table, one limb to each leg. When I was certain she was secure, I tended to my re-injured leg. I cursed as I cleaned the dirty wound. It took several towels to staunch the flow of blood. I winced as I put the skin back where it belonged. I braced myself for the sting of the antiseptic as I poured it over the wound. It smarted worse than I thought. The gash that Beth had so lovingly cleaned and bandaged was now a bloody mess with a large flap of loose skin that wouldn't stay in place. I wrapped it in gauze from the first aid kit and figured I'd have to go to the ER later. That wasn't so bad; it would give me a paper trail showing that I had been at the ER the night Beth disappeared. When you're given lemons, make lemonade.

I watched Beth as she started to wake. My fingers had left bruises on her neck. They were both the telltale and the harbinger of the coming end of her life. Red now, they would soon turn color if she lived that long. I had never grabbed anyone hard enough to leave a mark. All of this

114

was new territory for me. I felt powerful and terrible and exhilarated all at once. My head was swimming with the emotions and pounding from my racing pulse. Beth stirred and let out a small noise. Her eyes fluttered open, and she tried to reach her sore neck. She jerked fully awake when she realized she was bound to the table. She writhed and hissed and bucked and bounced, trying to find the limits of her tresses. She quickly stopped as she understood that I had been very thorough.

"What now?" Beth queried. "Why aren't I dead already?"

"Beth, Beth, Beth. It all could have been over now. It could have been peaceful. Beautiful even. But you had to fight me. Now you will have to pay for that before you die. You were trying to bargain with me. Screw me to save yourself. Give up every shred of dignity so I might let you live. But you kept fighting. Kept hurting me. My leg is a real mess. I'm going to have to go to the ER now. No way to avoid it. But I'm not going to the morgue. I will walk out of here. You, on the other hand, are going nowhere. Ever. Again. Sorry." I paced excitedly. "I was simply going to kill you. Quietly. Peacefully. Now I think I am going to have fun with you. Either way, you end up dead, but this way will be so much worse. You will lose everything, and then you will lose your life.... And I will be reborn and whole again."

Beth's eyes looked like dark marbles. Blank. Cold. Staring without comprehension. She had resigned herself to the inevitable. She knew this was the end. She was as good as dead. What more could I do? How could it get any worse?

I got out scissors and a knife. I pulled the tail of Beth's blouse out of her skirt. I took the scissors and started to cut the shirt from her body. Slowly, I cut up toward her heaving breasts. She closed her eyes. Her hands clenched into tight fists, but she didn't struggle. I took my time. I was enjoying every moment. I thought about how much I had loved unwrapping gifts at Christmas time. This was so much better. This gift was alive and breathing and warm and inviting. This gift was beyond anything I had ever had the pleasure of unwrapping. I took great care not to hurt her as I sliced her shirt open. Even though we had fought, I still had no desire to cause more physical pain than necessary. The pains of battle were just collateral damages, the unintended consequences of a struggle that could have been avoided. I finished my first slice and opened her shirt. She had amazing skin. Lightly tanned. No blemishes. Not a mark. Just perfect young skin begging to be touched. I stared for a moment. I placed my hand on her firm, taut tummy. It was like an electric jolt to my system when I first felt her warmth beneath my hand. She turned her head, twisting her body subtly away from me. She trembled a little. She gasped when I bent and kissed her just below her navel. She tensed, but she quickly relaxed because she knew that fighting would just make things worse. I traced the gentle curves of her abdomen with my fingers. When my hands reached her bra, I paused. Beth's breathing stopped as she waited for me to move. I slid one finger under the space between the cups and lifted it just enough to slide the scissors between her supple flesh and her bra. There was a pronounced snip as I squeezed the scissors and the bra opened a bit. Beth turned her head back to me and opened her eyes.

"I'm sorry I hurt you," she said. "I…I didn't want to. I don't know what I was thinking. I… please take me. I want you. I want you to make love to me. I…you should have just asked. I want you…"

"Bullshit. Don't do this, Beth," I said angrily. "I

know you are just trying to cloud my head. You just think you can lie to me and get me to let you live. Don't do this. I don't want to, but I will gag you if I have to. Just don't…don't…let me enjoy this…."

"I…. Please…anything…. I don't want to die. I don't want to die. I don't understand. I don't…. I just want to live…. I…I…I…." Her voice trailed off, replaced by crying.

I stroked her face and told her to calm down, that everything would be OK and that everything would be over soon. "Just wait and it will all be OK," I repeated. I turned my attention to her bra; I parted it, revealing perfectly formed breasts. I cut the straps so I could fully remove the bra. I did the same to her shirt. I stepped back to admire her young form. I couldn't have designed a more perfect example of young womanhood. I had to see more. I undid her belt and unbuttoned the top button of her skirt. I pulled the zipper down and parted it. I hesitated. Should I remove it or slowly cut it off? I decided to take my time opening my package. I got the scissors once more and began to cut over her right leg. It was hard to get through the hem at the bottom of the skirt. It took more force than I'd imagined. Thankfully, the scissors were new and sharp. I slit the skirt to the waistband and repeated the act on the other side. The sides of the skirt fell away, revealing her thighs. Her legs were shapely and muscular. Amazing. I lightly caressed her calves and moved my hands northward. I gently lifted the center section of her skirt and dropped it to the floor. The sight of her nearly naked was breathtaking. I slid my hand under the waistband of her panties and cut them off her with the knife. She was naked. Beautiful. Helpless. Mine.

I removed my shirt and pants. I left my briefs on. I climbed onto the table and lay on top of her. I marveled at the feel of her skin on mine. She was still and supple. She didn't fight, but she didn't look. She was quiet and accepting of her fate. The time was now. I slid my hands from her waist up her perfect torso and brushed her breasts, lingering there for a moment. I then placed my hands on her throat and gently began to squeeze. I slowly applied more pressure. She opened her eyes and looked into mine. Pleading one last time? I didn't care. I looked into her eyes and tightened my grip. I felt her pulse quicken. Her body tensed. She stared more intently into my eyes. She gasped and sputtered. She tried to get life-giving air into her body. I applied even more pressure. I kissed her cheek and whispered into her ear, "Isn't this better than fighting? It will be over soon. Thank you. Thank you. I love you...." I felt her pulse weaken and slow. Felt her muscles start to relax. I squeezed once more, even harder. I crushed her windpipe and released her from life. Beth went totally limp, her eyes went blank and she was gone. I lay on her lifeless form for a few more moments, totally spent and satisfied. This was better than anything I'd ever felt before.

*

I got up off the table and surveyed the shelter. The struggle between Beth and me had certainly wreaked havoc on my neat little place. Furniture in disarray, the chair Beth had tried to hit me with on its side in a corner, the bean can in another. Blood everywhere. That surprised me for a moment, until I looked down at my leg. Blood was flowing freely from my reopened wound. Even though I had rebound it, the exertions of the evening had made me bleed right through the gauze. I had to tend to it right away. The rest could wait. Beth certainly wasn't going anywhere. I looked back at her. Even in death, she was beautiful. Her skin was quickly losing its glow and would become sallow, but right now, she was still lovely. Bound to the table, she looked like how I imagined a virgin sacrificed to the gods in ancient times had looked. No time to admire my handiwork, though. I had to stop my leg from bleeding before I could clean up this mess.

I got my first aid kit out again and washed up the wound as best I could. I applied pressure to stop the bleeding. I wound the gauze tightly around my calf. I put a towel over that to prevent any more leakage and taped it securely. It was a little ungainly, but it would have to do until I could go to the hospital and have it properly attended to. I made a mental note to myself to look myself over completely to see whether any other wounds I had received would need to be covered or explained away when I went to the ER. The bite on my arm concerned me the most. Beth hadn't broken the skin, but it was clearly a bite. I hadn't planned for that eventuality. I needed to think quickly and clearly about that one.

I untied Beth's body from the table. I was planning to dump her in the cistern. I didn't own a boat—Lake Superior certainly would have been the best dumping ground for my victims. Not too far from New Worcester's shoreline, the lake deepened to almost 600 feet. It would be highly unlikely that any bodies properly weighted and dumped there would ever be found, but I didn't have that luxury. I also didn't want to risk being seen carting a body from my place to another location. I suppose I could cut my victims into conveniently sized chunks to do that, but that seemed too gross even to consider. So the cistern was my solution. It was very deep and big enough for a body to tumble down. The water was normally about ten to twelve feet below grade level. I had put a fair amount of quick lime in the water to deal with the smell. I simply had to pick Beth up, sling her over my shoulder, carry her up, and dump her in. Put the cover back on the cistern and she was gone. I had no worries about anyone seeing me doing this.

The shelter and cistern were far enough into my woods that no one could see them from the road. Under cover of darkness, I felt safe.

I bent over to pick up Beth. I put her rag doll form into a sitting position on the table, put my shoulder into her torso, grabbed her thighs, and stood up. I almost fell over because I was off balance. I steadied myself and turned toward the door. My first step was OK. The second was awful. Pain shot up my injured leg and I almost fell again. I gritted my teeth and moved my feet again. Each step was torture. I got to the door and realized I hadn't opened the lock. I put Beth down and spun the combination dial. I cursed my stupidity under my breath. I swung the door open and bent down to pick up Beth again. I didn't have the strength to lift her body from the floor. The pain in my leg and the toll of the night's exertions were getting the best of me. So I grabbed her arms and dragged her up the stairs, one step at a time.

"Sorry, Beth; didn't mean to have you go to your grave being dragged like a sack up the stairs. I'd hoped to carry you properly, but, well, you saw to it that I couldn't." I felt a little odd talking to a corpse, but after all, the situation was a little odd. I had just killed a good friend simply for the thrill. Even as beat up and dog tired as I was, the thrill of the whole evening was everything I'd hoped it would be and more. I felt alive again. I could sense blood coursing through my veins, thoughts in my head; I felt vital and involved and whole. This could definitely be habit-forming. I was already thinking ahead to my next play date, thinking about ways to make it safer for me and even more exciting. I knew I had a lot of loose ends to wrap up after tonight's entertainment, and I also knew I would have to wait a while before even thinking of doing it again, but I was pumped.

I dragged Beth to the cistern. Let her down and opened the cover. I pulled her so that her upper body was just over the edge of the cistern, face down. I moved to the opposite side and took her hands in mine. She was getting colder by the minute. She had taken on the pallor of death and was no longer a thing of beauty, just a lump of garbage to be disposed of. I pulled a little more and her torso was briefly suspended over the cistern's opening. I let go of her hands and her body bent at the waist; her head fell forward and into the well. I went back to her lower body, lifted her legs, and heaved her in. She made a quiet splash when she fell. I opened another bag of lime and dumped it over her and closed the cistern's lid. I went back down into the shelter to get dressed and gather my thoughts.

I had to deal with my injuries. I needed a plausible story to tell when I went to the ER. I looked myself over. Other than the leg injury and the bite, I was pretty much OK. Some minor scratches here and there, but nothing out of the ordinary. The bite was the problem. That would surely tip off the doctors that something was amiss. *How will I hide it?* I thought as I straightened up the bomb shelter. Nothing seemed to be coming to me. I couldn't come up with a story that I would buy as plausible. If I didn't think of something soon, I was screwed. I would have to go to the ER, and I would be caught because of a silly bite mark. As I gathered up the remnants of Beth's clothes, it came to me. A believable story that I could pass off. It was a little risky and a little dangerous, but it made sense to me. I stopped cleaning and headed back to the house.

I had to wreck my motorcycle. It would be a perfect cover story. I often rode late at night; anyone who knew me knew that I liked riding at night. I was a bit of an insomniac since Gwen's passing, so I would ride on a beautiful summer's night when I could not fall asleep. I usually wore a leather jacket or motorcycle jacket when I rode, but not always. I sometimes wore shorts and a T-shirt. I knew it was stupid, but I liked the feeling of freedom when I did. If I took the bike out and laid it down on a gravelly corner, I could explain away just about any injuries. I would have to work a little further on the bite on my arm, though. I couldn't guarantee that the crash would provide road rash right where I needed it to cover the bite. So I went into the kitchen and got out my cheese grater. Drastic times call for drastic measures. I took the grater to my arm and forced it across my arm. It hurt like hell, but after a few passes, it obscured the bite marks. I was shaking, it hurt so badly. But it would hopefully prevent me from having a new address and a roommate named Butch who really liked me. I scooped some dirt and gravel up and rubbed it into the wound.

I fired up the bike and headed out. Thankfully, there is no shortage of winding roads close to my place. I didn't think I could ride for long. I was spent and the pain was getting unbearable. The flap of skin on my leg was rippling in the wind like a flag. The freshly-grated arm hurt like hell. My head was starting to ache from everything. I wasn't looking forward to the pain when I laid the bike down, but it was necessary for my cover. I got to a sharp bend on Bay Road and goosed the throttle when I hit the shoulder. The rear of the bike flew out from under me. I spilled onto the shoulder like a rag doll and the bike skittered across the berm and down the ditch. I rolled a few times and came to an abrupt stop when my helmet hit a small sapling. I had new scrapes and bruises to complement my battle wounds. My head started to spin. I crawled over to the bike and pulled my cell phone out and dialed 911. I told the officer at Central Dispatch that I had just missed a deer and had wrecked my motorcycle. I tried to tell him where I was, but I could only mumble "Bay...mmm...." before I passed out.

*

"James, what the hell were you doing on your bike at two in the morning? Don't you ever sleep?" I opened my eyes and saw Doctor Terry Tomzcak looking at me. "You took a pretty good tumble. What the hell happened?" Terry and I went back a long time. He was one of the first people I had met outside the university community. I was glad he was working. It felt good to be in familiar hands.

"You know I have trouble sleeping. Have ever since Gwen got killed. I was just riding around to clear my head when a deer got all suicidal. Leapt right out in front of me. I stupidly swerved and lost it on the curve. At least I didn't hit it; I had a friend ride right through one once. It wasn't pretty." I winced as Terry cleaned the wound on my arm. He was doing his best to take it easy, but a lot of dirt and gravel were in the wound. I had made sure of that.

"Looks like the road bit you hard," Terry quipped.

"Huh? Bit me? What? I wasn't...." I stopped and caught myself. Terry was just commenting on the wounds, not saying that it looked like I had been bitten. Even with the pain meds starting to work on me, I was a little jumpy.

"Your tox screen came back pretty clean. You must have had a couple of drinks earlier, but you certainly weren't impaired." Terry looked at me closely. "Still having trouble sleeping? After all this time? I'm sorry, my friend. I know how much Gwen meant to you. I wish I could bring her back. You just aren't the same without her." I wished he could bring her back, too. A part of me had died when she was killed.

It took a couple of hours and a bunch of stitches to put me back together. The grater-induced road rash must have been convincing since Terry never noticed the human bite it was meant to conceal. Good thing because I would have felt cheated if all that pain had been for naught. The gash on my leg took an even dozen stitches. Terry apologized and told me it would never be pretty. I would always have a V-shaped lump there unless I wanted to spend a lot of money on a plastic surgeon. While the university provides good insurance, I didn't think it would cover plastics for a leg injury. If it were on my face, no problem. My leg? I doubted it. Besides, I wanted the scar to remind me to be a little more careful when practicing my hobby in the future. The cop who had come to the scene of my wreck, Joe Higgins, came to check up on me. Another friend, he had been first on the scene and had tended to me until the EMS crew arrived.

"How many times have I told you to stop riding that thing at night? Christ, James, you could have been killed. Thank God you don't ride very fast. What the hell happened? You were out of it when I got there." Joe was concerned, both professionally and personally.

"Damn suicidal deer. Jumped out right in front of me. I tried not to swerve, but I did. I think I hit the throttle when I hit the gravel and the rear just flew out from under me. It all happened so fast. I was just tooling along, heading home after a moonlight ride. When the deer popped out, all hell broke loose. One moment I was riding and the next I was sliding. Hurt like hell. Wish I'd been wearing my leathers and some riding pants. Stupid. Stupid. Stupid. Just as dumb as could be. I won't ever ride that way again."

"James, I hope you're not planning on riding again. Period. I hope this woke you up. Motorcycles are dangerous. I thought you were dead when I got to the scene. You were awfully still and pale. I don't want to lose another friend to a stupid motorcycle." Joe never missed an opportunity to lecture me about motorcycles. When he was a teenager, a friend of his drove one head-on into a semi. Died instantly. I think that is what made Joe become a trooper. I know it was what had turned him off to motorcycles. We agreed on most things, but not on the subject of motorcycles. I loved to ride. Joe was adamantly against it. Hated to see anyone on a motorcycle. Made sure anyone who would listen knew it, too. I knew this wreck would buy me a lot of grief from Joe. If he only knew the half of it....

Joe hung around to give me a lift home. It was almost dawn when we left the hospital. I was grateful for the lift until I realized there was still a bloody towel in the entryway and another in my kitchen. The cheese grater was in the sink. Another slip—I hadn't thought about who might come home with me from the hospital. I prayed that Joe wouldn't want to see me in when he brought me home. I also started to realize that I wasn't as bright as I thought I was. I hadn't planned well enough. I could be caught tonight. One kill, rather sloppy, and it could all be over. I wasn't ready for that. I liked my new hobby. I really wanted to do it again. And again. And again. Thankfully, Joe didn't come in with me when we got home. He helped me out of the car and started toward my door when his radio crackled to life. He excused himself and went back to his car to answer it. He came back to me a few moments later.

"You'll have to see yourself in, James. I just got a noise complaint over on White Street. Almost 7:00 in the morning and we're still getting noise complaints. Christ, it's been a busy night. I've got to go quiet things down. Do you want me to come by later to check on you?"

"Joe, you've done more than enough. I'm glad you

were the first on the scene. It was nice to see a familiar face, even if it did have a scolding look on it."

"James, you have got to get some help for your insomnia. And stop riding motorcycles. I know you'll never ride that one again; it looked pretty trashed at the scene."

"Oh, God, Joe, where will they take it? Where will my bike be? I'll need to get some stuff out of the saddle bags."

"I saw Lincoln Towing come to get it. I suppose you can call them later and they'll tell you where it is. I gotta go. Get some rest." With that, Joe headed off into the early dawn. I dragged my weary body into the house, uncharacteristically locked the door, and staggered off to bed. I slept the whole day through.

AFTERMATH—BETH

When I awoke, I was sore everywhere. I was excited though; I was going to get to watch the video of my play date with Beth. I got out of bed and limped to the bathroom. I looked at myself in the mirror. "You look like hell!" I said to my reflection. "It looks like you got into a fight and got the worst of it." I looked myself over. I did look nasty. I was glad that I had cancelled my usual Saturday tutoring sessions. I needed the time to recover from the evening's doings. I was in no shape to deal with anyone, anyone living, at least. I had to clean up the mess Beth and I had made and watch the raw footage my camera had caught the night before. Thinking about that made my manhood twitch.

I had more pressing things to attend to first, though. I needed to clean up my living room and kitchen before anyone stopped by to see me. The bloodstains in the entry and the bloody cheese grater were the most pressing. Then I had to dispose of Beth's personal belongings. Her purse was in the living room next to the sofa. Her cell phone was beeping, beckoning her to answer the missed calls and messages on it. I limped over to it and turned it off. I took out the battery and SIM card. I destroyed the SIM card and put it and the battery into the trash. I would deal with the purse later.

I got the mop and a bucket and scrub brush and set about the task of cleaning up my blood from the entryway. I took the entry rug and put it in a bag to bring to the cistern later. I scrubbed the dry blood from the tile and wall in the entry. I took the towels that Beth had wrapped my leg in and put them in the cistern bag as well. I didn't really need to dispose of those, after all; they were soaked in my own blood and I could launder them. But they were old and I could use some new towels anyway, so into the cistern they would go. I finished up the entry and moved into the kitchen. Not much to do there, just do the dishes and throw away the leftovers. Anything Beth had touched in the kitchen, living room, bathroom, or hallway got a thorough washing. I knew I couldn't eliminate all of Beth's DNA from my house, but Beth's being there from time to time was old news, nothing out of the ordinary. I knew that sooner rather than later, the police would want to talk to me about Beth. I had been the last person she had been seen with, so I knew it would not be long before I had to confront them. I hoped I could keep my cool when the inevitable visit occurred. I'd rehearsed that moment in my mind over and over; I just hoped I was as good an actor as I thought I was. I wondered how long it would be before her disappearance was noticed and how long after that it would be until I was questioned. Even that would be a fun part of the game. Keeping my cool while talking to the police would be a supreme test of my skills. I relished the thought.

I was exhausted after cleaning up, and my body ached everywhere. It was almost midnight. As much as I wanted to look at the video, I needed to take some more Aspocontin and go to bed. I needed to be functional and punctual in the morning. I had a Monday 8:00 a.m. class to teach. I was always in my classroom fifteen minutes before class time, and I wanted tomorrow to be no different. Everything needed to be normal…. I dragged my weary and beaten body to my bed and lay down. I fell asleep instantly.

*

I almost slept through my alarm the next morning. When I got up, I washed up in the sink; no showers allowed for a few days until my wounds healed more under my stitches. I dressed for work, and then I looked in the mirror once more before leaving. I still looked awful, but there was nothing I could do about that. Word of my motorcycle accident would have been on the local news, so word would spread fast. When I got to my classroom, Vince was already there waiting for me.

"Jesus, friend, you do look like shit. How bad is the bike?" Vince pulled my desk chair out for me and plopped into the chair in front of me. "Should you even be here? Haven't you ever heard of sick days? Use one, for God's sake!"

"I don't know how bad the bike is; I haven't seen it yet. Going there tonight. And I'm OK. Sore, but OK. I slept all day yesterday, and the pain meds seem to be working. I'd much rather be here than rattling around the house. You know I like to keep busy."

"James, you've got to get some help. You're still not slee—"

"Vince, I've heard this over and over. Yeah, I know, I still need more therapy. I need to find a way to move on and deal. I need to get over my insomnia. Blah, blah, blah. Boring. See how you would handle Sue's death. Trust me; this shit isn't easy." Of course, I didn't tell him that I had found a new hobby to keep me busy. Couldn't tell him that I was an aspiring serial killer. Somehow, I didn't think that there was anything in anyone's rules of etiquette that covered that particular scenario.

"I've got to get to my first class. James, take it easy for the next little bit. Try to rest, relax, and heal. OK?" Vince left and I was alone for a moment. I thought about Beth's skin, her breath, her pulse under my hands. The look of horror in her eyes. The struggle. Her bargaining and pleading. I smiled to myself. I wanted more. As tired and battered as my body was, I felt alive. I had something to look forward to. I had a reason to live again. I wondered how long I would have to wait until I could play again. The sounds of students entering jerked me out of my reverie.

"Dr. Martin, are you OK?"

"Bummer about your bike!"

"Anything broken?"

"Are you going to fix your motorcycle? I haven't had a ride yet...."

"How many stitches?"

As my class filed in, the questions and comments flew through the room. I patiently answered all their questions. I couldn't deny that I'd had an accident, so I might as well be open with them. At least, appear to be. I had to be on my guard to make sure my story was consistent with what I had told the police and the hospital staff. I didn't want to get caught in any lies already. I wanted to make it to my next play date.

The day continued on in the same fashion all day long. It was almost like the time immediately following Gwen's death—a blur of questions and condolences and concern. It was tiring dealing with it all, and I regretted my decision to come to work. I should have stayed home. I could have been editing my video. I could have been reliving Saturday night's fun. People were tedious. This was boring. I wanted to say, "Fuck it all" and head home, but I stuck it out for appearances' sake. I called Sarah and told her that I wouldn't make it to rehearsal, that she should just have the cast do a line glib. Run the lines as fast as possible, no feeling or inflection. Do it twice. I could certainly be excused from one rehearsal to nurse my wounds. Sarah certainly understood and told me that it would all be taken care of. Told me to get some rest.

My seemingly endless work day ended and I headed home. I winced as I got into my car. I hurt everywhere, more than I had on Sunday. I downed a couple more

Aspocontin and hoped that they would take the edge off. I had a long evening ahead of me. I had to clean up the shelter before I did anything else. It was a mess. Then I would sit down and watch the raw footage of my playtime with Beth. I was looking forward to that. I hoped that the camera had caught enough to enjoy. I hadn't planned on Beth fighting back and moving all over, so I was worried that we had been out of the camera's eye for some of the festivities. I'd know soon enough.

The shelter was an awful mess. Total disarray. It took me the better part of a couple of hours to gather Beth's cut up clothing and other paraphernalia that I needed to dispose of and thoroughly clean my playroom. Everything was out of place. She had made quite a mess of things with her futile fight for life. I spent a long time wiping things down, trying to eliminate fingerprints and hair and fibers. Then I reminded myself that it was likely that I would, someday, be found out and either have to flee and assume my new identity or face the music. Either way, there would be no doubt that I was the perp, so why bother trying to eliminate any of my playmate's evidence from this place? If the police were in here, they would find my videos, my equipment, everything they needed to convict me. If I hadn't successfully fled, I might as well not make it any harder on the local gendarmes. Just fess up and face the music like a man. No need to try to erase Beth or any of my future playmates. Just tidy the place up so it was livable and neat again; no need to scrub for DNA. My house was a different matter. I would be extremely cautious there. Here, in my hideaway, I would simply keep it neat for my own liking and pleasure, evidence be damned. That reasoning freed me up to watch the raw footage of my play date and enjoy.

I booted up my computer and loaded the raw

footage from the camera. I simply wanted to watch it first, take some notes, and then I would get down to editing it. My pulse quickened as Beth and I first appeared on the screen. How lovely she was. How innocent. Unsuspecting. Trusting. Her first uncomfortable looks when I locked the door were priceless. I looked stupid when she bolted away and ran to the storeroom. A fair amount of time was just our voices and shuffling sounds with an empty table in the frame. Then the fight with the chair and my struggle to subdue her. Once again, much of it off-camera or just an arm or leg flashing in and out of the frame. Sad—I had wanted to watch it all. But then it was all worthwhile again. Beth lashed to the table. Me cutting the clothes from her lithe form. And the final moments of her life slipping away. All delightful. My back obscured too much of what I really wanted to see—I hadn't been as aware of the camera as I should have been. I would have to buy more cameras so I could record from multiple angles. That would be much more satisfying. Still, this was a better souvenir than none at all. Much better than just a lock of hair or a snippet of clothing. And I certainly wasn't Ed Gein; I had no desire to keep any fleshy bits as trophies. This video, in its edited form, would be a wonderful reminder of this evening and the gift Beth had given me.

*

When I finished editing my recording and headed back to the house, it was almost 1:00 a.m. I would be a tired boy at school later this morning. It was worth it….

When I got to the house, my cell phone was beeping. Missed calls and messages. I opened it and dialed my voicemail. I had three messages, all from Sarah.

"James, I just got to the theater. Do you want me to tell the cast about your accident or just say you are ill? I mean, I'm sure almost everyone knows, but it is your call.

Call me back if you can before rehearsal starts. Thanks." Sarah was nothing if not thorough.

"James, Beth wasn't at rehearsal tonight. I tried her cell and got no answer. I had Brandi read her lines. Line glib went very well. Hope you feel better." The shit was going to hit the fan soon. People would notice that Beth was missing. This would get interesting, and fast. This would test my nerves, my planning, and my acting. I rather looked forward to it all.

"James, I called Kendra. She's out of town, but she hasn't been able to get Beth to answer her cell for a couple of days. I'm worried. Call me. Bye." Sarah had good reason to worry about young Beth….

*

It was another day before the police and the media got involved. Wednesday. The Wednesday morning local news reported that Beth had disappeared. They reported that she had last been seen walking out of her apartment building Friday evening and never returning. The news mentioned that she had been seen being dropped off at her apartment by a man on a motorcycle and that the police were interested in speaking to him. I'll bet they were. I was prepared for that. I was expecting it. I was looking forward to it. I debated whether to call the police and "out" myself as the motorcycle rider or wait for them to come to me. I decided that the former was the better course of action. I had nothing to hide, at least as far as Beth's disappearance, so I thought it would be best if I were as forthcoming as possible. The police wouldn't have to dig far to find out I was the rider. I was sure they would talk to members of the cast and crew of *Guys and Dolls* very soon. So I called the police station as soon as I got to my office.

"New Worcester PD. Officer Noble speaking," said the blasé voice on the other end of the phone.

"Bill, James Martin. How are you? How're Millie and the kids?" I had known Bill Noble and his family for a few years; they were friends of Joe Higgins, and our paths had crossed a lot at different events and parties. Less often since Gwen had passed, but Bill and I knew each other well enough.

"Hey, James, how are you doing? Feeling better after your wreck? Sorry about your bike. That was the one Gwen gave you, wasn't it? Can it be fixed?"

"Don't know, Bill; haven't had the time to go over to Lincoln and look at it. Actually, that's a lie. I really don't want to look at it just yet. Seeing any kind of wrecked vehicle gives me the creeps. So I really don't know. But, actually, the bike is why I called. The girl who disappeared, Beth, well you know she's a student at MNC. She's also a friend of mine from the Pearl. It was me on the video dropping her off Friday night. Thought I should call, see if there was any way I could help you guys out. I'd hate to think that anything happened to her. Nice kid; I really like her a lot. And I really don't want to replace her in the cast. She's a great actress and has a great voice. I know that sounds a little selfish of me, but I kind of have to deflect the thought of anything happening to her with my feeble attempts at humor."

"James, Joe was just getting ready to call you. The video isn't very good, but he knows you often give kids rides home from the Pearl. He figured you were probably the man we needed to talk to. When can you get over to the station? Do you have a break in your schedule this morning that would work for you?"

"Bill, I can cancel a class if I need to; just tell me when you want me there."

"James, no need to call off a class. Turns out that Beth had a habit of running away from home when she was younger. While we are certainly taking this seriously, we don't really know if there's any foul play involved or if she just fell into old habits. Talking to her mom, Joe found out that Beth ran away no less than five times from ages twelve to sixteen. Don't get me wrong, her mom is worried, but she was the one to suggest that maybe the stress of school and work was too much and that Beth had run away again. You never know with today's kids."

"My first class gets over at 10:00. I don't have another till this afternoon, so I'll come over to the station around 10:30. OK? If that doesn't work, just call me on my cell. I'll leave it on during class."

"Thanks, James. We'll see you then." With that, Bill hung up. I was surprised by what he had told me about Beth. I thought I had known her well, but she'd never mentioned anything about running away repeatedly. I wish I'd known that before; it might have hastened my choice of Beth for my first playmate.

I got to the station just a little past 10:30. Bill greeted me at the desk and buzzed for Joe. Joe and I went back to his desk to talk. Everything seemed normal, nothing threatening about Joe or anyone's demeanor. I was pleased.

"You want a coffee? Doughnut? Water?" Joe asked.

"No, I'm OK. Had a pretty good breakfast this morning. Still stiff, but I'm beginning to feel more like myself."

"James, what if one of your students or theater kids had been on your bike when you crashed? You could have seriously injured one of them. Hell, you could have killed Beth." I did my best not to react unnaturally to that sentence. Could have killed Beth? Ha-ha. Yes, I could have.

"Joe, you know I'm a cautious rider. Stupid

deer…but we really should talk about Beth. I'm so disturbed that she's gone missing. Nice kid; I really like her."

"You know me, James, always looking for another chink in the armor when it comes to you and your motorcycles. Maybe reminding you that you could kill one of your friends might get you to stop riding. I wish everybody would. You're right, though; I am preaching. Tell me about Friday night. Anything unusual about Beth's behavior that night? Anything to make you think she might be in trouble or stressed or just out of sorts? Any reason she might have skipped out of town for a little while?"

"Honestly, Joe, everything seemed perfectly normal to me. She was fine at rehearsal. She'd been bugging me for a ride all week, so I brought my spare helmet along so she could ride home with me if she wanted to. Normally she rides out to rehearsals with Lainey Bryant. They're pretty close, those two. When I asked if she wanted a ride, she said yes and buzzed off to tell Lainey that she was riding home with me. On the ride home, she told me her roommate Kendra was out of town. She mentioned that she didn't like it when Kendra wasn't home, that she didn't like to sleep alone in the apartment. We took the back road home; it's a nicer ride. I dropped her at her apartment and headed home myself. I had a drink and tried to read for a while. I was dog tired, but I couldn't sleep. I took a late night ride and then hit the deer. You know the rest of my story for that night…."

"Anything else? Did she say she was going to go out later? Meet any friends? Go to the bars or any parties? God knows it was a busy night. Hell, I was getting noise complaints all night. These kids party a lot harder than I did when I was in college. 'Thirsty Thursday' because most of them don't have Friday classes. 'Freaky Friday' when they get really wound up for the weekend. 'Suck 'em Down Saturday' for serious drinking binges. I don't know if there's a name for Sunday yet, but even they aren't quiet. Did she indicate that she might be meeting someone later on?"

"Nope. We talked about the show, Kendra's sloppiness, school, working at the sub shop…nothing about anything going on later. I didn't hear about any of the cast getting together, either. They usually try to convince me to come party with them; it's kind of a running joke because I seldom do, but I didn't hear of anything Friday. Sorry I'm mostly useless, but I haven't a clue what might have happened to Beth. I hope she turns up. Nice kid. Please keep me in the loop as much as protocol will let you…."

Joe thanked me once again for coming in so quickly. We chatted a little longer about my accident and life in general. I was glad that Joe was involved in the investigation. I knew Joe could never suspect me of hurting anyone. We'd known each other for too long. Joe knew I was a gentle man and couldn't intentionally harm anyone. He knew I would help in any way I could. Joe was a good friend to have in this situation.

I left the station and went back to my office to finish prepping for my next class. The interview had gone well, quite well in fact. I felt that I had stayed cool and calm, that nothing about my demeanor would give Joe any clues to Beth's actual whereabouts. It would be vital to my hobby that I keep my wits about me. I had to make sure that whatever story I told was simple and believable. I would have to make certain that I didn't trip myself up over details that could give clues to the girls' actual fates. I would have to start a log or journal on my computer in the shelter to keep track of each girl, the real and made up circumstances of her disappearance, and each visit I had with any authorities. School officials, local and State Police, the FBI if they ever became involved, anyone I talked to about any of the "missing" girls would have to be carefully documented. Those same files could, ultimately, prove to be my undoing if the police ever got into my shelter. But if they got that far, I would be done for anyway.

My work days passed uneventfully for the balance of the week. The whole campus was abuzz about Beth disappearing. Lots of crazy rumors flew around. Beth had gone to The Boar's Head Tavern and been kidnapped by a biker. Beth had been hitchhiking and a trucker took her away. Beth went for a moonlight hike and her body was in the woods, a victim of a wolf attack. Beth had run away because she was pregnant. Lots of silliness. Rehearsals at the Pearl were a little strange, too. At the end of the week, I had to tell the cast that we were going to have to assume that Beth was out of the show, that Lainey would assume her role. That "sealed" Beth's fate in the cast's eyes. We had been rehearsing as if she were simply absent; none of them wanted to think of her as gone, really gone. A few of the girls cried. I assured them that if Beth returned, we would put her back in the show. I told them all how much I missed her and hoped that she was OK, that she hadn't been the victim of any sort of foul play. As the days turned into weeks, Beth became less of an item on the news. The police had no leads and no witnesses. I was pleased....

THE WAITING GAME

In time, Beth slipped from the news. After a few weeks, there was barely any mention of her. Once in awhile, the paper would run a filler story saying that there had been no leads, that she had vanished without a trace. Blah, blah, blah. The local TV station had a similar story a month after she disappeared. I was pleased. I would get to play again. Nothing had led anyone to suspect me. Whenever Joe Higgins and I crossed paths, I would ask whether there was any progress. He always told me he was baffled, that Beth had simply vanished from the face of the Earth. The New Worcester PD had called in the Michigan State Police, but thus far, they had no more leads than the locals.

After my fun with Beth, I was itching for more. I wanted to feel another throat in my hands. I wanted to see the look of horror as my friend realized I was not whom she thought I was, see the realization of her impending doom in her eyes and her expression. The bargaining, the begging, the pleading. The empowering feeling that I got from controlling the ultimate destiny of another human being. The feel of her pulse under my fingers, weakening as I squeezed harder. I repeatedly watched my video of Beth, wishing I had had the foresight to use more than one camera. Still, I found the video endlessly entertaining. Her fine young body slowly revealed to me, her struggles, even her getting the better of me, all of it was thrilling. I needed more. I knew I had to bide my time. I had to let the hubbub of Beth's going missing fully subside before I made another young lady "vanish." I used my time to better plan my next play date. I would plan a scenario that would keep my victim front and center in the camera's eye. At some point, I would place more cameras around my playroom if needed, but first, I would try controlling the situation better.

Who would be my next playmate? Who was close enough for me to get the maximum pleasure? Who would arouse the least suspicion? The possibilities intrigued me. I thought about Jessica. After Gwen had died, I had shut Jess out of my life for a while. I knew it wasn't her fault that Gwen had died; it was Gwen's misunderstanding of my relationship with Jessica that had been Gwen's undoing. Still, seeing her was painful right after Gwen's death, so I had been very cold to her for a while. In time, though, I realized how much I needed her friendship. I needed her in my life to try to heal from the blow of losing Gwen. So Jess and I had resumed our friendship. She would be an ideal playmate. I found her attractive, more so when she was stressed. I thought about how aroused I had been when I had seen her after Marcus had abused her. Thinking about it made my manhood twitch. We had a deep history. We were as connected as any man and woman who had not been physically intimate could be. But I couldn't pick her. Not quite yet. Maybe later….

I thought about Lainey. Lainey was a sweet kid. She'd had a rough go of it over the past couple of years. Her long-term boyfriend had dumped her and she'd been feeling down for a long time. She'd dated a little, but nothing had clicked for her. She'd always had issues with her weight. While she was never model thin, there were times when she would tone up and look really fine. Other times, especially when depressed, she would pack on the pounds and lose a lot of her appeal to me. She always trusted me and treated me as "one of the girls." I knew more about her personal life than was probably normal for a straight man to know about a female friend's. I knew that she looked up to me almost like a second father. She was definitely in the running. If she knew what she was in the running for, she would do everything she could to lose the race. The biggest problem was how close she was to Beth. They were practically joined at the hip. Killing her would certainly raise alarm bells at the New Worcester PD, and I didn't need that. About the only worse choice would have been Kendra, Beth's former roommate. I moved Lainey off the list for now.

After mentally sifting through a few more potential playmates, I settled on Rene. Rene was very cute and a bit of a flirt. She was bright and a good student. She had taken a couple of history classes from me, and we had done a few shows together at the Pearl. She and I were close, not as close as I was with Lainey or Beth, and certainly not as close as I was with Jess, but we were still friends. She trusted me. She asked my advice and opinion on many things. She had aspirations to try her hand at modeling before grad school. She made no secret about that; she told everyone who would listen that she was going to pay for grad school with her modeling income. To my knowledge, she had never actually posed for a photographer. She had not posted any photos on her Facebook page that were professionally done, as many of her contemporaries had, but she had posted many pictures of herself on the beach or dressed in revealing Halloween costumes and the like. I browsed her photos on Facebook many times. She was a very appealing creature and seemed happy to share her beauty with her online friends quite freely. I decided I would appeal to that side of her and approach her about doing a photo shoot. I had posted some of my photos on my Facebook page during the past year. Nature shots mostly. Nothing remotely approaching professional quality—just some nice pictures of sunsets, flowers, Munising Falls, Pictured Rock, and other stuff around the U.P. I always brought my camera with me on the motorcycle and took a great number of photos. Asking Rene to pose for me would not seem that far out of the ordinary. I just had to wait a couple of more months to let Beth's disappearance fade a little further from the local memory before I got to play with my next mate. I used my time to prepare my playroom and plan our date. I gathered costumes for her to wear, thought about backdrops and lighting, and planned every other detail I could think of. When enough time had passed, I only had to ask her to put the plan into motion. I waited impatiently; I told myself to wait three more weeks. Two more. One more. And then, it was time. I could ask my playmate to join me.

I ran into Rene in the hallway of the Clinton Building on campus. I say "ran into," but, in truth, I made sure I was there when she was likely to be. Rene had not been at auditions for *Bye Bye Birdie*, which gave me a perfect excuse to want to talk to her. She had always told me she loved that show and really wanted to audition for the role of Kim. I had encouraged her to do so. I told her that Jim Waters, the director, was a fan and would probably cast her. She had seemed excited and positive. I was surprised when she hadn't shown up.

"Rene! Could I have a moment?" I stopped her in the hall.

"Hi, Dr. Martin. Sure. My next class isn't until noon. I've got a few moments. What's up?" Rene always insisted on calling me by my professional title when we were at school. At the Pearl, I was James, but here I was always "Dr. Martin." I actually found it to be charming.

"You weren't at *Birdie* auditions. Jim was disappointed. I was too. I thought you loved the show…."

"I do, but I am going to take summer session classes, so I just can't do it. Christ, I don't know what I was thinking when I signed up for three…."

142

The regular semester was just about over. MNC offered a "summer semester" for masochists, a very compressed class schedule that started right after the regular year ended. A whole semester's class work crammed into five weeks. Most people took one or two summer semester classes at most. Three was suicidal.

"Rene, what were you thinking? Oh, my God, three? That's nucking futs! I wouldn't do that. I like my life too much. Why?"

"I really want to be done in four years, and I needed to take these classes now to make it happen. It seems like everyone at MNC is on a four-and-a-half- to five-year plan. I just wanted to be out in four. So I'm taking three summer semester classes at once. Call me stupid, but here I go. So that's why I can't do the show."

I looked at Rene for a moment. "OK, if you really want to do it that way. I understand, but I think that two would be more than enough. I seldom even teach summer semester—it makes my head spin. I do have something else I'd like to talk about. A little project of mine that won't take too much time...." I smiled and waited for Rene's reply.

"OK, I'll bite.... What is it?"

"Rene, you know I've been doing a fair amount of photography. I post a lot of my shots on my Facebook page."

"Yeah, sure. I've seen some. You do nice work."

"Thanks. I am still just a beginner, but I am enjoying my new hobby. Anyway, I would like to try shooting a model. I have some new lights and stuff and would really like to shoot you, if you're game."

"That would be cool. I've wanted to pose for a while. You know I'm going to be a model after I get my degree. I plan to pay for my grad school by modeling. But

143

I've told you that before…."

"That's why I wanted to ask you. I know you have an interest, and we know each other well enough for me to ask you. I'm a little uncomfortable asking; I don't want to seem like some old creep…."

"James, c'mon. You? A creep? Far from it. You're the farthest thing from it."

Silly girl; if she only knew…. We chatted a little more. We agreed to meet at Starbucks to talk about the details. I told her that I looked forward to it.

We got together later that evening. We talked about what kinds of shots I wanted to take, set up a few ground rules, and talked about her fee. At first, she said I didn't have to pay her, but I insisted. I told her that if she were going to try her hand as a professional, she would have to get used to assessing just what her time and talents were worth and that she should not shy away from asking. I reminded her that she wouldn't go to work for free, so she shouldn't treat posing for me any differently. We agreed on an hourly rate. I asked her to be discreet. I told her I didn't want to ruffle any of the other theater girls' feathers because I hadn't asked to shoot them. I appealed to her vanity, and I hoped that it worked. I also reminded her that these were rather uptight times at NMC since Beth's disappearance. I would have to trust that this little girl would indeed be discreet. We finished our lattes and shook on our bargain. In only a few more days, this young one would be mine.

RENE

"I'm so glad you agreed to this shoot, Rene. I have wanted a model for this for a long time, but I was afraid to ask. Thought I'd sound creepier than I really am asking one of my friends to pose for me. I'm really enjoying my new hobby, but I'm ready to try photographing people rather than just things. I mean, I've shot people, you know, snapshots, but I've not had someone that I've done a photo study of. Thanks."

Of course, Rene had no idea what my real hobby was. She had seen some of my photos online and had commented on them. A lot of my friends had. I seemed to be getting a real feel for my camera and composition. Back in the day, I had a Canon AT-1 35mm and had done a fair amount of photography, but I hadn't been serious about it for years. Gwen and I had shared camera duties as the kids grew and when we went on trips, but we were just taking snaps, not "photos." Digital cameras had changed the whole photography universe. I had held onto my old film camera for a long time until digital cameras had replaced them. It was silly, but I missed the anticipation of waiting to see whether what you had taken turned out. Now I had instant gratification. I knew right away whether or not the photos were OK. There was another, darker reason that I liked my new digital camera. I could take pictures of anything and not have to worry about sending them to the lab. I could have a whole gallery of memories of my real hobby and "develop" them myself, no worries....

"James, you know you really don't have to pay me. This will be fun. We always have a good time doing a show together. You're my favorite director. This will be just like a show, only I am the only lead," Rene bubbled. "I am kind of excited. No one has ever asked to shoot me before." I thought, *No one has ever asked you to die before, either....*

"Rene, I do have to pay you. This isn't community theater. You aren't donating your time. You are acting as a professional model. While it sounds like fun, and I will try to make it as much fun as possible, there is a lot of hurry up and wait. Holding a pose while I get the light right. Costume changes. More time waiting while I fiddle with the settings and the lights. Your time is valuable. And honestly, I will feel better about asking you to do some of the things we've discussed if I pay you. It will help me to think of you as a model and not a friend."

"OK. This will be fun. And if it makes you feel better to pay me, well, like all college students, I am broke. Where are we going to shoot? You said your studio, but I know every inch of this house and I've never seen a studio. Your guest bedroom is too small and your basement too full. Where is your studio?" Rene looked around the living room as if she thought a hidden door might slide open.

"Follow me out back. I've got a secret." I started through the kitchen and out the back door. Rene followed along. When we reached the woods at the edge of my lawn, I turned to her. "I didn't even know this was here until just before Gwen died. It was such a cool find." I led Rene to the hatch for the bomb shelter. I pulled it open and flipped on the light switch for the stairs. Rene looked at the concrete stairs leading to the heavy steel door.

"A bomb shelter? I've never seen a real one. Cool," Rene said. "I watched something on The History Channel about the Cold War and knew that some people built them, but I never thought there would be any here in New Worcester."

"Rene, most of you kids here at MNC don't know that the airport used to be a full-fledged SAC base. B-52s, a fighter squadron, nukes, cruise missiles, the works. Here in the middle of God's Country, we were sitting at ground zero. I used to joke that if there was ever a war, I would just climb up on the roof with a beer and watch the south. The fireworks would have been spectacular. New Worcester would be wiped out. At least 80-90 percent casualties in the first month alone." I watched Rene's face as she listened to my story. Rene was bright and very interested in history. I thought she'd enjoy learning a little about my funhouse. "This place was really built. Deep cistern to hold rainwater, lights, generator, fresh air filters, large storeroom. C'mon down." I headed down the stairs and opened the door. Flipped on the lights. Rene eagerly followed.

"Cool. I like how you've done it up. It is so bright in here. Not like a cellar at all. It's a perfect private getaway." Rene looked all around.

I had set up my lights on one side of the room and arranged a couple of different backdrops on the opposite wall. I had a blue velvet drape on one side, deep burgundy on the other. I had boxes and things under the fabric to create different shapes and levels. I was looking forward to our photo shoot. I was looking forward to our real purpose. It had been too long since Beth, and I was eager to play. I had learned a lot from that first kill, and I hoped that this time would go a little smoother. I certainly didn't plan to end up in the ER this time.

"OK, Rene, why don't you go into the storeroom and put on your first outfit. Start on the left side of the rack; I am rather anal retentive. I've laid everything out left to right." Rene stepped into the storeroom while I powered up the camera, lights, and monitor. I put a chair in the middle of the blue fabric. I fussed with the placement a little while I waited for Rene to come out. The long white dress I'd picked for the first pictures fit her like it had been made for her. A silky gown, very formal and form fitting. Modestly cut neckline with beadwork detailing. A matching hat and handbag completed the ensemble. She looked stunning. She looked ready for a high society ball in Washington or a gallery opening in New York.

"This dress is fabulous! I love it! Where did you find it?" Beth was practically purring.

"Saint Vinnie's, if the truth be told. I love to rummage through there. Never know what you'll find. Some doctor's wife probably outgrew it and finally gave up on ever being able to fit it again, so it ended up at Vinnie's. Not a bad find for $7.10! You can have the dress when we're done, if you want. I knew you'd like it. I'm glad it fits so well. I have my sewing kit down here if we need to make any alterations, but this is perfect. Do you want it?"

"Duh! I don't ever want to take it off!" Beth gushed.

"Well, you're gonna have to after we shoot the first set of pictures. I think you'll like the other outfits, too." I had Rene sit on the chair while I shot a few test shots and adjusted my lights. I knew these pictures really didn't matter; the ones I'd take later were the pictures that would really interest me, but I had to keep up the act for a little while so Rene would play along. After I was satisfied with the lighting, I had Rene pose in a number of different ways. Formal. Serious. Flirty. Fun. I had her pull the hat down to cover one eye. "Like a movie spy," I said. She seemed to be enjoying herself. She took direction well; I already knew that. What I hadn't known was how much I would enjoy this playtime leading to the final act. I knew that as she got more comfortable, I could push her a little further. And then I could push her over the edge and revel in her unraveling as my true intentions were revealed. After about a half hour, I told her to take off that outfit and put on a robe so we could take a break. She bounced into the storeroom and came out in the heavy black silk man's robe I had for her. It covered her more fully than the dress, but it was still somehow arousing. I drank it all in.

"This thing is lush. Vinnie's again?" Rene asked.

"Guilty as charged. I bought it thinking that someday we'd need it at the Pearl. Didn't really have any specific need for it. Just caught my eye. An extravagant waste of $2.10. Do you want something to drink? I've been working you hard already. I've got OJ, Coke, beer, water, or I could make a pot of coffee."

"A little orange juice would be nice."

I found a glass and opened the little refrigerator I had hooked up in the shelter. After I found the juice, I poured it for her while she looked around for a minute and then said, "This is fun. Are you going to shoot anyone else?" Rene took the glass from me and smiled.

"Maybe. We'll see how this goes. I was really nervous asking. I don't want any of you guys to think I'm turning into some kind of creep now that Gwen is gone. 'Come over to my house. Alone. Let me photograph you,' sounds like some sexual predator's come-on or maybe a killer in a 'B' movie thriller. I've got to be careful. I try never to be alone with any of the female cast or crew at the theater. Got to watch out; things can be taken the wrong way. That's why I asked you to be discreet. I just don't want people getting the wrong idea...."

"James, anyone who knows you knows that you aren't a creep. A flirt, but not a creep. I can't imagine anyone worrying about you. You couldn't hurt anyone. Christ, if one of my boyfriends ever turned out to be a creepster, you're the one I'd come to you for advice or help. But I understand. These are weird times. My drama teacher back home had a strict "three-foot rule." He would never be alone with any of us, male or female, and he never touched us other than to place us when we were blocking a scene. I felt bad when I couldn't hug him after a show, but he insisted that he wouldn't take the chance."

"Glad you understand, Rene. These are stupid times. I worry so much about appearances that I am almost as strict as your high school drama teacher. Almost, but since I am with college kids and you are all over eighteen, I figure that we can be adult about things. So I am OK with a quick hug of greeting or after a performance. But I still make sure I'm not alone with you guys. Just overly careful, I guess." I waited for Rene to finish her juice. "Ready for the next set? I am."

Rene went back into the storeroom to change. I shifted the lights to the burgundy backdrop and fussed with the layout. Rene returned quickly in the silver flapper dress. It was short and sparkly. The strappy heels she wore made her legs look even more defined and longer than they really were. I really liked the look. Then I saw her bra strap next to the dress' strap. That wouldn't do….

"Rene, would you mind going back into the storeroom and removing your bra? The strap really contrasts with the dress."

"Sure. Didn't even think about it. Be right back." She slipped away and popped out quickly. "Better?"

"Perfect." And it was. Her shoulders and neck looked inviting and clean without the extraneous straps. The thin material clung to her little breasts and revealed their delightful true form. Bras, while a necessary evil on larger busted women, are a blight on the form of someone sylphlike like Rene. She looked so much more natural and beautiful without it. We got down to business. I handed her a prop Tommy gun to pose with. A shiny hip flask. A prop revolver. We shot some "Bonnie Parker" gangster shots. Rene was once again a willing and eager model. I asked her to stand in semi-profile with one leg up on the chair. I gave her a garter and had her place it on her thigh. I asked her whether it was OK if she put the garter a little higher on her thigh to reveal a little more leg. She did and I almost groaned at the result. She was beautiful. She was sexy. She was mine, although she didn't know it yet.

"OK. Are you game for some Roaring Twenties pinup action?" I paused. "Nothing really revealing. Hell, you wear far less at the beach."

"Sure. I feel sexy. This is fun."

"You should feel sexy. This is sexy. We now show so much skin in movies and stuff that the tease is lost. Burlesque shows hardly ever showed more than a shoulder or thigh, but men went crazy for them. Now any girl willing to wiggle out of her skirt can 'dance' in a club. It isn't hard to get a man's attention when you rub your boobs in his face. Don't get me wrong; there's a place for strip clubs, and I don't mind going once in awhile, but this is more titillating than naked."

"You're funny, James. How do you want me?" *Naked and struggling for your life in my arms*, I thought. What I said was "Drop the straps down around your arms. If you have to, unzip the back a little so you can lower the neckline and clutch the fabric to your bosom. Show a little cleavage, but not a lot. Leg up on the chair. Your other hand on your dress, pulling it up a little past the garter. Yeah, like that." She got it right away. I shot several pictures of her in variations of this pose. A few minutes later, I told her to change back into the robe and take another break. We'd look at the photos on the monitor when she came out.

I played with the pictures a little. Added a sepia tone to some, made some look like faded black and white. I love Photoshop and all the things you can do with a picture with just a few mouse clicks. When I was younger, this would have all taken hours of trial and error in somebody's darkroom. I had never developed my own film or made my own prints, other than in a high school photography class. Never had the money or time to devote to the hobby.

Rene came back out wrapped up in the robe. "More OJ? And do you have vodka down here? I would love a screwdriver," Rene said.

"I just might have vodka. Ice, too." I mixed her a drink and handed it to her. We looked at the pictures. Even with my hasty doctoring, they looked period-appropriate and turned out really well. Rene seemed to enjoy them very much. This pleased me. She pleased me. I hoped this would be so much different than Beth had been. I actually enjoyed her fight and struggle, and most of all the pleading for her life, but I didn't want Rene's death to have to be so violent. I had a romantic notion that it could be a sensual experience like the vampire seductions in Anne Rice's novels. I wasn't kidding myself; I knew that when the time came, Rene would fight too. Who wouldn't fight to stay alive? I just hoped I was better prepared for it. After a few minutes, Rene went to get changed again. I looked forward to her returning.

Rene came back in the black leather miniskirt and halter I'd picked for her. I was stunned. This girl looked so freaking hot in this short skirt and top that I thought I'd lose it right there. I had to turn toward the monitor to compose myself.

"This leather is so soft. More Vinnie's?" asked Rene.

"No, not this. I bought it especially for this shoot. It is deer hide. So soft and supple. You can even wash deer hide. It is neat stuff. This really was a splurge, but I thought it would be worth it. Seeing you now, I know it was. Rene, don't take this the wrong way. I'm not hitting on you or anything, but you look amazing in that leather...." I kind of stammered as I said the last few words.

"Thank you. I feel hot. This feels so good against my skin. I like the fit. I've never worn anything like it. I'm afraid to ask, but how much did it cost?"

"Rene, you never ask how much a gift costs...."

"What? I can't take this. It's too much...and I am a little uncomfortable thinking you bought it for me." Rene started to tense up a little. I needed to defuse that, and quickly.

"Rene, I bought it for the photos. I really hadn't planned on giving it to you, but when I saw you in it, I...well, I couldn't imagine anyone else wearing it. Sorry if I made you feel uncomfortable. Do you want to call it a day and change back into your own clothes? I'm sorry...."

"No. I'm OK. You just caught me off-guard. I...uh...um...no...I'm OK. But I can't keep this. I wouldn't know where to wear it anyway. May I have another drink before we start?" Rene paused. I sensed that her defenses were going back down and that she truly was OK. She wouldn't be for long, but that would be on my timeline, not hers.... So I mixed her another screwdriver and one for myself. We sat and talked a few minutes until she told me she was ready to start again. She seemed to be enjoying herself again. I knew that I was.

"Rene, do you trust me? Really trust me?" I asked. I looked into her eyes and waited for her answer.

"You know I do. What's up?" she asked a little warily.

"When we talked about doing this shoot, I told you that I wouldn't ask you pose nude. And I still won't. But I do want to push the envelope a little. May I continue?" This was getting to the moment of truth, so to speak.

"Yeah...I think.... What do you want?" Rene asked.

"You look so hot in the leather. I'd like to shoot some fetish shots. Nothing really crazy, nothing too dirty, whatever dirty really means. I know we talked about some slightly racy content, but I had to ask again. I want to make sure you are OK, really OK with it. I would like a few shots of you with leather straps on your wrists and legs. If you don't like them, I'll let you delete them from the hard drive. I know this is a lot to ask, but man, would they be smoking hot." I looked to see whether Rene was totally freaked or OK with my proposal. With or without her assent, she would end up bound....

"Maybe I *should* be worried about you, James." Rene said this with a spark of mischief in her eye and a tone that said she was all right with what I had asked. My heart skipped a few beats as I waited for her to continue. "OK. A few," she agreed. "But turn the monitor so I can see them right away. And you have to promise to untie me immediately if I ask. And you'll let me delete them if they make me uncomfortable?"

"Of course. Anything you want. You don't think I'm a total pervert?"

"I would if you wanted to take these pictures of little boys, but I think you're probably pretty normal. A little strange, but I've known that as long as I've known you. And when we talked about me doing this shoot, you did ask whether I would be OK with some racy content as long as we drew the line at nudity. So yeah, I'm OK. They might make a fun gift for my boyfriend, if I had one." Rene smiled. I got the straps and then turned the monitor so she could see what my camera saw. I had always planned to turn it so she could see, but not to make her comfortable. I tied the straps to her wrists and to each other. She still had some freedom of movement. I didn't want her to freak out just yet. I had her sit on the chair and told her to look at the camera. Told her to look forlorn. Wary. Worried. She complied. I then tied the straps to her ankles. I asked her whether it was OK to tie each ankle to a chair leg, just for a minute. She nodded, "Yes," so I did. I then went over to the steel door and slid the bolt noisily home. I put the lock in place and spun the dial. "For your privacy," I said. Rene nodded again.

I shot a couple of pictures of her this way. She looked so pretty sitting there. Her long brown hair flowed over her shoulders. It glistened under the lights. Her eyes shone. I asked her whether I could put her hands behind her back for the last couple of pictures. She said, "OK" and I did. Even better. She looked totally helpless. She was mine now. It was time. I walked over and gently stroked her face. She turned up to me, puzzled. I kissed her on the forehead and told her not to worry—that everything was fine. Then I untied the top of the halter. I left it on her, just let the straps rest on her shoulders. She shuddered.

"James, this is not OK now. Untie me and let me change now. I am weirded out by this. This was definitely NOT in our discussion of the photo shoot." Rene's voice had a wavering tone to it with an underlying fear. Fear and understanding that things were terribly wrong for her.

"Rene, we need to talk a little more. Actually, I need to talk and you need to listen. Very carefully. The next few things I say will be very important to you. Do you understand me?" I smiled as reassuringly as I could. "I regret to inform you that your trust has been misplaced. I am not the nice guy you all think I am. In fact, I think that if you all really knew me, you would consider me a monster. But I'm not a monster. I don't have any deep emotional trauma. I don't have a scarred childhood in my past. I don't have little voices in my head. I prefer to think of myself as a 'self-made man.' I made a conscious decision to be who and what I am. I chose my path; it didn't choose me. And I chose you as my plaything. It's nothing personal. Well, actually, it is. Anyone can snatch strangers off the street for what we're about to do. But what fun is that? This is *so* much more fun when it *is* personal. I get off on it being personal. I like watching your growing horror. I like knowing that I have violated your every trust. It makes me feel. It makes me whole. I hate to keep losing friends, but at least I'm with them to the very end."

During my little speech, Rene's face fell further and further. Her eyes reflected first her disbelief and then her terror as she realized that I was not kidding, that I was, in fact, planning to do something terrible to her for my own amusement. And total revulsion followed when she realized I would have nothing but satisfaction from it. No guilt, no remorse, just pleasure. It was golden.

I had left the camera focused on Rene's face so she could see herself reacting to my revelations. I used the remote to snap a few shots along the way so I would have pictures of her psyche shattering. I hoped that the video camera was catching it all, too. My video of Beth was rather unsatisfying. I wanted this one to be perfect.

Rene started to make some non-verbal sounds. Best described as whimpering, I guess. Her tears started to flow and she started to shake. I loved every minute of it. I snapped a few more shots.

"See yourself on the monitor? Beautiful." I grinned. I stroked her hair and then moved behind her so we were both in the frame. "Now, I need you to listen a little longer. Then you can make whatever noises you want to. It really won't matter. No one can hear what goes on down here anyway. A good cry and scream or two will probably do you some good. But not quite yet. More painful truths first." I paused, waiting for the inevitable screams. Rene didn't disappoint. I simply waited her out, let her scream a while until she realized it was indeed futile. When she stopped, I continued. "Now the rest of this can be fairly pleasant or really horrible and painful. You get to decide that. I get to decide everything else. Beth chose unwisely. It did not end well for her."

"BETH! What?!" Rene screamed again. "You did what to Beth? Where is she? What did you do? Where? What..." I let her go on for a few moments. I had learned from Beth that I needed to let them tire themselves out. If Rene wanted to waste energy screaming about her lost friend, who was I to interfere? It would certainly be to my advantage. I decided to "twist the knife" a little and turned the Beth video on for Rene to watch. I rubbed her shoulders and gently turned her toward the monitor so she could see Beth's final few minutes. She cringed at my touch, but that was just fine with me. I liked that she was revolted. I didn't expect her to vomit when Beth died. I thought she would scream again or try to bite me or something. I never thought she'd get sick. An awful orange goo flew from her mouth and out of her nostrils. It went everywhere. I got a towel and a mop and cleaned it up. Rene just sat and quietly cried.

"Rene, this just won't do. You're a mess. I'm going to get another towel and a washcloth and get you cleaned up." I turned the camera feed on and switched off the video. Rene could see that she had vomit on her chin and cheeks. A little clung to her hair and some on the halter. I got a pan of warm water and some soap and a washcloth. I tenderly cleaned up Rene's pretty face and did my best to clean up her hair. She just sat staring into the monitor. She recoiled from my every touch. I talked to her in very quiet and soothing tones, just like I had to my kids when they were little and sick.

"What happens next? What are you going to do to me? Why are you going to kill me? Who are you…?" Rene went on for a little while like this.

"Rene, who said I was going to kill you? Remember when I told you that Beth made some bad choices? That's why she ended up dead. You don't have to." I was lying, but Rene didn't know that. "Just listen and cooperate and live. Can you do that?"

"Uh-huh," Rene whispered as she nodded. "I don't want to die."

"That's good because I care too much about you to see you die. I know this sounds strange, but I really don't want to hurt you. That's not what this is all about. I just want to have a little fun. This is my hobby. I hope you will play along. We can have a good time. Just relax…." I kneeled down in front of her. "I am going to take a few more pictures now. I want you to struggle. Try to get free. Really try." I wanted pictures of her straining against her bonds. I also wanted to know that she really was secured well before I went any further. She couldn't escape this place even if she did break loose, but I didn't want another Beth situation either. The scar on my leg still smarted and itched from time to time to remind me of Beth's kicks. As I moved over to the camera, Rene started to struggle in earnest. She first tried to free her hands. Her torso twisted and rose from the chair as she moved her hands behind her. She tried jerking her hands violently. She tried pulling them apart. She tried to untie the straps. Nothing worked; she was bound securely. She began to sweat a little from her exertion. A light sheen of perspiration highlighted her neck and chest. A drop of sweat ran from between her breasts down her abdomen toward her navel. I focused my camera on her torso to document the drop's convoluted path southward. She tried to bounce the chair by flexing her body up and down. The only thing she succeeded in doing was making the left side of the halter fall away from her breast. I excitedly snapped more pictures. She tried to twist and shield her now naked breast from me, but there was no way to accomplish that.

"Rene, why don't you take a break for a few moments? I know all this has tired you, and you are starting to perspire. Would you like something to drink?"

"I just want you to let me go. I am sick of this. Let me out of here. I don't want anything from you," she spat. "Please let me go. I won't tell anyone. I won't say a word about Beth. Just let me get dressed and let me go!"

"Sadly, Rene, that just isn't going to happen. Sadly for you. Much to my delight. This is just a small break so you can catch your breath. We have a long evening ahead of us. How long depends on you. Would you like some sort of refreshment? A drink? A sandwich? I will untie one of your hands so you can eat, if you'd like. Only one, of course. And only if you behave yourself." I waited as Rene thought of a response. I could see that she was weighing the pros and cons of accepting my generosity and trying to devise a plan to use that one free hand to her advantage.

"Some water. And I have to use the bathroom. You'll have to let me up from this chair." Rene looked hopefully at me as if I hadn't thought of this request.

"Which first, drink or restroom?" I asked.

"Restroom, please." Rene was getting into the spirit of things; she was cooperating and remembering the simple niceties such as "please" and "thank you."

I got a short metal rod, about 18" long, fitted with leather cuffs at each end. I tied one cuff to Rene's left ankle and tied the other to her right. Only then did I release her

159

legs from the chair. I tied a long leather strap to her left wrist and secured it to her left ankle so her left hand would have a very limited range of movement. I tied her right wrist securely to her torso. I then instructed her to get up and make her way to the bathroom. She was hobbled by the metal rod, but she gamely made her way to the bathroom's open door. I reached in and switched on the light. She entered the bathroom and turned, looked at the toilet and then back to me.

"Will you help me sit down? I'm not sure I can do it without falling...."

"Gladly." I helped her sit down. "Rene, you will have to do your best with your left hand. I suggest you hike up the skirt and pull your panties down. Probably the simplest, although I'm not well-versed in female bathroom habits."

"Are you going to close the door?" Rene waited.

"No. I don't think so. I need to keep an eye on you. Can't have you trying to escape or fight with me. I learned from my time with Beth, Rene. You'll have to forget modesty." She had some difficulty pulling her panties down one-handed, and they wouldn't go down very far due to the position of her legs. She squirmed and got the skirt moved. When she finished, she reached to pull the panties back up. I stopped her.

"You really won't need those any longer. I'll take care of them." I stooped to cut the panties free from her legs. She strained and tried to prevent my doing so. I took her face in my hands and made her look at me. "Rene, you need to cooperate or things will get bad. I thought you knew this already. Now sit still so you don't get hurt while I cut your panties off." I put one foot on the rod and kneeled down to finish what I had started. She tried to lift her legs, but my foot was firmly planted on the bar. I took my time with the knife, slowly sawing at the fabric. The soft skin on her firm thighs felt delicious on the back of my hands as I removed the panties. I tossed the spoiled garment aside and led Rene back out into the main room of the shelter. I stopped her in the middle and untied the strap that bound her hand to the metal rod. I then tied it to a hook in the ceiling. I took her other hand and untied it from her waist and tied it to the same hook. Perfect. Next, I removed her halter. I got behind her, undid the lower strap, and slowly peeled the leather halter from her damp and trembling form.

I stood behind her and looked at us in the monitor. Her breasts and torso looked like they had been crafted by Michelangelo himself, sculpted from an alabaster-hued marble. I ran my hands up and down her sides, not touching her breasts, but simply tracing the outline of her form with my hands. She whimpered and started to cry; she tried to twist and move, but I tightened my grip on her sides. I leaned forward and kissed her shoulder. I then slid my hands to her breasts and cupped them in my hands. I told her she was beautiful, told her that they were perfect. I felt my manhood swell and harden. I'm sure that she did, too. That couldn't be helped. I am, after all, just a man. I moved my attention to the leather miniskirt. I put my hands under the hem and lifted slowly to reveal her beautiful buttocks. So wonderfully formed; a perfect heart shape. I placed my hands on her bum and gently massaged. I moved my hands forward and lifted the skirt to reveal her womanhood. As I did I felt every muscle in her body tense. When I touched her there, she screamed. I put one hand over her mouth and pulled her to me with the other. She fought and twisted, trying to escape, but it was futile. The hook in the ceiling was securely bolted to a support beam, and her legs had very limited use; there was nothing she could do but struggle in my arms and sob. I loved how alive she felt in my arms. I needed more….

She tired after a while and stopped struggling. I held her close, stroked her hair, ran my hands over her marvelous young body. I touched her wherever and however I wanted. I cut the skirt from her. I just sat back and admired her naked body. She was broken and beautiful. Most of the fight had left her; she just stood there and stared sullenly back at me. After a time, I asked her whether she wanted me to release her hands and whether she needed anything. Again, she simply asked for water. I let her make her way over to the chair by the table and sit down. I got her drink and offered her some food. She took half a sandwich and a cookie and sat there naked, eating her last meal. Not much of a repast, but it would do. Had I been a cruel man, I would have kept her a prisoner down here for a long time—toyed with her over and over. But that's not me, not really. I had my needs and those needs didn't involve pain and torture and imprisonment. The care and feeding of a prisoner is tiresome and time-consuming.

When she was finished eating, I told her to move over to the blue velvet side of the room. I had her lie down on the lush fabric. I tied the ends of her wrist straps to the metal rod between her legs. She had some use of her hands, but she couldn't get very far.

There was a mattress under the fabric so she wouldn't be too uncomfortable. I told her to pose some more so I could have a selection of pictures of her in her naked bound glory. I kept telling her how beautiful she was and reassured her that everything would be all right. I told her that her cooperation was appreciated and would be rewarded. I made her think she had some chance of survival. I told her whatever lies she needed to hear.

"Rene, you have been wonderful to work with. Just

a few more pictures and we can talk about letting you go," I said. "Are you ready for this to end?" She nodded quietly and waited for my instructions. "I'm happy that I haven't had to keep your hands tied to the hook. While you are so enticing bound that way, it does limit your movement. And I do like to watch you move. Your naked form is exquisite, a treat for the senses. I'm going to ask you for a few more simple things and then we'll be done. OK?"

"OK. Anything. I just want to go home...." Her voice trailed off and she started to sob again.

"I want you on your knees, pretty bottom facing the camera. Face down on the velvet. Reach back and play with yourself. I want to watch."

"No! I will not! I won't!" she screamed

"Rene...we're getting close to the end. Don't blow it now. Just do as you're told if you want to live. Now, face down on the velvet, lovely bottom toward the camera, hands busy. Just a few more moments. Then you'll be done and I'll release you." She remained motionless. "Rene, I do not want to force you. I don't want to hurt you. Please, indulge me this one last time. This is the last thing I'll ask. You're so close to the end of all this. So close."

I paused. Rene started to comply. She turned her back to the camera and got down on her knees. She slowly lowered herself to the velvet. Her hands went to her vagina. She stopped. Paused. I cleared my throat. She worked a finger into herself. I started taking pictures. She worked her pussy more vigorously. I encouraged her, gave her direction. I quietly removed my clothing and stroked myself a little. I rushed over, grabbed her hips, and thrust myself into her. She screamed and twisted. I put my arm around her throat and thrust harder, forcing her flat on the floor. I marveled at the feel of her skin and muscles writhing underneath me. I put my hands on her hips and thrust faster.

This felt so...wrong. I couldn't believe it. I felt dirty. I pulled myself out of her and told her I was sorry. "Rene, I'm so sorry. That was wrong of me. I'm so, so sorry." And I was. I had decided I would have sex with her before I killed her. I hadn't with Beth, but I figured that once I was caught, a little more DNA evidence wouldn't matter. I had thought I would enjoy myself, thought that sex would contribute to her undoing and add to my pleasure. But it didn't. Even though I had subjected her to many indignities and would ultimately strangle her, this was wrong. I felt remorse, something I hadn't felt when I killed Beth. Nothing that I had done with Rene thus far had given me even a twinge of guilt, but this was wrong on so many levels.

Rene rolled and wrapped herself up in the fabric and cried. I wondered what to do next. I couldn't let her go. I wasn't sure I could still kill her. I had a problem.

"Rene, I am so sorry. I never wanted to hurt you. I never meant to force myself on you. I am—"

"Never wanted to hurt me?" Rene screamed. "You fucking scum! You creep! What the fuck do you think all this has done? Built my ego? Think this is fun? You fucking pervert! All this has done is hurt! Fuck you! Fuck you! If I could, I'd kill you!" Rene shrieked and spat. I deserved it. I let her have her say.

"Rene, please, you don't know how terrible I feel. Please, let me make it up to you. Just calm down and be still and I will unbind your legs and let you get dressed. Just get a hold of yourself and calm down. I promise. Just calm down and rest and I will untie you."

Of course, not everything I told her was true. I was going to untie her. That much was true. Let her get dressed? Maybe. Let her go? Never. I couldn't; then my new hobby would end now, and I was not prepared to give it up just yet. I was still learning. I had so much more I wanted to do.

Rene did calm down a little. She was sobbing, her entire body shaking as she did. I felt terrible for having violated her, but I was still thrilled to look at her naked body in front of me. Seeing her in a crumpled heap, really just a pretty rag, was more than I can describe. Her spirit was gone, her will completely broken. Her universe had been forever ripped apart. I was the dark and terrible god who had done it, and I loved the feeling. Next, to end her life, holding her close as the life forces slipped away. My member twitched at the image and I had to work to control it. I was still naked, after all, and I had no easy way to hide my growing erection. When I felt Rene was calm enough, I kneeled down beside her. I spoke in the most soothing tones I could muster.

"Rene, I am going to remove the tresses from your arms first. Please give me your left arm." After I had undone the leather strap, I asked for her right. All her struggles had made the knot very tight. "Rene, I am going to get my knife and cut this strap. Don't worry; I am not going to use the knife for anything else. I would appreciate it if you didn't try to either. I am bigger and stronger than you are and have not exerted myself as you have. A fight for the knife would only end up with a lot of unnecessary blood and cuts, but it would still end up with me the victor. I am going to release you from your bonds as long as you don't try to grab the knife. Can you do that? Can you promise to be good a little longer? This is almost over, dear one. Just lay flat on your back and I will release you."

"Uh huh. I promise." Rene didn't look at me. No eye contact. She was basically in total submission, like a dog offering up its own throat to another dog to show surrender. I got the knife and carefully cut the leather on her right arm. She was true to her word.

"Rene, I am going to take this binder from between your legs. Again, I remind you not to fight. We're so close to the end, so close. Just be good a little longer. You're so close." I figured she was no threat anymore, that she had lost the will to fight. I wasn't fully off my guard, but I felt confident. As I touched her ankle to begin releasing her, I felt her body tense like a spring. I paused and tapped her calf. "Rene...don't do it. Just relax." She let out her breath and relaxed. I undid one ankle and then moved to the other. "Keep still, Rene. Almost done." I released the binder and moved it from between her legs. "There. As promised, you are free. Let me help you up so you can get dressed."

I stood up and reached my hand to her. When she reluctantly took it, I pulled her to her feet and spun her into my waiting arms. I put my arm around her throat and started to squeeze. She flailed and clawed and clutched at my arm, trying to loosen my grip on her neck. She kicked her legs up into the air to try to make me lose my balance, but I anticipated that and dropped to my knees as her feet left the floor. As she fell, I guided her so she would land face down on the fabric, me on top. I loved the feel of her skin on mine; I delighted in the feel of her pulse under my arm. She was weakening. I put my face next to hers, cheek to cheek, and whispered in her ear, "Thank you, Rene. Thank you so much for this. I've had the most splendid evening. Sorry for my brief rudeness; you didn't deserve that. Thanks for everything you've given me. I'll always cherish the memory of our lovely evening together." I kissed her cheek and applied more pressure. As she faded, my cock grew hard between her thighs. One more squeeze and she was gone. I collapsed on her lifeless body, totally spent.

I lay there for a few minutes, savoring the smell of her person, her sweat, her womanhood. I didn't want it all to end, but I knew it had to. Too soon she would start to get cold and just become a disgusting piece of rotting flesh. I needed to clean up and dispose of my lovely Rene. As I got up, I saw a large gob of my semen clinging to her thigh. I didn't remember climaxing, but I was so focused on the beauty of her death that an air raid siren could have gone off and not disturbed my rapture.

I washed up a bit and looked at myself in the bathroom mirror. Rene had left a few scratches on my arm when she struggled. Nothing too serious and nothing that couldn't be explained away easily. Nothing like what Beth had done to me. No trip to the ER. No stitches needed. No bruises. Just a few scratches. I smiled. I had been much better prepared with Rene. I did have a learning curve, after all. I was pleased. I pulled my jeans and shirt on and opened the combination lock on the door's bolt. I slid the bolt and pushed the door open. The fresh night air felt good. I stepped out onto the stairway and breathed it in. It was energizing.

I went back in and looked at Rene. She was very obviously dead. Her skin already looked dull. Her hair straw-like. She was so still. I bent down and gathered her up. I threw her over my shoulder and started up the stairs. Over to the cistern. I had to put her on the ground as I moved the heavy cover aside. I picked her up and dropped her head first down the cistern. She made a muted splash when she reached the water. I wondered how badly decomposed Beth was by now. I went back down into the shelter to get a sack of lime. Lugged it upstairs and emptied it into the cistern. The lime had seemed to do the trick with Beth—I'd never caught a whiff of foulness emanating from the cistern since I'd placed her there.

I went back downstairs and cleaned up the place. I gathered anything that Rene had brought with her: clothes, purse, underwear, makeup, laptop computer and books, and put them all into a large box. I put that box into the storeroom to be dealt with later. I finished tidying up the rest of the shelter and took the disc from the computer. I removed the tape from the video machine and closed up the shelter. I would enjoy my souvenirs later. Now, I needed my rest.

Before I made my way back to the house, I scattered brush and leaves over the opening to the shelter and the cistern cover. I tried the best I could to obscure my path through the woods in the same manner. It wasn't perfect, but I hoped it would do. After I had chosen my hobby, I had tried to vary my path to the shelter each time I went out there. I wanted to keep it a secret as long as possible. It had been nearly impossible to stay out of it after Beth. I just wanted to sit there and soak up the memories, but I was disciplined enough to stay in the house.

I went into the house and put my disc into my computer. I looked at the images for a little while before turning in. I grew excited as I viewed them. My pulse quickened and I relived every minute. I had a very good evening. I was proud of my night's work. I was already looking forward to my next play date.

MAURA

It had been several months since my play date with Rene. The memories and videos could only satisfy me for so long. I needed to play again. I needed to feel a throat in my hands. I needed to cause the complete and utter collapse of a playmate. Beth and Rene were only occasionally mentioned in the news or in the paper any more. The police were still actively looking for them, but they had vanished without a trace. I had done my best to help with the investigations, offering as much insight into their connection and their friends, habits, and the like that I could. I was a model citizen. But I was also a needy one. I really liked my new hobby and was ready to play some more. I knew that waiting was smart; it just wasn't satisfying.

I decided that I needed to pick my next victim a little "out of pattern," not that I'd had enough really to establish a pattern. I figured I should pick a young lady (or young man, for that matter) who was more on the periphery of my circle of friends and acquaintances, and maybe one who was not as physically appealing. While the police had not connected Beth and Rene, I didn't need to risk them starting to do so. I had to find someone who would satisfy my needs, but be different enough from Beth and Rene that the crimes would seem unrelated. I mentally "shuffled the deck" of people I knew, trying to find the right candidate. Who to play with next? It was a tough choice. It shouldn't be someone I knew at the Pearl. For one, I couldn't afford to lose another actress. And that was too small a circle; I would be caught too easily if I kept mining that vein. So I ruled out any of the theater friends. My students were a larger universe to choose from. My class sizes ranged from fifteen to sixty and I taught four of them. And all of those students had at least three other classes they were taking that semester. But who should it be?

After mulling it over for several days, I had narrowed it down to two. Maura was a shy girl, a little overweight, awkward, but bright enough. She was a better than average student and really seemed interested in my classes. School didn't come easy for her—she had to work hard to keep up her GPA. In a way, I admired her. School had always been so simple for me. I never really had to develop any solid study or work habits until I was working on my PhD. She had taken her just slightly better than average raw materials and forged them into something better. Maura would stop by during my office hours to discuss an assignment or to get clarification on something I had said during class. She had some potential.

My other prospect was Breanne. She was fairly attractive in a very conventional way. Blonde, blue eyes, Jessica Simpson build, not my cup of tea, but the male population of MNC seemed to dote on her every move. She was also a spoiled little brat. Mom and Dad had money, cubic dollars, but the money wasn't enough to buy her way into anything other than a state school like MNC. This kid defined "average" when it came to smarts and much below average when it came to common sense. She was whiny and demanding. She had a sense of entitlement that I resented. She treated everyone as if they were servants. I loathed this girl. I would probably enjoy killing her, knew that I would enjoy ripping her apart mentally, but I reasoned that she was too high profile to play with no matter how much she deserved her fate. So Maura it was.

I had no real pretense to bring Maura to my house. She wasn't in my circle of theater friends. I seldom had students other than the theater clan over. When Gwen was alive, we sometimes would have some "holiday orphans" over for Thanksgiving dinner, but that was about the extent of my involvement with my students at home, other than the theater clan. Theater folk were different. When we were doing a show, we were family. Old and young, veteran or rookie, we all had to work together to make the magic happen. That tended to make us a more tightly-knit group. So those people I would normally have over. Drinks after a rehearsal. The occasional cast party. Community members and students together. Age really didn't seem to matter. In community theater, it was not impossible for a twenty-year-old man to be "married" to a forty-something woman onstage. You had to work with what you got, and sometimes the age range was very diverse. Yet we all got along as if we were all peers. I found it invigorating and fascinating. So I tried to keep those people close at home, more so after Gwen had died. So I had to devise some way to get Maura somewhere I could comfortably have my play date with her.

After a few more weeks of research, I was ready to play. Maura really had a very small circle of friends. She didn't really seem to fit in anywhere. No clubs, sorority ties; she didn't frequent the bars…. Maura was pretty much a loner. She spent most of her time either in her dorm room, in class, or at the library. She seemed to get along well with all her professors and did tend to visit their offices. I wonder whether she visited us not so much with real questions, but as a substitute for genuine social interactions. The prof-student relationship offered a pat set of rules of engagement. It was a safe type of social setting. Since she did well in her classes and was regarded as a hard worker, she probably felt more comfortable in our presence than she did with her classmates. It was a pathetic existence. She wouldn't be missed by many. I had everything prepared at home; I just had to wait for the right opportunity to present itself.

"Dr. Martin, do you have a moment?" It was Maura at my office door.

"Sure, how can I help?" I smiled at Maura and motioned her toward the chair in front of my desk.

"I just wanted to double-check which chapters were going to be covered on the test on Monday. And I'd like to talk to you a little about Chapter 23..."

"OK, no problem. The test will cover Chapters 23, 24 and 25. Middle of the Depression till the start of World War II. What did you want to discuss...?" I waited while Maura pulled some of her meticulous class notes from her backpack.

"I just want to get some of your input on Herbert Hoover and how responsible he really was for the Depression. I mean, this book paints a pretty negative picture, but I've read others that don't show him in such a bad light. Some scholars seem to feel that Calvin Coolidge was more to blame, that Hoover got a bad rap. Coolidge worked harder to do nothing than any President, before or since. So I wanted to talk to you more in depth about the Depression's causes." Maura smiled at me and seemed to be waiting for some sort of approval, like a dog that has just brought you its favorite tennis ball to play with.

"OK, Maura, you seem to want to cover a lot more ground that I have time for during my office hours today." She looked a little dejected when I said this. "I do have some errands I need to run, and I need to prepare for my classes tomorrow, but I think this could be a fascinating discussion. Do you have any more classes today? We could continue this, but you'd have to tag along with me on some errands. Boring, but I hope that the conversation would overcome the mundane nature of my routine...." Maura visibly brightened at my suggestion.

"I'm done for the day. I usually go to the library now, but if I wouldn't be in your way, I'd love to talk to you more about the Depression and today's class. If you don't mind...."

"Not at all, Maura. Not many students have the interest in the subject matter that you do. Glad to have you along. Let's get out of here." I got up and headed out the door. Maura followed and I locked the office door behind us. I had some concern about the security cameras on campus, so I had been parking a block or so off campus for the past few days. It wasn't uncommon for me to walk to work, so the image of me walking off campus wouldn't be out of the ordinary. And I would walk in the company of a student or two fairly regularly, so that shouldn't raise any eyebrows. I just needed for Maura and I to be seen parting ways on camera. That would be the trick. Maura and I walked toward the faculty lot. I stopped and turned to Maura.

"I am rather absent-minded. I didn't park in the lot this morning. No space. Ever since they started the repaving project on the other side of Upham Hall, my regular lot has been fuller than usual. So I'm over on Eighth Avenue. Silly me. I'll have to double back to get my car. Why don't you stop by your dorm and drop off your backpack, and I'll buzz back to my office since I've forgotten the papers I need to grade, and I'll meet you at my car. It's on Eighth, in front of the church."

Maura smiled and nodded her assent and we parted. As soon as she was out of sight I headed directly to my car, not needing to go to the office. I simply needed the cameras to see us part amicably and see me head off campus. The dorm camera would show a student stopping at her dorm and heading back out, obviously done with classes for the day. Perfect, I hoped.

I got to my car and sat down, waiting for Maura. When she arrived a few minutes later, I reached over and pulled the handle to let her in. When she plopped into the seat, I noticed just how overweight she really was. Very unappealing. Her skin was pasty white. Obviously, she never got out into the sun except to cross campus from dorm to class to library and back. I smiled at her and started the car. We chatted a little about the Depression and the relative merits of Coolidge and Hoover. We talked about the other causes of the Depression. We stopped at the drycleaners, and I went in to pick up my suit. I really did have errands to run. I didn't think the lady at the cleaners would pay any attention to my car—the counter was very busy. I got back into the car and drove off.

"Maura, would you mind if we made a little detour? I want to drop my suit off at home before doing my other errands. After paying $18.50 to get it dry cleaned, I just don't want to get it wrinkled or risk it falling of the hanger onto my car's dirty floor."

"Sure, that would be fine. I'm enjoying our talk. This is much better than studying at the library."

You wouldn't say that if you knew what was going to happen next, young lady. I drove to my house and up the drive.

"Do you want to come in for a minute? I feel a little rude running in for a bit and leaving you outside in the car like a dog." I paused. "I have to take a quick look in the pantry and whip up a list—I left my shopping list at my office. I guess the stories about the 'absent-minded professor' must be fact-based, because I surely am today." I hoped that Maura wouldn't realize how trite and contrived my conversation was. I don't make "small talk" very well, especially not with people I don't know well. I'd had Maura in a couple classes and did see her during office

174

hours, but our conversations were always focused on history. I found it hard to sound "natural" while talking to her. I just didn't feel any connection with her, so conversation was a little stilted. I thought about aborting the mission then and there, but I needed to feel a throat in my hands.

"Umm, sure, I would like to come in. I promise I won't reveal your secret."

"Secret? I don't follow." What secret did she think I had?

"I won't blow your cover. Everybody knows that all the profs sleep in their offices and have no real lives. Kind of like vampires, only with books. I won't tell anyone that you have an actual house." Maura laughed at her own joke. I led her in.

"Do you want to see a real piece of history? Real American Cold War history? Right here in New Worcester? I guarantee you've never seen anything like it. You're the first student I can think of with enough interest in history to appreciate it." Although a couple of others had seen it already. Briefly….

"Sure. Is it something you found here in the house? A Civil Defense helmet or something like that? Cold War brochures about being prepared for nuclear war? A fallout shelter sign? You said it was Cold War era…so what is it?" I had piqued Maura's interest.

"You won't believe it. Follow me out into the backyard." I started toward the back door when Maura caught me totally off-guard.

"Do you have a bomb shelter? The houses in this neighborhood were all built in the late '40s and early '50s. Is that what you are going to show me?" Maura looked genuinely enthused at the prospect.

"You guessed it. Very perceptive of you. This house

was built in 1948. The bomb shelter dates to the mid-1950s. It is very cool. I have restored it. Not entirely to period, I have made some improvements, but it is quite serviceable and representative of the era. I use it as a private hideaway and studio." I was impressed that she had guessed it. More impressed that she knew the town as well as she did. I knew that she came from downstate, somewhere near Lansing, so her knowledge of the neighborhood showed an interesting bit of initiative on her part. She was one of my better students. Until now, I hadn't really appreciated just how hard she studied or how interested in the subject matter she really was. I led her to the shelter, opened the hatch, and headed down the stairs.

"This place is amazing. I never thought I'd get to see a real one. So many of the bomb shelters have been filled in or turned into wine cellars. Did this factor into your decision to buy this place?" Maura looked around excitedly. Her words poured out of her very quickly, sentences running together.

"Slow down a minute. One thing at a time." I chuckled. Maura and I talked about the shelter and the former airbase and other bits of local and regional history. She really had a good head on her shoulders. I had little interest in her head, though. My true interest lay just below. Having a playmate here in my shelter was practically making me salivate like one of Pavlov's dogs. I knew that my reward was coming soon, and I just couldn't wait. It had been too long. I was ready for a dance with my third partner. And yet, I was somehow hesitant. I couldn't put my finger on it, but something was missing. I ached for the kill, but I didn't know whether I really wanted to kill her. Logically speaking, straying from my fledgling pattern was a good choice. But even though Maura was bright and interesting and easy to converse with, I just didn't feel any real connection to her. Would I enjoy it as much? I just didn't know, but since I had brought her here, I would go through with it. I couldn't let anyone know about my little playroom but me. I needed to keep it a secret from my future victims and the police for as long as possible. By bringing Maura down here, I had sealed her doom. I was just having second thoughts about my choice. I decided I would have to make the best of it and enjoy it as much as possible. I was a worrywart; I needed to learn to let go a little more and enjoy life as it came to me.

"Dr. Martin, may I use the bathroom?" Maura asked.

"Of course. Be my guest." I waited for the door to close; then I went to the storeroom and grabbed a few necessary supplies. I got a pair of handcuffs and some extra-long zip ties. When Maura returned, I would have to act quickly, use the element of surprise to avoid a conflict like Beth and I had. I certainly didn't want to go through that again, and I couldn't use another motorcycle wreck to cover any injuries. I switched on the video cameras and hid the handcuffs and zip ties from easy view. I waited for Maura to emerge. My heart raced a bit in anticipation.

I didn't have to wait very long. Maura returned and sat down. As soon as she made herself comfortable, I snapped one end of the handcuffs to her wrist and the other to the chair. She jumped and screamed. I pounced into her lap and grabbed her other wrist and quickly zip-tied it to the chair. She struggled under my weight and flailed her legs about. She yelled and screamed. I liked it. I didn't like the feeling of her fat body squirming around under me; I found the soft flesh and sallow muscle tone to be almost disgusting. When I had her arms secured, I turned my attention to her legs. Her thick ankles and fleshy calves felt like Silly Putty in my hands. I shuddered a bit. Nothing like the pleasure I had felt when I touched Beth or Rene.

"Maura, you need to stop screaming and listen to me…. What I am going to say to you is very important." I waited for her to stop yelping.

"Dr. Martin, what are you doing? I don't understand…. I…. What is wrong with you?" Maura had thankfully lowered the volume a bit, but now she was sobbing out her words.

"Maura, just be still and listen. I know this is all a bit abrupt and a bit of a surprise, but it doesn't have to be unpleasant. I need you to stay calm and just go with the flow. Think of this all as a game and you will be just fine. You don't think I would actually hurt you? When this is all over, we will laugh about it together. Trust me." I tried to sound as soothing and reassuring as I could. I doubted that she believed a word.

"Why did you tie me up? And why do you think it is OK to tie me up? And what do you think I will ever find funny about it?" She looked at me and waited for an answer.

"OK, so I admit my methods are a little strange. But I want to share something with you, and securing you was the only way I knew that I could get you to share it with me. The only sure way. I just want you to watch a little video with me…."

"What? I still don't get it. You should have just asked. I would have gladly sat here and watched something with you. I just don't get it…."

"Let me turn this on and we can watch for a few minutes. Then we'll see about me untying you and watching the rest. OK?"

I didn't wait for her to answer; I just flipped on the TV and started the video of Beth. Maura's eyes got wider and wider as she started to understand what she was seeing.

She started to scream again, and she clenched her eyes tightly shut. I paused the DVD and spoke to Maura.

"OK, so now you see why I tied you up. You certainly wouldn't sit still to watch this. And we haven't really gotten to the good parts yet. So I must insist that you open your eyes and watch the rest of this DVD. Please? For me. And for your immediate future. Trust me; everything will be much easier for you if you cooperate. Watch and see...."

"I can't. I heard about that girl. She disappeared. No one knows where she went. I don't remember her name, but I know that police are still looking everywhere. And you have her? You took her...?" Maura started to cry harder now. Giant sobs wracked her body. Giant sobs sent waves rippling through the fat on her torso. My god, a GI Joe could surf those waves. I almost couldn't look. It was gross. I wasn't sure I could touch this girl any more. This was not going according to plan. I should be getting more excited. I should be looking forward to holding her body close and feeling the life forces within. Instead, I wondered whether I could even feel her heartbeat through her insulation. I had to get a grip. I had started this whole thing, I had to finish it. No other choice.

"Maura, please stop your crying. Please just open your eyes and watch the rest of the video with me. I really enjoy it, and I want to share it with you. Think of it as a historical record; think that you are watching footage of recent events in history, which, in truth, you are. Detach yourself just a little. You didn't know this girl, did you? You've watched the footage of Dachau or the Cambodian killing fields, so you can watch this."

"Dr. Martin...I...you? How could this be you?" She looked at me incredulously. I had shaken her perception of reality at little. At least this gave me some pleasure.

"I'm going to do something I've never done with the others. I'm going to tell you why. You deserve at least that much." I looked at her intently as I spoke. The word "others" had certainly hit a nerve. Maybe this wouldn't be so bad after all. I turned the DVD back on so she could see a little more before I spoke again. Maura gamely tried to watch as Beth and I struggled. She seemed to be having some trouble deciding whom to empathize with, Beth or me. This was interesting. Maura looked from the screen to me as Beth kicked viciously at my wounded leg. She winced as Beth fought for her life. I couldn't tell whether she reacted to my intent to kill Beth or Beth's ripping my leg apart with her kicks. It was easier to tell how she felt when I tied Beth's unconscious form to the table and unwrapped my present. Maura was definitely in the Beth camp at that point. I had certainly fallen into the realm of monster in her eyes. When I lay on Beth and squeezed the life from her, Maura cried out. I smiled. I paused the DVD again.

"Yes, Maura, Beth did not simply disappear. In fact, she's still quite close. In the cistern next to the shelter with a new friend. I do like to keep my friends close to me...." I smiled at her again. She shuddered.

"Why? What did Beth do to you? And you said 'others.' How many? And who?" She looked blankly at me, not sure how to feel, not sure she wanted the answers.

"Maura, sadly there has only been one other after Beth. A beautiful young woman named Rene. As you'll see soon, I had a much different play date with her. And you'll be number three. My little hobby is relatively new. I'm glad you chose to join the game. I really need this; Rene was months ago. I need to feel again...."

At that, Maura started to scream. She strained to free herself, the cuffs and zip ties biting into her doughy flesh and leaving ugly red marks. It was futile. I watched amusedly as she tried every way possible to free herself. All she succeeded in doing was making a sweaty mess of herself. It was not an attractive sight. Her screaming gave me little pleasure. Was it because of the ugly visage she presented? Did the unappealing nature of her appearance dull my enjoyment of her screams? I was quickly becoming disgusted with myself for choosing this mountain of blubbering protoplasm to be my toy. I certainly had better taste than this. I got a dish towel and stuffed it into her mouth to shut her up. I used another to tie around her grotesque face, hiding all but her eyes and forehead from my sight.

I switched the DVD back on and sat back to watch the beautiful Rene meet her demise. This was much more interesting than looking at Maura. I didn't care about her on any level any more. While she may have been an interesting student and was a good conversationalist, as a plaything, she was an utter failure. Doing this thing would be about as satisfying as masturbating with an ice cube in my hand. But I had started down this path, so there was no way I could let Maura live now. I had to kill her. What a waste of my efforts.

Maura kept trying to turn away from the video screen. I finally had to stand behind the mountain bound to my chair and hold her head firmly so she could see my beautiful tango with Rene. God, that woman was stunning. And sexy. Not at all like the frump awaiting her doom. Why had I been so stupid? I should have risked Breanne. At least I wouldn't be repulsed by the sight of her. Would I at least enjoy Maura's actual demise? That would be the ultimate irony, risking arrest and prison and getting nothing out of it. Oh well, I was still just learning about myself and my new hobby. Nobody's perfect.

When Rene was gone, I stopped the DVD. I untied the towel from Maura's face and pulled the towel from her mouth. I expected her to start screaming. Instead, silence. She just sat there, silently staring at the blank screen. A couple of tears formed at the corner of her eyes, but she just sat still. I sat down and remained quiet myself. I was as patient as a cat stalking a bird. We just sat there, not moving, not making any sound, just waiting for the other to break the silence. Dead air takes forever to pass. The moments stretched into minutes; minutes seemed to take hours to pass. Yet we sat still, silent. Finally, Maura spoke. She asked a simple question.

"Why? You said you would tell me. Why?" For a woman about to meet her doom, she was surprisingly calm and collected.

"Why indeed? A good question. I expected nothing less from you. You are a good student. I have always appreciated that in you. You work hard and are genuinely interested in the subject matter. I wish more of my students had that attitude. Teaching American History 204 is such a drag sometimes. I know the bulk of the students are only taking it because they have to get out of this place, but you seem genuinely enthralled by it. Honestly, so many of the kids we are wasting our tax dollars on should be in trade schools rather than college. We are over-educating the masses and not really paying attention to the students who might actually make a difference. It's a sad state of affairs…but I digress. You asked me why…." I paused a moment.

"Do you want something to eat or drink? I've been an awful host." I waited for Maura to reply. I did my best to seem "normal"—whatever the hell that really was.

"I really don't have any appetite. Dr. Martin, I am tied to a chair! I'm really not interested in eating or drinking anything. I just want to get out of here…." Maura squirmed a bit, but she stopped quickly as the cuffs and zip ties bit further into her flesh.

"OK, I see your point. I just didn't want you to see me as rude or thoughtless. I really don't want you to be too uncomfortable here in my little hideaway." Just because I was going to kill this disgusting pile of flesh didn't mean that I couldn't be polite to her. I continued on with my narrative.

"I have always been a little, umm, 'emotionally constipated.' I was really pretty much a loner until I met Gwen. Being the smartest kid in the room isn't easy. I was always on the outside looking in. I never thought the way the other kids did; I never fit in. When I was a college student at the ripe old age of fifteen, I was really a fish out of water. I was always prepared mentally, but emotionally and socially, not so much. Gwen was the first woman ever to take an interest in me. My whole world revolved around her. After she was killed, I kind of died inside. Nothing gave me pleasure. Sure, I enjoy doing theater and the people I am with, but that is fleeting. When I am not doing a show, I am lost. Teaching is OK, I still like what I do, but it doesn't really bring me any joy. I don't feel anything, Maura. Nothing. I am just an empty shell going through the motions of life. I decided that I needed to do something different, something radical, something totally outrageous to jumpstart me again. I gave it a lot of thought. Mountain climbing? Bungee jumping? Motorcycle racing? Stand-up comedy? A lot of ideas, but none of them got me going. I jokingly thought to myself that I should become a serial killer. Maybe that would jolt me back into the realm of the living. I examined that idea a little further. The ultimate extreme sport. Hunting and killing humans. The story 'The Most Dangerous Game' really had it right. Human prey was the only thing interesting. Having a quarry as well-equipped as me was the only real challenge. So I decided that maybe I would try it. I played with the idea in my head for a while. I decided I needed to take it one step further. Anyone could pull strangers off the street and kill them. Jeffrey Dahmer killed dozens of victims before he got caught. So did Gacy. But they were picking victims that had little or no connection to them. No personal involvement. Far less risk of getting caught. What was the fun in that? I decided that if I was going to do it, I would kill people close to me. People who trusted me. I would begin to feel again if I could start by ripping their little worlds apart. No one would ever suspect me, modest unassuming James Martin, of being a killer. Everybody thinks I'm a 'nice guy,' that I couldn't hurt a flea. The real challenge is finding a way to pick off people in your own inner circle without arousing suspicion. It is both a mental challenge and it has a certain visceral appeal. So I decided to try it. And guess what? I found that I really liked it. A lot. Even though Beth got her licks in, I never felt more alive than when she was struggling for her life. Feeling her life slowly ebb away under my hands was delicious. Rene, too. I still regret my little indiscretion with her. I never meant to rape her. I am a gentleman, after all—not some filthy rapist. But the sight of her luscious body and the feel of her skin in my hands was a delight beyond words. I like my new hobby. I feel more alive and more powerful than I ever have in my life. So, there you have it. The 'why' of it all. I am simply doing this because I want to feel alive again, and I am willing to make a few small sacrifices to make that happen...." I paused. "Sorry if I was a little long-winded there. I am rather passionate about my new hobby...."

Maura sat there dumbfounded. I don't think she had

any way to process what I had just said to her. I really didn't know where to go from there, either. I had just laid out my whole raison d'être to her. Where to go from here? How to segue to her demise? I was at a loss. No script and no director to ask. How to move forward? It would be rude and abrupt simply to choke the life out of her without any warning or further play. But I really didn't know how to proceed from here. I'd just spilled my guts to her. Now I was to kill her? Just like that? Where was the pleasure in that? I needed more....

"Why me?" she asked. "I'm not pretty like the other two. I'm sure you don't want to have sex with me. I know you don't want to touch me like them. Why me? Why do I have to die for you?" Maura looked right at me. Why indeed? How was I going to salvage this and get some joy out of it? She was right; I didn't want to touch her, and I certainly didn't want to look at her naked. The thought was repugnant. Was this girl going to talk me out of it? I couldn't let that happen. I couldn't let her live now. And I couldn't let her prevent me from playing with partners whom I really could enjoy later. I had to find some way to enjoy this and see it through. I decided I would have to try to fuck with her head a bit. Maybe that would make it worthwhile for me. I hoped so.

"Maura, you are a mistake. Yes, a mistake. I figured that I needed to pick someone who was 'out of pattern' for my next victim. So I picked you. Close enough that you would be shocked to find out who I was, but at arm's length, not in my inner circle. And not pretty. Definitely not pretty. Don't want the FBI profilers to have too easy a time of things.... So I picked you. Sorry, but I need another dance partner. I need to feel someone's life forces ebb beneath my grip. I am having some second thoughts.... But I brought you to my little play room, so you will have to die. Sorry about that, but I can't let you leave, alive, to blab to the world about my little hideaway."

I paused for a moment to see how she reacted. I was disappointed. She didn't really react at all. She sat there like the lump that she was, doing nothing. No tears. No sound. Nothing. Not a word. This was disheartening. I needed something out of her to make this even a little worthwhile. But she was giving me nothing. I couldn't understand; earlier, she had been crying and screaming. Why silence now? I decided to press on.

"Maura, you are oddly quiet. You seem very calm for someone who has just been told that she is going to die. I'm impressed in a way. How are you able to do this? You are too young to be ready to die. Most people your age haven't even accepted their own mortality, and yet here you sit, silently waiting for the end. Do my words fall on deaf ears? Are you as unfeeling as you seem now?"

"Dr. Martin, I realize that nothing I say or do will change my fate. You've already played your hand; you told me that I had to die. What's the point? If I scream, I assume that it will give you pleasure. If I struggle, you'll enjoy it. No matter what I do or say, I end up in your cistern. The only power I have is denying you anything. So you might as well just kill me now. I don't care. I'm smart enough to know that I'm already dead." With that, she crossed her fat arms and just glared at me.

The nerve of this girl! How dare she ruin this for me? The situation went from bad to dismal. This pig was robbing me of any fun, any feeling, any release. It was a smart move on her part, I suppose, but I was supposed to call the shots in this place. No one else. I resented this impertinent snot more and more with each passing minute. Sadly, though, even the building anger did little to satisfy me. She would die, but she had won. I cursed myself for

186

choosing her.

"OK, Maura, you are right. You have ruined this for me. You leave me with no choice but to simply throttle you now. No play time, no fun, just a waste of time. We could have had a delightful few hours, but you had to fuck it up. I hope your death is painful and miserable, you fucking pig!" I grabbed a zip tie, wrapped it around her neck, and pulled it tight. It bit the flesh on her neck like a garrote. I should have throttled her with my own hands or at least have held the rope, but I was so angry with this pig and disgusted with myself that I didn't care to have any more intimate involvement with her death.

She gagged and sputtered. Her eyes bulged. Her face turned red, then purple, and then blue. Her mouth fell slack and her blue tongue fell out. She slumped forward in the chair and expired. Her bowels and bladder both let loose immediately after. The room was filled with the foulest stench. Disgusting. A terrible end to a terrible day. I took no pleasure in watching her die. While I was enraged, that gave me no energy or enjoyment. Seeing her pay for it with her life was no reward, either. Just a useless death. And a smelly mess for me to deal with. Beth and Rene had made a mess of this place, but cleaning up after the exquisite pleasures they had provided me with was almost a joy in itself. This would simply be work.

I cut the zip ties and released the handcuffs on Maura. She fell forward out of the chair and onto the floor into her own urine. As she fell, more noxious gases emanated from her guts. I had to switch on the ventilation system and spray Febreze to try to quell the growing stench. I gloved up and grabbed Maura's hands. I had planned on carrying her up the stairs to the cistern, but when I pulled, I realized she was too heavy for that. I started to drag her putrid corpse across the room. I wasn't sure I'd have the strength to get her up the stairs. I shuddered to think I might have to butcher this cow to get her out of my lair. I'm not squeamish, but cutting a corpse into easy-to-carry pieces was certainly not in my plans. Not now, not ever. I didn't want to deal with the blood, and I certainly didn't want to touch her any more than I absolutely had to. In a pinch, I could just cut her legs off. Lots of bone and muscle mass there. In a pinch.

Of course, I couldn't just phone a friend. I imagined the conversation. "Yeah, Fred, I just need you to come over for a little while. Yep, I need your help carrying a dead girl out of my secret room and dumping her into the cistern. Yeah, lunch next Thursday would be fine. See you in a few…." Yeah, that just wouldn't do. So I doubled my efforts and dragged her to the door. At the door, I cursed myself again. I hadn't bolted it shut. Had Maura managed to get loose, she could have rushed to freedom. Sloppy work, Martin; sloppy work. I had to get a real grip on myself before my next play date.

I put all my effort into hauling Maura up the stairs. I dragged her up, one step at a time, her head hitting each step as I heaved her along. I had to stop and rest several times. I was sweating profusely. I opened the cistern and dumped the corpulent beast in. The Walrus made a huge splash as she hit the water. I shoveled some lime in, closed the cistern up, and returned to the shelter to clean the filth this ungrateful walrus had left.

KIM

My time with Maura left me worse than unsatisfied. It left me wanting. Hungry. Anxious for a real dance with a proper partner. I knew I still had to be careful about whom I chose. Whomever I chose had to be on the periphery of whom I knew. Couldn't risk raising too much suspicion. But I now knew I had to have a victim who had some physical appeal. I needed the visual stimulation that an attractive young thing provided. I couldn't bear the thought of looking at another quivering pile of flab. The only pleasure I had derived from Maura was just before I killed her. Verbally abusing her and making her fall apart had been OK, but just OK. The actual kill had been rather hollow. Very little release for me. A waste.

The press and police had very little to say about Maura. Even they weren't interested. I never got so much as a call or inquiry about her. Not a one. It was almost as if she'd never existed. The police had never made any public announcement that they thought any of the disappearances were connected. They were spaced far enough apart that they really didn't raise that kind of attention. I was pleased, but I ached for another kill. I wracked my brain, trying to think of someone who would meet the criteria. Someone interesting to look at. Someone who knew me well enough to trust me, but not close enough to start fitting a pattern. I kept drawing blanks. No good ideas came to me. But I ached to watch a beautiful woman crumble as she realized what was about to happen to her. I needed the feel of warm flesh and a pulse in my hands. Needed to experience the flowing of my partner's life from her as I willed. I felt these needs growing stronger every day, yet I still couldn't think of a proper choice of victim. I couldn't let my needs get in the way of rational thought and caution. Getting hasty and sloppy would result in me losing my freedom. I certainly wasn't ready for that. I was enjoying my life again and was relishing the experimenting with my new hobby. Testing what it was I really wanted, what really satisfied me. Maura was just a bump in the road. Even she served a purpose, even though she didn't fulfill my needs. It was frustrating me not being able to choose. As it turned out, fate would choose my next playmate for me.

One fairly nasty night, I was coming home from the Bay Bell Inn in Bayville, about twenty-five miles from New Worcester. I had gone up for the Friday fish fry. Fresh lake perch and whitefish, all beer battered and deep fried. All you can eat for just ten bucks. Hell of a deal. I usually go there once a month to indulge. I wish I had the metabolism to go every Friday, but I would be a blimp in no time if I didn't watch it. Gwen and I loved to go there. It reminded me of the good times we'd had together to eat there. After dinner, I stayed for a little while to have a couple of their micro-brews. They made a particularly good stout that I enjoy. I left around 9:30.

About two miles out of Bayville, all hell broke loose. I heard the loudest crack of thunder I'd heard in years. A bolt of lightning struck a huge old white pine next to my car, and the tree practically exploded and came crashing onto the highway right behind me. I stupidly hit the brakes and swerved into the gravel. Thankfully, I didn't lose control and brought the car to a stop. This tree had to be at least seventy-five-feet tall and easily ten feet around at the base. The lightning had ripped the thing apart, creating quite a mess on the roadway. No traffic would be coming back from Bayville any time soon, that was certain. I reached into my pocket for my phone, then realized I had forgotten it at home. I really wanted to call Central Dispatch and let the authorities know about the tree, but I had no way to do so.

I herded the car back on to Bay Road and cautiously headed toward home. It was dark as pitch. Even on a clear night, Bay Road was fairly dark as the canopy of trees shielded it from the starlight. On a stormy night like this, I might as well have been driving in an inkwell. My headlights were a feeble match for the darkness and the torrents of rain. I had to drive the twisting Bay Road very carefully indeed. As I got closer to town, I approached the corner where I'd purposely laid down my bike after my dance with Beth. I reminisced about the thrill of that first kill. I lost my concentration on the road for a moment and drifted a little wide as I entered the turn.

At that moment, a figure appeared on the shoulder, a figure of a young woman, soaked and waving frantically at me. I jerked the wheel to avoid hitting the apparition and skidded the car to a stop on the gravel. But she wasn't an apparition. I wasn't seeing Beth in my mind. The young lady was real and ran to my car. I hopped out as she got there.

"I'm sorry; I didn't see you there! Are you all right?" I yelled a little louder than the conditions called for. My pulse was racing and my heart pounding from the adrenaline rush after the near miss.

"I'm OK, but my car is wrecked. Do you have a phone?" The woman motioned to a dark lump bent around a tree. It was almost exactly where my motorcycle had ended up when I crashed it.

"Get in; you're soaked!" I jerked open the passenger door and helped her get in. I shut the door and dashed around to my side. I was drenched, and I'd been out less than a minute. This poor girl must be freezing and soaked to the bone. The rain was cold as ice and the wind was fierce. "How long have you been out here?" I asked.

"About half an hour. Nobody is out tonight. Yours is the first car I've seen. I slid off the road and into that tree. I didn't think the car was so bad, but I couldn't start it, and I couldn't move it. I don't know where my phone is. Stuff flew everywhere in the car. My ears are ringing from the airbag." She paused. I could hear her teeth chattering.

I turned the heater up full blast and switched on the dome light. This girl seemed familiar, but I couldn't quite place where I knew her from. She wasn't one of my students, present or former, but I did think I knew her.

"You're 'double mocha latte with skim milk!" she blurted out.

"Pardon me…oh, wait, you used to work at Tall Timbers Coffee! I thought you looked familiar!" This young lady had worked at the drive-thru coffee shop I frequented. She'd been gone from there for about a year, but I'd not forgotten her smile. My colleagues and I used to joke that Tall Timbers Coffee was called that because the staff was sure to give all the male patrons serious wood. A fairly crass and crude joke, but based on fact. The owner of Tall Timbers made sure all his servers were eye candy of the first order. He encouraged the girls to dress to thrill, and for the most part, they did. The women in town referred to it as "The Porno Coffee Shop," but it wasn't all that bad. Just pretty young things displaying what "God gave them" and smiling at the male patrons. The girls were all very personable and easy to talk to. I'm sure for a lot of men, it was the only pleasant interaction with an attractive female they had in their week. This girl had been quite sweet to talk to and was, in my eyes, a goddess. Dark brown hair, olive complexion, eyes so brown they were almost black, and a lean, athletic build. Not a wasted ounce anywhere.

"I'm sorry, but all those times you waited on me, I never did ask your name."

"Kim. I'm Kim Waters. I never got yours, either. Silly that we saw each other two or three times a week for a couple of years and never asked for a name."

"James. James Martin. Now, what the hell were you doing out on Bay Road on a night like tonight? I went to the fish fry up in Bayville. It wasn't so bad when I went up there. I should have just got a room. Nasty stuff, this storm. So why aren't you safely sitting at home?" I couldn't help but notice that, in the dim dome light, her eyes really did look like black velvet dots in her head. The gentle light made interesting shadows on her face. What a delightful specimen of young womanhood.

"I was out at one of the cabins on Harrow Lake with a few friends. We ran out of beer and rum. I'm the only one old enough to buy, so I got elected to run into O'Dell's and get some more. In the woods, it really didn't seem this bad. I've had a few drinks, but not too many. When I got onto the road, I almost turned back. I should have. I kept thinking I was seeing deer or coyotes or dogs running out in front of me; couldn't see much other than rain. I lost it on the corner and ended up in the ditch against the tree. I tried to get my car out, but I stalled it, and it wouldn't start back up. I knew no one would see my car, so I stood on the side of the road waiting. Bay Road is usually pretty busy, isn't it?" She stopped and looked at me.

"Not tonight. Nothing is going to come down from Bayville. Huge tree came down right behind my car. I wanted to call the authorities, but I left my cell at home. And no one in their right mind would head out tonight. If I had known it was going to get this bad, I would have gone to the fish fry at The Shores or Big Al's. I sure wouldn't have headed up to Bayville. Can I give you a lift home? Then you can call the police and a wrecker. Where to?"

"James, I moved away last summer. I transferred to

Michigan State after my sophomore year here. Home is the cabin for the week. There's no cell service out there, so I can't call the girls or call the police from there. I don't know what I'm going to do." She kind of pouted and looked down at her lap.

Being the nice guy I am, I figured that I could offer her a ride into town. We could go to the police station, and then I could take her back out to the cabins if she wanted. Then I had a better idea.

"Kim, I live pretty close. Do you want to come over, use my phone, and call the police and wrecker from there? It would be no trouble. I could give you a lift back out to the cabin, if you wanted."

"Thanks, James. That would be great. I don't want to be any trouble. I could call one of my friends from your place. I couldn't ask you to drive back out to the cabin tonight. My girlfriends at the cabin will be worried, but too bad. I want to get warm and dry and don't want to go back out. Not at all. So I'll find some place to crash in town. Thanks."

"Not at all. My pleasure. I'm sure that someday I'll be stuck and need help again, too. I like to think of this as 'paying it forward.' If there is any such thing as karma, I want as much good karma as I can get." *I'll need it after what I've been doing lately*.... "Is there anything else you want to get from your car before we go? Where's your purse? Do you want to take one more look for your cell?" I reached across the car, "accidentally" brushing my arm against her knees as I opened the glove box and got out my flashlight. I had a small folding travel umbrella, too. I grabbed that and retreated to my side of the car. She didn't seem to notice me brush her legs, but I certainly did. I knew that I wanted Kim to be my next dance partner. She was perfect.

194

"I do need my purse. I've got a backpack, too. When we got to the cabin, we all just headed in and started to party. I never got all my stuff moved in for the weekend, so I've got my backpack with some of my clothes and stuff. I just don't want to go back out there. It's warm in here, and I'm still cold. Do you think it will let up any time soon?"

"Kim, is your backpack in the car or in the trunk? I'll go get it for you…."

"No, I can't ask you to do that. I'll get it. I didn't mean to whine."

"Kim, you didn't ask; I offered. My Boy Scout good deed of the day. I've got my umbrella; it shouldn't take but a moment. So where are your purse and your pack? I'll grab them and be right back." She looked grateful. She looked so pretty. I wanted to take her home. I wanted to play. I wanted to kill. I was excited. This would have to be better than Maura. Of course, almost anything would.

"James, really, I'll go get it. No need for both of us to be cold and wet."

"Kim, not to argue the point, but I got drenched when I stopped and picked you up. I'm going home where I have clothes and blankets and a hot shower waiting. Is your purse in the front? And your pack?" I waited.

"The backpack is in the backseat. Yellow with red flowers. There's a boring green one, too, but that is just school stuff. Leave it. My purse is somewhere up front. Yellow, too. Medium sized. There's a lot of stuff all over, I hope that it isn't hard to find. Thanks, James. This night has been awful. You have no idea."

I zipped my jacket as high as it would go and opened the door. I put the umbrella outside and opened it. Just like a cartoon, the wind ripped it apart in an instant. I swore and then laughed. Kim laughed, too. I jumped out of the car and raced over to her wrecked Taurus. I opened the door. No dome light. I hopped in and swung my flashlight around the interior. It was a mess. Kim had way too much crap in her car, and the jarring stop at the tree had scattered it everywhere, as she had described. What a freaking mess. I couldn't imagine that it had been too much neater before the wreck with so much detritus scattered around. Empty Mountain Dew cans, fast food bags, lipstick containers, magazines, a little bit of everything. The purse was on the passenger side floor. Easy to spot. I took a quick peek into the open glove box. The usual assortment of papers and crap. And a pistol. What? A pistol? What the hell was she doing with a pistol in her glove box? This was a surprise. I removed it and put it into my jacket pocket. I would think about how to approach the subject of her pistol later in the evening. I hoped that my jacket pocket didn't bulge too much.

"Nasty! I'm almost as soaked as you. A warm house and some dry clothes and coffee sound great to me right now. Let's get out of here. By the way, I left your car keys up above the visor. Make sure you tell the tow truck guys that. They'll need them when they pick up the car. I didn't lock it. I don't think we have to worry about anyone stealing anything tonight." I laughed.

"Thanks again. Thanks for stopping. I was beginning to think I would die by the side of the road from exposure! I know I wouldn't have, but it did seem like forever before you came along." She smiled at me. I smiled, thinking she would be mine soon.

I pulled back onto the road and headed back to my place. When we got to my neighborhood, I noticed it was darker than expected. No streetlights, no lights at all in any of the houses along my street. Nothing. I pulled into my driveway. My security lights didn't turn on. This was intriguing….

"It looks like we've got no power. Let's go in and see if we have any phone service." I parked the car and grabbed Kim's pack. She got her purse and we dashed to the front porch. I unlocked the front door and led her in. I flipped the light switch, but nothing happened. I turned on my flashlight and motioned her to the sofa.

"Let me go into the kitchen and grab a couple of candles so we can see. Then I'll find my cell and we can call the police and tow truck and get you situated. Can I get you a blanket first? You must really be chilled; I can hear your teeth chattering." She nodded her assent. I grabbed a blanket from the guest room and handed it to a grateful Kim. She wrapped up in it quickly. I went to the kitchen to get a candle. I lit it and returned to the living room.

God, she was stunning in the candlelight! My heart raced a bit. I was ready to play. This girl was tailor-made for my pleasure. Happenstance had put her right in my lap. I started to plan the evening's fun in my head. I picked up my phone and listened for a minute. Nothing. Of course, since I had phone service with my cable provider, I had no phone at all when the power was off. That was a happy thing for me—less so for dear Kim.

"Phone's out. No service without power. Let me grab my cell."

"OK. Thanks again. This blanket really helps. Sorry to put you out like this." She smiled in the candlelight. I trembled inside. Soon this little thing would be begging for her life. Soon she would be struggling and fighting and dying in my arms. I could hardly wait.

I went into the bedroom and got my cell off the dresser. I popped the back off and took out the battery. I certainly didn't want my phone to work. What would the fun be in that? I went back and gave Kim the sad news.

197

"Kim, my cell battery is dead. No way to plug it in without power. So I guess we'll just have to head over to the police station in person. Back out into the storm...." I paused and waited for her reaction. A huge crack of lightning, followed almost immediately by deafening thunder, punctuated my sentence for me. Perfect.

"I don't want you to have to go out in this again. I don't want to go out if I don't have to. Is it OK if we wait out the storm for a while? I don't want to intrude, but I am a little frazzled by this whole thing. I've never had a wreck before."

"You're not intruding; you're an invited guest. Can I get you anything? Coffee? Tea? Are you hungry? I ate too much at the Bay Bell Inn, but I would be glad to fix you something if you wanted." It was only fitting that I offer the girl a last meal.

"Ummm...tea would be nice. But how are you going to heat the water? The power's out."

"I have a gas stove and matches. We may not be able to make a phone call, but we can cook. Are you hungry?" I smiled at my quarry. "I can whip up an omelet or, well, really whatever. I'm a pretty good cook, and I keep a fairly full pantry for a bachelor. I'll make the tea while you ponder food." I lit the stove and a couple of more candles. I put the water on and looked over at Kim. "No way of knowing how long this storm will go on. Worst I've seen in years. The wind is really whipping out there." I got out two cups, the sugar and milk, and some cookies. When the kettle whistled, I took it off and brought the tray into the living room. "Tea's on. I've got several choices, suit yourself. Cookie?" Kim took a tea bag and a chocolate snickerdoodle. She made her tea and then took a bite of cookie.

"This is good. Where did you get them?" She took a

bigger bite.

"From my oven. I confess. I bake. If you'd been here last weekend, you could have had some of my parmesan basil bread. That never lasts. Bread is one of my downfalls, I'm afraid. I spend a lot of my time at the YMCA working off bread. I'd probably be skinny as a rail if it weren't for bread."

"James, you are a good man. Most men just don't cook or bake, let alone do the dishes or clean. From what I have seen in the candlelight, your house is beautiful. My hat's off to you." Kim nodded and did a mock bow on the sofa.

"Thank you. But I am a terrible host. Do you want me to build a fire in the fireplace? That would help you warm up and would take the fall chill out of the air in here."

"Don't go to any trouble. But I would love a fire if you were planning on having one anyway…."

I quickly built a fire in the fireplace. In no time at all it was roaring. Kim moved over to the hearth and practically purred with delight. She allowed the blanket to open so the heat from the fire could warm her and dry her clothes. I wished the blanket was the only thing that she was wearing. Maybe later. The thunder and lightning intensified and the wind ramped up even more. I usually don't get nervous during a storm, but this one was something else entirely. I excused myself and went to get my battery-operated weather radio. I turned it on just as the house shook from another thunder crash. Kim jumped when it happened. I started to worry that I'd lose a tree or two in this intense storm. The weather radio crackled and sputtered. I fiddled with the knob and got the local station tuned in. The disembodied, computer-generated voice was droning about the weather conditions. Then the annoying alert tone sounded.

"There is a severe thunderstorm warning in effect for the following counties: Alger, Baraga, Dickinson, Gogebic, Luce, and Marquette. Winds gusting up to sixty miles per hour and damaging hail are possible. Avoid travel. Remain indoors. Stay away from windows. The severe thunderstorm warning will remain in effect until 1:00 a.m. There is a severe thunderstorm warning in effect...." The voice repeated the warning a couple of times, and then the regular weather broadcasting resumed. Kim and I just looked at each other and shrugged. I looked at my watch.

"It's 11:15. We've got a couple of more hours before the Weather Service thinks this might calm down. Have you thought of anything you'd like to eat? I'd like an excuse to cook. Or something. I just feel like doing something rather than just sitting and waiting. Not that I don't enjoy your company, but I don't sit and do nothing very well." I looked hopefully at Kim.

"A couple of scrambled eggs would be nice. And some toast? If it's not too much trouble."

"Coming right up. Plain eggs, or can I doctor them up a bit?"

"Surprise me. I eat everything. I'm not very picky."

"Good. Eggs in a couple of minutes. More tea?"

"Um, would it be out of place to ask for a drink-drink? A rum and Coke would be really nice. That's what I was out for; beer for the other girls and rum for me..."

"No problem. Here's a Coke, and here's rum. A glass, ice.... I'll let you mix your own while I whip up your eggs." I diced up some onions and olives and some ham and browned them up a bit before pouring the eggs in. A quick dash of seasoning and some cheddar cheese, and in no time, I had a nice plate of eggs and toast for my dance partner. She attacked them with gusto. I enjoyed watching her eat. I would enjoy watching her squirm even more.

"I was hungry. Thanks. They were great. It seems like the storm is letting up a bit. Maybe the power will come back on soon and you can get rid of your surprise visitor."

"It is no trouble. I rattle around this house alone a lot; it is nice to have company for a change. Ever since my wife died, well, this place seems big and empty. I…sorry…um…it does seem that the storm is quieting down a bit. That's good. Maybe we will be able to get you back out to your friends after all. They must be worried." I paused for a moment. I wondered just how comfortable she was. "The water heater is gas…there is hot water. Do you want to take a shower and get into some of your warm clothes? I could light a couple of candles in the bathroom for you."

"I've been enough of a bother already. I'll be OK."

"Excuse me, but are you Catholic? Jewish? I haven't heard someone more guilty sounding than you in a long time. You have been no trouble at all. I just hope you are feeling OK after your evening. If you tell me you've been a burden one more time, I will scream. You are just fine." God, she was fine….

"Thanks. Guilty as charged. I'm a recovering Catholic. Went to a Catholic grade school. I think every third word I said as a kid was 'Sorry.' I would love to take a hot shower, if it really isn't any bother."

"OK, I won't scream…. It is no bother at all. I'll light a candle for you in the guest room and put some towels and shampoo and stuff out for you in the bathroom. Please make yourself at home." I puttered off to get things ready for her. I would get my own things ready for her while she was in the shower. I still wanted to find an

201

excuse to take her to the shelter. I wanted to try the new camera setup. But how? What would convince her to go back out into the storm after she had cleaned up and put on dry clothes? I didn't want to have to force her, but…THE GUN! I could use her own gun to 'persuade' her to leave the warmth of the house and head to the shelter. What a delightful idea.

Kim went into the bathroom and started her shower. I got a couple of my ties and some twine and stashed them in the kitchen. Not as effective as zip ties or handcuffs, but I didn't dare keep those in the house. I played out several scenarios in my head as she showered. My pulse quickened as I thought of this delectable creature bound and serving my whim. I almost hyperventilated thinking about what her skin would feel like next to mine, how her throat would feel in my hands. Patience, patience. Just a few more minutes and I could start to work on moving things into my playroom. I paced a little in the dimly lit room. I rubbed my hands together. I actually think I was salivating a little. I was worse than Humbert Humbert in *Lolita*. A couple of gentle flashes of lightning and some pleasant rolling thunder snapped me out of it. The storm seemed to be breaking. I would have to work quickly. I hoped that the power didn't come on too soon.…

Kim came out a few minutes later in a nice pair of jeans, bare feet, and a worn white Oxford men's shirt. Her hair had been towel dried, but it still clung to her neck and shoulders. I almost gasped looking at her. How could something this simple, something not revealing at all, be so incredibly sexy? The contrast of her dark eyes and hair against the weathered old white shirt was exquisite, as was her flawless olive complexion. I am a "devout atheist," but if I were to be persuaded that there was a God, she would be part of the proof. It was hard to believe that random pairings of chromosomes had resulted in this. There must have been divine inspiration in her design. She would more than make up for Maura.

"Thanks for letting me take a shower. I'm finally warm and feel human again. Thanks you." She crossed the room and gave me a friendly hug. "The storm seems to be pretty quiet now. That's good. Maybe we can think of going to the police station soon, although I'm in no hurry to get wet again." She smiled at me and started to move back toward the couch. Just then a huge lightning bolt struck the giant maple at the end of the drive and the house shook as the thunder crack roared. A huge branch fell off the tree and blocked the end of the driveway and the road leading to it. Kim jumped and screamed when the tree split. I jumped, too.

"I guess we're roommates for the evening," I said. "No getting around that tree without my chainsaw and several hours of work. The guest room is all yours. I hope your friends are OK out at the cabin…" As I spoke, the wind howled and whipped beyond its former fury. The rain came back down in sideways sheets. The treetops sawed back and forth violently. I'd never seen a storm like this in the U.P. in all the years I'd lived here. I went back to the weather radio and turned it up. After a few moments, the warning tones sounded and a real human voice came on.

"There is a tornado warning, repeat a tornado warning in the New Worcester area. Two confirmed sightings of funnel clouds approximately three miles west of the city, heading east by northeast at forty-five miles per hour. Take shelter immediately. This is not a drill. Take shelter underground if possible. Repeat, there is a tornado warning…."

"Kim, we've got just a couple of minutes before it gets here. I've got a safe place out back. Grab your jacket and follow me. Now!" My voice was commanding. Kim didn't question; she just grabbed her jacket and followed as I headed out the back door. I tossed her a flashlight. "It's going to be nasty, and we've got to haul ass to my shelter. Stay close and run!"

When we got out the back door, the wind hit us like a freight train. The trees danced back and forth. Branches snapped and broke and debris flew through the air. The rain came in sheets, sideways sheets, and was bitingly cold. We ran as fast as we could through the melee and quickly got to the hatch leading to my playroom. I threw the hatch open and led Kim down the stairs. I unbolted the heavy door and yanked it open. I motioned Kim in and followed her in, slamming the door behind.

"That was awful!" I exclaimed. "I've never seen a storm like this in the U.P. And never this late in the season. Imagine if this had happened a month or two from now. We'd be ass-high in snow with twenty-foot drifts. I'm soaked again." I panted from the exertion. Kim was out of breath, too. She stood, catching her breath and panning her flashlight around the shelter.

"Let me fire up the generator. Then we can make ourselves comfortable and wait out this mess."

"Generator? What is this? 'We're not in Kansas anymore,' are we?" She looked around and took it all in.

"I'll start the generator and tell you all about it." I went into the utility room and fired up the generator and the ventilation system. I flipped on the lights and went back out into the main room.

"This is a Cold War era bomb shelter. Probably built in the mid-1950s. I've been restoring it and modifying it for the past few years. I use it as a studio and kind of private hideaway. It's quite safe down here. Even if a tornado levels the neighborhood, we won't notice a thing with so many feet of concrete and dirt above us. I've got some food and drink and plenty of fuel for the generator. While we only need to make it until morning, this place was designed to keep a family safe for weeks. I just never thought I'd have to use it for real. I don't ever remember a tornado actually being sighted and touching down in New Worcester before. I just wonder if we'll be in Oz when we emerge? Will a wicked witch be under the corner of my house?" I laughed.

"This is cool. Other than no windows, you'd never know you were underground. It is cozy. I hope that nothing happens to your house. Hope the tornado doesn't hit." She got an awful look on her face. "I hope the girls are OK at the cabin. Oh God, what if they get hit? They've got no place to hide out there. The cabins don't have basements or even crawl spaces; I could tell that just by looking. Oh, God; oh God...." Kim started to pace and tears started to well up in her eyes. I did my best to calm her.

"There's no way to know and no way to help them right now. Tornadoes are unpredictable and do tend to hop about...the odds are good that they are OK. Scared, I'll bet, but OK. Just calm down and we'll wait it out together. We'll go to the police as soon as we can.... I'll get my cell charged up and we can call. They'll know something when we call, I'm sure. I wish I'd brought my cell with me; I could have charged it. We'd still have to wait until we could leave the shelter...no cell signal at all down here. In fact, no nothing down here. We are as alone as if we were on a desert island. But safer. We'll be OK and I'm sure your friends will be, too."

I paused to assess Kim's state of mind. She seemed to be getting a grip. She had stopped pacing and appeared to be attentive to my words. I took my wet jacket off and put it on the back of one of the chairs. I had to be careful how I hung it as the butt of the gun was slightly visible in my pocket. Her gun had some interesting possibilities for the evening's fun. I'd never used one with a playmate since I didn't own one, but here it was....

"Are you as soaked as I am? I don't have any women's clothing down here, but you are welcome to change into some of my things if you'd like. They'd be a little large on you, but they would be warm and dry." Just then, I noticed her feet. She had been barefoot when we had dashed down the path to the shelter. Her left foot had a fairly good-sized gash that was starting to bleed enough to say so. The adrenaline rush from our sprint to safety must have numbed her to the injury. I suspected that she had no knowledge of it.

"Kim, you're bleeding. The run out here was a little rough on your feet. Please, sit down and let me take a look at it." Kim looked down at her foot and turned pale. Apparently, she was a little squeamish when it came to blood. She gasped and quickly sat on a chair. I went to get a towel, washcloth, and the first aid kit. I also switched on the power to the three cameras. I didn't want to miss any of what was to come. This would be the first time I'd had the opportunity to use the three-camera setup with an interesting subject.... I was hoping the three camera angles would eliminate the blind spots that my previous efforts had. I really wanted to watch this girl from all sides. I had used the three-camera setup with Maura, but I had never even edited the video of my time with that hippo. Not worth my time and effort.

"I didn't feel anything when I did this," said Kim when I returned. "It sure hurts now. I'm sorry if I'm a little weird. I...ugh...I sometimes faint when I see blood. I...." Her eyes rolled a little in her head. She leaned her head back and shut her eyes tightly. I kneeled down in front of her and attended to her foot. I carefully washed her cut with warm soapy water and dried it off with a fresh towel. The cut would require stitches, but that would have to wait until, well, never since she wouldn't live long enough to go to the hospital. I applied pressure to her foot to staunch the flow of blood, and I put a gauze pad over the wound to try to catch the blood that continued to ooze out. I had a few butterfly bandages in my kit. I worked to slow the flow as much as possible before applying them. Then I bound the foot in gauze, fairly tightly. All the while, I marveled at how smooth her skin was. I don't have a foot fetish, but I couldn't help noticing how pretty even her feet were. I was smitten. This girl was a knockout, even her feet. I needed to see more.

"Do you want anything for the pain? I've got Tylenol down here. Depending on how bad it is, I do have some Aspocontin, but only if it is really bad. I don't want to give you anything that strong unless you really need it."

"It's really starting to hurt," she admitted. "I'll try some Tylenol. You don't have anything to drink down here? Stronger than water?" She looked hopefully at me.

"I have a fairly full liquor cabinet down here. I spend a fair amount of time down here. What's your poison? More rum? I'm not sure I have Coke, and I know I don't have ice...."

"I'd like a shot of brandy, if you have it. I'm a Wisconsin girl; we drink more brandy than any other state. Funny statistic, but it's true...."

"Brandy, no, but I do have a bottle of B&B, one of my personal favorites. Will that do?"

"Yes, please. And a couple of Tylenol, please."

I got the B&B and the Tylenol. I thought it was funny that I was tending to Kim's wounds like Beth had tended to mine before I killed her. I didn't plan on being as cruel as Beth, though. I had no intention of using Kim's injury as a weapon. Kim washed the Tylenol down with a swig from the bottle of water that I handed her, and then she sipped the B&B.

"Nice. I like that. Thanks again. James, this has been a hell of a night...."

I agreed with her. I asked her whether there was anything else I could do to make her more comfortable. She asked for a towel and some dry clothes. I gave her a bath towel and some of my jeans and a flannel shirt and showed her the bedroom. She gingerly hopped over and went in to change. I looked forward to seeing her in my clothes. I looked forward to seeing her out of them. This was going to be quite the night. Quite the night.

Kim came out in a few minutes and made her way back to the chair. I fired up the space heater and gave her a blanket to wrap up in, if she needed it. She said she was comfortable and warm now that she was dry again and I'd fired up the heater. She had a pained look on her face, though. I asked whether she was OK.

"My foot really hurts. The Tylenol hasn't touched it. You said you had something stronger...? Would that be OK? This really hurts."

"I do have something stronger. Have you ever taken Aspocontin or anything like it before?" I hoped that she wasn't really familiar with it.

"When I had my wisdom teeth out, they gave me Tylenol 3 with codeine. That really helped. Other than that, nothing. But I'd eat half a bottle of those right now. My foot is throbbing. I don't mean to sound like a wimp, but it hurts."

"We'll have to get you to the ER when we're able to. I cleaned it up and bandaged it well, but in my humble opinion, you'll need stitches. I can believe it hurts. I remember how things felt after my motorcycle accident one summer. That's when I got the Aspocontin. It really helps. Let me get you a couple." The proper dose for someone her size would have been one, but I got two and a glass of water. "Here, take these. When the doctor gave them to me, he told me to take two every four hours. They really work." I gave her the pills. She swallowed them eagerly and gulped some water.

"Once again, thanks, James. You're my hero. I could still be out in that storm. Thanks. I hope the girls are OK." She put the blanket around her shoulders and snuggled into it.

"It's getting late; do you want to lie down? You should elevate that foot. You can have the main bed; I'll just hang out here and pop my head outside to see what's going on. Hopefully, soon I'll be able to get you to the hospital and the police station. You should get some rest...." I motioned toward the bedroom. She smiled and started to walk toward it. Her foot must have really smarted. She winced each time she put any weight on it at all. I put her arm around my shoulder and supported her as she made her way to the bed. I helped her get in and asked whether she needed anything else. She told me no and said that she was getting very sleepy. I smiled and told her to have pleasant dreams. I went back out into the main room and waited for her to fall asleep. It didn't take long.

I decided to try something new. Since I had her gun, I decided I wouldn't bind her in any way. I would just use the power of the gun to make her do what I wanted. It was risky on some levels, but she couldn't go anywhere. I would make sure she knew the door was bolted shut. Besides, between the drugs and her foot, she would be none too mobile. In a short time, she fell asleep. I heard her breathing get deeper and more regular. I waited a few more minutes, and then I entered the bedroom. Let the games begin!

I approached her sleeping form and gently pulled the blanket back. She was sleeping on her back and like the dead. The double dose of Aspocontin combined with the B&B had certainly worked their magic. Now it was time for some of my own. I carefully undid her first shirt button. She didn't stir. I undid the next. And the next. Still no movement from her. The next button revealed that she hadn't put her wet bra back on, much to my delight. I undid the final two and let the shirt fall open. Her body was as perfect as I had hoped it would be. In the dim light of the bedroom, I could make out the gentle curve of her belly around her navel, the cut lines of her firm abs, and the exquisite outline of her perfect little breasts. This girl must either have the most amazing genes ever or spent some serious time in the gym to be this toned. Didn't matter how she got that way, I just enjoyed the view. I traced the contours of her abdomen with the tips of my fingers. Electricity flowed through me as I touched her flawless olive skin. Like silk, smooth and sleek, warm to the touch. I kissed her just above the waistband of her pants. Her skin was heaven on my lips. This was going to be divine.

Just then, she stirred a little. I pulled her gun out of my waistband and held it at the ready. It was heavy and cold in my hand. A Colt pistol, .32 caliber; it would put a sizeable hole into anything it was pointed at. Not as messy as a 9mm or a .45, but it was certainly effective. It had a full clip—I checked—but I planned on using no bullets. This goddess deserved a gentle touch, not the fiery blast of death from a hot round ripping her flesh open. My hands on her throat, slowly and lovingly applying more and more pressure until she quietly slipped away—that was what she deserved. The gun was just for persuasion. Nothing more. It was a visual bond, a mental restraint, nothing more. The threat of the gun would be enough to get her to do my bidding. I dared to kiss her navel. She stirred more and started to wake. Good. I wanted her awake now. I wanted to see how much the drugs had affected her and how far I could play with her before our final dance. I wanted to see what this girl was made of.

"Kim, sorry to bother you, but the storm seems to have blown itself out. Do you want to get up and head back to the house now? The power's on." All lies, but she needn't know. I was aching to get on with it. I wanted to make her my puppet, make her do things for my pleasure; I wanted to touch her and hold her and finally strangle her. I needed this. I needed this to wash the foul taste of Maura from my memory. She reacted to my words. She stirred and her eyes fluttered open. Her hands went to her chest and found it bare. She sat bolt upright and screamed. She tried to cover herself, but I grabbed one wrist and shoved her gun under her chin.

"Morning, Sleeping Beauty. I wouldn't try that. In fact, I wouldn't try anything. Just lie back down and listen for a moment. Be quiet and listen." Of course, she didn't. She screamed and twisted and tried to cover herself. I jabbed the gun harder against her.

"Do you recognize this? Feel the cold steel on your chin? This is your gun. You should know what it will do. I am not afraid to use it. I'd rather not; I have other plans for you, but I will if I have to. Now lie down and be still!" I glared at her and pushed her back onto the bed. I flipped the lights on so I could take in her beauty and her fear. She didn't disappoint. Even in the harsh fluorescents, her skin was amazing. She looked at me with venom in her eyes. It made her even more beautiful to me. The anger and rage were almost an aphrodisiac. I smiled at her. I told her to lie still and be quiet. She complied. She tried to cover her breasts with her hands, but I waved them off with the gun. Powerful tool, a gun. Never thought about using one before. Didn't know if I ever would again, but I was having fun now.

"I'm sorry to say that I am most definitely not your hero. Yes, I did take you in out of the storm. Yes, I gave you food and drink and tended to your wound. And, if I hadn't been missing my hobby so much, maybe nothing more would have happened. But I see finding you on the roadside in the storm as fate. You were destined to be my next dance partner. We know each other; you are beautiful, young, desirable, perfect for a playmate. So here we are, about to start on a journey together. You can decide how pleasant or awful it will be. Just do as I tell you and things will be painless and fun. Fight me and it will be terrible. Your choice. I'm a gentleman; I let the ladies decide…." I stopped to let her take this all in. She looked at me, then at the gun, then back at me again.

"Who the fuck are you? I thought I had some notion. You seemed like a nice guy. But what the fuck is this? What happens now?" If looks could kill, I would have been annihilated. She was mad. She was, however, in control of her words and emotions. Her speech was direct and measured. If the drugs had any effect on her, it was impossible to tell by listening to her. This was getting better and better every moment.

"I could ask the same thing. What twenty-something young lady carries a .32 caliber pistol in her glove box? Explain that…." I waited. Kim gathered her thoughts and started to speak. Then she stopped. Paused. And started again.

"May I cover up? I'm a little cold. You've been a good host up till now, and—"

"Quiet!" I interrupted in my most commanding voice and with a flourish of the gun. "You may not cover up. I like to look at you laying there. I like your breasts and love your taut tummy. You are delicious to look at. Clothes are such a waste on you. I want you naked. Please, finish what I started. Shuck off my jeans and let me take a good look at you."

"I'd rather die!"

"Too soon for that. Strip. Now." I waved the gun at her and used it to motion the jeans away. "Take the pants off. Now. If you weren't hurt, I'd have you dance for me. But I'm too much of a gentleman to have you do that. So you can stay on the bed, but remove the pants...or I will...."

She pondered this for a moment and then undid the button on the jeans, pulled down the zipper, and slid the jeans off her hips. She got them down to her knees and then kicked them off with her feet. She covered her womanhood with one hand and tried to cover her breasts with the other. I let her have this little bit of comfort for a moment. The view was still a delight. Her legs were well-muscled and shapely, toned and not over-developed. I wanted to touch her, but I couldn't risk getting that close when she wasn't bound in some way. I was beginning to understand the limitations of my steel friend. The threat that the gun represented could cause my playmate to comply, but it hobbled my ability to enjoy fully the fruits of my labors. Frustrating.

"I asked you about this," I said, motioning with the gun. "What are you doing with this? I guess I'm not the only one with dark secrets around here."

"No dark secret. My dad's a cop. He taught us all to shoot when we were young. He taught us how to use a gun safely, to use it as a tool. My sisters and I all have concealed carry permits. I always have a gun with me.

Habit."

"That's interesting. Does it make you feel safe? Do you feel safe now, lying there naked in a locked cell with your own gun trained on you? I'll bet not. I'll bet you feel pretty unsafe looking down the barrel of your own gun. I've never owned one myself. Shot a few times. Gwen's dad was a collector and hunter. He wanted me to be 'one of the boys,' but I never developed a taste for the things. I know how to use it, but I choose not to…usually. Now it is a useful tool, though. Very useful. How's your foot?"

"How's my foot? You have me lying here naked with a gun pointed at me and you casually ask, 'How's your foot?' What are you?" She glared at me. I smiled.

"Good question, that. What am I indeed? I'm just your average guy with a hobby. You are part of my hobby. And now that you're up, let's take our little party out into the main room. I have something for you to watch, something that will answer all your questions."

"I'm not getting up or going anywhere unless you let me cover up. I won't have you gawking at me like I'm some fucking stripper. I'm going to put the blanket on, and then I will go out into the other room." She sat up and started to wrap the blanket around her.

"Stop that. Now. I like you much better this way. Remember, you have a choice about how the rest of your life goes. Easy or hard, it's up to you. I would choose easy. Now get your pretty little ass out of the bed and out into the main room. Now. I don't like to repeat myself." She sat resolutely. She started to reach for the blanket again. "Did I stutter? Didn't you hear what I said? Let go of the blanket and get your delicious body out of bed. Be glad I am only asking you to walk into the other room. I can think of many more things that I would like to watch you do. I can think of even more that I would like to do to you. But for now, just get up and go into the other room. I really don't want to have to hurt you. I'm not really a violent man." I motioned her off the bed with the gun.

This time, she rose and got to her feet. She was unsteady. She was careful not to put too much weight on her left foot, and the Aspocontin was making her a little woozy, I assumed. She fell back a little. I quickly put the gun on the shelf and caught her before she fell. I loved how she felt in my arms. She recoiled from my touch, but she did let me help her into the other room. I sat her down in a chair and hastily got the gun again. A gun, while a powerful persuader, was definitely an inconvenience. I needed both hands free to have any real fun. I would have to bind her after all.

"I do want you to know that I am not a rapist. As tempting as your naked body is to me, I won't violate you. That I promise. I hope that makes you feel a little better…."

"Getting the hell out of here is the only thing that will make me feel better. Clothes would make me feel better. I can't feel any better knowing that some sick pervert is 'promising' me that he won't rape me. Big deal. What are you going to do to me?"

"Just a little dance. Most of what we do together, you will do to yourself. I won't touch you much. Not until the end…." I smiled. "I'm a man of simple pleasures and excellent taste. You, for example, are proof positive of my taste. You are lovely. I dare say flawless. I am honored to have you in my company. And I will have memories of you to cherish forever. We are on camera now. I want to be able to look at you whenever I want, so I am recording the night's fun. Once again, I want to assure you that none of the images captured tonight will end up posted in any public forum. No nude photos of you on the Internet. I want to keep you for my private collec—"

"Like that is supposed to make me feel better! I'm locked up naked with a freak, and your reassurances are supposed to make me feel better? What the hell! I want out. I don't care about the storm, my foot, anything. I just want to go. Now! Open the door. I'll leave naked; I just want out! This is like some psycho-slasher flick or something. Let me go!"

I pointed out to her that I wasn't touching her. I couldn't let her go because I wasn't holding her. I wanted to, but I was not. She was not amused by my gentle joke. She spat at me and started screaming. I let her scream for a while. It was probably good for her. I liked it. After a short while, though, it did become tiresome. I told her to be quiet. Enough was enough. She did finally quiet down. I asked her whether she wanted to watch some TV to pass the time. She looked at me strangely, but nodded. I smiled and turned on my "greatest hits" video.

Kim watched in horror as Beth appeared on screen. She started to tear up and whimper. When Beth was breathing her last, Kim wailed. Rene came on the screen. More gasps and whimpering from Kim. It was very satisfying. When I had my little indiscretion with Rene, Kim looked at me and screamed, "You lying fuck! You raped her! You're going to rape me, too! You sick, twisted piece of shit!" I thought it amusing that she was so fixated on my brief violation of Rene rather than Beth and Rene's deaths. Was rape worse to her than death? I couldn't understand women. I knew that I never would. Maybe that was part of why I liked playing with them so much. Each one was an enigma unto herself. No predictability. Other than tears and crying, each had reacted differently to their situations.

Suddenly, my train of thought was disrupted when Kim lunged at me for control of the gun. I had not expected

216

this—her injury and fuzzy head had made me think she wouldn't try anything stupid. I was the stupid one. She threw herself at me with all her strength and grabbed at the gun with both hands. Normally, I would have enjoyed wrestling with a naked goddess, but the stakes were very high. I put my free hand over both of hers and tried to pry them off my right hand and the gun. I pushed my weight onto her and managed to get her to the floor. We struggled for the gun. Her finger slipped into the loop over the trigger, and as we fought for control, her finger pressed against mine. A blast louder than thunder followed as the gun went off in this very small space.

Kim made a tiny noise and then went limp. My face was wet. She was very still. The floor under her had a rapidly growing puddle. I let go and got up so I could survey what had happened. The bullet had gone into her throat and upward into her head. I couldn't see any exit wound, but the entrance wound was pumping and spurting blood like a BP oil well in the Gulf of Mexico. I screamed "No!" and dropped down next to her. I checked for a pulse, checked for a heartbeat, but found none. She was dead...and a mess. I was terribly disappointed. I had never wanted this to happen. I had intended so much more playtime with her. I needed to feel her death. A gunshot was no more intimate than a video game. I had been robbed of my prize.

POLICE ACTION, PART ONE

I had to cool it for a while. The news was talking about Beth, Rene, and Marua more and more. They started putting two and two and two together. While there had been no bodies found, the media was starting to talk about a serial killer. Officially, the police and the FBI were still calling the girls' disappearances probable abductions. They reported few leads and no suspects. I didn't know if that was a smokescreen or the truth. I wasn't too nervous. I had covered my tracks well, I thought. Still….

When I embarked on my hobby, I had started preparing for the worst. It was ineveitble that I would have to leave New Worcester at some point. I had started to craft a couple new identities for just such an eventuality. I had the luxury of very deep pockets. Anything can be done with enough time, effort, and application of cubic dollars. I shifted assets into accounts offshore, into my new identities' accounts. I had to be prepared.

BRITTANY

After a couple of disappointing play dates, I felt it was time to return to what I knew was satisfying—women I was close to and who trusted me. And, as my experience with Maura had shown, I needed women who were physically attractive. While I didn't feel Kim's disappearance would really have any bearing on my wait time between play dates, the media attention about the others was giving me some cause to pause. The news was positing that Kim must have injured herself in the crash and wandered off, incoherent. Because of the conditions, no foul play was suspected. The months passed slowly as I waited.

Brittany was bright and interesting. Honey-blonde hair about shoulder-length. Fuller of figure than most women who turned my head, but certainly not Rubenesque by any means. She had a lovely hourglass figure, a perfect complexion, and a beautiful smile. She and I had always gotten along well. She went out of her way to be involved in shows I was doing. If I were directing, she always auditioned. If I were tech directing, she was at every build and worked backstage. If I auditioned for a show, she did as well. She was a good friend and a bit of a flirt. I certainly didn't mind a beautiful twenty-something flirting with me. It felt good to be noticed and the banter was fun. I knew nothing would or could ever come of it—like most of my theater friends, I was old enough to be her father. But it was still fun to pretend….

I had decided to step back in time to Rene. The photo shoot idea had worked well. Overall, Rene had been very satisfying on many levels, other than the brief moment when I had lost control and was rather rude to her. I wouldn't let that happen again. After all, I am a gentleman, not some filthy rapist. I'm sure that in Rene's brief time alive after that unfortunate incident, she never believed how remorseful I was. For that, I am truly sorry. I wish she had died knowing that raping her was something I regretted and would have taken back, if only I could. Oh, well, there was no use crying over it now. I had made the mistake and would never do that again. I do have my morals, after all.

"Brittany, can I talk to you a minute?" I asked after a rehearsal.

"Sure. What's up?" she asked.

"I need to talk to you about a private matter. Can we go up to the balcony for a moment?"

She looked quizzically at me and nodded her assent. We climbed the stairs to the balcony. When we got to the top, Brittany turned to me and asked, "Was I so bad tonight that you couldn't talk to me during notes? I mean, I may have been a little distracted—" I cut her off with a gesture.

"Brittany, your performance was fine. Not your best, but OK. This has nothing to do with the show. I want to talk to you about something a little awkward for me to ask. So I wanted a little privacy to do it."

"Whew. That's a relief. I thought I sucked it big time tonight, so you were going to have a little 'balcony talk' with me. I remember when you were having so much trouble with Andy in *Forum*. He looked like shit when you got done with him." I laughed a little. I am a pretty easy going director, but when Andy had missed not one, but two entrance cues during first dress of *A Funny Thing Happened on the Way to the Forum*, I was *not* amused. I did march him up to the balcony and talked to him very seriously about his performance and the importance of timing in comedy. I was a little hard on him, but I had been having trouble with him since the very first day of rehearsals. If he hadn't had that "god voice" of his, I would have bounced him out of the show the first week. So it amused me that Brittany thought we were going to have a "balcony talk."

"Brittany, you know that I do a little photography as a hobby. I want to talk to you about a job modeling for me. Would you be interested?" I paused a moment. "Before you say yes or no, I want to tell you a little more about what I am looking for. I want a model with a fairly, um, open mind and attitude. I want to shoot some pictures that are a little racy. Nothing hardcore, no nudity, but a little 'off color' for some. I would need you to be discreet. While you aren't one of my students and are certainly of legal age, I don't want to get any more of a reputation as a dirty old man than I may already have. These are increasingly stupid and uptight times, so I don't want to risk my job for my hobby. I will pay you as a professional, have you sign appropriate releases and such, and will give you final say over what gets saved or deleted. All I ask is that you are discreet...." Brittany was quiet for a moment. Then she grinned.

"James, I've been a life model for a few art classes. You could shoot me nude, too, if you wanted to. I am OK with it. I like to model. I would be comfortable with just you, more than with sixteen kids I see every day here on campus. Yeah, I'd love it if you wanted to shoot me. When?" This was a pleasant turn of events. I had hoped she'd say, "Yes," but I didn't think she'd be this eager. I didn't know she had posed for the Art Department, either. This was easy, almost too easy.

"Can you do it Sunday afternoon? We don't have rehearsal. We could shoot in the afternoon, and then you'd still have time to finish any homework you have before classes on Monday."

"Sunday afternoon would be great. If we finish early enough, you can buy me dinner, too!" Brittany flashed her infectious grin at me again. *You won't really be interested in dinner when you're dead*, I thought.

"Perfect. Sunday it is. One o'clock." I started to head down the balcony steps. "James, is there anything special you want me to wear? Anything you need me to bring? I've got some really cool boots and some fence-net stockings. A corset? I have a lot of stuff you might like...." Christ, this girl was getting to me already and she was fully clothed and not in my playhouse. I was getting more anxious for the next couple of days to pass. I was going to have a very good time with young Brittany. Just what I needed to get my spirits back up after my last couple of outings.

"I've got some costumes for you," I replied, "but feel free to bring whatever you want."

"I'll be sure to pack my birthday suit," she said with a spark of mischief in her eye. She caught me off-guard with that. I just looked back at her and blushed.

*

The next couple of days could not go by fast enough. My one Friday class seemed to take a week. Rehearsal Friday night was at least a month long. My Saturday took eons. I found myself looking at my watch every couple of minutes and cursing that the time wasn't passing faster. I busied myself with the preparations for Sunday's fun. I picked out the outfits that Brittany would wear. Got the cameras and lights set up. Laid out props. Reselected outfits. Fiddled with the lights some more. Tested all the equipment. Cleaned every nook and cranny of the shelter. Made sure that I had food and drink and restraints and cuffs and other toys. I paced. My heart raced. My palms sweated. I looked at my watch again. I was a ball of nervous energy about to explode. I tried to relax by watching the videos of Beth and Rene and Kim. That just made me want the time to pass even more.

Saturday's rehearsal wasn't much better; I couldn't focus. I turned the reins over to Sarah and had her do a line-glib with the cast. After rehearsal, I went home and had a couple of drinks and tried to read so I could sleep. I was worse than a kid on Christmas Eve waiting for Santa Claus.

Sunday finally dawned bright and clear. It was one of those special U.P. days: crisp, clear, flawless. I was happy. I was going to get to play again, enjoy my hobby to the fullest. I went out for a light breakfast, worked out at the gym for a while, came home and took a relaxing shower. I was fresh and clean shaven and anxious. A little nervous. That surprised me; I should be more comfortable with this after four play dates, but Brittany's attitude had me worked up. I knew she wouldn't disappoint. A couple of minutes before 1:00, she knocked. I opened the door and gasped to myself. She was standing there in a trenchcoat and some very sexy boots. I imagined she had nothing on underneath, but I knew that couldn't possibly be true. She carried a medium-sized canvas duffel bag. I just stared for a moment and then caught myself. So did she.

"James, are you going to invite me in or just gawk at me like a high school kid?"

"God, sorry Brit; come on in. You just caught me a little off-guard. You look great, not that you don't normally…." I was feeling rather awkward. She did her best to make me feel comfortable.

"James, it's OK. I know you look, and I like it when men look at me. If I didn't want your attention, I would wear pants and ugly penny loafers with this coat. You are going to be taking pictures of me in a lot less than this…." She smiled and slipped in the door, just barely brushing me as she passed. There is plenty of room in my entry, so was the brush deliberate? Or was I just projecting my own desires into her actions? She was quite a flirt at times. I never read much into it. I was old enough to be her father, and she flirted with other men and women all the time. She was certainly attractive enough that she could have her pick of more eligible and age-appropriate men; she couldn't be interested in a middle aged man like me, so I dismissed her flirting as just harmless fun.

"James, where are we going to shoot? I must admit to snooping around here a little at the last cast party, and I don't think I know of any place to do this. Your basement is full of stuff, your living room is charming, but not right.... Where are we going to take these pictures?" She looked at me and waited for my reply.

"Brittany, I have a secret out back. It is perfect for a studio. This place has an old bomb shelter in the backyard. I fixed it up and use it for a study/studio/private getaway. I don't tell anyone about it because I like to keep it private. You'll be the first person, other than Gwen, who has ever been down there."

"Lead on, MacDuff. Let me see your private lair." She picked her bag up and waited for me to show her the way. I led her out the back door and into the woods. I lifted the hatch and flipped on the light switch for the stairway. Even in broad daylight, the stairs are fairly dark at the bottom. We made our way down the stairs. I turned to look at Brittany's face as we descended. She was fascinated by the looks of it. I slid open the bolt on the door and swung it open. Flipped on the lights. Motioned Brittany in before me.

"This is cool! Can you live down here? Do you ever? We should have the next cast party down here! Why haven't you told anybody about this? It is so dope!" Her face shone.

"Whoa there! One thing at a time. I take it you like

my playroom?"

"Hell, yeah! James, this is awesome. I'm glad you haven't told us about it—none of us would ever get anything done; we'd be bugging you to hang down here. Do you have a TV down here? Stereo? Computer? Can I look around?" She could barely contain herself. I was pleased. This was going to be better than I thought.

"Brittany, feel free. The bathroom is over there, the storeroom next to it, the bunk room on this wall, and you can see the kitchen facilities behind that burgundy fabric. This place was built for a small family to inhabit after a nuclear exchange; it is quite complete. Make yourself at home. The storeroom will be doubling as your dressing room; I've got your stuff laid out. Take your time; look around. I'm glad you like it." Once again, I had blathered on like a professor. It was a wonder my victims didn't die from boredom before I had a chance to play with them. She might as well like her final surroundings. No need to die in a dark alley or some other shithole.

Brittany took a little while to scope the place out. She put her bag in the storeroom and checked out the kitchen area. She made quiet comments to herself about how cool the place was and how clean and bright. She obviously was comfortable. At ease. That would make everything later so much sweeter. So happy. So trusting. So unsuspecting of the fate awaiting her. I relished the thought of her face when I revealed the truth to her, when I played the "greatest hits" video I had edited just for her—the horror she would feel when she realized that I was not going to release her from her bonds and that she would not leave this place. Ever. Not under her own power, anyway.

"Brittany, ready for the first set? Anything you need?"

"I'm ready. I hope you are…." She smiled that

mischievous smile of hers again.

"Why don't you take off your coat and stay a while then?" I used one of my dad's corny old lines. "Unless you're cold. I can crank the heat up a little more if you need me to."

"I'm fine. I'll go change now. Which costume first?"

"I'm pretty anal retentive…they're all on the rack in the storeroom, grouped left to right. Footwear directly underneath each outfit. I'm nothing if not organized." She disappeared into the storeroom. I heard her giggling as she got dressed.

I flipped on the switch to turn on the lights and the three hidden video cameras. While I hadn't enjoyed my time with Maura as much as the others, hers had been the first three-camera shoot. I got great footage and edited the whole experience into what was probably a very marketable snuff film. Maybe someday when I felt the police's noose tightening around me, I would "leak" that video out onto the Internet. I was sure there were many others like me who would appreciate it.

Brit came out a few minutes later.

"James. A school girl outfit? Couldn't you be a little more original than that?"

"Brit, I am a teacher…." I grinned and motioned her over to the chair. "I know it's a little cliché, but the little plaid skirt/white stocking thing really works for a lot of guys. Me included, if you must know."

"OK, but I was hoping you'd have a little more imagination than that…." She winked at me and sat down. She would shit if she knew just how vivid my imagination was. I had her simply sit while I checked light levels and adjusted the color balance. I could fix a lot later with Photoshop, but I liked to take good shots up front. Kind of took me back to my old film camera days. When I was satisfied, I started having Brittany pose.

"OK, Brittany, loosen the tie. Can you unbutton the next button on the shirt? Thank you. Leg up on the desk. Turn a little more to the left. OK. Next to the right. Got it. Head up a little. Wink." This went on for a little while. I was feeling out the boundaries, seeing what Brittany was comfortable with and what she wasn't. So far, nothing seemed to make her uncomfortable. I was pleased. I decided to push a little farther. "Brit, could you go back into the storeroom and take the bra off? Tie the shirt like a halter and really loosen the tie. Mess up your hair just a little too." Brit smiled and turned her back, opened the shirt, and removed the bra. She tied the shirt and then turned back to me.

"Like this?" She flashed a quick grin. "Is this what you want?"

"Perfect. You look great. Back to work." I had her go through another range of poses. She seemed to enjoy herself and the camera loved her. I loved her attitude. After a few more shots, I told her it was time to take a break. She could change into a robe or stay in this costume while we broke, whichever she preferred. She chose to stay in costume. She sat on the edge of the table and asked for a bottle of water. As I handed it to her, she leaned forward more than necessary to take it from me. The shirt fell a little away from her breasts, and I couldn't prevent myself from staring at the fullness of her cleavage. When she sat back up, she caught my eye and I blushed a bit. She just smiled.

"Do you want me to change now? Are you ready for more?" Brittany asked.

"Any time you are. You're the one working. I'm just hitting the shutter button." Brittany hopped off the table and scooted into the storeroom. I grabbed a Dr. Pepper and waited for her to appear in the next outfit I'd chosen for her. I hoped she wouldn't chide my lack of imagination after putting on this one. Thus far, this had been going swimmingly. Better than I could have hoped for. I was very pleased with my choice of Brittany. I wanted to see more and couldn't wait to feel her in my hands. I could tell that I would be able to play for a long time. Brittany was attitude-appropriate for our afternoon delight. Brittany came out of the storeroom in a shiny latex corset, latex elbow-length gloves, fence-net stockings and high-heeled boots—all in a ruby red that looked marvelous against her creamy white skin. She practically strutted when she came out.

"OK, you are forgiven for the school girl outfit. This is much nastier. Don't you think?" She ran her hands over the shiny latex, accentuating her womanly curves. "I like the zipper and buckles on the front of the corset. I could adjust it and make my boobs look just right. They are just right, aren't they, James?"

"Brittany, they are perfect. I mean…ummm…you look perfect. Just right for the shoot." I stammered a little. I got back to business and started having Brittany pose. The more I asked for, the more she liked it. I didn't think she was faking it; I think she was getting off on our shoot as much as I was, if not more. I decided to push a little further….

"Brittany, would you be OK with a ball gag for a few shots?"

"Sure thing. Whatever you want. You're in charge."

"I'm not entirely sure of that young lady." I wasn't anticipating an enthusiastic response like that. So I asked another question. "Would you mind if your hands were bound?" She just looked at me blankly for a moment. Then she smiled a Mona Lisa smile and said, "I thought you'd never ask." I got the gag and straps and put them on. I bound her hands in front of her and had her kneel on the floor. Then I eagerly began to take pictures. I swear she was smiling behind the gag. I felt a familiar rise in my nether regions. I wanted to put my hands on her now, feel her pulse and squeeze, but I wanted it to last. I felt like a sixteen-year-old boy getting his first piece of tail, I was so eager. But I had to reel it in, had to make it last. This girl was priceless and meant to be ravished and relished. After a few more shots, I untied her hands and removed the gag.

"I know latex is hot and sweaty. Why don't you put on the robe in the storeroom and come back out for a breather?" I know I was hot and bothered and needed a break. I hoped she did too.

"OK, although I really like it. I like knowing you have a wild side too, James. Makes you much hotter. Much." She disappeared into the makeshift dressing room. What did she mean by that? Why would she care that a fifty year old had a "wild side?" Was there something about this girl that I didn't see? I knew it had to be my imagination. I was reading way too much into a simple tease. Brittany returned in the silk men's robe that had looked so nice on Rene. It certainly did the trick on Brit as well. We sat and talked a while, shared some cookies and some water and some laughs. Brittany said nothing more that teased. It was as if she never had. Puzzling. Oh, well. She'd find out soon enough just how wild my wild side really was.

After a couple of more minutes, Brittany went in to change into our last outfit for the day. I had picked out a set of black leather short-shorts, a leather bra, a dog collar, and leather arm cuffs with sturdy D-rings. Thigh-high black leather boots completed the ensemble. The D-rings would make binding her so much more secure. I liked the look of the dog collar, although I planned to remove it when I was ready for the final act. I planned to remove it, all except the arm cuffs, before I throttled the life out of her. I do like to look…. But when she came out, I was more than a little confused.

"James, I hope that you won't be mad, but before you shoot me in the leather, could you take a few of me in my coat? I think you'll like it…." Once again, I saw a conspiratorial gleam in her eye. Who was I to refuse one of her last requests?

"Sure. I don't have to shoot in any particular order. If this will make you happy, fine." I moved to my tripod and camera. Brittany moved over to the chair on the red fabric like I asked her to. She was a natural. She put one leg up on the chair, unbuttoned a couple of lower buttons of the trenchcoat, and revealed quite a bit of shapely leg. She moved well and responded immediately to any requests I had. She even suggested poses I hadn't thought of. Her smiles were real, not fake or forced. She loved the camera, and it loved her. She undid a couple of her top coat buttons, baring some of her ample cleavage. When she leaned forward for a shot, I didn't see a hint of a top or a bra. The shadow hid her bosom from view, but I was intrigued. What did she have on under her coat? I'd know soon enough. I'd know all the secrets of her young form in due time. I felt my cock stiffen a little at the thought.

Brit looked at me and suggested she turn her back to the camera and look over her shoulder. Once again, who was I to deny a dying girl a polite request? She had been so cooperative and pleasant that I was starting to have second thoughts about killing her. Maybe just the photo shoot would be satisfying enough. But I couldn't carry just the shoot far enough to enjoy myself thoroughly. And then what? She would know about my playroom. I couldn't trust anyone with that secret, not if I were to continue with my beloved hobby.

Brit looked back at me and smiled. She undid a couple of more buttons, draped the coat below her shoulders, and looked back. She winked. I gawked. Her back was bare. No straps, no top, just creamy skin and sexy shoulders. She lowered the coat a little more. It was draped to just above her buttocks and still not a hint of clothing. Had she really come out in just the coat and boots? I hadn't planned on this. I never expected this. I thought I would have to coax her a little like I had Rene to get her into something revealing. And here she was, doing a striptease for me, unbidden. I snapped several shots in quick order. A little sweat formed at my brow. She half-turned toward me. Her breasts were barely covered, really just the nipples and the very bottoms were covered by the coat. I could see the lovely curve of her belly and her cute navel. It was unbelievably sexy. This girl was rocking my world.

"Is this OK, James? Do you like it?" She paused. "Can I undo the last button? Would you like that? I would." She reached for the button with one hand and held the fabric together with the other. I could see the entirety of one of her breasts now. While I've never been a fan of large-breasted women, Brittany was stunning. I couldn't answer. I just looked at her and nodded. She slowly undid the final button and let the coat fall to the floor. She stood there in all her glory, naked as the day she was born, save for the black leather boots. I was speechless.

"Aren't you going to take a picture?" She positively purred. I stood there, dumb. I couldn't think, speak, or move. All I could do was look at this magnificent creature standing before me.

"James, are you all right?" Brittany looked concerned. I took in a deep breath and gathered my wits about me.

"Brittany, this is indeed a surprise. I don't mean to just stare, but you certainly caught me off-guard. I, uh…." I stopped. Brittany stepped forward. She moved toward me slowly, seductively. I really wasn't prepared for that. I involuntarily backed up a step.

"James, I'm sorry. I didn't mean to offend you. I just wanted…." I interrupted her by moving forward and putting my hands on her shoulders, and I said, "We have to talk…." I picked up her coat and put it around her. I led her to the table and had her sit across from me.

"James, I have a little confession. I have a crush on you. A big one. I…when you asked if you could photograph me…I…uh…James, I've had a crush on you like… forever. I'm sorry. I…."

"Brittany, don't be sorry. Christ, woman, how could I be offended? Surprised. But offended? Never. You are young and talented and beautiful and everything that a man could ever desire. I am just rather surprised, that's all. I really don't know how to react." And I didn't. What the fuck! This lovely twenty-something was actually interested in a used up old crust? Was she nuts? Was I? How was I supposed to react? She got up, walked around the table, and sat on my lap, straddling my legs, facing me.

I started to say something, but she stopped me with her finger on my lips. She shrugged her coat off and started to unbutton my shirt. She kissed my chest as each button revealed more. She took my shirt off and undid my belt and the top button of my jeans. She paused and pressed her lips to mine and kissed me. I kissed back. Her lips parted and her tongue found mine. My arms were around her and I held her tight. I ran my hands all over her beautiful young body, and she held me in her arms. She lifted herself off my lap and onto the table and returned her attention to my jeans. She unzipped the fly and pulled my rigid member free. She started to lower herself on to me. I put my hands under her lovely bottom and held her off.

"Brittany…what about a condom? Birth control. Sorry to be a wet blanket, but I am not prepared for this. I never dreamed tha…" She put her hand on my mouth and made a shushing noise.

"James, I am going to tell you something I've never told anyone here at MNC. I had cancer when I was young. Very young. Fourteen. Ovarian cancer. They tried to save my ovaries, but they saved me instead. I can't get pregnant. And unless you have much darker secrets than I think you do, I don't think we have to worry about nasty diseases. So are you going to let me finish this or not? I really want to do this. Now. Here. With you. I've wanted you for a long time." I moved my hands to allow her to follow her desired course.

"Silly girl. I could be your father." But that was my last objection. We spent the balance of the afternoon and most of the evening exploring each other. Pleasuring each other. I'd not been with another woman since Gwen had died, other than my rudeness with Rene, nor had I been with anyone before Gwen. This was new ground for me, and I was loving every moment. We had made love on the table, on the floor, wrapped in my backdrop velvet, everywhere in the little shelter. The shelter was a mess when we finally lay in a crumpled tangle on the bed, sweating and panting and shaking and laughing, exhausted and exhilarated.

"Is it dinner time? I'm famished!" Brit propped herself on her arms and smiled at me.

"I'm hungry; you gave me quite a workout. There's a reason why old guys like me don't get to sleep with beautiful young women. We can't keep up." I touched her glistening skin and kissed her gently.

"You're not old, and you more than kept up. I'm not complaining. I'm just hungry. Feed me. Soon. Or I'll get ugly and grumpy." She bit at my finger and laughed.

"OK. Shower first? I'm sure I smell of sweat and sex." I swung my legs off the side of the bed and started to get up. Brittany grabbed my shoulders and pulled me backwards. When I fell back, she planted her lips on mine and kissed me hard. When she let me up for air, I said, "I think I'm going to have to keep you locked up down here and use you as my toy. I'll come down when I want sex and when you need to be fed. Otherwise, I'll just keep you locked in my own private dungeon." She smiled a sly smile and told me she would quite willingly be my toy, but I didn't have to keep her locked up. She wanted to be here with me and wanted me to have sex with her again. Soon. Often.

I had a problem. A serious one. While I was certainly flattered by her attentions and loved the idea of having her again, having a "girlfriend" could certainly complicate things. As much as I wanted both the social contact and the physical release of sex, I wanted to pursue my hobby more. I lusted for the feel of a throat in my hands, craved the look of horror in my playmates' eyes when they realized my intent, and I couldn't be comfortable with anyone living knowing of my little hideaway. I didn't want to have to account for my whereabouts to a significant other. Didn't want to try to keep track of any more lies than I had to. Didn't want to risk being found out because of a slip of the tongue or talking in my sleep. No, Brittany was definitely a problem. A stunning problem, but a problem nonetheless. I really should have killed her right then and there, but I also wanted to add a twist to the game.

Maybe I would see her for a while, really get her

attached beyond what any of my previous playmates had been, and then kill her. Could I trust her to keep our "relationship" a secret? Could I trust her to keep this place a secret? Could I keep myself from getting too attached? Could I let her into my life and still keep my hobby hidden from her? If she spent any amount of time down here, she could stumble on my collection of videos from my other play dates. They weren't hidden; they were neatly labeled and in a file drawer with my other discs and camera paraphernalia here in the shelter. So keeping her around for even a little while was fraught with potential problems, but the challenge was enticing. What to do…?

When she got up and started toward the shower in all her naked glory, my "little brain" made my decision for me. I would toy with her for a while before the kill. Seeing her perfect hourglass figure, hips swaying seductively as she walked, covered in a sheen of perspiration that I had caused, I couldn't resist her. When she looked over her shoulder and asked whether I was coming to shower with her, I had no will to do anything but follow. I turned the water on and we enjoyed some good clean fun in the shower. We stayed in there as long as there was hot water, exploring every inch of each other with our hands and mouths. The hot water streamed down her perfect form. I was in awe of the goddess in my shower. I was delighted to be an invited guest, to be encouraged to touch this young nubile girl. I made sure that she knew just how it made me feel and how special this was to me. I let her know that there would be more special times to come. I could hardly contain myself. I told myself it was a good thing that I had listened to my penis instead of my head. Told myself that the kill would be so much sweeter this way.

When the hot water ran out we got out and toweled each other dry and got dressed. We made our way back to the house. I opened a bottle of wine and made a quick dinner. Spinach salad, asparagus with balsamic vinegar and pine nuts, some pasta with a parmesan sauce and two juicy rib-eye steaks. I told her there was a definite advantage to dating old men rather than boys—we can cook and are more attentive than testosterone-poisoned twenty-somethings can ever be. She laughed and agreed. She told me that none of her boyfriends had ever cooked for her. She said she could easily get used to this kind of treatment. I knew it was time for a little talk....

"Brittany, I don't mean to spoil things by bringing up a delicate topic, but I'm afraid I must." She stopped eating, put down her fork and looked across the table at me. I continued, "I want to see you again. And again. I haven't felt like this for a long time. Thank you. But, well, we need to talk...." I paused.

"James, is something wrong? Second thoughts? Did I do something?" She looked worried.

"Oh, God, no. You're perfect. I just have some concerns for you and for me. Brittany, you do know that I am fifty? That I have kids older than you? Our age difference is certainly a concern. More important, though, is that I am a prof at MNC. Now I know you are not one of my students. And you are an adult. And we are both consenting adults. But the 'Miss Grundys' of the world are out in force these days. We have to be discreet. You can't risk your reputation, and I can't risk my career. I don't think there is anything wrong if we see each other. I know there is nothing legally wrong, either, but...."

"James, I understand," she interrupted. "I know we have to keep it quiet. I've watched you for a long time and wanted to say something for a long time. But I knew how careful you always were. You are never alone with any of us for very long. Even when we flirt, you are careful not to cross any lines you shouldn't. You're a gentleman. I'm a big girl; I understand your worries about appearances. I know the university frowns on this kind of thing. The last thing I want is trouble…well…other than the fun kind!" I looked across the table at this beautiful creature. Could I trust her? Could I really trust her to be discreet for a while? Could I trust myself to keep cool? If the answers were "yes," then this could be a fun ride. And the end…I couldn't wait. I tingled with excitement just thinking about it. If the answers were "no," I would have to kill her now rather than later. I decided that the ayes had it….

We both ate with gusto, our afternoon's exertions having fueled our appetites. Dinner was full of laughs and silly glances, pleasant conversation and sexual tension. I hadn't felt this alive in what seemed like forever. I had this beautiful creature in my home, a plaything waiting for the ultimate game, yet she had no idea what game we were really playing. She was playing "Bang the Old Professor" and I was playing "Kill Her with Pleasure." We'd both get our enjoyment from our games. I suspected that in the end I would find mine more satisfying. I wouldn't end up in a cold cistern full of corpses.

"James, I want to stay the night, but I have got to get going. I have to finish my homework. Stupid paper. Ugh." She pushed her chair back and got up. I followed her to the door. She turned and put her arms around me. Kissed me deeply. Flashed that smile again. Kissed me again and slid her hand to my crotch. "I guess you really don't want me to go either!" I blushed as I felt my cock stiffen and try to burst free from its denim prison. I told her she was right, but I understood. I had to prepare for classes tomorrow; I said I had some papers to read and grade. I put my arms around her and pulled her closer. I cupped her perfect buttocks in my hands and squeezed her tightly to me. I kissed her once again and then spanked her lightly on her bottom. "Get out of here before I take you right here and now. Go home little girl…." She laughed and gave me one last quick kiss and was gone. I closed the door and plopped myself into my favorite chair.

No sooner had she left than I started to panic. What the fuck was I thinking? How could I be so stupid? I had showed her my shelter and let her live to tell the tale. I thought I knew her, thought I could trust her to be discreet, but could I trust her that much? Stupid, stupid, stupid! James, you are letting your cock think for you. This girl will get you caught. Are you ready for that? I kept arguing with myself all night. How could I know she wouldn't tell anybody about us? How could I trust a kid to keep her mouth shut? And what were her motives, really? Why would a beautiful young thing like her have any interest in an old guy like me? She could have her pick of young suitors. Why me? Why now? What did she hope to get out of this? Surely she didn't see any future with me. I'm not the most attractive man on the planet, so what was up? Still…the sex had been great. I certainly looked forward to more. I liked looking at her naked form. I loved the feel of her skin on mine. I loved feeling her muscles tense and relax as we coupled. Her mouth, her breasts, her firm bottom, her lovely curves, her attitude, it all was appealing. I would have to try to keep my cool and to keep tabs on her without seeming paranoid. I would play along and finish her when I felt there was any danger. Yeah, that was it. I would be able to sense when she was getting wise to me. And the rumor mill at MNC was such that I would know if she had spilled anything sensitive. So I calmed myself enough to wash the dishes, pour a double shot of B&B, and grade papers. I had a problem and I liked it.

The next few days passed uneventfully. I just went

to class, went to rehearsal, did everything as I normally would. I was careful not to pay any undue attention to Brittany at rehearsals, just acted as if nothing new was up. I really didn't know how I was expected to act. This whole affair thing was new to me. I'd never even thought of having one while Gwen was alive, and I had never even dated before I met Gwen. What was the proper etiquette? What did Miss Manners have to say about a fifty-year-old serial killer and his twenty-year-old fuck buddy? I doubted there was any online advice for my own situation.

*

It turned out that Brittany took the reins. I didn't have to worry about proper etiquette any longer. After Wednesday's rehearsal, I was talking with a small group of cast members about the rehearsal. Brit naturally joined the discussion. I tried not to notice her any more than any of the other cast members, but her short skirt and scoop-necked top conspired against me. One by one, we all said our goodbyes, and then, Brittany and I were alone in front of the Pearl. She was obviously pleased, as was I.

"Do you know how hard it has been sitting through rehearsal and not touching you? James, I just wanted to come sit next to you when I wasn't onstage. I wanted to kiss you. I wanted to do a lot more than that, but I figured I'd better keep my distance. It's hard being quiet. I just want to feel you next to me. I want to feel you inside me again."

"Nice to see you, too!" I laughed. "You are rather direct, young lady. And I like that. I have had it rough the past couple of days. I don't know if I'm a good enough actor to keep my thoughts from showing. I tried really hard not to look at you tonight, but I was undressing you in my head all night. I…um…I'm really awkward at this. I've never 'had an affair' before. New turf for me." I paused.

Now what? I wondered. *Take her home?* I was tempted.

"James, I think I forgot something in the theater. Can we go back in and look for it?" She grinned at me and let her hand gently brush my jeans. "Please…?" I got my keys out and unlocked the front door. I locked it again as soon as we had crossed the threshold. She took my hand and led me into the dark auditorium. It was eerie with just the exit lights and the ghost light on.

As soon as we were out of sight from the street, she stopped and put her lips on mine. Her hands found the buttons on my shirt, and she started to open it. I fumbled with her top and bra. I was far from smooth. Bra clasps are like bank vaults in my hands. She laughed and finished the job for me. I grabbed her now bare waist and pulled her close. We kissed our way to the floor. I pushed her skirt up and found that she had no panties on. "I took them off in the dressing room just before I came out. I hope you don't mind." I didn't. She undid my belt and pants and freed my rigid member. She lowered herself on to me and I ran my hands over her marvelous hips and waist. I grabbed her firm breasts and felt them heave as we thrust ourselves onto and into each other. I climaxed quickly. I was embarrassed, but she was pleased. She collapsed onto me and we held each other in the aisle of the dark theater. She found ways to coax my member back to life, and I gave her the attention she properly deserved. A while later, we were hot and sweaty and spent.

"James, you are never to call yourself 'old' in my presence ever again. None of my younger lovers have ever made me feel that way. I don't know how many times you made me come. I hope I can keep up with you." In the pale glow of the ghost light, I could see her face and she looked happy. Satisfied. Perfect. She had the special "just fucked hairdo", and her face was glistening with a light sheen of perspiration. I stroked her face and kissed her gently. Neither of us wanted to move. Neither wanted to break the spell. The sound of someone fumbling at the theater's front door did that for us.

"Shit! Who is that?" I grabbed my pants and hurriedly pulled them on. Brit grabbed her clothes and started dressing frantically. We heard more rattling at the front door. Then it stopped. We looked at each other and laughed. "It must have been one of the Northton cops checking the door," I said. "They do that as they walk their beats at night. Scared the crap out of me one night when I was working on a set after midnight."

"It certainly got my attention!" said Brittany. "I almost peed myself."

"You're so wet there already," I said, "how would you know anyway?"

Brittany slapped my shoulder. "It's your fault. You're to blame. I was saving myself," she quoted from *The Rocky Horror Picture Show*. We both laughed and fell into each other's arms. We finished getting dressed at a more leisurely pace.

"Do you want to come back to my place?" I asked. I hoped she would; I was ready for another round already.

"Can't. Homework. I'd love to, but we'll have to wait." She frowned and continued, "I'm having a hard time juggling class, work, theater, and friends as it is. Now I find myself wanting to spend all my time naked with you. What's a girl to do?"

"Put on sexy leather and screw me in that. That way you won't have to spend all your time naked with me!" I grabbed the back of her neck and drew her near so I could kiss her just under her ear.

"Sounds great, but I really gotta get this homework done. I'll see you tomorrow at rehearsal. Sweet dreams."

With that, she smiled and headed up the aisle. I watched as best I could in the dim light. Damn she was sexy. This little girl was full of surprises.

*

We carried on in a similar fashion for the next couple of weeks. Brit had a wild side that I found quite exciting. She kept pushing me further and further. While I had certainly imagined some of the things she wanted, I had not experienced most. My sex life with Gwen had been satisfying but, I realized now, somewhat limited in scope. Still, no matter how much I was enjoying the ride, I had to keep my eye on the prize. The feel of her young body next to mine was exhilarating. The feel of her life ebbing beneath my grasp was even more tempting. I knew I had to bring this to a close, and soon. I didn't know how much longer I could trust myself, how long I could stay relatively detached, and how long I could rely on Brittany to keep our secret. Almost getting caught in the aisle of the Pearl had made me realize this had to be short term. Once again, Brittany surprised me and offered up a gift that I had never hoped for in my wildest dreams.

"James, can I make a confession?"

"It is hard to keep any secrets when you are naked. Go on…."

"James, I am, hmmm, no beating around the bush. I am bisexual. I have a girlfriend. I hope you aren't mad that I've kept this from you."

"Brit, I am thankful for everything that we share. How could I be upset about a girlfriend? I'm actually rather turned on by the idea. May I ask who she is? Do I know her?" I propped myself up on my elbows to get a better look at my young friend.

"Stephanie. Stephanie Watson. We've been lovers since I got to MNC, almost three years now." That was

242

interesting. Stephanie was a delightful young woman. She didn't do theater, but I had met her at a couple of cast parties. I'd never noticed whom she had arrived with.

"Does she know about us?" I tried to make sure I sounded interested rather than concerned. But I was concerned. Very.

"She's not stupid; she knows I'm seeing a man. I smell like sex when I come home and she has, ummm, tasted you on me sometimes. But, no, she has no idea who you are. Just that you are the best male lover I've ever had. And she wants to meet you. I told her you were very private and a little shy, so I told her I'd have to ask. I like what we have too much to violate your trust. So I haven't even hinted who I might be seeing." This was good and bad. She was reassuring me that she had not revealed us to anyone else, but that someone knew she was seeing someone on the sly was not good. It did present another interesting possibility, however.

"Is she into fat old men, too? Is she bi?" Brit bit my shoulder. Hard.

"Pig! You dirty bastard!" She smiled a sly smile after she said this so I knew I wasn't really in trouble. "Yes, she is bi and she likes men. And I'll bite you again if you call yourself fat or old again."

"This strikes me as a tricky situation. If I tell you that I'm not interested, you might think me prudish and boring. If I say I am, you might think I'm not satisfied with you. Quite a dilemma...."

"I would like it very much if you would take pictures of us. Together. I would like it more if you joined us after...if you think you can handle two wild women at the same time, you old man, you!" It was my turn to "punish" her. I slapped her bare bottom lightly with my hand. "That's for calling me old, you little wench!" We wrestled a little; I got the better of her and took her over my knee and threatened a right proper paddling. She just laughed and told me to bring it on. So I did. Fairly gently at first. A little harder with each spank. She became more aroused and vocal with each slap of her behind. I had left a good-sized handprint on her butt. She just purred her approval. I grabbed one of my ties from the bedside table and tied her hands together. She asked whether I was going to restrain her feet, too. I got a couple of more ties and put her face down on the bed; then I tied her ankles to the bedposts.

"Is this what you want? Is this what you need?" I climbed onto her and put my hands around her, cupping her breasts in my hands. I pinched her nipples and entered her. I thrust so hard that the bed shook. I was so excited that it was over way too fast for me. She just giggled and asked me whether I'd like to do that with her and Stephanie. I told her I would.

*

Stephanie and Brit were going to come over the following Saturday. I had never thought of a double, but killing one while the other watched was too tempting to pass up. The photo shoot would be fun, too, but the kill would be the thrill. I was almost salivating as I imagined the absolute horror that the second victim would experience. I was practically shaking as I laid out the wardrobe for the shoot and prepared the cameras, then returned to the house to wait for them.

When Brit and Stephanie arrived at my front door, I was blown away. Brit was in a tight little skirt and a halter top. Stephanie was dressed in a simple shirt-dress and sandals. And a blindfold.

"I thought this would add to the mystique," said Brittany, "so I told Steph that the only way I would bring her here was if she let me blindfold her. Does that meet with your satisfaction, 'Mr. X'?" Brit flashed her smile. I just nodded and stepped out of the door so they could come inside.

"Before I take off your blindfold, Stephanie, I need to swear you to secrecy. I'm serious."

"OK, Brit, OK. Just take this thing off me. I want to see this man you keep telling me about. I want to have some fun!" Stephanie obviously had the same attitude as Brittany. I looked forward to the rest of the evening. More than I could ever tell.

"OK, Brittany, enough cloak and dagger. Release your prisoner…." Brittany removed Stephanie's blindfold. Stephanie looked around the room and then directly at me. She certainly looked surprised.

"Dr. Martin. You? I am ah…um…oh wow! I need to sit down." Stephanie moved over to the couch. "Brittany, are you for real? Are you having an affair with Dr. Martin? I'm waiting for you to yell 'April Fool' even though it isn't April."

"Stephanie, no joke. He's it. The real deal. Are you OK with this?" Brittany sat next to Stephanie on the couch. She reached over and took her hands into her lap. "If you aren't OK, you can go home. But you can't blow the whistle on us. This is too good for me to give up."

"You just caught me off-guard. You told me you were fucking an older man, but a prof? I just need a little time to digest this. I love you, Brittany. I trust you. Can we just do the photos, you know, just you and me? That sounds like fun, but I don't think I can fuck a fossil. No offense, Dr. Martin." Stephanie looked over at me and then back at Brit.

"Brittany, who said anything about me having sex with Stephanie? I thought we were just going to take

245

pictures of two hot young women...." I lied and hoped Brittany would catch on and play along.

"James, I just wanted to surprise you. I should have told you what I really had in mind, but...I'm sorry. I hope I didn't queer this whole thing." Played like a trouper! Brittany was fast on the uptake. Of course we had talked about a threesome. I just wanted her to put Stephanie at ease. I had big plans for the evening, and they certainly involved Stephanie. Now that she was in on our little affair, my plans for the evening would have to include her. I could never let her out of my sight again. Brittany was enough of a risk. I couldn't chance anything more with Stephanie. I would have to kill them both tonight.

We sat and talked in the living room for a few minutes. I got drinks for all of us. Brittany and I worked well together, defusing Stephanie's apprehension. Brittany was a good actress. I'm sure Stephanie bought it. We had a couple of more drinks, and then I asked whether they were still up for photos or they wanted to call it a night. Brittany leaned over, kissed Stephanie, put on her "sad puppy dog eyes," and asked Stephanie whether they could go into the studio. Brittany promised that she'd make it up to Stephanie for the shock she'd given her about who the "third man" was. I told Stephanie I would let her review any of the pictures and give her final say over what was kept and what was discarded.

Slowly, the alcohol and persuasion worked; Stephanie agreed to head to the studio. I let Brittany lead us to the shelter, let her have the fun of sharing how cool the place was to her lover. Stephanie was as fascinated with the shelter as Brittany had been and seemed fairly well at ease. Damage control had been a success. After a little while, I told Brittany to take Stephanie to the storeroom to get dressed. When they were changing, I slid the bolt home on the door and locked the Master lock. I powered up the cameras and waited for them to emerge.

Brittany and Stephanie came out in the leather corsets and boots I had for them. Stephanie had on the dog collar and leash. Brittany had the wrist and ankle cuffs with the sturdy D rings. Perfect. I was so ready for this. Fucking around with Brittany had been great fun. I loved making her sweat and moan. But I was having more difficulty dealing with my growing paranoia. I ached for a kill. It had been a long time, and the last two had not been as satisfying. I would do my best to change that tonight. A doubleheader, so to speak. I asked them whether they were ready to pose. They both said they were, so we got down to business. I had Brittany "walk the dog" with Stephanie. I had them kiss. I had them improvise however they wanted. Without my even asking, they started to undress each other. Stephanie undid the laces on Brittany's corset and exposed her breasts. Brittany did the same to Steph. They laid down and started to fondle and suckle each other's breasts.

They were less and less aware of me as time went on. I just watched and snapped the shutter. The action got hotter and hotter. Stephanie pushed Brittany's panties aside and played with her pussy. Soon they were both naked, save for the cuffs and collar, and going at it full bore. I stopped snapping stills—I knew the video cameras would capture it all. After a while, Brittany stopped and looked up at me. She smiled and motioned me over. I shook my head "No" and then spoke.

"Sorry to interrupt, but can I pose you again? Is that OK with you two?"

"Not yet, James. Can we see the pictures so far? Can we take a little break first?" Brittany looked up at me and then back to Stephanie. "I'm sure Stephanie would like to see them as much as I would." Stephanie squeezed Brit's hand and nodded.

"Sure thing. I'm ready for a little break too. I must confess that after a while, I stopped taking pictures and just enjoyed the view. You two…shit…I never imagined I'd ever see anything like you two going at it in my life. Not for real, anyway. Oh, my God. Go put on whatever you want to wear while we're looking at the pics. I eagerly await your return."

I got drinks for everyone and turned the monitor for them to see. They had both put on silky robes that I had in the dressing room for them. I put the pictures on "slideshow," and we sat and watched. Brittany and Stephanie were obviously aroused by seeing themselves on the screen. They cuddled closer and cooed with delight. What dirty-minded little girls these two were! An admirable trait, one every sweet young thing should have. My idea of a perfect woman was one who was a saint on the streets and a whore in the bedroom.

When we got to the end of the stills, I asked Stephanie whether there were any that she wanted me to delete. She smiled and told me there were a couple that made her look fat that she wanted to make go away. We all laughed since Stephanie is tall and willowy, but I let her scroll through and delete the ones she thought made her look fat. I thought she looked mighty fine in all of them. Didn't matter, though. I had video of the whole shoot. She could delete the entire file if she wanted. I'd have a greatest hits video edited in a couple of days to enjoy at my leisure.

After our break, I told them it was time to shoot some more. When they asked what to wear, I told them I wanted to pick up where we had left off, if that was OK with them. They exchanged a sly glance and shucked off their robes. They both stood in their naked glory with just the leather collar and cuffs for accent. I told them to stand

and embrace and caress each other. I busied myself snapping pictures as they kissed and fondled each other.

After a time, I told them I wanted to change things up a bit. I handed Stephanie four leather straps and told her to tie Brittany to the chair. She put the straps through the D rings on the cuffs and bound Brittany very securely. I was pleased. One restrained and one to play with. Perfect. Just about time to reveal our true purpose. Time for the world to come crashing down on them both. I told Brittany to struggle a bit, to test the job Stephanie had done. Brittany was going nowhere. Stephanie had her expertly tied. I wondered whether bondage was on their normal menu. I told Stephanie to take a break while I shot a few pictures of Brit bound to the chair. Stephanie sat down on another chair, and I took a few pictures of Brittany struggling in her chair.

"Stephanie, your turn. Could you go sit on Brittany's lap, facing her? I want you to tease her a bit with your body. Tempt her, tease her, torment her a little. Brush yourself close and let her try to reach." Stephanie practically leapt at the suggestion. She positioned herself as I told her to and teased the hell out of Brit. Once again, I shot rapidly. After a few minutes, I told Stephanie to take another break. Brittany looked genuinely frustrated and aroused. I liked the look. I would like what would come next even more.

"Stephanie, would you get the leash and the riding crop from the dressing room? Thanks. Brittany, not much longer. I'll turn you loose and we'll change things up in a couple of minutes. You OK?"

"Yeah, this is fun. I'm just fine. I'm making a little mess on your chair. I am so wet from all this that I am practically sitting in a puddle here. Someone better be planning on taking real good care of me soon."

Stephanie came out with the leash and the crop as requested. I asked her whether it would be OK if I put the leash onto her collar. She slowly nodded an "OK," so I fastened the leash to the D-ring on the collar. I then told her that I wanted her next to Brittany, on all fours. I gave the end of the leash to Brittany to hold and snapped a few pictures. I was getting bored with all the pretense, so I decided I would start in on the main course now. I took the leash from Brit's bound hand and led Stephanie to the middle of the room; then I tied the leash to the ring on the ceiling. She had some freedom of movement, but not much without the collar choking her. I wanted her to have a little wiggle room. I wanted her to be able to squirm. I took a couple of pictures just to make her think we were still really on track with that. Then I grabbed the crop and gave her a couple of short raps on her bottom. Sharp enough to leave a mark. She jumped and gasped and quickly found the limits of her lead.

"Not cool! That hurt!" Stephanie looked at me in surprise.

"No it didn't. Not really. Not as much as this will!" I slashed her thigh with the crop and held nothing back. She jumped again and gagged when she reached the end of the tether. I whipped her again on her other thigh and then again on her calf. She screamed and jerked away. Brittany screamed as well. I had never thought I would derive pleasure from inflicting physical pain, but I found I rather enjoyed this. Seeing the welts rise on Stephanie's legs made me smile inside. Hearing Brittany scream in anger and disbelief just added to my pleasure.

"James! Stop that now! Untie me this instant! What the fuck is going on!" Brittany's eyes were full of venom and anger. "Why are you doing this to Stephanie? What the fuck is wrong with you?" Stephanie's hands were at the collar, trying to unbuckle it or unhook the leash. I rapped her hands with the whip and told her to stop. "Stephanie, I wouldn't do that. Not unless you want to find out just how badly you can hurt. Put your hands down. Now!" She complied. How easy this was. She could at least put up a little resistance, try to defend herself. Oh well, I was sure she would soon enough.

"James, I still don't get it," Brittany exclaimed. "What is wrong with you? Who the hell are you? Why do you think this is OK? This is wrong on every level. Let us both out of here. I never want to see you again. You sick fuck!" Brittany was furious. I loved it.

"Don't worry, sweetie; this is the last time you'll see me. Trust me; I am a man of my word...." I walked over to her chair and licked her neck and cheek. I ran my fingers down her shoulders to her breasts and down her abdomen to her navel. "We have a very long night ahead of us, so you might as well relax and enjoy the evening's entertainment." I now noticed Stephanie was trying to free herself again. "Excuse me, dear Brittany, I have to attend to a very bad young lady...." I raced over to Stephanie, grabbed her hands, and yanked them firmly behind her. She lost her footing and was briefly suspended by the leash and collar. She sputtered and gasped, but I stood her back up quickly. "Can't have you hurt yourself, young lady. That is my department." She shuddered in my grasp. This was the first time this evening that I had held Stephanie close. I liked the feel of her skin next to me. I reveled in the softness of her hair. She was in good shape; she had a nicely toned body. I would have to take my time with her. We had all the time in the world, after all. They both had the rest of their lives to devote to my evening's pleasure. I let her go and got another strap. I pulled her hands behind her and tied her wrists together. She fought it a little, but she was wary of the whip and the choking effect of too much movement. When I was done, I stepped back to admire my handiwork.

"Ladies, it is now time to tell you about the rest of the evening. I'm sure you'd like to know what is on the agenda for tonight. First, a few rules. Oh, wait—there really aren't any rules. I know I don't live by any now. You will have to live by only one rule, my rule. You will do what I tell you when I tell you. It is that simple. You are no longer people. You are just my toys. Sorry, but that is just the way it is." I looked at the two naked, bound lovelies and smiled.

"James, how could you? I loved you! I had a crush on you! I thought we had something…. I…." Brittany sobbed. Her head dropped; her chin hit her chest with an audible thud. Tears splashed on her chest. Then her head jerked back up and she spat at me. "You fucking asshole! You scum! I wish I could tear your heart out, you fucking pig! I'll kill you!" She strained against her bonds and bounced the chair violently back and forth. It tipped over and she crashed to the floor. I walked over and stood there looking down at her. I bent down and righted the chair. I kneeled down so I could look her in the eye. "No, Brittany, you won't kill me. It will be quite the opposite. And you'll have to watch Stephanie die first. It's really nothing personal. Just a little hobby of mine…." All color left her face. Her eyes went blank. All human dignity disappeared in that moment. My heart raced. My palms sweat. My hands shook a little with anticipation of the rest of the act. I leaned forward and kissed her left breast. I sucked on her nipple. It hardened and I bit. Hard. She jerked as much as her binding would allow, which increased the discomfort level. I put my hand on her thigh and released her nipple from my mouth. "Brittany, you can decide how easy or hard this is. If you are cooperative, it doesn't have to hurt. I really don't want to hurt you. Really. You have been a fun companion, a great fuck buddy. I've enjoyed every moment with you. You are quite the little vixen. It will be a shame to see you go...." I slid my hand forward. "Still wet, I see. Good...." I rose and returned to Stephanie.

"Young Stephanie, I am sad that your girlfriend dragged you into this. I never planned to have company, just planned on having my way with Brittany. But this is too good to pass up. You are quite a beauty. I will enjoy our brief time together. I'm sorry that you probably won't, but that is certainly understandable. Now, make yourself as comfortable as you can, standing naked and bound. I have some 'home movies' to show you both. A 'greatest hits' video, if you will. Enjoy...." I ran my hands over Stephanie's firm body. I hadn't decided on everything I would do to her this evening; I was improvising a little, but I was going to enjoy whatever path I took with her. I had already surprised myself by enjoying the whipping; maybe I was "evolving" as they would say on *Criminal Minds*.

First things first, though; time for movies. I put on my latest version of my "greatest hits." When Beth appeared on the screen, both girls gasped. Beth and Brittany had known each other fairly well, and I assumed that Stephanie had known Beth as well. I was sad that the video quality wasn't better, but I did have a learning curve. The later videos featuring Rene and Kim would be much better. The girls screamed as the action unfolded on the screen. Brit tried to turn away but was unable to. She closed her eyes and started to sob. I took the riding crop and slapped at her thighs.

"Open your eyes and watch. I don't want to have to hit you again!" I turned to Stephanie. She had turned her back to the screen. I grabbed her shoulder and violently turned her toward the screen. She lost her footing and stumbled a bit, suspending herself briefly by the collar. She choked and screamed. I steadied her. She recoiled from my touch and stepped back a step. Once again, she reached the end of her leash and had to stop. I raised the crop and told her to stand still and watch the video. She complied.

When I started to finish Beth off on screen, the girls both started howling and screaming again. I enjoyed every noise they made. These two were providing me with so much more enjoyment than any of the previous girls, and we really had just begun. I couldn't wait to see Brittany's horror as I slowly tortured and killed her girlfriend. The final act of snuffing out Brittany's life would be the whipped cream on a banana split. Rene's time here in my playroom came on next. Brittany and Stephanie had, of course, known her too.

"How many girls have you killed?"

"What kind of monster are you?"

"Turn it off! I can't watch it anymore!"

"You sick fuck!"

"Turn it off, turn it off, turn it off!"

"Help! Help! Somebody help!"

The girls' screams turned into a jumble; I couldn't tell who was screaming what. I didn't care; I just wanted to feel their terror build. I felt stronger and better with each scream, each yelp, each whimper, every sob. Stephanie turned her back to the TV again. I kicked her feet out from under her. She hung from her collar for a moment, the wind knocked out of her. Her feet were scrabbling for purchase as she tried to right herself. When she was close to getting her balance, I knocked her feet away again. She struggled and sputtered. She found her footing more quickly this time.

"I strongly suggest that you stand still and watch the

254

rest of the video, unless you want me to tie your feet together and then kick them out from under you again. Trust me, I will, too. Just try me. Now stand there and watch the rest of this. You'll live a little longer if you do." I jerked her body back into place and stood behind her for a moment. I whispered into her ear, "There, that's better, isn't it? Just stand here and watch with me. Relax. The video will be over soon and we can all go back to play time." I ran my hands over her sides and firm abdomen. I licked the side of her cheek and moved my hands to cup her breasts. I could feel her revulsion, but she didn't try anything stupid. She just stood there and let me touch her. She kept her eyes on the screen as ugly Maura appeared and quickly died. I held her hips in my hands and ground my crotch into her naked ass. Still, she kept eyes forward and watched the video. Brittany kept mouthing some objections to my treatment of her trollop, but I paid little attention. Stephanie would be the center of my attention for a good long while. I had plenty of time for Brittany later.

"I hope you enjoyed my home movies, girls. I know I did." Stephanie and Brittany just stared blankly at me. "Now it is time for some real fun. Stephanie, I think I will spend a little time with Brit, if that's OK with you. I'll be back soon." I pulled a chair next to Brittany and sat just behind her right shoulder. I leaned forward and talked softly into her ear. "Brittany, I have to thank you for bringing Stephanie along to play. I know we discussed a different sort of play date, but this is so much richer—so much more entertaining for me. I intend to put on quite the show for you with your young friend. Stephanie is going to suffer. A lot. And you're just going to have to watch every minute of it. Helpless to change it. And then, after I am through with her, you and I are going to have our special time together. It will be the time of your life, I promise...."

I kissed her gently on the neck and shoulder. I really liked this girl, it would be hard to kill her. I had no choice, though; my hand had been tipped. Nothing could stop her death now. I sighed at the thought and kissed Brittany on the cheek. "Enjoy the show, dear. I know I will." I strode over to Stephanie.

"Stephanie, I wish I could tell you that this isn't going to hurt, but I would be lying, and I don't want to lie to you. So I will tell you the bald truth. The things you are about to experience will be extremely unpleasant. Painful. Humiliating. Ultimately fatal. Sorry about that. But, being honest, I'm not really that sorry. I will revel in every moment. Would you like to sit down? I can get a chair for you and let you sit if you'd like. You have been standing a long time. I'm sure you must be getting a little tired."

"I don't care! You fucking pig! It doesn't matter what I say or do, I'm going to end up like the others. I'm going to end up dead like Beth and Rene! Just get it over with. I don't want to look at you any longer than I have to, you sick fuck!" She spat the words at me with venom and vigor. I was pleased. This was going to be even more interesting than I had thought.

I was tempted to cut her hands loose so she could scrap with me a little. She could not escape. The door was securely locked, and they certainly didn't have the combination. It might be fun to let her think she had some hope and see how much fight was left in her. I was tempted, but not stupid. I kept her bound for now.

I went to the closet and got out a cat of nine tails. I snapped it a couple of times and circled Stephanie. She turned and tried to stay face to face with me. I flicked the cat at her calves. It connected and made a satisfying sound as the tails bit at her flesh. She let out a small scream and jumped back a bit. I flicked it again, harder. A nice crisscross pattern raised on her calves. I flicked again, full force, and hit the fleshy backs of her thighs. Welts instantly rose. She yelped and jumped. I whipped her again before she had finished the jump. It caught her off-guard. She fell backwards and was caught by the leash and collar. Brittany started wailing in the background. I just grinned and raised the whip again. I snapped the tails across her inviting bottom. The whip cut her skin in a couple of spots, and she began to ooze a little blood. This was new turf for me. I'd never physically tortured anyone like this. I liked it. I liked the feeling of power. I liked watching the tears well up in her eyes, liked seeing the marks that my whip left, liked hearing her scream and cry. I looked to see Brit's reactions. She had been very vocal, but I needed to see what was in her face. I needed to look into her eyes and see what she really felt. I turned and saw that she had her eyes closed. I told Stephanie, "Just hang out here; I'll be right back..." and crossed over to Brittany.

"Young lady, I will tape your eyes open if you don't open them yourself and watch what's going on. This is for you, you know...." I leaned forward and put my fingers on her eyelids and gently opened them. I held her cheeks and looked directly at her. "Brittany, things will go easier on you if you are a good girl. Keep your eyes open and watch. If you don't want to have the same pain that Stephanie is getting, just watch...." I kissed her cheek and went back to Stephanie. "Brittany is having a little trouble watching this. Maybe we'll have to give her something more interesting to keep her attention." Stephanie stared blankly back at me. I reached up and released her leash from the ring on the ceiling.

"Would you like me to untie your hands? Would you like to take a break before we continue with the evening's entertainment?" I said this in as soothing a tone as possible. Stephanie just stood mute. "If you don't need one, well, we can just press on then...." I walked Stephanie over to Brittany's chair and tied her leash to one of the chair's arms. "Brittany can get a better view now that you are up close. Sit on her lap and get comfortable if you want." Stephanie climbed onto Brittany's lap and buried her face in Brittany's shoulder. I let her stay that way for a few moments, and then I snapped the cat across her back without any warning. Hard. As hard as I could manage. She screamed and the whip left ugly cuts on her back. Brittany screamed some obscenities at me. I laughed and lashed Stephanie again. And again. I whipped her a third time and stopped to look at my artwork. Her back was now crisscrossed with sharp red cuts all oozing blood. The girls cried and screamed and sobbed. I just drank it in. Then I had an inspired idea. I left the room to get a washcloth. I quickly returned with a washcloth and a small pan of soapy fluid.

"Steph, I had no idea the whip would cut you like that. I feel terrible. I am going to clean up the cuts with this washcloth. I am sorry; you are too pretty to scar this way." I was not sorry at all, no; I liked the way the mosaic on her back was coming out. I was going to like the "cleaning" even better. I dipped the washcloth in the fluid and dabbed at her back. She bolted and screamed as the salty, soapy water bit into her wounds. I grabbed her collar roughly with one hand and firmly rubbed more of the stinging concoction into her wounds. She tried to kick, tried everything she could to escape the torture of the salt and soap and rough fabric. I pushed her more firmly against Brit so she could not escape Stephanie's pain and screams. I rubbed the wounds more vigorously. The cloth was red with blood. Stephanie was reduced to a moaning and panting animal. Brittany just looked on in horror. I was giddy with all the feelings swirling in my head. I felt powerful and terrible and godlike. I ached to finish Stephanie off. I was beyond ready to feel her throat in my hands and watch as she drifted away in my grip.

This was rich! I could do anything, be anything, and there was no one to stop me. No remorse. No guilt. Just pleasure. I was evolving, growing, my skills increasing. I had no limits now. I had felt bad when I had raped Rene, but I only felt pleasure as I tortured Stephanie. Having Brittany to witness it all made it so much better. Knowing that I would have her to play with after I was finished with Stephanie was a gift beyond words. Knowing that her watching this was breaking her down, turning her into little more than a shadow, an empty shell of a person, and hurting her far more than the physical pain that Stephanie felt was satisfying beyond description. I decided to experiment a little more with Stephanie before I killed her—to see whether I truly had left any feelings of guilt behind.

I went to get another washcloth and clean water. I gently cleaned Stephanie up. She offered no resistance once she realized I was not rubbing in harsh-feeling chemicals, but actually cleaning her wounds. I don't think she had much fight left in her anyway. After I finished, I got a pillow from the storeroom and put it in front of Brittany. I instructed Stephanie to kneel on it with her head in Brittany's lap. I untied her hands from behind her back and tied them around the back of Brittany's chair. I removed the collar and leash since they were no longer needed to keep Stephanie secure. Stephanie was now ready for her final indignity before her death. Her head was cradled by Brit's thighs. I smiled at Brittany and said, "Watch this…." Brittany looked like a ghost and just stared back at me.

Stephanie had been brought here as a gift to me by

her lover. The girls had been planning on a threesome until Stephanie had balked at my age. I disrobed and got behind Stephanie. I played with her tits a little and fingered her pussy. She just sobbed in Brittany's lap. Brittany looked at me and mouthed words, but no sound came. I pushed my now rigid cock into Stephanie's vagina and thrust for all I was worth. Both girls screamed. Stephanie bucked and tried to twist to keep me from fucking her, but it was no use. She had limited movement. I put one hand on her throat and pulled her head up so she could see Brittany and Brittany could see her. Unlike when I had tried to rape Rene, I had no feelings of remorse. Why should I? Brittany was my "girlfriend" and she *wanted* me to have Stephanie. "So I'm too old for you to fuck?" I now shouted. "Bullshit! I am fucking you and will as long as I want." I thrust hard enough to lift her knees off the pillow. Every noise the girls made caused my prick to harden more, or so it seemed. I felt as if I could go on like this forever.

I tightened my grip on Stephanie's throat as I thrust my cock deeper and deeper into her. She gasped and gagged. I loosened my grip and stopped thrusting. I pulled myself out of her and she collapsed forward onto Brittany's lap. I let her catch her breath and then violently forced my cock into her tight anus. She screamed louder than I have ever heard any human scream. I put both my hands on her throat and jerked her head as far back as possible so Brittany could watch as her slattern slipped away. I buried my cock in her ass and squeezed her throat. Thrust, squeeze, thrust, squeeze. I repeated the pattern over and over. Stephanie was on the brink of losing consciousness. I tightened my grip and thrust myself even deeper and stayed there. I held her throat in my hands and felt the life leaving her body. I squeezed even harder and felt my cock erupt inside her. She twitched twice and then crumpled in a heap, dead. I collapsed on top of her, utterly spent and happy. Brittany just made a keening sound and sobbed. After a while, I pulled my cock out of Stephanie's dead ass and walked over to the bathroom to clean up.

"You bastard! You can't leave her this way! Get her off me! You sick fuck!" Brittany went on for a few minutes, ranting and screaming. I took my time in the bathroom cleaning the blood, sweat, and semen off of myself. I leisurely walked out of the bathroom, got my clothes, and started to dress. Brittany renewed her screaming at me. "How could you? Get her off me! You sick fucker! Untie me! I want to go home!" She ranted and raved at me as I dressed. I walked over to her and quietly said, "I'm going back to the house to get a bite to eat. I'm rather hungry after this. Why don't you just hang out here with Stephanie for a while?" I turned, went to the door, and opened the combination lock. Brittany yelled a jumble of curses and shrieks as I did it. I just laughed and stepped out into the cool night air, closing the door behind me. I locked the door and walked back to the house.

I was hungry after the evening's fun. I made a quick sandwich and a salad—a light supper so I would have energy for round two. I was eager to see the videos that had captured our games so far. Maybe Brittany and I would watch the raw footage together before we resumed our fun. I wondered how she was coping with having her dead lover on her lap, bound and unable to move, as young Stephanie got progressively colder and uglier. I was sure Brittany could never recover from the experience if she somehow managed to survive and escape. I imagined that her psyche was basically putty at this point. Her will to live must have vanished. How delightful.

I had surprised myself when I hit Stephanie. Brittany and I had engaged in some playful spanking, which was fun, but when I whipped Stephanie, it was different. I hit her with the intent to hurt, not arouse, and I liked it. I really liked it. Every cry of pain, each mark I left, every drop of blood made me feel more alive and more potent. Beth and I had fought, but the pain I inflicted was of an incidental nature, a side effect of the battle, not the point of the fight. But to hit Stephanie and make her lose her footing and choke herself on the leash was great fun. And I felt nothing but pleasure when I raped her. Physical and emotional pleasure. The firm young flesh. The taut snugness of her cunt, the tightness of her bottom, her screams of anguish as I sodomized her, all were exhilarating and exciting beyond belief. Feeling her arteries and veins under my hands as I squeezed her life away and pounded her anus was heaven. Her blood on my skin, mixing with my semen and sweat, was a magical elixir. Having Brittany feel it all, up close and personal, was divine. I was divine. In my little shelter, I was the only god. James the Destroyer. James the Defiler. All powerful.

I really had no idea how I was going to top this when I went back to kill Brittany. After all she had given me, I certainly felt she deserved an even grander send off. How could I make her sink even lower than I already had? Sitting alone tied to the corpse of her lover should have destroyed her emotionally. What more could I do to make her suffer even more for my pleasure? Simple physical pain alone wasn't enough. I wanted to push it even further. I wanted her to beg for death, wanted her to ask me to end it for her because everything was too terrible to live with. What to do, what to do? I pondered this for a time while sipping a B&B. Drinking it felt like sipping heated velvet. Truly a gentleman's drink. Just one, though. Didn't want to cloud my thinking or dull my reflexes. Brittany and I had a long dance ahead, and I wanted to enjoy every aspect of it.

I returned to the shelter feeling renewed and refreshed. Ready for another go. This "two-fer" was quite enjoyable. I knew it was a rare treat so I needed to savor it. I doubted that a situation like this would ever present itself again. I opened the door and smiled at the scene. Stephanie was quite obviously dead. Her slack body was covered with scabby wounds. Her skin had a deathly pallor. Semen and blood mingled and crusted her thighs. Her legs were starting to discolor due to the blood collecting in her lowest extremities after her heart had stopped. Brittany was slumped over as much as her straps would allow. There were streaks from her tears on Stephanie's corpse. She raised her head slightly as I entered the room, but then she just let it fall back to her chest. She just made guttural noises and labored breathing sounds. Then I noticed the smell. Urine. The shelter reeked of urine. I noticed a puddle under Stephanie. Her bladder naturally had let go when she passed. It was wet under Brittany's chair, too. She must have peed herself in my absence. That inspired me.

"Brittany, I'm afraid that you and Stephanie have made a mess. I will need you to clean it up." She raised her head and sullenly glared at me.

"Fuck you, you fuck. Fuck you." She said this quietly, but defiantly.

"I don't think so. I might fuck you one last time, but I haven't decided. I have decided that you will clean up this mess. Stephanie can't go to meet her maker looking like this, and I can't have my little hideaway smelling of piss. So 'fuck you,' you are going to clean it all up." I crossed to her so I could untie Stephanie's hands and place her on the table. Brittany spat in my face as I leaned over to reach the straps. She had more fight in her than I thought she would. This could be interesting.

"That was stupid, Brittany. You are still tied to that

263

chair. You can't go anywhere. You can't do anything unless I let you. Don't piss me off." She spat again. I backhanded her face. "Want to do that again?" She just shrieked and twisted in her bonds. I laughed and finished untying Stephanie. I lifted her up and put her face up on the table. "Now, Brittany, I am going to get the cleaning supplies so you can get started. I want you first to clean up dear Stephanie and then attend to this mess. You will be on a tether, of course, but you will be able to move around a bit. Don't get the idea that you have any hope of escape. The door is locked, and only I know the combination. If you don't want your last few hours to hurt like Stephanie's, I'd suggest you be a good little girl and do what I ask." I got a longer leash and tied it to Brittany's waist. I got a bucket of warm soapy water and a clean washcloth for her to clean up Stephanie with. I untied her arms and legs and told her to do a good job cleaning up her friend.

I sat in my chair and watched as Brittany tentatively dipped the cloth into the soap and started to cleanse her friend's battered body. She started to sob anew, but she soldiered on. I could tell that doing this was tearing her apart inside. I loved it. Her hands trembled and her body shook with her sobs. She tenderly dabbed the blood from her lover's wounds. When she was done with the front, I turned Stephanie over so Brittany could attend to her friend's backside. There were many more cuts on Stephanie's back, and the wounds were pretty well scabbed over, so Brittany had to use more than a little elbow grease. After she finished washing up Stephanie, I took a little bit of a risk; I got the mop and a bucket for Brittany to use on the floor. I considered that a mop could actually be quite a formidable weapon, but with Brittany tethered, I didn't expect too much trouble.

"You and Stephanie have made this place smell

awfully bad. Part of it is my fault. I should have asked if you needed to use the bathroom after I finished with our friend. Terribly inconsiderate of me. But you do need to clean it up. You certainly could have told me that you needed to use the facilities rather than ranting and raving at me." Brittany looked at me in disbelief as I spoke. Was I missing something? I mean, she could have told me rather than just pissing on the chair and the floor. Did she think me rude enough to deny her the use of the bathroom? Young women are rather emotional creatures…. I suppose the sight of her lover beaten, bleeding, raped, and sodomized just might have taken her mind off her own hygiene. "Would you like some shoes while you mop? I know that the cleaning solution can be rather harsh on your skin. The floor will get a little slippery while you're mopping, too, so shoes would really be a good idea. Wouldn't want you to slip and hurt yourself." At that Brittany screamed some obscenity and swung the mop full force at me. Her aim wasn't true and she scored only a glancing blow.

I was rather amused. Didn't she realize that the best case outcome of her action was both our deaths? If she succeeded in overpowering and killing me, she was signing her own death warrant. The door was firmly bolted shut and only I had the combination. If I died, she would die from starvation. No one knew of this place; no one would think to look for her here; she couldn't make contact with the outside world, and there weren't the means to break the lock. Slow death by starvation. A horrible way to die. There was food for a few days; I always had some snacks down here. She would have plenty of water. She could survive for quite a while if she ate my rotting corpse, but I doubted she would. A few miserable weeks and she would be dead. I offered a much better future for her. She would still die, would still endure pain, but it would be very brief in comparison. Hadn't she thought this out? Apparently not. Time to think for her.

I grabbed the mop from Brittany and swung it at her knees. I connected and knocked her to the floor. I tossed the mop aside and pounced on her, pinning her to the floor with my hands and body. She was lying face down on the floor in a mixture of blood, urine, and spunk. It could not be pleasant. My clean clothes were getting soiled, but I had anticipated that they would anyway during my last dance with my lover. I had not planned on getting them spoiled with this mess, however. She would pay for that….

"Brittany, you surprise me. I would have thought you would understand that cooperation is your best hope. This was a very stupid course for you to choose. You—"

"Fucking SHUT UP! It doesn't matter what I do, you are going to kill me. So fuck you; I hope I hurt you as much as I can before I die!"

"What a foul mouth you have, my love. Any more unpleasantness emanating from it will result in me washing it out for you, and I won't use plain old soap. Watch yourself, Brittany…." I shifted my weight a little and loosened my grip on her to see how she would react. She didn't make any move of any kind; she just lay there in the slime, panting from the exertion and panic. "I'm going to get off you now. I'll get you the mop again so you can finish cleaning up. Just watch your behavior. Don't think of trying to clock me with the mop again and keep a civil tongue." I got up, brushed myself off as best I could, and motioned for Brit to stand back up. She slowly got to her knees and then to her feet. I handed her the bucket and mop and told her to resume cleaning. She just stared blankly at me and shook her head. She dropped the mop and plopped herself back into the chair.

"I don't care. Fuck you. There's nothing you can do to me anymore that will make a difference. You can't hurt me anymore. I'm done playing your sick fucking games. You sick piece of shit. Fuck you, fuck you, FUCK YOU!" She screamed the last "Fuck you" at the top of her lungs. I'd had it with her and her attitude. This game was about to end, and end badly for Brittany. I jumped across the room, grabbed her tether, and wrapped it around the chair. I tied it quickly and tightly. She twisted and struggled and tried to bite, but I got her secured. I went to the storeroom and got a roll of duct tape. I wrapped it around her torso and the chair, further securing her. I taped her hands behind her back.

"Now it is time to deal with your foul mouth, Brittany. I told you that any more obscenities would result in your mouth getting washed out. I thought by now you would know that I am a man of my word. This will be unpleasant…for you. I think I will rather enjoy it." I got the bottle of bleach and a rag. I soaked the rag in the bleach and stuffed it into her mouth. I duct-taped her mouth shut with the bleach-soaked rag inside. She twisted and struggled. Her eyes watered and bulged and turned red. She gasped and snot began to run out of her nose.

After a couple of moments, I jerked the duct tape from her mouth and pulled the rag out. She spat and gasped and sputtered. I got a bottle of water and flooded her mouth with it to rinse the bleach from her mouth. I didn't want to poison her to death. I was still looking forward to putting my hands on her throat for the final squeeze. I was, however, enjoying the torture I was putting her through more than I had ever thought I could. I never thought this could be so much fun. Why hadn't I tried this with my previous play dates? I guess I was simply growing. Evolving. Maturing. Time to play some more!

I decided the duct tape had so many possibilities that I couldn't ignore it. I wrapped some of it around her midsection to secure her further to the chair. I then put random pieces of it all over her body. She looked at me quizzically but said nothing. The bleach had shut her up quite effectively. I pressed the tape firmly to her body. I made sure it was good and stuck. When I finished making my mosaic, I stood back to admire my work. The poor girl looked very tired and frightened and hurt. Her eyes were very red and bloodshot. Her nose still ran. I was sure that her every breath burned from the chlorine. I reached out and grabbed the end of one of the pieces of tape and ripped it from her as fast as I could. She jumped and yelped, but she didn't utter a word. I tore another piece off. And another. Each one produced a wince of pain and a little shriek, but still no words. I was pleased. The next piece was on one of her nipples. I ripped it off as slowly as I could, watching the skin languidly pull from the sticky surface. The old Band-Aid dilemma…which hurt more, fast or slow? I had my answer. Slow. No question. Brittany screamed as the tape grudgingly let loose from her tender nipples. She glared at me, but she still said nothing. I smiled and grasped another piece of the silvery wonder. Fast this time. And another before she'd even had time to react. This was fun. I found myself getting hard again. Was my erection due to her pain? Must have been because there was nothing sexy about the way she looked now. Interesting….

After a short while, I grew bored with the duct tape game. I was ready for my second kill of the night. What a treat. Never in my wildest dreams had I thought I could have the pleasure of two playmates at once. And so many discoveries. My horizons had definitely expanded on this day. I'd always thought myself incapable of inflicting real pain on another human being. I'd always been a peaceful man. Little did I know I could not only purposely inflict physical pain, but it could be very arousing. When I decided to start this journey of mine, I thought the emotional pain, the psychological stomping of my victims, would provide me with the most pleasure, but the torture was almost as delightful. I'd missed the boat with my earlier playmates. No use crying over unspilt blood, though. I would simply have more fun and games from here on out.

"Brittany, you look awfully tired. Has this evening worn you out? I've found it rather invigorating, but then I'm not the one all tied up, bruised, and hurting. And I'm not the one who's about to die. You are. So I guess I can understand why you don't look your best." Brittany looked up at me. She was spent. Physically. Emotionally. In every way. While not beautiful in a conventional sense, she was beautiful to me. Artwork. My handiwork.

"Please. Just end this. I can't take any more. Just kill me…." Brittany looked pleadingly into my eyes.

"More than happy to oblige." I stripped down to just my underpants and sat on her lap. I wanted to feel her skin next to mine one last time. Wanted to feel the last gasps of breath leave her body as I crushed her windpipe. I hugged her close. Even as battered as she was, her young flesh felt so good next to mine. I kissed her cheek and nuzzled her neck. I leaned back and took her face in my hands. She tried to turn her head, tried to avert her eyes, but I wouldn't let her. I had a few final words for her.

"Brittany, I cannot thank you enough for your gift of Stephanie. I know that what happened was not what you intended, but it was the ultimate present to me. You made me so happy when you offered up your lover to me. Feeling her body spasm around me as she died was a real treat. I wish you could feel something even remotely as exquisite; I hope that you did when we made love. And, Brittany, I know that this may sound strange, but you are only the second woman I have ever loved. I never told you this while we were together. I needed to keep myself a little detached. I'm sure you understand. But I do love you. And I am so happy that I not only got to share your amazing young body and your vast appetites, but I get to share your death as well...."

I tried to kiss her on the lips, but she bared her teeth and spit at me. How rude! I put my hands on her throat and began to throttle her. She struggled against her bonds, but she knew it was futile. Even though she had begged for her death, her body's survival instincts fought against it. I took my time with her. I brought her to the edge of unconsciousness several times, and then I let her have just enough blood and breath to sustain her a little longer. I held her close and felt her heartbeat next to my chest. I felt her tense up as I started to squeeze, and I felt her muscles slacken as she started to fade. Again and again, I let just enough air back into her lungs to keep her alive for a few more precious seconds. Finally, I miscalculated and she slipped away. Not dead, but now no longer aware.

I tried to decide whether to let her wake once again or finish her then. I ran my hands over her sleeping form one last time. I untied her tether and cut the duct tape that held her to the chair. I carried her sleeping form to the table and gently laid her on it, face up. I crawled onto the table and laid on top of her, feeling her shallow breaths and gentle pulse. It was so peaceful. Calm. Quiet. I put my hands over her nose and mouth. She tried to breathe in, but to no avail. Her eyes fluttered open one last time. I kissed her eyelids and moved one hand back to her throat, keeping the other over her mouth. I applied a little more pressure.

She was awake and free to fight, but she was far enough gone that she didn't realize it or had resigned herself to it. I applied just a little more pressure. She went limp. Her eyes went dark. Her heart stopped. She was gone.

Her dead form didn't repulse me as some of my other friends had. I stayed cuddled up on her lifeless body for quite some time; I'm not sure how long. I knew that she was dead—I had killed her after all—but holding her was still comforting. I thought about her remarkable sexual appetite and the pleasure she had given me. I thought fondly about the fact that this sweet young girl had wanted to be with me, that she was the initiator, that she had been forward enough to ask this old man to bed her. In another life, maybe she'd still be alive and we'd be together. If I hadn't developed this hobby of mine, we could be a couple. May-December, dirty old man and young girl, call it what you will, the time I spent with Brittany would always be cherished. Her last few hours especially….

YES WE GOT TROUBLE, WITH A CAPITAL T...

Two missing at once. A big risk. But it was a thrill. So worth it. I missed Brit, missed her fiery appetite and her very willing body. I missed her companionship. I took time to edit her video. The three-camera set-up was just what I needed. I didn't miss anything with Steph or Brittany. I got to see their luscious bodies, their faces, the crop and the cat biting into them, every detail. I anguished over the final edit, wanted to make sure that the video was a fitting tribute to them both. The pleasure that they'd afforded me was a once in a lifetime thrill; I didn't want to give the memento short shrift by hustling the edit.

It was a couple of days after our glorious play date that the media announced the two girls missing. Even if the police hadn't started to put two and two together, the news staff at the local TV station was howling louder. They started to ask why the police didn't consider all these disappearances as linked events, save for Kim's. A young and very ambitious reporter was leading the report and he was good. Obviously destined to move up to bigger stations in the near future, this young man asked hard questions and drew some scarily accurate conclusions. He charted the parallels in their lives, the connections at MNC and other activities. He posited that there was a serial killer or kidnapper in our town, a very clever one. He had no true leads; nothing had ever been found anything belonging to the girls or any evidence that they had met with foul play, but he planted seeds.

I watched the news with interest every night. The local paper picked up the cry as well. After a week, the local Michigan State Police captain announced that the police were considering all the cases as the work of one person or one group of people. They were going to go back and re-interview everyone they had interviewed before to try to shed any light that they could on the cases. I was getting a little nervous. I really liked New Worcester and really did not want to leave, but I was prepared to assume my new identity at a moment's notice, if need be. I had known this day would most likely come….

POLICE ACTION, PART TWO

Joe Higgins called me to his office. He was almost apologetic about it.

"James, you know how silly I feel right now, asking you here? I've known you for years. I know you have told me everything you know, everything you've seen. But I have to ask you to try to dig deeper. Is there anything else you know about any of these girls that might help us out?" It seemed odd that Joe still did not consider me as a suspect. I'd always thought him to be brighter than that. I was actually a little disappointed.

"Joe, I really can't think of anything. I've always felt weird about Beth, me being the last person recorded as being with her. Makes me wonder if I had taken the highway, gotten her home at a different time, maybe she'd still be here. Still nothing to indicate if she was taken or killed? Have you found anything at all? On any of them? That is just weird for them all to vanish without a trace. You'd think if they'd been taken, that somebody would be looking for money or something. And if they were dead, at least one of their bodies should have been found. This has to be frustrating for you and the department…."

Joe looked at me for a moment before he spoke.

"The strangest thing is the kinds of connections between the girls. Some of them knew each other quite well. Maura knew nobody. All but Maura were very pretty. They all were bright. Good students. Weirdly, most had been students of yours at one time or another. And a good number did theater out at the Pearl. If I were a better cop, I'd be trying to make a case with you as a suspect." He paused for a moment. He smiled a strange smile and looked me right in the eye. "But I've known you forever. Even though you've changed since Gwen's death, I just can't see it. Maybe I should turn the lead on this one over to someone else. I'm getting nowhere. I'm tired of running around with the State guys, and I sure as hell hate spending time with the Feds. I'm just a small town cop. I'm not cut out for this shit. Maybe some fresh eyes will be able to figure this out…."

Joe and I talked a little longer. I did my best to recall anything that might help, anything at all. I gave a bravura performance, I thought. I don't think I tipped my hand at all. Still, I was a little concerned about the pause and smile. Was Joe fishing? Did he suspect something? I just couldn't read him. I began to worry. I put things into motion. Time for James Martin to vanish. Time to leave town. Reinvent myself. Save myself.

I started to bleed my local accounts down. Moved the money someplace safe. Fattened up my other identies' accounts. I moved the money through a couple shell companies and offshore accounts to muddy up the trail. I scoured the house for any evidence of any of the girls. Washed everything down. Left no stone unturned. I didn't worry about the shelter. If the police found it they would find a complete record of what I had done and a nice letter. I'd be long gone by the time they got to the shelter. No sense making their jobs any harder after they got that far. I am a gentleman after all. Fair is fair.

JESS

A few days later I was taking a break from my final preparations. My overnight bag was packed, I had my chosen ID in my wallet. My "getaway" car was fully feuled and stashed a few blocks away. I had plenty of cash. I had an encrypted hard drive with my beloved videos. I was leaving in the morning. The police were getting too close. The previous night they had announced that they had a "person of interest" that they were going to question. Fuck.

I was sitting in front of my TV watching a rerun of *The X-Files*, one of my all-time favorite shows. My favorite episode, "Home," was on. No matter how many times I'd seen that episode, it still creeped me right out. I admired the quality of the writing and the imagination that went into the show. It seldom disappointed. I had been channel surfing, grousing because there was nothing of interest on even though I had over 150 channels to choose from. When I'd been a kid, with only six channels, I never lacked for something to watch. Why couldn't I find something new and interesting to watch on a Thursday night? A puzzle.

About halfway through the show, I heard a violent knock at my door. Fuck. The police? Was I too late? I paused the DVR and walked to the door. I flipped on the porch light and saw Jess standing there, her eyes red and swollen from tears, her hair wet with them. Jess? What the fuck? I opened the door and noticed that she was wearing a faded old T-shirt, panties, and one flip-flop. When I looked at her face, she let her head slump forward on her neck and hid her face from me. "I'm sorry," she mumbled and she collapsed into a crumpled heap on my doorstep. Her body shook as she sobbed. I scooped her into my arms, carried her to the couch, and gently placed her on it.

"Jess, what's wrong? Jess…Jess?" She didn't

respond; she just kept sobbing. I knelt on the floor in front of her and tried to comfort her. I reached forward and put my hand on hers. I put my other hand on the back of her neck and gently guided her forward into my arms. I cradled her head on my shoulder and stroked her hair, and I softly spoke to her, asking what was wrong. She just rocked in my arms, my shoulder getting wet from her tears. I held her and rocked her. "I'm sorry I came…. James…I'm sorry…. I…." Jess' voice was weak and uneven.

"Nonsense, Jess, you know I am always here for you. This house is always a safe place for you. Take your time. Relax. I am going to get on the couch and sit next to you, if that's OK." Jess just nodded her assent, so I got off my knees and sat next to her. She buried her head into my chest and melted into me. We sat there silently for what seemed an eternity. Jess stopped sobbing. Her breathing become slow and regular. I stroked her hair. She shifted a little and snuggled back in. I realized she had fallen asleep. I sat there on the couch with her cuddled in close. I liked feeling the warmth of her skin next to mine, enjoyed feeling her breath. I would be quite content simply to sit there holding her all night. Her soft scent, her delicious little body next to mine, it was peaceful and powerful. I found myself stirred by her presence.

I got up carefully, trying not to disturb her sleep, and got a down comforter from my spare room. I gently moved her into a more comfortable position and covered her up. When I touched her legs, I felt a tremendous rush of energy course through my body. I tried to shake it off, but to no avail. Jess had an appeal to me like no other. I wanted her, wanted her badly, but I couldn't act on it just yet.

Jess and I hadn't seen each other much since Gwen's death. I never blamed Jess, not really, but I couldn't help but feel uncomfortable around her. The few times that we had tried to recoonect it had been awkward. We tried to talk, tried to connect, but it just didn't work. I told myself it would get better in time. I told myself that we could be friends again. Now here she was, obviously in trouble again. So was I. I didn't have time for this. I had to get the hell out of here. But still, I couldn't deny the strong attraction. I couldn't deny myself the pleasure of that one final kill before I left….

*

Jess slept through the night and well into the next morning. I had already called in to work and sent an e-mail to my students, cancelling my classes. I was planning on being gone for good this morning. I wanted Jess more than I ever thought I could want anything in my life. She'd come here for solace. I didn't think that I could feel this way about her. This woman had a grip on my soul. I had checked on her a few times during the night. She must have had a nightmare at some point because when I looked in on her around 4:00 a.m., she was lying askew on the sofa and the comforter was on the floor. I stared at her in the pale moonlight streaming in through the window, the shadowy light playing over the subtle curves of her body.

She'd not changed much in the years that I had known her. Her form was still spare and lithe, not an ounce wasted and beautifully sculpted. But her face didn't have the innocence of the seventeen year old I was first smitten with. The years of bad relationships and stress had combined with the natural aging process to add more character to it. There was a subtle scar from the night Marcus had beaten her and she'd almost bled out here in this room. I shuddered a little at the thought of that night, the memories of my fight with Gwen, the accident, and all that had followed. I shook it off and looked back at Jess. I couldn't help but notice the lean muscle in her legs, the gentle curve of her pert little breasts, and her taut little tummy. I wanted to touch her, wanted to hold her, and, for the first time ever, felt that I wanted to kiss her. I just stood there and drank it all in for a few minutes before gently covering her back up and returning to my room.

My head was spinning. Nothing could have prepared me for how I felt at this moment. I'd spent plenty of time with this young lass over the years, always been attracted to her, but never felt the physical desire for her that I did in that moment. I had trouble going to sleep. I kept thinking about her skin, her hair, her lips, her everything. I checked on her a couple of more times before morning. Each time I had to fight my desire to curl up next to her and hold her in my arms. I needed to run. But I needed to stay. Just till I was done with Jess.

*

"Morning, Sunshine. Thought you were going to sleep until noon." I grinned and handed her a cup of coffee. "Strong and black, just like your men, right?" She sat up to take the coffee from me. Her T-shirt was a little off one shoulder and very sexy. I tried not to look, but I couldn't help myself. I hoped she didn't notice.

"Thanks, James. Strong and black, but I think I am going to forget about men for a long while. I've had enough to last a long time."

"Pardon me for saying this, but you are a loser-magnet. I don't know how you do it, but every creep in the whole U.P. must have you in his sights. What's up with that?"

"I wish I knew. I should have some sort of sixth sense by now to warn me of impending jerks, but it is even less developed than my gaydar. I wish I was a better judge of character; then I wouldn't end up on your doorstep in the middle of the night looking like zombie. I'm sorry I landed here. I just didn't have anywhere lese to go. I understand if you need to send me away. I know how you must feel about my part in Gwen's death. I wish I could change all that. I am so sorry that I came here, but I had no place else that seemed safe."

"Jess, you know you can always call me. I will always be here for you. Always. Even though it has been a few years since we we've been close." *We will be very close very soon,* I thought. We chatted for a few moments before I asked what had happened the night before.

"Brett seemed so much different than any of my past boyfriends. He's cute and sweet and thoughtful. He seemed kind of shy, and he took a long time after we met before he even asked me out. I thought I might have finally found a good one. He wasn't even upset when I told him that even if we were dating, sex was off the table for a long time. He told me he was OK with that—that he could respect that. We've been dating a little over a month and we went to a movie last night. Afterwards, we went to his place for a drink and snuggles. He lives in those new duplexes off Union Street, just a few blocks from here. We've been having such a good time. He's a great kisser. We've kind of fooled around a little, no sex, but some skin to skin time…." She stopped and looked at me. I must have had some strange expression on my face because she kind of verbally back-pedaled and continued.

"TMI. I'm sorry; I didn't mean to embarrass you with details like that."

"That's OK. I'm 'just one of the girls' Jess. You don't need to paint too much more of a picture for me." *My mind could fill in those blanks just fine, thank you.*

"Anyway, we were kissing and cuddling and clothes were coming off. I was OK with that; I was really OK; it felt right. Then he started to press me about wanting more.

280

About how he'd been patient, but he wanted sex. He wanted sex, or he wanted to break it off. He said he liked me, but I needed to put out or he'd have to rethink our relationship. I told him I just wasn't ready; things were going just fine, but I'd let him know if and when we could go any further. I was on his bed with him, just like we'd done before. I didn't understand his sudden change of attitude. I asked him if one of his friends was giving him a hard time about 'not getting any,' as if it was anyone else's business anyway.

"He got really angry when I said that. He grabbed me and pinned me down on the bed and put his hand over my mouth. He called me a little bitch and a tease. He's a big guy. He's like 6'5" and about 250 pounds of muscle. I was pretty much helpless. I apologized and started to cry. That just made him madder. He yelled, 'I'll give you something to cry about you little cunt,' and he twisted one of my nipples so hard that it made me scream. Then he grabbed my panties, pushed them aside, and forced his fingers into me. I screamed 'Stop!', but he didn't care. He pulled them out and grabbed my hair and forced me face to face with his cock. He jammed my head down on his cock. I clenched my mouth shut and tried to get away, but he just pulled my hair harder. He used his other hand to pry my mouth open and then he shoved in his prick. I gagged, but that just made him laugh. He pushed me even harder until I bit him as hard as I could. I gagged and vomited and ran as he screamed. I saw a little blood mixed with my puke as I was leaving. I hope it was his.

"My flip-flops were by the door. I grabbed them as I threw it open and ran away. I don't think he came after me; I'm sure he was really hurt. I bit him hard. I don't know where I lost the other flip-flop. I put them on about a block from his place and then started to run again. I was so tired when I got here.... Well, you know the rest."

Jess had started to cry a little as she told me her tale. I sat there, dumbfounded. How could anyone do something like this to Jess? Then I stopped and laughed inside. *How indeed? Considering my hobby, I really wasn't one to judge.*

"Jess, we should call the police. This guy can't get away with this. I know it was hard for you when you had Marcus prosecuted, know you don't want to go through all that again, but Jess…Jess, you have to. He has to be stopped." *What the hell did I just say? Call the police?* Jess looked blankly at me.

"James, I can't. I can't. Besides, what if he wants to prosecute me for biting him? I'm just as bad as he is…." She collapsed into my arms and sobbed. I have no idea what she said after that. It was just an outpouring of hysterical syllables and sounds. I tried to comfort her, tried to reassure her that she was not to blame, that he was the beast. It was self-defense, clear as could be. It was a long time before she calmed back down. My shoulder was drenched with tears. Her T-shirt was splattered with them. We just sat still, holding each other for the longest time.

"Jess, as fetching as your outfit is, can I try to find you something else to wear? I should have something more for you to wear than panties and a T-shirt."

"Thanks," she sniffed. "I'd like that. I don't want to wear these any longer than I have to. I just keep seeing Brett on top of me, hands all over these. I'm sorry to be so much trouble. I don't know why you ever open your door if it's me. I don't mean to be a burden. I really don…." She started to sob again.

"Enough tears, young lady. And you are forbidden ever to apologize to me again. I love you, Jess. You are my best friend. Anything for you. Always." I hugged her and kissed her cheek. She hugged me close, got on her tiptoes and put her lips against mine, and softly kissed me.

"Thank you. James, you are the best." I released her from my embrace and went to find something for her to wear. I knew I had plenty of clothes that I'd like to see her in out in the shelter, but I wasn't ready to reveal its existence to her. I checked in the spare bedroom. Gretchen usually had some clothes stashed here at the house. It would be a little odd seeing Jess in my daughter's clothes, but maybe that would temper my growing desire to a more manageable level. I needed a clear head to think. Did I have time for this?

I found a nice pair of jeans, a white button-down shirt, and some new panties still in the wrapper that Gretchen must have left here after a visit. Perfect. Gretchen was a little taller than Jess and a few pounds heavier, but I thought Jess would be more comfortable in this than in what she had been wearing.

"Here you go. I don't have a bra for you, but I actually found new underwear and a nice pair of jeans. They're Gretchen's; hope that's OK. These should do until we can get you home and you can get some of your own things." I handed the clothes to Jess. "Go on into the spare room and change while I look for some shoes or something." She got up and walked down the hall to the bedroom. The sway of her hips and her perfect legs got to me instantly. Looking at her walk away was almost enough to make me start believing in a creator. She was perfect.

"Are you hungry?" I called down the hall. "You must be. I got you coffee, but you've been up for hours and we haven't had a thing to eat yet. Anything I can make for you?"

"James, I'm starving. I hadn't thought about it until you asked, but I didn't have dinner last night. We had popcorn at the movie and were going to get a bite...." She stopped and tears welled up in her eyes again. Her tears were the ultimate aphrodisiac. I had to turn slightly to conceal the rising tent in my pants. I felt like a silly middle-schooler with his first hard-on in class.

"Jess, no more tears. There will be enough salt in your food without tears." We both laughed a little. "Chicken salad, OK? I've got a couple of chicken breasts leftover from last night. I make a mean chicken salad. Will that work? On some homemade parmesan-basil bread?"

"James, you're never going to get rid of me at that rate. You will spoil me."

"I wouldn't mind that at all. I'd like to spoil you. Someone should." I went into the kitchen and made up a bowl of chicken salad. I put it on the table and got some plates and utensils. Jess joined me shortly after. She'd taken a shower and came in with her hair still damp and clinging to her. The jeans were a little too big and the shirt loose, but in my eyes, there had never been a more beautiful goddess. The shirt had the top two buttons open, not enough to be revealing, but enough to make me think.... Her skin glowed from the warm water and the towels. I was, for once, speechless. Thankfully, she broke the silence.

"James, this is a feast. I am famished." She sat down and made a huge sandwich with the thick bread and chicken. She ate like a man from a desert island having his first meal after rescue. It pleased me greatly.

"God, I'd forgotten how well you cook. When are you going to teach me? I need a recipe to boil water, I swear."

"You've never asked. I'd love to. You name the time and I am your tutor." I flashed a grin at her and continued, "How do you survive on your own without

284

being able to cook? I can't imagine eating out all the time. Ugh, I'd be 500 pounds."

"I eat a lot at the restaurant next to work. The manager and I are good friends; she always calls me and asks what I'm doing for lunch. I practically have to fight to get her to let me pay. Other times, ramen or mac 'n cheese. Or I'll just eat a pint of ice cream for dinner. I really don't eat as well as I should."

"Jess, you really do need to learn to cook. Next time you are over, we'll cook dinner together. Simple but tasty stuff that you can make. We'll work up to more complex stuff as time goes on. Deal?"

"How could I refuse? I'd love it." We finished our meal and I cleaned up quickly.

"Ready to go home and get into your own clothes? I'm not rushing you off, but you probably have to call in at work. They'll be wondering where you are. There's probably an APB out for you by now."

"I'm off for a few days, so no problem there. And James, umm, I really don't think I'm ready to go to my apartment. I'm worried Brett will be there. Can I stay tonight, too? I don't mean to be any bother, but I'm kind of scared." *Stay tonight? Fuck. I should already be gone!*

"What did I tell you about apologizing? Of course you can stay. I know I sound like a broken record, but whatever you need is yours. Do you want to go out and pick up some clothes? Not your apartment, but some new clothes. We could go shopping. My treat."

"No, that's silly. I'll be fine. I'll be able to go home tomorrow; I won't need anything else. I promise."

"No problem. We can start teaching you to cook later. "Jess, we've been through a lot together. I can't tell you just how much you really mean to me. From the moment I met you, back when you were a seventeen year old at The Pearl, I knew you were special. I knew there was something different about you. About us. I know there is a huge chasm between us in age. I could be your father, but I need to be honest with you. I think I may be feeling something more for you. I—" *Telling her I loved her would make what was to come so much richer.*

"Stop. I think I know what you want to say next. I have to ask you not to, not yet. I have a confession of my own." I looked at Jess. She continued. "James, now that I'm not a student and not a kid any more, I can say this to you. Over the years, you have been so much more to me than just a friend. More than a mentor or a protector. More than my 'local dad.' You are the only person who has been true to me. One hundred percent. All the time, even when it risked your marriage. When I was having my troubles with Marcus, I knew I could call you. I knew you'd be there. I knew I'd be safe. I am so sorry for what it cost you, all the loss and the torment you've been through. And I feel so guilty because of it. I never thought I'd ever see you after I caused Gwen's death." I started to object, but she stopped me by putting her hand gently to my lips. "James, I know that you never blamed me, but I have always blamed myself. I stole your wife from you; she died because of me, and yet you still remained my truest friend. Even right after when you couldn't see me, you never shut me out completely, you never turned away from what we had. You tried to reconnect. It didn't work out, but I always knew that someday we would figure it out. You are a part of me. I rely on you and always will. Even though it has been years, it feels like we saw each other yesterday. I never thought about telling you how I feel before today; I thought you'd dismiss me as a silly little girl, but James, I am in love with you. I have been for a long while, I've just been afraid to say it and afraid you'd reject me. Now, if I'm wrong about what you were getting ready to say, I'm really going to have to crawl into a hole in the ground and die."

What an appropriate choice of words, I thought.

I answered her by taking her into my arms and kissing her tenderly on the lips. Gently and tentatively at first, gradually allowing my passion to take control and my tongue to probe for hers. Her lips parted and her tongue met mine. We melted into a tangle of arms and hands and lips and hair and heat. I moved my hands from her face to her neck and shoulders. She moved closer and guided my hand into her shirt. I felt her perfect little breast and cupped it in my hands. She was warm and alive and inviting and exciting. She unbuttoned the rest of the shirt and I helped her wriggle out of it. The shirt fell to the floor as she laid back on the loveseat. I took her breast into my mouth and teased her nipple with my tongue. Her back arched and her hips moved seductively. I caressed the rest of her lovely torso, my fingers tracing the flawless curves of her nubile form. She moaned gently and then more vigorously. Her hands clutched at my back and she pulled me closer. I kissed my way back up her neck and softly whispered into her ear that I loved her. She pulled my shirt over my head and started to kiss my chest and shoulders. She reached to undo my belt. I stopped her and said, "Not yet..." and kissed her some more.

I undid the top button of her jeans and slowly unzipped them. I parted them, but I did not start to remove them. Instead, I kissed her taut tummy and worked my way to the triangle of heaven that had been exposed by opening her jeans. I gently stroked her body and kissed her everywhere I could. Her hips rose to meet my face every time I kissed her below her navel. I slid my hands under her bum and slowly peeled her jeans from her. I moved between her thighs and kissed them. The sight of her completely naked, writhing and clutching, yearning for me, was almost too much to bear. I gently placed my hands on her thighs and started to stroke her on the outside. I stopped. A memory of the last time that I'd touched her there flashed through my head. I saw a towel, wet with blood and her pale face looking at me as the life were flowing from her. I rested my head on her belly and tears formed in my eyes, falling onto her naked form. She looked at me and stroked my cheek.

"James, are you OK? I…oh, God…that night…I am so sorry, James. I never should have said anything, not here. I…." I raised my head and put my finger to her lips.

"I'll be all right. I was just thinking how close I was to losing you then; I could have lost you *and* Gwen that night, and then this never would be happening. I'm so happy right now. Feeling you next to me is exhilarating. I want to kiss you…ummm…down there, but I was worried about your recent rough treatment. I don't want to do anything to hurt you."

"James, you're sweet; thank you. I think I'll be just fine in your care …." She stroked my hair and made it quite obvious where I was to go next. I gladly obliged, bringing her to a shuddering climax with my mouth. I savored the sweet smell of her, drank in the wonderful nectar that flowed from her as she came. I gently stroked her body and delighted as I felt the aftershocks flow like electricity through her. I laid my head on her belly again and caressed her thigh lazily. We stayed that way for a while, listening to each other breathe and the fire crackle.

"Jess, I have another confession. I am woefully ill-prepared for this. I want to make love to you completely, but I don't have a condom. I've never been with anyone but Gwen. I've dated a little, but it was disastrous. I never bought any…."

288

"James, I don't think I can get pregnant, not after Marcus. I don't know for sure…."

"Jess, I wasn't worried about that, I'm 'fixed.' After our second child, Gwen and I decided it would be best. We didn't want any more kids. I just wanted you to feel safe. I'm sure I'm disease-free; I am a hermit, after all."

"I'm not worried. I want to feel you. Please…." Who was I to refuse? I stood to remove my pants. Jess scooted forward on the loveseat and assisted in the best ways possible. I loved watching my cock disappear into her sweet mouth. Her head moving up and down my shaft made me harder than I'd ever been, harder than I'd been with Brit and Stephanie. In time, I gently moved Jess down to the loveseat and entered her wetness. Her hips rose to meet mine. We coupled passionately. Powerfully. Tenderly. I did my best to please her and she to please me. When I could hold back no longer, I released a torrent of my seed into her, and we collapsed into a sweaty heap, panting and gasping and utterly spent.

After a brief recovery, we went to my room for round two. And three. We spent the day holding each other, laughing and kissing, promising that we would let the other get to sleep. And, just as one of us would start to drift away, the other would find a way to prevent it. I have no way of knowing how many times we coupled that day and night. Being with her seemed to summon an inner strength that I didn't know my aging body possessed. The sight of her perfection in the moonlight, her lips on my body, the feel of her buttocks in my hands as I entered her, it all conspired against sleep and reason. I didn't have time for this, but I couldn't resist it. I had to get the hell out of Dodge. Now.

Somewhere around dawn, sheer exhaustion won out and we slept, Jess' head on my shoulder, my hand cupping one of her breasts. It was the sweetest and deepest sleep I'd had in years. While I slept, I dreamt of the pleasures to come—the ultimate thrill that would be her death. I couldn't wait to feel her throat in my hands.

*

We got up around 10:00 a.m. I hardly ever sleep in, so 10:00 felt like half the day was gone already. I had no plans that would take me anywhere, nothing that needed my attention off my little compound, and I had my new toy with me. What could be better? I rolled over and found Jess lying on her stomach on top of the covers, legs slightly parted. The sight of the full sun on her skin made my cock stir to life again. I ran my hands along her neck and back and down the valley between her buttocks. I gently traced the folds and found her to be still wet from the night's activities. I kissed the back of her neck and slid my finger into her. She moaned and her bottom rose to meet my hand. I rhythmically moved my fingers in and out until she opened her eyes and smiled. We played a little while, and then we got up and took a long, soapy shower together. I made a quick breakfast and we both ate heartily. I was in heaven.

A little later, after we'd gotten dressed, I decided the time had come for some real entertainment. As much as I was enjoying my time with Jess, I knew it couldn't evolve into anything further. I couldn't have a partner or a lover and continue to pursue my hobby. I suppose it was possible, that some serial killers had normal families they managed to keep in the dark about their true natures, but I was not willing to risk it. Worse, I had to vamoose. I certainly couldn't have Jess tagging along with me to my new life. I was a couple days late leaving already. I was going to miss Jess. She was the closest thing I had to a soul mate, despite her lack of years, but the payoff in my own growth in my hobby would far outweigh her value as a friend. I was ready for this, ready to take my hobby to a whole new level. The only thing more exhilarating than killing Jess would be to kill someone from my own family, and my kids were off the table....

I found some more of Gretchen's clothes in the spare room. A skirt that was too short and tight for her to wear anymore and a nice white tank top. I found a pair of flip-flops that fit as well.

"Fresh clothes my love. I still haven't found a bra for you, but we can get one later when we go out."

"I don't need a bra. You should know that quite well by now. I'm practically flat." She looked at me with a salacious grin. "Or have you forgotten already?"

"Jess, you are not flat. You have the most delightful and perky breasts I've ever had the privilege to see, let alone touch. I worship your high little treasures and your rosebud nipples. I have no taste for giant bags of flesh stuffed into a woman's blouse. It just doesn't do anything for me at all. But yours..." I opened the robe that she'd put on after our shower and licked her nipples playfully. She squirmed with delight.

"James, we'll never get dressed at this rate." She tried to look upset by this, but the glint in her eye told me otherwise. I let the robe fall closed and did my best to look like a scolded puppy. She kissed me and laughed.

"How do you know that I ever intend to let you get dressed? Maybe I am going to keep you here as my sex slave. Naked. Chained to the stove or the bed. Doing my bidding. Using you as I see fit. Hmmm?"

"That doesn't sound so bad. If you didn't have to leave all day for work, I would like that just fine. But I'd get lonely during the day without you."

"Jess, you know I only work because I want to.

Gwen left me set for life, really she did. I could stay home all the time and just pleasure myself with my new toy. Hmm, I think I'll start that letter of resignation right now. Woman, drop that robe. Now." She did, much to my surprise. "Put your hands on the back of the sofa and bend over. That's it. Perfect!" And it was. She looked amazing bent over, waiting for me to make my move. "Rub yourself with one hand…." Again, she complied. This was jolly good fun. But I wanted to play a little harder, and I didn't dare do that here in the house. Or did I? I shook that thought from my head. Mustn't stray too far. We'd spent too much time in the house already. I worried the police were coming, and if they found us in our little love nest, I'd never be able to finish what I really wanted to do. I'd lose everything. The thrill of the kill was so much more powerful than any sexual release. My only regret was that I couldn't indulge as often as I really wanted to. I had to pace myself, and that was proving to be agonizing at times. I had to kill Jess now and get the hell out of here.

I watched Jess play with herself for a couple of moments. When I could see her fingers glistening with her dew, I thrust myself into her. Hard. More vigorously than before. I thrust so hard that I lifted her feet off the ground and she was supported by her hand on the couch, my cock, and my hands on her hips. She seemed to like it. I put my hand in her long brown hair and pulled back as I thrust. Harder and harder, feet lifting with every thrust. I came quicker than I'd hoped, and we both fell to the floor, spent again. She looked into my eyes and asked, "Was that what you wanted? Did I behave properly?" I couldn't verbalize. I could only summon the strength to grunt a positive response and nod. My chest was heaving from the exertion and the excitement.

We cleaned up again and Jess got dressed. She

looked like a walking wet dream, her ever-erect nipples clearly visible through the thin white fabric. The skirt fit her well. When she walked, it was indeed poetry in motion. I had a hard time keeping my hands off of her. I had to remind myself that I had no time. I had to escape. Time to ask her to come into my special place with me.

"Jess, now that we are finally dressed, can I show you something? Something really cool? Something secret?" Her face lit up.

"You are a man of surprises. What is it?" She looked around the room, her eyes darting into every nook and cranny. "Is it in here? Somewhere else in the house?"

"Outside, actually. Follow me. I'm going to take you to my secret hiding spot, someplace no one but Gwen and I have ever been." I led her out the back door. "First, you have to promise that you will never tell anyone about what you're going to see. Seriously. This is my private place. My secret."

"Cross my heart and hope to die. Your secret will die with me."

"That's the spirit. Follow me…" I led my beloved Jess to my favorite place on Earth. My goddess and my favorite place and my hobby, together at last. I was almost shaking with the anticipation.

"Here we are. My secret lair." Jess looked around, puzzled.

"Call me stupid, but I don't see anything. What am I looking at?"

I kicked the leaves and other debris off the cover to the stairs. Her eyes lit up.

"What is this? A dungeon? Did there used to be a castle here?" I just smiled.

"Castle? Wrong continent. Nor a fort. This leads to a '50s-era bomb shelter. Watch." I pulled the ring and lifted the cover to reveal the stairs. I reached in and flipped on the light. "Go on down. It is the coolest thing ever."

"James, you know I am claustrophobic. I don't know if I can." I hadn't thought about that. Jess was claustrophobic. I'd known that for a long time. When the theater built a haunted house as a fundraiser, Jess could not go through the maze or into the 'trash compactor' because of her claustrophobia. She couldn't take a sauna or use the restroom on an airplane. Riding on a plane was hard enough for her. I had to get her down there. I'd shown her the door; she knew its location. I could not let her live after this. I had to find a way to coax her down there. Coax her or force her. It really didn't matter. What mattered was that I get her into the shelter now that she knew where it was. I had to think on my feet. I didn't want to have to overpower her; that would detract from her reaction once she was inside and I tore her world apart.

"Jess, you trust me. You know I would never do anything to hurt you. I couldn't scare you. It is bright and cozy inside. You'll never know that you're not just in somebody's living room or camp once you're down there. You can close your eyes without fear. You do sleep every night. Couldn't you just close your eyes, and I could carry you down? Not open them until we are safely inside and the lights are on? Wouldn't you try, just for me? I really want to share this with you. I haven't had anyone but Gwen to share this with. It's my favorite place. Please?"

"I just don't know. I just don't think I can. I'm sorry. Let's go back to the house." She was getting pale.

"Please just wait here. I will go down, unlock the door, switch on the lights and the ventilation system before we even start to descend. Then I will carry you safely in my arms. Would you try?" She looked at the steep stairs descending into the earth and shuddered. "You could

294

pretend that it is your duty as my slave. We could role play, and I could order you to do it? Make a game out of it. Pretty please?" I jokingly thrust out my lower lip and batted my eyes like a pouting little girl. "If I have to, I'll squeeze out a tear or two. It means that much to me to take you here." She pondered it for a moment.

"If you open it up and light it up before I go down, I will try. For you. And you must promise not to close the door. I couldn't take it."

This was going to add a whole new layer to my pleasure. Making her confront one of her deepest fears and then, immediately, violating her trust was a delectable thought. I could already hear her gasp when I slammed the door shut and rammed the bolt home. The look would be priceless.

"Jess, I promise. I'll keep the door open. If you are uncomfortable in any way, I will get you out of there as quickly as humanly possible. You have my word." I went rapidly down the stairs and spun the dial on the combination lock. I made sure to open the door as quietly as possible, and I left it wide open when I went in to turn on the lights and the ventilation system. I also turned on the recording system and got a couple of tough leather straps and some cable ties ready for the evening's entertainment. I put the binders in a concealed compartment under the table in the middle of the room. I called out reassuring things to Jess as I worked. I came back up and asked her whether she was ready.

"No, I am not. I'm sorry, I just can't go through with it. I cannot go down there, even with my eyes closed. I can't do it. Period. Sorry." She looked at me, knowing that she had disappointed me.

"That's OK. I understand. Let's go back to the house. I'll come back later and lock up." As I said this, I started back toward the house. Jess stood by the trap door and peered down into her doom. Then she trotted over to me, took my hand, and stopped me. She got on her tiptoes and kissed me.

"James, I'll try. For you. I can see how much it means to you." I smiled at her and kissed her again. I stooped down and put her on my shoulder like a sack of potatoes.

"Not very romantic, but if you keep your head pressed into my back you will be in there before you know it." I felt her tense up as I picked her up and started toward the trap. I quickly followed the stairs into the shelter. I felt her heart rate go through the roof as we descended. I thought her heart would burst out of her chest before we got into the comfort of the shelter. When we reached the bottom, I put her on her feet in the middle of the room next to the table.

"We're here. You can open your eyes, my sweet." I put Jess down and placed my arm on her shoulders to steady and reassure her. She opened her eyes and looked about. I had every light burning as brightly as possible, save for the bright photographer's lights in the corner. The place did look warm and inviting. A little more Spartan than your average living room, but not too bad. Jess must have felt that way as well—I felt the tension release from her shoulders as she took it all in.

"This is actually nice. If it weren't for the narrow stairway down, I really wouldn't mind coming out here. It is kind of homey."

I took Jess on a tour of my playhouse. Showed her the storeroom, the bedroom, the heating and ventilation system, talked about the process of restoring it. Made sure that everything seemed normal to her.

"I am pleased that you wanted to share this with me.

It is sweet, in a weird way. This would be a nice hideaway. No phones, no distractions, just you and whatever you want to do. Private. Peaceful. Are you still planning to have parties out here? Your secret is out; I've seen the place. I won't share unless you tell me to, but it would be a cool place to have a cast party." I smiled.

"No, I plan to keep it private. Just you and me. No one else. I don't want to share it with anyone but you." I took her in my arms and kissed her. "Jess, you make me feel like a person again. Loving you is just what I need."

"Loving me? James, did you just say the 'L' word?"

"I did. Jess, I love you. There, I said it again. I love you, Jess. I want to be with you. Now. Tonight. Tomorrow. Every day. Always." She hugged me hard, kissed me, and a tear formed in her eye.

"James. Oh, James." She melted into my arms and we embraced and kissed. I wasn't lying to her; I did love her. Loving her would make what was to come even better for me. The ultimate. I was anxious to move on to the next stage.

After a few minutes, we parted and sat at the table. I opened a bottle of wine and poured a glass for each of us. We sat and drank quietly, looking at each other's face and giggling like young lovers do.

"I don't mean to spoil the mood, but I think we need to take another step here…."

"What are you talking about?"

"It is time to conquer one of your fears. You feel OK down here now. You don't feel like you're in a hole, do you?"

"No, I don't. It is nice, just like you said. I feel happy here. But I don't think I would if the door were closed. That would frighten me."

"Really? Even now? Even here with me? Let's

see...." With that, I leapt from the table to the door and slammed it shut. Jess gasped and turned pale. She started to whimper. Her breathing got faster and shallower. She was hyperventilating. I was getting hard.

"James," she panted, "please open the door. I...can't...breathe...." I smiled and slid the bolt home and clicked the lock shut loudly. When I spun the dial, she screamed. She flew to the door and tried to push me away. I laughed and caught her in my arms.

"Quiet. Quiet, sweet Jess. Be still. This is for your own good...." She looked in my face with abject horror written on hers. She struggled to get away, struggled to get at the bolt. I let her go and watched her futile attempts to break out.

"James, this is not funny. Let me out! How could you? You love me and torture me? What?" I laughed again.

"Jess, close your eyes. Let me hold you. Face this fear. Trust me." She struggled in my arms. I held her tighter, hoping it would increase her claustrophobia. I was not displeased with the result. She struggled and moaned and whimpered. She kept repeating my name and looking at me as if she'd never seen me before. I relished every moment of her agony. I looked forward to more. After a few more moments, she stopped fighting me. She was running out of breath and out of strength. I picked her up, carried her to the platform, and put her on it. I pulled a couple of zip ties out of the concealed drawer and quickly bound her legs to the platform's legs. She screamed a blood-curdling scream and twisted and bounced, futilely trying to break free. Tears streamed down her face and her body was wracked with sobs. All she could say was "Why?"

I quietly went about my business and more thoroughly bound her legs to the table. I bound her ankles and knees to the platform's legs. She had no hope of escape, but she still had some desired mobility. I pushed her back onto the platform. She fought her way back to a sitting position and tried to claw at me. I just dodged out of her reach and grabbed a pillowcase. I pulled it over her head. She ripped it off. I grabbed her arms and zip-tied her wrists together. Then I put the pillowcase back over her head.

"Jess, I need you to calm down. I think I'll just turn out the lights and take a little break in the house. Hopefully, you'll be in the proper mood to continue when I get back." Jess screamed and sputtered some unintelligible nonsense at me. I just unlocked the door, turned out the light, slammed the door, bolted it loudly, and went back to the house to freshen up. A few minutes in the shelter on her own would be just the thing....

*

I did take a little break in the house. I checked my new IDs and bank balances, made sure that everything was ready for me to leave. I knew that after Jess was gone, I would need to be, too. I'd stupidly stayed too long already. My conversation with Joe, all the media attention, images of being caught, they all swirled in my head as I checked and doubled checked everything. It would be hard to leave, but it was the right time. I did not relish relinquishing my freedom, couldn't fathom rotting in jail.

I went back to my shelter for what was most likely the last time. Poor Jess was whimpering on the table. The pillowcase billowed and fell with her breath. She'd given up struggling. I cut the tie holding the pillowcase in place and pulled it off of her head. She gasped in a huge breath, let it out, and then gasped in another huge gulp of air. Her eyes burned as she looked at me.

"Why? Why? I just don't understand.... James,

you've always been there for me. How could you do this? How could you?" She started to sob.

"Jess, I'm sorry, but I have to. I love you. I love you more than I've ever loved any woman, any person, save Gwen. But I have to leave, and I can't leave you here, alone, unprotected. I have bared my soul to you. I've shown you my innermost secret. And I am going to tell you the truth. And that is why I have to do this…."

"That is the most senseless pile of crap I've ever heard. You have to kill me because you love me? That makes no sense at all…." I put my finger on her lips and shushed her. I then told her everything. I spared her watching the videos; I just told her about my emptiness, my rebirth, about Beth and Rene and Maura and Kim and Brittany and Stephanie. I explained to her how and why she fit into it all. I held back nothing. I'd like to think that she understood. I'd like to think that she realized how beautiful it all was and what a gift we were exchanging. The most intimate and personal exchange that two people could ever share.

I'd like to think all that, but I know better. I know she was in shock. In terror. Broken. Beyond appreciating anything so exquisite as what we were about to share. It was a pity, but there was nothing I could do to change it. I kissed her deeply. She fought it, but I kissed her anyway. And I took her lovely throat into my hands. I looked directly at her and squeezed. I felt the breaths slow. I felt her heartbeat slow, the pulse weaken. I watched as the light left her eyes. I was elated beyond description. I held her tiny dead form in my arms for quite some time. I cried at the beauty of what I had just witnessed. I didn't want to break the sanctity of that moment. But I had to put her to rest, gather my things, and move on. I was done in New Worcester.

I left Jess in the shelter. She wasn't just one of the girls, she deserved a special place apart from them. I wasn't coming back here. It didn't matter. Nothing mattered anymore except escape. I'd been here too long, but I felt it was worth it. Jess had been everything I'd hoped. She bought it when I told her I loved her. Maybe I did too. But that just made it all so much richer in the end.

POLICE ACTION, PART THREE

I looked around the shelter one last time. I'd miss it. I looked at Jess on the table. Beautiful. What an exquisite experience it had been. I turn off the lights and headed out. I shut the door, spun the lock, climbed the stairs and started to close the hatch. Sirens! Lights! Fuck. The police were at the house and more on the way. I had no reason to think they'd come back here. I'd not left anything I really needed in the house. Everything was in the car waiting. My pulse quickened. I could hear faint echoes of the cops' voices through the woods. Caught glimpses of the flashing lights on the cars. I headed through the woods toward the University property. I'd have to take a roundabout way to the car. Hoped I didn't see anyone I knew. The branches and brush cut my hands and face as I ran, but I didn't feel it. I was running for my life and I knew it.

Fuck! *FUCK!* I knew I had taken a risk with Jess. I knew I should have left right away, not stuck around for a couple days. But the chance to end things in New Worcester with her was too powerful an attraction to me to pass up. At least I had stashed the minivan in my garage over on Water Street. I chuckled to myself as I ran through the woods. I was probably the only one who would get the joke in my new name. Chance was the main character in *Being There*. A gardener with no last name, no past, just a position in the estate of an old man. A slow-witted but gentle man who manages to land on his feet in every situation. Peter Sellers' greatest role, in my humble opinion. So I would be Chance Sellers for a while. Chance had property in Oxmoor, Ohio. Before Jess, before the cops' untimely arrival, I had planned to drive my car over to the garage, park inside, leave in my boring white Chrysler Town and Country and drive to the airport in

Milwaukee to fly to Rio for some cosmetic surgery and a little R&R before assuming my new life in Oxmoor. Now I had to haul ass to the garage, slip in quietly and get the hell out of Dodge before the cops tightened the noose and put out an APB for me. Fuck.

I made it through the woods without incident, other than a torn shirt and a little cut on my arm. As fast as I was booking it, I am surprised I didn't have more damage to concern myself with. I quickly walked the ten blocks from the edge of the University property to the garage. The early evening didn't provide me with cover of darkness. But it was better than mid-afternoon. I saw no one I knew, nor did I see any police cars. I was lucky. I prefer to be smart. Once in the garage, I was smart again. I was relatively safe. I had my bags in the car, Kim's gun, three different passports and other necessary papers for each of my three new identities. I had planned this day carefully…except for the almost getting caught part. I wondered how long it would take before the police found the shelter. It had taken me several years before I found it. The house would yield very few secrets. Obviously they had put enough together to finally view me as a suspect, no, more than a suspect. *The suspect.* I hadn't wasted the time to count, but I was sure there were at least 4 or 5 squads there from the number of lights I saw. I debated whether to leave immediately or wait a bit longer for the dark of night. Each answer had its appeal. Making the right choice was crucial. I had one bit of unfinished business I wanted to attend to before leaving. I decided that I would leave immediately. Make the one stop I needed to and get out of town.

Brett's apartment was in an older building on the edge of town. I'm glad that Jessica had told me where he lived before we had our playdate. Brett was an ass. He didn't deserve to live. The way he treated Jess was

303

unthinkable. She was a wonderful girl. Certainly didn't deserve to be in the hands of a masher like him. I needed to avenge the treatment he had given her. I felt I owed it to Jess for all that she had given me. Marcus was still safely locked up in a state prison or I would have paid him a visit as well. *How could people like this even exist?* Treating women this way? Other than the satisfaction of saving other women from Brett, killing him would give me little satisfaction.

I knocked on his door. "Brett? Are you there?" I waited a moment. I heard a bit of scuffling and shuffling and a mumbled "Be right there" from inside. I waited. The door opened. Brett was half dressed, just some shorts and an inside out tank top. I could see past him to the couch where a very attractive young thing was pulling a ratty sheet around her. Brett wasn't wasting any time getting what Jess wouldn't give him. He was just making this even easier for me.

"Who the fuck are you? I don't know you! What are you doing here?" Brett looked curiously at me.

"I'm a friend of Jessica's, Asshole. What you did to her was wrong. Time to pay up."

I didn't care that his new plaything saw me. Didn't matter. I was out of here immediately after I was done with this. I pulled the gun from my jacket pocket and stuck it in his face and pulled the trigger. It made a muffled report, Brett's face acting like a silencer of sorts. His brains exploded out of the back of his head. I didn't need to waste another bullet. He was dead on his feet. The cute little thing on the sofa screamed. I pushed past the dead on his feet Brett and quickly covered her mouth.

"Shh. I won't hurt you. You aren't part of this. So sorry you had to see this." She struggled a bit. The sheet slipped and exposed a very pretty breast and torso. I held her still with one hand and pulled the sheet up with the other. No time to take a peak, but she was lovely. I explained to her that I had to tie her up and gag her so I could leave. I apologized again. She had no part of this. I wanted her to understand that. I knew that she would be able to ID me, but I didn't care. It should be a little while before the police found her. I'd be long gone by then. I'd be Chance Sellers.

EPILOGUE

The little town I am in now is nice. Not quite as charming as New Worcester, but few places are. The little theater that I bought is almost ready to reopen. A former vaudeville house/movie theater built in the late 1920s, just like the Pearl. It had been foreclosed on and sat vacant for years. I got it for a song. The bank was happy to be rid of it. I was glad to have it. I am looking forward to our first production. I love *A Thousand Clowns*.

I can't wait to make some new friends. Life is so much richer when you have friends…

Made in the USA
San Bernardino, CA
27 May 2016